NEPTUNE'S
ACCOUNT

To Laura,
I hope you enjoy Neptune's
unique story!
Best wishes,
Mike Maffett
9/25/96

Templeton Reid Ten-Dollar Gold Coin, 1830. This was the first privately minted gold coinage in the United States. Photo courtesy the Smithsonian Institution.

NEPTUNE'S ACCOUNT

MICHAEL MAFFETT

WOODVALE PRESS

ATLANTA, GEORGIA

This book is printed on acid-free paper which conforms to the American National Standard Z39.48-1984 *Permanence of Paper for Printed Library Materials.* Paper that conforms to this standard's requirements for pH, alkaline reserve, and freedom from groundwood is anticipated to last several hundred years without significant deterioration under normal library use and storage conditions.

Published by Woodvale Press, Atlanta, Georgia
Manufactured in the United States of America
Design by David Laufer
First Edition
ISBN 0-9644618-0-3

For my parents

Acknowledgments

I would like to thank my friends Pat Gowdy, who first heard Neptune's story on the trail up Hooper Bald, and Hunter Tison, who gave me encouragement when I had little else. In addition, I would like to recognize Dr. John Ellis and Dr. Dan Byrd for allowing me access to their wonderful collections. I am grateful for the hospitality of Dr. and Mrs. Jim Bland, custodians of "Carter's Quarters," where echoes of the old times can still be heard. My special thanks goes to Alexa Selph, David Laufer, and Fred Thompson for their invaluable assistance in editing, designing, and producing Neptune's story. And lastly, I offer my deepest gratitude and love to my wife, Beaty, as well as my children, Dale, Fletcher, and Clay, for their great patience and understanding during the writing of this book.

The Cherokees
A Historical Note

Like all American Indian tribes, the Cherokees know nothing of their origins other than generation myths, and the archaeological record tells us little more. Even the exact meaning of their name has been lost, although some have suggested as a root word *tcikoli,* a Muskogean Indian word meaning "people of a different speech." Curiously, the Cherokee language is indeed distinct from that of their immediate historical neighbors, and linguists have shown Cherokee to be of the Iroquoian family of native American languages, an association suggesting a past migration from the north. Although the site of their original homeland remains subject to debate, we do know that by the time of Spanish contact (Hernando de Soto) in 1540, they were well established on both sides of the Appalachians, their influence extending from Kentucky and Virginia southward into Georgia, North Carolina, Tennessee, and Alabama.

With the abandonment of the outpost of Saint Elena near present-day Beaufort, South Carolina, in 1586, the Spanish largely ended their contact with the Cherokees, a vacuum of influence later filled by the English and to some extent the French. English traders from Virginia and the Carolinas traveled and lived among the Cherokees as early as 1673, and over the next century the English became their primary trading partners. During the Seven Years War, or as it is called in America, the French and Indian War, the English sought to block French influence from the West by the construction (1756–57) of Fort Loudoun near the confluence of the Little Tennessee and Tellico Rivers, a site at the geographical and spiritual heart of the Cherokee Nation. The security of this outpost, based to a great degree upon the Cherokees' increasing dependency on manufactured goods, was short-lived. At the instigation of the French and because of the ever-increasing incursions by the English onto their lands, the Cherokees renounced their new alliance with the British and besieged and took the fort in the summer of 1760. In the resulting warfare, the Cherokees suffered greatly, ultimately ceding a good deal of their land in return for a very transient peace.

During and following the American Revolution, the pressures placed on the Cherokees by the ever-expanding frontier once again led to warfare. In this instance the victors were the Americans rather than the British, and their demands for land proved insatiable. As before, the Cherokees lost tens of millions of acres, forcing them to abandon their ancient capital at Chota on the Tennessee River in favor of a new capital, named New Echota, in northwest Georgia.

In July of 1791 this cycle of war and peace was broken by the signing of the Treaty of Holston. By the terms of this landmark treaty, the relationship between the Cherokees and the United States government was defined, granting Washington controlled access to tribal lands and in turn giving the Cherokees considerable autonomy to conduct their own affairs. More important, the federal government promised to give assistance to the Cherokees in assimilating their culture with that of the whites.

Under the provisions of the treaty, the Cherokees made remarkable social progress. With the aid of various missionary groups, literacy in English spread, as did education in agriculture, various cottage industries, and the basics of a mercantile system. Intermarriage with whites was not uncommon, giving rise to a new class of Cherokees possessing a unique, but sometimes confusing, cultural identity.

In 1821, after a labor of many years, Sequoyah, a Cherokee silversmith who spoke no English, introduced an alphabet in Cherokee, the first syllabary of any Native American language. In New Echota the tribal leaders set into operation the rudiments of a democratic government with its own legislature, judiciary, and bilingual newspaper, *The Phoenix*. Ironically, every advancement brought the Cherokees into an ever greater dilemma in their ambivalent relationship with the whites, a situation that would make its final resolution all the more painful.

The beginnings of a solution, at least from the point of view of the federal government, was initiated by Thomas Jefferson, who at that time was the president and the primary force behind the just-completed Louisiana Purchase (1803). He suggested that the best interests of all the eastern tribes would be served by relocating them to lands west of the Mississippi River. This suggestion was presumably based on a genuine concern for the Indians' welfare, but curiously, this sort of thinking paralleled that of the non-altruistic, economically motivated white majority. This official attitude was to give the whites all the unofficial leverage they needed in removing the southeastern tribes.

A discussion of the legislative and judicial events that led to the downfall of the Cherokee Nation and its ultimate displacement to Oklahoma is beyond the scope of this brief explanation. It remains one of the most regrettable episodes in American history, a sad scenario unimaginable by the standards of today's national ethic. In short, the Cherokees' fate was sealed by the election of a pragmatic and unbending Andrew Jackson as president and the subsequent revelation of a long-unappreciated bit of geologic happenstance.

According to local tradition, in 1828 in northeast Georgia, on a ridge somewhere between the Etowah and Chestatee Rivers, a man named Benjamin Parks was deer hunting. While chasing his dog, he happened to kick up a curious stone that caught his eye. The quartz rock he had uncovered was veined with gold. Within a matter of months, thousands of prospectors swarmed into this unsettled frontier area in what became the first large-scale gold rush in North America. The pressure of their numbers and the fact that much of the gold-bearing ore lay on Cherokee land brought about a ready excuse for the state of Georgia to completely disenfranchise the Cherokees.

With gold as the pivotal issue, the Georgians wasted no time in stripping the Indians of their few remaining civil rights, and formed a paramilitary group, the Georgia Guard, to enforce the state's edicts. The Cherokees fought back, not with bullets and war clubs as in the past, but through the courts. Although the Supreme Court under Chief Justice John Marshall was to ultimately rule in their favor, President Jackson chose to ignore the decision, thus allowing the state government to continue in its illegal actions.

The Cherokees themselves became highly divided on the issue. One group saw continued resistance to the whites as futile and advocated relocation of the tribe to the Indian Territory. The majority, however, disagreed, and under the leadership of Chief John Ross steadfastly opposed removal. A stalemate of sorts existed until December 29, 1835, when the Treaty of New Echota was signed by a group of men representing the pro-removal minority. In retribution, three signers of this treaty were later assassinated by more conservative members of the tribe. The final implementation of the treaty was to take three more troubled years and the eventual intervention of the United States Army. All Cherokees who resisted removal were rounded up at bayonet point and herded into internment camps before being forcibly marched to the Indian Territory. This journey, the infamous Trail of Tears, was to result in the deaths of approximately four thousand people due to starvation, disease, and exposure. No apology or recompense was ever offered.

Small bands of Cherokees remained in the East, however, and were later joined by a few Indians who avoided the army patrols or became disenchanted with Oklahoma. These people were culturally more traditional than those who went west and were fortunate to reside deep within the southern mountains, far removed from the mainstream of the American economy. The state of North Carolina, largely due to the patronage of a few sympathetic whites, took a more benevolent attitude toward these remaining Cherokees, a policy later adopted by the federal authorities. A reservation, the Qualla Boundary, was established in 1889 for their protection.

THE BALL GAME

Before removal of Cherokees to the West, a great game was played near the present site of Jasper, Georgia, between the settlements of Coosawatee, in which there were eighteen players on a side, and the chiefs of the rival settlements wagered $1000 apiece on the result.

—JAMES MOONEY, *CHEROKEE BALL PLAY*

Coosawatee District, Cherokee Indian Nation
August 1834

Unbeknownst to the participants, this would be the last game played by the old rules. The old ways were passing away—anyone could see that. No longer were the Cherokees in control of their fate. The ancient blue mountains that held the nidus of their power were being taken away. The majority held to the hope that somehow, either through the courts or perhaps even divine intervention, they would be allowed to keep their ancestral lands, to live as they had for uncounted generations. But there were those who did not share in this optimism, for whom despondency had given way to pragmatism. This small minority viewed resistance as foolhardy, and believed that the eventual abandonment of the Cherokee Nation would be their only salvation. They advocated moving west as the government in Washington dictated, to begin new lives in a land beyond the Mississippi River.

William Hand, a half-breed Cherokee who owned a prosperous farm on Chickamauga Creek, was one of those who saw removal as unavoidable. Perhaps because his father had been white, Hand had at first looked the other way in face of the growing discord, assuming that his personal prosperity would not be affected by the government's decision makers. But one cold morning in February his indifference was shattered by a flinty-eyed white man who appeared unannounced at the door of his farmhouse. This grimy intruder declared that Hand's home and barn and fields and orchards were his by law, awarded by virtue of a land lottery, a game of chance designed specifically by the state of Georgia to disenfranchise the Cherokees from their rightful property. With his wife and children cowering at his back, Hand met this unwelcome declaration with loud argument, first on the porch of the house, then spilling down the steps and into the red clay yard. In response to one particular epithet, Hand struck the man, knocking him to the ground and bloodying his mouth, but this outburst brought scarce advantage as the two bearded men accompanying the usurper came to their cohort's aid, and the half-breed took a fearful beating.

To compound this dire turn of events, a warrant for battery was issued by the Georgia authorities, forcing Hand to flee the state, since as a Cherokee he possessed no rights before the courts. He retreated to an abandoned cabin across the Tennessee River, beyond the jurisdiction of Georgia law. He considered plotting a violent revenge, but he could see that the odds against him were too great, that the law was openly unsympathetic toward him and his kind, and that any attempt to regain his land would be futile. Hand understood that he had no place in the new order. He would have to leave the Cherokee Nation without regard for what it might cost him.

After several weeks of brooding, Hand left his family and traveled six hundred miles to see the new land for himself, first by horseback to the great Mississippi and then up the Arkansas River aboard a steamboat owned by an immigrant Cherokee. It seemed a harder land, rocky and blessed with less water, yet there were possibilities here; prospects that would require capital and considerable hard work. Because of the warrant for his arrest, Hand had received none of the limited remuneration due him under the terms of the lottery, and despite the sale of two slaves and his wagons and his stock, the amount of money in his possession would not provide the nest egg needed to begin anew. He must somehow, some way, find more. He returned to his borrowed home a more desperate man.

As his few options dissolved in tandem with the autonomy of the Cherokee people, Hand sank into a deep depression, a darkness magnified by his isolation and fueled with cheap liquor. His dreams awash with intemperance, he became morose and abusive. His wife admonished him for his drinking, and he struck her on several occasions. In the spring following his eviction, she finally left him and went to live with her sister, and the drafty hovel on the banks of the river fell silent.

In July, Hand was visited by his half brother Jiya, who operated a small drayage operation along the Federal Road leading from Augusta to Nashville. Arriving in the late afternoon, the younger man discovered a disheveled, wasted figure hardly recognizable when compared to the face he remembered from only a few months before. The two men displayed little of their shared heritage. Hand was taller, close to six feet, and was thin and rawboned. His dark skin and shoulder-length hair spoke of his Cherokee mother, but in dress, manner, and speech he appeared to be white. In contrast, Jiya appeared to be exactly what he was—a full-blood. Shorter in stature, more muscular, endowed with an agile gait, he favored traditional dress, a loose-fitting hunting shirt, a green turban concealing his long hair, and earrings of native silver. His English was heavily accented when he bothered to use it, and although quite intelligible, it was obviously his second language.

Shocked at seeing his brother in such a state, Jiya had flown into a rage, breaking several jugs of whiskey against the side of the house. After threatening bodily harm, he pushed the pathetic drunkard outside into the light and swore at him for a full hour, forcing William Hand to face the sad reality of his condition. Jiya ordered Hand into the bed of the heavy freight wagon, before heading south with a malnourished, burr-infested horse in tow.

The direction of their travel caused Hand much consternation, but Jiya would not be deterred.

For an entire day, Jiya, a man not given to extended discourse, showered verbal abuse on the tremulous drunkard, as he sought to renew any residual self-esteem and to challenge the man's pride as a Cherokee. He spoke of the old ways and of their strengths, lecturing at length on family and the importance of a good name, and talking of their shared hopes for the future. As Hand became reacquainted with sobriety, he crawled into the seat beside Jiya, pulling his hat low over his face to avoid any chance of recognition, slumping forward to listen in grim silence. As the second day of travel began, Jiya continued his admonishment, but now Hand interrupted him, readily admitting to his weakness and his guilt, and pledging to improve himself, to start anew. This promise defused much of Jiya's fury, and as the long miles passed, the trail talk turned to more mundane things.

In the course of conversation, Jiya mentioned the upcoming ball game. After all, it was big news, and more important, he was married to a woman from Hickory Log and was himself a former player. On the basis of his experience, he had been chosen to lead the selection committee for the Hickory Log side, a position of considerable prestige. As the veil of alcohol passed from Hand's thinking, he found himself listening to Jiya's casual report of the challenge with more than passing interest. In particular, he was struck by the rumor of an extravagant wager, and suddenly, as if it had lurked there all of the time, a plan, an opportunity, came to mind. As Jiya proceeded with the dialogue, a smile spread across Hand's lined face, and his dark eyes widened with inspiration. How simple it would be. It was the answer to all his prayers. A fix. They would predetermine the outcome of the game!

"You have gone crazy. The whiskey has damaged your brain." Jiya said, tapping the side of his head with his finger.

"No, little brother. It is possible. We need only a few special players."

"And considerable good luck."

Hand nodded in agreement. "We must provide that too."

Their discussion of the options occupied the balance of the day and continued late into the night. The game was a mere three weeks away. The following morning Jiya continued his errands while Hand mounted his horse and rode toward Talking Rock, a settlement close by the Federal Road, to attempt a reconciliation with his wife. She was heartened by his sobriety, but at the same time suspicious of his motives. He briefly mentioned seeing his brother and scarcely spoke of the upcoming ball game, but his cheerful manner disturbed her. In light of his previous despondency, she sensed that he was not telling the complete truth. She also sensed that this secret somehow involved her brother-in-law, Jiya, whom she had always eyed with suspicion; the man was undependable and lived none too well by his wits. Despite her persistent inquiries Hand would not reveal anything further about his plans, other than the fact that their prospects for money were much improved.

— · — · — · —

The day before the ball game Hand camped among a grove of white oaks crowning a low hill overlooking the playing field. After securing his horse, he shouldered his saddlebags and walked slowly downhill while considering his options. A five o'clock sun cast shadows across the rectangle of riverine land and the river beyond it. The field was ample, as Jiya had described, and sloped ever so slightly toward the water that bordered the south side. He noticed that the goal sticks were in place and that the earth comprising the playing surface was soft underfoot and well covered in small hummocks of closely trimmed grass. The conditions favored a fast-paced game. Satisfied by his inspection, he began a casual stroll among the campsites.

Hundreds of people, entire families, had already arrived, camped out under the trees that surrounded the field, and the smell of chestnut bread and hominy hung in the cool, humid air along the river. Snatches of conversation came and went under the summer foliage, and somewhere in the distance, Hand felt the percussion of a drumbeat. The Coosawatee team was beginning the final night of ceremony.

The sight of so many of his countrymen heartened him, and for a brief moment Hand put aside their shared misfortune. Perhaps the conservatives were right. Possibly by some unexpected stroke of good fortune, they would be allowed to hold on to this green and fertile land, but his optimism quickly passed when he encountered two white men loitering in the shadows. One he recognized as John Bullington, the owner of a tavern on the nearby Federal Road.

"Well, I be damned if it ain't ole William Hand," the man exclaimed. He offered his fat palm while rotating his thick neck to introduce his companion. "This here is Levoitt Greene. Owns a farm up my way. How you been? Heard you lost your land."

"It was taken from me."

"Well, that's what I mean. Now, Hand, you know me. I ain't got no quarrel with the Cherokee. I think it's terrible what the Georgia Guard is doin', but what in the hell am I supposed to do?"

His declaration of innocence brought no response from Hand. The fat man pulled a brown bottle from the waist pocket of his coat and removed the cap. "Hows about a drink? We come all the way up here to see this ball game. Never seen one before, but I hear there ain't nuthin' like it." He took a long draw from the bottle and handed it to his friend, who did likewise before passing it on to Hand. Hand looked down at the bottle. He wanted to cause no offense, for he sensed the men had money to wager. The aromatic liquid tore at his healing throat.

"Thanks," Hand grunted between clinched teeth. He wiped his mouth with the sleeve of his dusty coat.

Bullington stepped close and lowered his voice, as if he might be overheard. "I hear tell there's a lot of money ridin' on the game."

"That's what people say."

"You know anything about it?"

"You know the Cherokee—we'll bet on anything."

"How would a man like myself get in on some of this bettin'?"

Hand's face remained impassive. "I know somebody. I can help you." He anticipated Bullington. For all his buffoonery, the innkeeper was honest.

"I hear the smart money's on Coosawatee."

"Some say that."

"What's the odds?"

Shaking his head, Hand said, "No odds. It's all even."

"So ole Jola's gonna win it all. Ha!" He reached into his trousers and brought out several bills and a small leather bag. "Could you put this down for us, uh," he said as he counted the money. "Twenty dollars in paper and thirty dollars in gold dust? The weight's true."

"Who do you want?"

"Like you said—Coosawatee. I know that Jola," Bullington said, referring once more to the Coosawatee chief. "He's a tough damn nut. He ain't gonna lose."

Hand accepted the money and the gold. He opened his saddlebags and took out a small ledger book, a pen, and an inkwell. With a set of hand scales he double-checked the weight of the gold and made the appropriate entry. "I'll meet you in that grove of trees on the hill tomorrow afternoon if the game goes your way," Hand said, pointing to his left. They shook hands on the wager.

The Hickory Log encampment was one mile away, distant enough to provide some secrecy, but at the same time in reasonable proximity to the field. Jiya had been influential in choosing the site, shaded, remote from any house, and close by a clear swift stream. The eighteen players, selected by solemn council, were beginning the final hours of the preparatory ritual. In accordance with religious dictum, this select group had immersed themselves in the frigid water for a last time and were now considered purified.

The aged conjurer, Kingfisher, sat by the fire, chanting quietly to himself while consulting his divining crystal. On signal, a line of dripping, naked men formed before him, prompting him to rise to his feet. Dappled sunlight fell across the players' bronzed backs, refracting in the droplets of water adhering to their skin. Not a man moved. The shaman began speaking in a low voice, moving his gnarled hands in concert with the words. He spoke of other games and of other players, of the honor and the essence of the game, of what each player must do to win, and of the positive signs given him by the crystal. He recalled his myth-dream foretelling their victory and referred briefly to the familiar tale of the ball game between the animals and the birds, and how the birds won through the efforts of the bat and the flying squirrel who had been rejected by their fellow animals because of their size. Using this analogy, he reminded each player of his value to the team. At last he removed his own breechcloth and began a solo song. His voice was steady and strong. He appealed to Yuwi Gunahi'ta, the sacred spirit of the river:

O Long Man, I come to the edge of your body. You are mighty and most powerful. You bear up great logs and toss them about where the foam is white. Nothing can resist your waters. Share with us your strength in tomorrow's contest and grant that the enemy may be of no weight in my hands—that I may be able to toss him in the air or dash him to the earth at will.

Slowly, alone, unsupported by his walking stick, he descended into the water until the slack skin about his buttocks disappeared beneath the surface.

The role of the opposing conjurers was critical in any big ball play, for the conflict was as much a contest between the occult powers of the two men as it was a battle between the two teams on the field. Under Kingfisher's direction the players had lived out the weeks preceding the game. He had pointed out the taboos, the rules of diet and behavior, performed the incantations, and supervised the ceremonies. He had concocted the bitter ball game drink of Virginia pine and wild crabapple, and under his direction five of the strongest players were ritually scratched across the torso with the fangs of the rattlesnake and the bones of the wild turkey. He himself had cleansed the wounds and rubbed them with herbs. His healing art had prevented the shallow scratches from festering, a most positive sign indeed, and accordingly he had bestowed an eagle feather, an emblem of immense power, upon each of these fortunate men.

Although buoyed by this spiritual influence, the two brothers, in particular Hand, placed great faith in Sam Ax. Ax, as he was usually called, was Hand's ringer, a player possessing extraordinary skill. In a strict sense Ax was ineligible for the game by the rule of residence, but if his eligibility was challenged, it could be said that his mother's father had once lived in Sixes Old Town, but that had been years before, and Sam himself lived far away in Lookout Town, beyond the mountain of the same name. He was a man endowed with an almost unnatural athletic ability. He was tall in stature, six feet three inches, and cloaked in a lean muscularity. Hand had seen Ax play at Echota when he was hardly more than a teenager, and remembered his dominant role in that game.

Ax's friend Iya, the Pumpkin, was an anomaly in many ways. By birth he was not even a Cherokee, being half Muskogean and half white, but by circumstance he had lived among the Cherokees since his youth. He was a squat, almost square, man, but displayed uncanny speed and quickness for one of his build. He was also very strong. Ax told the story of watching the Pumpkin win a hundred dollars from a white man by outrunning one of the man's Negro slaves, who by all accounts had never been beaten. The Pumpkin was fast, very fast, but he still finished three strides behind Sam Ax at one hundred paces.

Jiya and Hand had paid these men well to play. To lose the game would leave the brothers with nothing. The information they received about the Coosawatee side cost them twenty dollars alone, and its usefulness was questionable. The informant was vague, other than to name the key participants. The only player unknown to Jiya was Tawodi, or Hawk, a local, the spy said, but Jiya doubted it. By all reports the opposing conjurer was second-rate, a man of inferior powers, chosen solely because of his friend-ship with the boastful Coosawatee chief, Jola. The conspirators had manipulated every variable available to them in their efforts to ensure a favorable result, but the final outcome of the game would now hinge entirely upon the skill of the players and the magic spells of the venerated Kingfisher.

There are times, when the ball gets to the ground, and such a confused mass rushing together around it, and knocking their sticks together, without the possibility of any one getting or seeing it, for the dust that they raise, that the spectator loses his strength, and everything else but his senses; when the condensed mass of ball-sticks, and shins, and bloody noses, is carried around the different parts of the ground, and for a quarter of an hour at a time, without any one of the mass being able to see the ball; and which they are often thus scuffling for, several minutes after it has been thrown off, and played over another part of the ground.

—From an eyewitness account of a Choctaw ball game of the 1830s by George Catlin, *Letters and Notes on the Manners, Customs, and Conditions of North American Indians, 1832–1839*

On the day of the game, Hand wandered about as he had the night before, winding his way among the spectators, talking to everyone who represented a potential wager. John Bullington brought over a couple of white men—traders, he said—who put down forty dollars each. This time Hand refused any whiskey. He kept an account of each transaction and by noon had collected over six hundred dollars. The primary wagers, those of the players and others involved directly with the teams, would be placed in full view of all just before the commencement of play. The stakes were tied into bundles made of blankets to be watched over by a neutral party. These wagers not only represented a tangible reward for victory, but were an integral part of the ritual surrounding the game.

The Hickory Log team appeared soon after the noon meal. Kingfisher followed by wagon, stopping on the riverbank a few hundred yards upstream from the field. A blanket was spread on the ground for his comfort, and on it he arranged the medicines he would need. One of his assistants removed the ceremonial drum from the wagon and began a small fire using coals brought from the team's campsite. Without delay, they renewed their chanting, knowing full well that the beginning of the game was an hour or more away.

During this time the teams continued their leisurely warm-up. The opposing game sticks, or goals, were set into the ground at a distance of 150 paces from one another. Halfway between the sticks, at the exact center of the field, was a bare circle of hard-packed earth, some twenty paces in diameter. The sidelines were demarcated with ribbons of various colors affixed to short lengths of cane. A herd of small boys, operating under the watchful eyes of the adults, spread across the field picking up any residual obstacles, stones, sticks, or pieces of hickory shell that might tear the bare feet or exposed skin of the players. Once this sweep was completed, a contingent of men walked to the center of the field, followed by the two chiefs and their entourages, and finally by the players themselves. The spectators, now numbering some three thousand, ceased their talking and spilled across the sidelines to encircle this assemblage. A canopy of high thin clouds had formed, admitting a hot, filtered sunlight. Hand consulted his engraved silver watch. The time was two o'clock.

At the head of the group was a man called Old Rabbit, a respected elder of the Coosawatee team. Upon his arrival at the central circle, he waited for the crowd to grow silent before beginning a lengthy and impassioned speech. His message was impartial, delivered for the benefit of both teams, reminding them once again of the great importance of this undertaking, of its meaning to the Cherokee peoples, and appealing to their spirit of fair play. When he finished, the bundles of stakes were brought forward, including several hundred dollars wagered by Jiya in the name of his players. These wagers were handed to a pair of trustworthy men previously selected to guard them. At the conclusion of the opening ceremony, an unexpected silence fell over the throng of people; there was no applause or cheering, no additional testimonials, no whistles or hurrahs, only the rush of many feet as everyone but the players and officials cleared the field.

The opening toss-up was not cleared by either team, and the ball was contested on the ground by a writhing mass of players. Within five minutes the first injury occurred as a Coosawatee player suffered a bloody nose when struck in the face with a ball stick. The first point was scored by Coosawatee when two of its players broke free from a melee in front of the Hickory Log goal. For the next hour, the teams matched goals until the score stood tied at six-all. The play loosened as fatigue became a factor, and the defense marked the offense less closely. Neither team seemed able to pull away from the other until Hickory Log gained a two-goal advantage on plays coordinated by Ax.

Several more injuries occurred, including a broken jaw, and in each case the injured man's immediate opponent, although usually unhurt, left the field also, for the rules allowed for no substitutions and were very clear on the point of equal numbers for each team. When word of an injury reached Kingfisher, he would consult his medicine bags and change the rhythm of the drumbeat. His tone become one of exhortation rather than mere litany.

Hickory Log's advantage proved short-lived when the score reached ten-all. The game was approaching its third hour. There had been no halftime or time-outs, and indeed there was no timekeeper. Only the passage of the sun and the score marked the progress of the game. Hand no longer looked to his watch, but stalked the sidelines in silence with his fists shoved into the pockets of his coat. Once he caught Sam Ax's eye, but offered no acknowledgment. The score was much closer than either man had anticipated, and victory remained uncertain.

The surviving players were by now covered with dust and smears of grass. The injuries mounted. One of the Coosawatee players was knocked unconscious, and another injured his wrist and retired from play. Each side was reduced to twelve players, and several of these were limping noticeably. Exhaustion mounted, and the ball frequently fell to the earth only to be covered by a swarm of struggling men. From one of these brawls Tawodi emerged without the ball, or so it appeared. He walked away from the pileup swinging his vacant sticks, but soon broke for the goal without pursuit. He had scored easily with the ball concealed inside his mouth. The drivers were unimpressed with the protests of the Hickory Log coach, and the tally man awarded the red team their eleventh point. The Coosawatee side was one goal away from victory.

The sun was well into its descent when the game was decided. Shadows were returning to the field when the ball was thrown over the head of a red player and rolled to the base of a beribboned piece of cane. As he stooped to retrieve the errant play, the Pumpkin struck from behind and sent the man sprawling into several spectators. The force of the impact sent the ball flying straight into the air, where the Pumpkin, having never left his feet, caught it cleanly and headed down the sidelines at full speed. Two other red players had an angle, but he cut inside to avoid them, running straight for the goal. Two more players tore at him, but he fended them off until he could throw a short pass to Ax running freely at his shoulder. All that remained from the point of the pass was a forty-yard sprint for the score.

This extended effort left Ax standing in the shadow of the goal sticks, seemingly exhausted, his breath coming in short gasps, his hands resting upon his knees. As he stooped in pain, the remaining players moved back toward the center of the field for what could be the final toss-up. A runner carried news of the score to Kingfisher, who rose to his feet gripping his crystal to his chest. He signaled the drummer to stop. From the opposite end of the field, somewhere beyond the trees, another, now solitary, drumbeat continued.

The question of whether Sam Ax's fatigue was real or simply a feign became academic once the ball returned to the air. Tawodi, having been consistently outjumped the entire game, went under a stiff arm to catch the taller player at the knees. Ax, at the time fully airborne, snared the ball just before impact and, as he rotated toward the earth, was somehow able to deflect the ball toward one of his blue teammates. The speed of the play exceeded the man's reflexes, and the ball struck him squarely in the chest, falling at his feet. For a fraction of a second everyone on the field seemed motionless, unable to follow the path of the ball, and then, from the edge of vision a blur of motion covered the ball.

Hand could not believe what he was seeing. Ax, rather than falling to the ground as expected, somehow maintained his balance and scrambled toward the ball. He snatched it from the ground in one motion and then crashed into his dumbfounded teammate, who recoiled from the blow. The force of the collision also staggered Ax, but he performed a full pivot, darting to the right and then the left before veering into the open field. Tawodi, the fastest player left to the Coosawatee team, gave pursuit, discarding both his sticks in the process. Now unencumbered, he called upon all of his residual strength to catch the tiring Ax after thirty yards.

After leaping onto the runner's back, the tackler was carried for another ten strides before two more red players hit Ax from either side. The stumbling convergence of bodies slowed, stopped, and then, as if in slow motion, toppled to the ground. The ball was ripped from Ax's grasp as he fell, and Tawodi, who somehow rolled free of the tackle, bounded to his feet. As Coosawatee's last hope leapt toward the errant ball, the Pumpkin appeared at his shoulder and struck him hard across the ear with a crushing forearm, sending Tawodi spinning onto his back.

With the ball in hand, the Pumpkin turned downfield, racing into the face of a dying sun. The nearest Coosawatee player made a feeble attempt to trip him, but the mercenary warrior hurdled the offending stick and leaned forward as he accelerated toward the goal, his breath sounding like the pulse of an engine, the impact of his bare feet churning up small clouds of dust with each stride. The moment had come—only a single, limping straggler now stood between the Pumpkin and a final score. Hand saw what was about to happen and took a step onto the field.

The unfortunate defensive player was tired, exhausted to the point of walking, and now as chance would have it, the entire prospect of victory or defeat had fallen upon his stooped shoulders. His static play had placed him directly in the path of the Pumpkin, who, recognizing the impending hit, took the ball in his left hand and cast his sticks to the ground, all without any perceptible loss of speed. The collision occurred some twenty yards in front of the Coosawatee goal. The wounded player did his best to stop the score by throwing his body against the Pumpkin's churning legs, but the attempt was to no avail. A driving kneecap struck the diving man in the forehead, allowing the hero to drive through and over him and to cross between the goal sticks for the twelfth and winning point.

Jiya, who ran along the sidelines parallel with the final play, raced onto the field to embrace the scorer, who by now had lifted his arms in triumph. His teammates surrounded him, raising their ball sticks into the air, and shouting with joy. Hand did not join in the celebration—that would all come later. He must keep his mind on business. After adjusting the brim of his slouch hat, he shifted the weight of the heavy saddlebags thrown across his shoulder and turned toward the appointed meeting place. All accounts must be settled now—the sooner, the better, for the serious drinking and storytelling would soon begin.

According to the victory plan, the brothers met the following morning and followed a little-used trail deep into the virgin forest. Jiya brought two riderless horses, also a part of the winnings, in addition to his familiar sorrel. Once satisfied of their privacy, they dismounted and spread a blanket upon the ground. They counted out a profit of over twelve hundred dollars, almost three hundred in silver coins, mostly Mexican reales, mixed with several dozen gold pieces, along with four hundred dollars in paper money, stacked in an array of different colors and sizes, the balance being in bags of gold dust and odd nuggets and a smattering of promissory notes. Consistent legal tender was rare to nonexistent on the southern frontier, and the bulk of all personal transactions were by way of barter. And this total did not take into account the value of the horses. They were ecstatic with the boldness of their success.

"Were Ax and the others satisfied with their share?" Hand asked.

"How could they not be?" Jiya replied. He had paid them from the team stakes.

"Good." Hand removed his hat and ran his fingers through his long oiled hair. "I never expected this much."

Jiya laughed, "Never frown on good fortune."

Giving his brother a playful shove, Hand replied, "You are right, but our work is not yet finished."

"Will you still go west?"

"Oh, yes. There is no doubt in my mind. There is nothing for me here. I would like to leave before the winter comes, if my wife will have me. And you?"

"I will stay for now. Perhaps Old Hickory will change his mind." He referred to the American president, Andrew Jackson.

"Do not be foolish. That man will never change. You should come with me before the whites take it all."

This was a familiar topic of discussion. Jiya was not as entrenched in his pessimism as Hand. He counseled for patience, perhaps because he had less to lose.

"I am not frightened of them. They cannot hold me. I will go wherever I chose."

"Ha! You talk like a child. Will you burrow in the ground like a mole? We have tried to live with the whites, and they will not have us. We must go our own way. They will not rest until we are out of their sight."

Jiya did not answer for a moment. He began to pace about in front of Hand. "I have the answer. I will become a raven. Kingfisher knows the spell." He then rose onto his toes and began to strut about, flapping his arms at his sides. "Yesss! I will become a great, black raven and fly far, far away."

Even the serious Hand had to smile. "My dear brother, I see that my counsel is indeed worthless. This money runs contrary to clear thinking. Sit back down and let us discuss further the matter of our windfall."

The problem lay in the conversion of the paper, most of it

written on state or private banks, into either coinage or the basic gold, both of which would be accepted as currency under any circumstance. Also, they had to consider the sale of the extra horses.

"They will bring top dollar in the gold fields," Hand observed.

"And how did you plan to get them there?"

"I think we should ride over to the Etowah." He referred to the river that marked the eastern boundary of the Cherokee Nation. "You wait for me there, and I will take the horses and the paper and convert them into gold."

Jiya was not about to put up an argument. Although Hickory Log lay alongside the same river, it represented a tangible barrier between his life experience and another. His knowledge of the white man's commerce was rudimentary at best, and he was uncomfortable at the thought of dealing with the enemy in his own environment, but he could think of no other option. They rebundled their winnings and rode to the northeast.

Hand stayed clear of the wagon roads, and the brothers crossed Amicalola Creek without incident. Before reaching the Etowah River, they turned due east and on the second day left the trail and rode along a small streambed. As the stream began to climb, they encountered a large rock shelter protruding from the hillside. They had hunted here often as young men. At the cliff's base was a clearing and the remains of numerous campfires. At twilight Hand looked over the extra horses, commented on their relative merits, and did so again the following morning, deciding on second look to keep the bay. After all, a good horse was a functional substitute for money. He said good-bye to his younger brother and announced his intention to return before nightfall. Jiya watched him disappear down the trail before reaching for his pipe and pouch of tobacco.

Not five miles beyond the campsite, Hand encountered the first signs of gold mining—piles of turned earth and fallen trees, cut for timber and fuel. Soon he heard the shouts of men and the tinny report of metal striking against rock. He passed from the despoiled woods into an alien landscape that looked as if it had been overturned and torn by the frenzy of some giant animal, a waste of barren hillsides stripped and eroded in the frantic search for gold-bearing quartz. Within the space of a mile, he arrived on the banks of the river itself, which had turned blood red, polluted by countless tons of silted clay and gravel. Teams of men and horses were at work all around him, and the smell of wood smoke and sweat replaced that of the forest. Clumps of miners stood along the riverbank shoveling rock and gravel into sluice boxes set close by the water. He paused before the nearest group and asked for directions into town.

Only one of the men, a lean fellow with a wild, prophet's beard, bothered to answer. He jerked his thumb over his shoulder and said, "Follow this here road along the river. There's a bridge around the bend there. It'll carry you up the hill to Auraria."

The bridge was makeshift at best but obviously strong enough for heavy wagon traffic. Hand paused and fell in behind two such wagons loaded with green lumber, content for the time being with the slower pace and the trail dust. The road was deeply rutted where it climbed up from the water, and the teams of oxen strained against their yokes. As the road leveled, the first buildings appeared, new affairs of the same unpainted, rough-sawn lumber as that carried in the wagons. A few hundred yards beyond the outskirts, Hand encountered an intersection, the crossing road running north-south, identified by a neatly painted sign as the Gold Digger's Road. He stood at the center of the boomtown of Auraria. Along the thoroughfare to his left was a substantial two-story building with a broad front porch. It was identified by a large sign reading "Miner's Hall, Hotel, Spirits, and Stable." He intended to dispose of the horses first.

After dismounting to the near side of the hotel, he stood for a time, mesmerized by the whirl of activity around him. Within his line of sight, he could see at least one more hotel, another smaller building marked "Western Tribune," two bars, three lawyers' offices, two banks, both of which he duly noted, a dry goods store, an assayer announced by a hand-lettered sign advertising "Gold, Ninety Cents per Pennyweight," and a tailor's shop, not to mention dozens of men of all shapes, sizes, and manners of dress, sober and drunk, talking loudly and softly, gesticulating with their hands and contorting their mongrel faces as they made deals of one sort or another. The drama before him became even more incongruous when he considered that these few acres of land had been hardly more than a parcel of untouched wilderness not two years before.

Leading the horses down an alley toward the rear of the hotel, he was brushed by a finely dressed man with silver hair covered by a broad-brimmed hat, the type favored by planters. His expensive black boots were splattered with red mud. The gentleman wore a stern expression and did not acknowledge his passing contact with Hand. Some ten paces to his rear came a stout black man, laboring under the weight of two heavy carpetbags.

Hand asked him, "Is this the way to the stables?"

The man took the opportunity to rest the bags on the ground and catch his breath. After adjusting his spectacles, he pointed behind him, "Yessa. They're just around the corner there."

"You work here?"

"No, sah."

"Do they trade in horses?"

"I would expect so." The Negro continued with an easy laugh, "They seem ready to trade for about anything in this town."

Hand returned the smile and walked on, pulling at the resistant animals. He slept in the stable that night with his head upon the saddlebags. By noon of the following day, he had disposed of the extra horse for a good price and had succeeded in changing most of the paper money for either silver coinage or gold dust.

Following a less direct route back to Jiya's encampment, he paused several times among the trees to make certain that he had not been followed. These precautions seemed wasted when he discovered that his brother was not alone.

Hand squatted by the fire and pulled at a piece of dried meat. "So where did you find this one?"

"Ha, he came to me. Down the trail there. He made such a noise that I was able to step under the rock and surprise him."

"And so, my black friend, how is it that you speak our tongue?"

"My father was a Cherokee."

"And who might that be?"

"Jackson Adair. He is long dead now."

Hand stood up and shrugged. "I did not know him." He walked over and eyed the stranger from under the shadow of his hat. "I remember you from the town. I had never seen a Negro wearing spectacles before." He then turned and took his brother aside, and they talked in confidence for some minutes. Neptune stood quietly with his back to the rock.

In time, Hand returned. "What is your name?"

"Neptune."

He laughed his peculiar laugh. "Such a strange name! It suits you." His mood darkened. "Neptune, you may join us for now if you so choose. I do not relish leaving anyone to the whim of our white brethren. But do not seek to take advantage of our charity," he said, pausing to rest his hand upon the large knife at his belt, "for you are in our country now."

ELDON

The affection and the respect that you will command from this day forward as doctors of medicine—these are not things of your own making. These things have been earned for you by the decency and by the humanity of countless generations of good men of all faiths over the past three thousand years. These men are dead and for the next few years you will hold in your own hands this magnificent heritage. I trust that when it comes time for you to pass it on to your children not one of you will be ashamed.

—CHARLES DUNLAP, M.D.

Pyott, Arkansas
October 1978

The only animation apparent within the darkened office was the silent blinking of a call light on the telephone. Someone out there was trying to get through. A man sat behind the room's solitary desk, unmoved, watching the white point of light come and go, one, two, then three times, before the line fell mercifully dead—the answering service was now dutifully engaged. He would not have long to himself.

Before him, centered among a clutter of papers, stood a common kitchen glass filled with ice taken from the laboratory ice machine. With a deliberateness approaching ritual, he pulled a single key from the center drawer and unlocked another close by his right foot. From the drawer, he withdrew a half-empty bottle of domestic vodka, a black plastic ashtray, and a package of unfiltered Camels. He lit one, took a long drag, and placed the glowing cigarette next to the spent match in the ashtray. During exhalation, he poured four finger-breadths of vodka into the glass and swirled it twice, leaving the colorless liquor to chill while he continued his smoke.

He did not indulge in tobacco much anymore, once, maybe

twice a day at the most, and when he did, the acute effects of the nicotine were all the more pleasurable. He sipped at the vodka and, finding the temperature to his liking, followed the sampling with a large, cold swallow that filled his chest with heat. Now fortified by secret sin, he closed his tired, puffy eyes and found the courage to activate the beeper clinging to his sagging belt. This was to have been the doctor's afternoon off, but as the community's senior physician, his habits were well known. As far back as anyone could remember, his office closed at noon on Wednesday, but that did not really matter, for whether it be Wednesday afternoon, the Fourth of July, a Christmas Eve, or even the seventh game of the World Series, illness knows no holiday, and more often than not, his rare day off became simply another day.

On this particular Wednesday, the doctor in question, Eldon Weatherford, was not feeling well himself. He had awoken that morning with his usual backache, and the ibuprofen he took at lunchtime gave him heartburn, to which he applied a liberal dose of antacids. Before his nurse could bar the front door, Mrs. Elmore, the Methodist preacher's wife, dropped by with one of her nervous attacks, and then came Buddy Pruitt with a sprained ankle, and Arthur Weeks, who had lacerated his arm over at the shop, and now here it was almost five o'clock and Rheba Elliott was trying to have a miscarriage. The glass was now empty save the melting ice, and the Camel was pulled down to the barest of butts; it was time to move on. He fished a breath mint from the clutter on the desktop and struggled to his feet.

Standing on the back porch, Eldon began to grapple about in the pocket of his rumpled plaid sport coat, where his overburdened key chain had become entangled with a tightly coiled stethoscope. After being pulled this way and that, the keys suddenly jerked free and arched into the air. Before he could begin swearing, something moved at the corner of Eldon's vision, and he paused to glance toward the gravel parking lot. In an instant, he gained all visible control of his temper. He was being observed.

The lot was covered with fallen oak leaves. Dr. Weatherford's brand new blue Buick sedan was parked at the foot of the steps, and beyond it, against a wall of dense privet, sat an aged Ford station wagon that had once been some shade of maroon and was now largely given up to rust and primer. Mustering what little grace remained in him, he retrieved the wayward keys, secured the door, and continued toward his car. As he stepped down into the sunlight, the driver's door of the Ford opened to reveal a black man dressed in a gray cotton uniform. The man crushed out a cigarette among the stones before coming forward. He appeared to be in his mid-forties, and above his right shirt pocket was an industrial monogram outlined in red, stating the man's name. If the doctor was either surprised or disappointed at this unplanned meeting, his impassive pink face did not show it; he possessed the control of a person long experienced in presenting a consistent demeanor.

"Afternoon, Docta Eldon." The two men shook hands.

"Good afternoon, Dexter. You off shift?"

"Yessa. I'm lucky to be workin' in the daylight these two weeks."

The doctor jingled the keys for a short second before asking, "What can I do for you?"

"Paralee sent me."

"I figured as much. She must be doing mighty poorly if she sent you all the way over here to wait in this sun." Although mid-October, the temperature was well into the seventies.

"Well, Doc, it's hard for me to say. She may be and she may not be. She don't look no worse, but she's done started actin' mighty peculiar the last couple a days."

"How do you mean?" Dexter seemed to be searching for words. Eldon continued, "Like out of her head?"

Dexter shifted his weight from foot to foot as he talked. "Kinda. She wouldn't let me call you. She's been a-carryin' on all day long, raisin' hell, sayin' I had to come and fetch you personal. Said it was almighty important."

Foreseeing a more prolonged discussion, Eldon turned toward

his car and motioned for Dexter to join him. He switched on the ignition and lowered the electric windows to allow the accumulated heat to escape. The car smelled new. The passenger smelled of tobacco.

"When are you going to give up those cigarettes, Dexter?"

The question produced the standard reply, "Any day now, Doc, any day now."

Eldon stared straight ahead. "Now tell me again, exactly what's been troubling her?"

Dexter shook his head. "Well sir, I don't rightly know what to tell you other than all this talk 'bout dyin'.'"

"Now Dexter, we both know that your aunt will be dying soon enough. We have heard her discuss her predicament to no end. We both know that she has already had me out to the house twice before to witness to her imminent death, and we can both testify to the fact that she is very much still with us."

"You're exactly right, Doc, one hundred percent right, and Lord knows I'm embarrassed to be here, but let me swear to you she is indeed actin' mighty strange, strange even for Paralee, and swore to me she wouldn't last three days. Then there's all this stirrin' about in the house, movin' this and that, gettin' her affairs in order so she says. She 'bout broke my back bringin' in things from out back. Then last evenin' she starts raisin' Cain 'bout you gettin' over there—says she has somethin' to give you 'fore she leaves."

The doctor expired a long sigh and said, "Dexter, she has given me all that will ever be necessary."

"I know that, I know that, but she kept a-swearin' you'd try not to come, that the evil side would keep you away. Then she started to moanin' and told me what to tell you—to get you to come." He stopped there. He did not move or say anything further until Eldon turned to meet his dark stare.

"Well?"

"She told me she wants to give you somethin' of Shine's—somethin' he left special for you."

"Shine? Joe Shine?"

"That's who she was speakin' of. That's just what she said."

"Hellfire, Dexter, that is ridiculous. Shine's been dead most of ten years now."

"Docta, like you said, we both know that, but let me tell you, whatever she wants to say has to do with Shine."

The car fell silent. Both men sensed the conversation had come to an end. The older man was dog-tired and had yet to go by the hospital. The messenger was uncomfortable and wished for another cigarette.

"Okay, but I've got to go by the hospital first." Eldon thought on the problem for a moment. "Just tell her I'll stop by after supper."

Dexter's smile was bisected by a single golden tooth that flashed briefly in the failing sunlight. "I want to thank you for all you've done, Docta Eldon." He took the doctor's right hand and grasped it in both of his. His hands were rough and strong. "May the good Lord smile on you for this. Thank you, thank you."

The Ford smoked its way out into the street and was gone. The weary man sat in his new automobile, letting his forehead rest upon the rim of the steering wheel. He was trying to decide what might be wrong with the woman. Perhaps the tumor had reached her brain—not much he could help her with there. Perhaps it was some sort of side effect. After all, she was forever getting confused about which pill to take when. Who knows? He started the engine and slipped the transmission into reverse. Just short of the hedge, as he braked to shift into forward, a curious feeling, the vaguest of premonitions crept into this thinking, based upon a lifelong association with his patient—maybe, just maybe, the poor soul was calling her own end.

Eldon had known Paralee Williams for the majority of his professional life. The circumstances of their first meeting were as curious and inexplicable as the woman herself. Soon after his arrival in Pyott, fresh from the army and Korea, with one small child and a wife close to having a second, he had assumed the care of a widow woman, a Mrs. Loudon, well into her eighties, who was confined by age and heart disease to her large home at the edge of town. As was the custom in those days, he made house calls when necessary, and since the patient was both demanding and an invalid, he began to visit her almost weekly. In the course of these frequent visits, he got to know her housekeeper, a thin black woman, herself approaching middle age. This woman was Paralee.

One gray day in early December, Doctor Weatherford was called to the Loudon home for a final time. The older woman had expired in her sleep. To this very day he could remember standing in the sickroom at the foot of the great mahogany bed with Paralee at his shoulder. The two of them looked out across the sea of bed-clothes at the tiny, shrunken face framed by banks of musty pillows.

"She sure passed peaceful," Paralee offered.

"Yes, she did."

"Peoples come and peoples go," Paralee said, shaking her head slowly.

"Yes, they do, Paralee." He turned to collect his bag.

"I heard your wife was expectin' any day now."

"Why—uh—yes, she is." The question surprised him, first by being inappropriate in view of the present circumstances, and second, how did she know about the pregnancy? He completely failed to see her intent.

"She gonna be needin' any hep with that new baby?"

"I honestly haven't thought about it," Eldon said.

That ended the conversation for the moment. Three weeks later, in the midst of the holidays, the baby came. Compounding the situation, their older child contracted strep, and the baby nurse was ill with the flu, along with everyone else in town. Eldon was desperately in need of immediate help, and shortly after the dawn ending that first desperate, sleepless night, Paralee magically appeared at his office without the first sort of summons.

"I heard you callin' for help," she laughed. She never did quite explain herself, but then, as he soon found out, that was Paralee's way of doing things. She went on to work for the Weatherfords in one capacity or another for the next twenty-five years, and the premonition that provoked her appearance at his office proved to be neither the first nor the last of such visions. In the beginning he found it difficult to view them as any more than blind luck, but in time he grew to suspect that Paralee saw things that other people did not. Her "gift," as she called it, was well known thereabouts, and she was often called upon as an advisor in matters of the heart.

Paralee lived in Sula, which lay five miles west of Main Street along Sula Creek. The community boasted eighty-six inhabitants, all more or less related to one another, along with seventeen houses, a Baptist church, and the usual complement of domestic animals. The people were poor and black and isolated, but in spite of their humble means, they were a prideful bunch, bound by a self-esteem rooted in the land, for they were not tenants or migrants or shiftless "no-counts." Historically, they owned Sula outright: it belonged to them, all nine hundred acres, down to the last pig and chicken. In their oral tradition, as well as the county tax records, their collective inheritance came to them through the foresight of Paralee's ancestor, Manus Adair, a freedman of unusual foresight. He was rumored to have come from Georgia and had fathered nine children, six of whom survived to adulthood. Eldon knew little else about him.

At one time or another Eldon came to care for most all the people of Sula, a quiet advocacy that extended beyond the ever-expanding responsibilities of his practice. As was the custom in a rural practice, more often than not he was paid by barter, and indeed he first came to know Joe Shine, Paralee's brother, by way of reimbursement. In his youth, Shine had fooled around with illegal liquor, even did some time, but upon his release had repented and become a part-time gravedigger and yard man. One afternoon while pruning one of Mrs. Elda Tison's apple trees, he fell from the ladder and fractured his forearm. Mrs. Tison was known to be the most tight-fisted woman in town, and she predictably offered only a pittance toward his treatment. Shine wanted no charity, and in lieu of money, he offered Eldon his services.

Like his sister Paralee, Shine was not all that he seemed to be. He was indeed an excellent gardener, and under his influence the Weatherfords' lawn gained genuine respectability. But he had another side, however, a private facet of his life about which he never spoke. Eldon had noticed that folks frequently stopped by the house while Shine was working, and Eldon had always assumed that they were either paying social calls or were inquiring about other work. Then one Saturday afternoon he watched from the kitchen window as Shine and Olan Smith, a local farmer, stood talking out by the fig bush in the side yard. To Eldon's surprise, Olan opened his mouth wide, just as if he were undergoing an examination, while Shine leaned forward and peered inside. The black man then stepped back and seemed to offer an opinion, prompting Olan to close his mouth and nod in agreement. The two then walked out to a battered pickup parked at the curb where, from a locked wooden toolbox in the bed, Shine withdrew a small bag and handed it to the customer. They talked for a moment longer, money changed hands, and Olan left.

Eldon confronted Shine as he walked around the house. "What were you and Olan up to?"

Shine seemed embarrassed. "Oh, nothin'. We was just passin' time."

"What in the world were you doing looking in his mouth?"

"He just had some mouth sores he wanted me to take a look at."

"What was in the bag?"

Shine smiled as if stating the obvious. "A cure for them mouth sores."

"What do you mean by cure?"

With this admission Shine allowed himself an uneasy laugh. "Just some ole alum root." He paused and squinted one eye in

Eldon's direction. "Doc, I can see by the look on your face you don't know about me, do you?"

At that moment Shine, the gardener, let Eldon, the physician, in on a secret that was in actuality no secret at all. It seemed that Shine was also an herbalist, a plant doctor, the best for miles around, people claimed. At first he was reticent to talk about his work, but with reassurance he began to share a portion of his knowledge, and as he did, Eldon's curiosity grew. The physician was well aware that such things went on, the tiny bags tied about baby's necks with cotton string, the herbal teas and home remedies, but he had dismissed them as superstition or at best placebo. Now, as he stood chatting with Shine in the privacy of his back yard, he began to see a parallelism to his own work.

Eldon began to surreptitiously jot down what he heard, at first on odd bits of paper, and then as the list grew, ruled notebooks, numbered in order of their telling. He made a deal with Shine, a modest financial arrangement, and in return Shine shared with him all he knew about plant cures. Many of these dialogues were captured on his office recorder to be later transcribed by his secretary. The two men were often seen together in Shine's old truck, out on the dirt roads, walking the fields and forests, stalking the rocky hillsides and the damp courses of creeks, the portly doctor with his notebook and camera, the thin, wiry black man with a canvas bag worn over his hip.

Shine looked upon the plant world as his sacred ally and spoke of it with deep respect. He talked of the different plants and their cycles, their individual characters and ways of being, and of his mother and grandfather, who had been his teachers. "She used to say her daddy was part Cherokee Indian," he said. "Said he was from Georgia."

A bond grew between the two men in the course of their work, and from this collaboration came greater plans, for as Eldon's exposure to Shine's craft grew, he felt a growing need to document what he saw, to organize it and to put it in writing. He dreamed of writing a book that would give credence to Shine's self-taught pharmacopoeia, but the idea of making public this knowledge seemed to make Shine uncomfortable.

Over time Eldon supplemented his fieldwork with a modest library and assembled extensive files on whatever he observed or read. He made an exhaustive study of other sources and compared them with his own experiences. He took photos whenever possible and started a slide file. On several occasions, he amused himself with self-experimentation, using Shine's herbal formulary for his own minor complaints, trying to compare his anecdotal experiences with the known scientific profile of the plant.

Perhaps it was the incongruous nature of his and Shine's friendship or merely the diversion it provided, but by any measure, Eldon came to value it above his more conventional relationships. By this time in his life the newness of the practice was past, the endless litany of maladies had begun to exact their toll, until the thrill of the diagnosis and the thankful cure had become a routine aspect of his professional life. The time he spent alone in his study, or afield with Shine, or exchanging letters with a botanist at the state university, or awaiting a book in the mail, was never wasted; it provided a stimulus, something new, something invigorating, something to give balance to his existence. It kept him going.

But fate would have it another way, for not three years after falling from the apple tree, Shine dropped dead from a stroke. He was fifty-two years old. Eldon had watched many a friend and patient leave this world, but Shine's death hurt him deeply. Whether it was solely the shock of death, or merely the natural progression of Eldon's maturing cynicism, Shine's passing took the spark from Eldon and he now had nowhere to hide, no way to avoid the rising, unavoidable tide of more pressing responsibilities. A thousand times he tried to start writing again, but his heart was no longer in it. There was always a previous obligation, to family, to patients, to friends, until now, ten years later, the stacks of notes, the tapes, the sketches, the specimens, the boxes of photos and slides lay gathering dust in forgotten corners, victims of neglect and the amnesia for self that is spawned by excessive commitment to others.

Eldon parked in the empty doctors' lot and walked into the stark emergency room of the county hospital. He spoke to Mrs. Elliott and her husband, conducted a brief examination, gave them the good news, no miscarriage, and sent her home to bed for a week. The cafeteria closed at seven, and he made it with ten minutes to spare—chicken-fried steak, butter beans, and mashed potatoes. After all, his wife was in Little Rock with friends, and with the kids all gone it did not make any sense to go home for dinner. The sun was almost gone when he set out for Sula, driving slowly, for he did not relish talking to Paralee.

Once past the city limits, he reached onto the floorboard and dragged a black leather medical bag onto the seat next to him. By feel alone, among the jumble of pill bottles, reflex hammers, tongue depressors, and sample ballpoint pens covering the bottom of the bag, he located a blue glass bottle, a magnesia bottle by its shape but without an identifying label. Without so much as a glance, he unscrewed the cap and took two measured swallows. The familiar warmth reappeared within his chest, a mild flush swept across his face, and he reveled in the volatile aftertaste of the vodka. He chased it with two breath mints taken from the glove box.

After turning off the pavement just past the creek, he eased the Buick through a series of large puddles and cursed himself for not bringing the truck. Once past the openness of the church yard and its attendant cluster of houses, he made a second turn and passed into the trees. The road climbed a low hill, and at its crest he saw a yellow, unnatural light breaking through the screen of otherwise colorless foliage.

The house was frame, two stories, and had once been painted white. A front porch wrapped around the front and one side. The light in the forest came from a single bulb, the type meant to repel insects, centered above the front door where it cast a garish oval down the front steps and across the yard. Dexter's Ford was parked on the high grass to one side, and Eldon pulled in beside it and turned off the engine.

The steps were in need of repair, and he climbed with care. Once clear of them and onto the relative safety of the porch, he paused to catch his breath. To his right was a decrepit metal glider covered with faded canvas cushions. The sight of this relic brought back memories of afternoons sitting with Shine, sorting out their specimens and drinking Paralee's minted iced tea until the sun set behind the hills. This mental picture disappeared when the screened door moved toward him with a groan, stopping at halfway. A voice came from the dim hallway behind it, "Evenin', Doc."

"Howdy, Dexter."

"I'm sure glad you could come out. She ain't shut up since I got back. She so scared my wife she says she ain't comin' back up here, and I can't say that I blame her."

"Where's Paralee?"

"This week she's upstairs in her daddy's old room. She says she's nearer to the Lord there."

The stairs were narrow but extended to the second floor in a single span. The wooden floor creaked mightily as they entered the sickroom where the dying woman lay upon an iron-framed bed covered by layers of colored quilts. There was a mirrored bureau, a bedside table covered with medications and several containers of candy, and a single straight-backed chair. An electric heater sat in the corner, its element glowing red. A faded portrait of Jesus hung above the bed. The room was too hot and smelled of dust and sickness.

"Well, it's about time you got here. You're fortunate I'm experiencin' a slow death, or you'd a sure missed it."

Eldon smiled and pulled the chair to the bedside, setting his bag on the floor alongside. He took her hand. It was passive and cool to the touch. Dexter stood in the doorway and said nothing.

As Eldon drew closer to her, he sensed that his amusement might have been premature, for he saw in her face the certain signs of deterioration.

"What's the matter, Paralee?"

Her manner grew calm. "I'm goin' to leave you soon, Docta Eldon. My time's 'bout passed." She attempted to push herself up in the bed, but was unsuccessful. "You're one of the finest men God ever placed upon this earth. My brother said you was the finest white man he'd ever been acquainted with—said that the very day he was taken, and Lord knows you done more for this po' old woman than she ever deserved, and now I'm 'bout to join him and the time's come for us to settle up."

Eldon felt mildly uncomfortable under the weight of her adulation. She is not making good sense, he thought. "Paralee, I always helped you willingly. You've never been a burden. You don't owe me a thing. It's I who owe you."

She did not seem to hear him. Instead she pointed toward the far corner of the room. "Shine told me to give you that chest and all that's in it. He made me promise for the both of us—said only you would know what to do with it."

He adopted a more solicitous tone, "Now, you know that Shine's been gone a long time and . . ."

She held up her free hand to silence him. She somehow managed to push herself up from the support of the bed, and her voice went up an octave, "He ain't gone. He's only left the world of this po' flesh. He's still with us. He's with us right now." Her eyes grew wider and she peered toward the door, past Dexter and into the hall, causing her nephew to glance nervously over his shoulder. "He told me what to do, yes, Lord," she continued. "He done told me everything."

Dexter whispered "Amen" at Eldon's ear. The room had grown insufferably hot from the emotion of her words.

The dying woman went on, using the last of her strength, "He made me swear to it." Her voice fell back to a whisper. "He said it was a secret. He said you was to be paid for your kindness."

Eldon did not immediately answer her. Spent from her effort, she sank back onto the pillows in silence. He took her pulse and blood pressure, felt her brow, listened to her thin chest with its missing breast, peered into her mouth, and passed his hand across her abdomen. She shook her head no to each of his inquiries.

Finally he left her and examined each of her medications in turn. "This one is for mild pain and this one is for severe pain. I'll mark the bottles." She would not look at him.

"Paralee, this medicine is here for a reason. Dexter can't be here all the time. Do you want me to put you in the hospital?"

"No."

He turned to Dexter, who attempted to look apologetic. "I want you to see that she takes these pills correctly. Do you understand?"

"I will, Doc, I will. I understand."

"Is anybody helping her with the cooking?"

"Yessa. My wife or one of the other ladies is up here a couple a times a day."

Paralee spoke again. Her voice remained soft but seemed to increase in its lucidity. "Oh, Docta Eldon, will you please take the chest for me and Shine?" Tears welled in her tired eyes. "I can't plead with you no more. Please take it. I want to be square with you."

Eldon sat down again and hugged her wasted shoulders. "Paralee, I will accept Shine's chest as your legacy to me. I appreciate the kindness you have shown my family through the years. We all love you. Now will you promise to take your medicine as Dexter says and stop all this foolishness?"

"Yes," was all she whispered.

The two men stopped on the porch to talk.

"Who's staying with her tonight?"

"One of my boys is comin' up after supper."

"Now, Dexter, are you sure you don't want your son to tote that ole chest on down to your place?" the doctor said. "You could just make up a story to tell her—say he was taking it over to my house."

Dexter cleared his throat. "Well sir, she said you was to take it, and I wouldn't feel right goin' against her. It wouldn't be the right thing."

"Okay, okay. You win." Eldon sighed and pulled out his wallet and handed Dexter twenty dollars. "Would you mind seeing that somebody gets it over to my house on Saturday? Have 'em set it around back in the garage."

"Sure thing, Docta Eldon, sure thing."

The doctor descended the front steps and passed under the unyielding glare of the porch light. He reached for his keys and felt consumed by sadness.

The more I read, the more I was led to abhor and detest my enslavers. I could regard them in no other light than a band of successful robbers, who left their homes, and gone to Africa, and stolen us from our homes, and in a strange land reduced us to slavery. I loathed them as being the meanest as well as the most wicked of men. As I read and contemplated the subject, behold! that very discontentment which Master Hugh had predicted would follow my learning to read had already come, to torment and sting my soul to unutterable anguish. As I writhed under it, I would at times feel that learning to read had been a curse rather than a blessing. It had given me a view of my wretched condition, without the remedy. It opened my eyes to the horrible pit, but to no ladder upon which to get out. In moments of agony, I envied my fellow slaves for their stupidity. I have often wished myself a beast. I preferred the condition of the meanest reptile to my own. Any thing, no matter what, to get rid of thinking! It was this everlasting thinking of my condition that tormented me. There was no getting rid of it. It was pressed upon me by every object within sight or hearing, animate or inanimate. The silver trump of freedom had roused my soul to eternal wakefulness.

—NARRATIVE OF THE LIFE OF FREDERICK DOUGLASS, AN AMERICAN SLAVE (1845), FROM CLASSIC SLAVE NARRATIVES, EDITED BY HENRY LOUIS GATES, JR.

The following Saturday Dexter and his oldest son delivered the chest as promised. Paralee died in her sleep that same night and was buried next to her brother in the cemetery behind the Sula Baptist Church. The funeral was well attended by people of both races. Her memorial was carved from pink Georgia marble. She had picked out the stone herself soon after she was diagnosed as having cancer and had stipulated as its farewell message "Nearer My God to Thee."

In the wake of Paralee's death Eldon almost forgot about the chest, although it was far too heavy to move in from the garage by himself. It was not much to look at, made of tulip poplar, formed in a plain style, and closed with a hinged top. Originally painted blue-green, much of the color had faded into bare wood at the corners. Along the base were two deep drawers, only one of which retained its original brass pull, the other having no pull of any kind.

On cursory examination, it seemed to contain a hodgepodge of junk mixed with an assortment of outdated magazines, but rather than empty it there, Eldon waited several weeks for the return of his son and a friend from college. The younger men muscled the chest down to his basement shop, where under the glare of banked fluorescent lights, it endured Sara Weatherford's initial evaluation.

"Honey, this is truly a beautiful primitive," she began, assuring him repeatedly of her approval. "You must find out more about it," she said. She gave Eldon the assignment of cleaning out the chest, repairing it where necessary, and making it otherwise presentable, in preparation for placement in the upstairs entry on trial display.

In the course of fulfilling her request, Eldon found the contents of the upper compartment to be stratified. Just below the layer of magazines were two tattered quilts and beneath them a tangle of old clothes, long unworn and smelling of mildew. At the bottom were several neat stacks of even more yellowed newspapers and magazines, many of which appeared to have been shredded along the edges by mice. Wedged between the stacks of papers were a few personal effects, such as a pair of wire-rimmed spectacles, badly bent, a bone-handled shaving brush with most of the bristles gone, a number of small bags of mummified herbs, a thin bundle of letters bound with string, along with a disintegrating box of photographs and postcards, many of which had been spoiled by exposure to moisture. At the bottom, pressed against the wood, was an ancient Sears catalog.

The only items that seemed to be either salvageable or of immediate interest were a collection of handwritten notes concerning herbalism. Stuffed into a dog-eared manila folder, they were written in faded pencil, many accompanied by crude illustrations. On several of the pages Eldon read the signature "Burma Adair Williams," and a variety of dates ranging from 1914 to 1925. He also discovered, once the storage compartment was clear, the name *M. Adair* and the date *1868* carved into the floorboards of the chest.

Eldon laid the notes aside with the intention of carrying them to his study for closer examination and turned his attention to the two lower drawers. Neither of them worked smoothly; in fact, the one on the left could only be coaxed forward a few inches even with the gentle aid of a screwdriver. After some effort the right drawer, the one with the remaining pull, came free. It appeared to be a catchall for odd socks and a single cotton shirt, all of which had succumbed to dry rot, a collection of broken pencils, rusted paper clips, a cardboard fan from Cates Funeral Home, an incomplete deck of playing cards, a chipped glass paperweight, and at the very back, a single 1938 penny.

He now returned to the more stubborn drawer on the left. To improve leverage and ease the strain on his back, he lay on his side while attempting to shine a flashlight into the drawer's interior. Finding no apparent reason for its not moving, he hooked a single finger into the narrow crack and swept along the upper margin of the drawer compartment, hoping to find the source of the problem. About midway, he encountered a small piece of wood, a slat of some sort, obstructing the drawer's passage. The piece was movable, and by pushing it upward and out of the way, he was able to remove the drawer completely. Strangely, in contrast to the more functional drawer, this one was almost empty save for a solitary die and three 410 shotgun shells.

With the drawer out of the way, he once again lay down with the light in hand. The offending piece of wood was obvious, but upon adjusting his glasses, he saw that the obstruction was part of a bracket, one of a pair, fastened to the underside of the floorboards. On first impression, he could see no purpose in these brackets. However, when he reached into the cavity with his free hand, he was surprised to find that these brackets held a packet, a long thin parcel wrapped in brown paper, that had escaped his notice.

By again resorting to the screwdriver, he was able to further loosen the right bracket and free the parcel. Laying all else aside, he regained his feet and stood holding the discovery with both hands. By weight and shape, it felt like a book. The paper around it was fragile, brittle, unmarked as he could tell, and was bound along each axis by a length of frayed twine. He stared at the packet for several long seconds. Looking up, he paused to listen for sounds in the house above. There were none. Without bothering further with the drawers or the contents of the chest, he hurriedly climbed the basement stairs and eased down the carpeted hall to his study, closing, then quietly locking, the door behind him.

Eldon reached into the foremost desk drawer and withdrew a set of chromed scissors. He carefully clipped the string and turned back the paper.

The prize was indeed a book. It appeared to be a journal, bound in darkened leather. He laid the wrapping paper aside, and centered the book under the bright circle of light from the desk lamp. Pausing once more, now to wipe his bifocals clean of debris, he replaced them squarely upon his nose and tilted his head slightly back to gain the full power of the near lens. Without the slightest notion of what the book might contain, he ceremoniously opened the cover.

The paper was of high quality, and in such good condition as to belie its age. It was white, delicately lined in blue, and framed with a faint brown stain of age along the edges. The pages smelled of dust. The writing was in black ink, formed in an ornate, highly schooled hand. Eldon began to read.

The signatures were written as if the author had been practicing, as in a school lesson, using a slightly different hand with each repetition. He turned to the second page.

September 8, 1834

One week ago I crossed the Etowah River in search of my freedom, and God willing I have gained it. I believe I am now among friends and am well hidden in these unfamiliar mountains. Good fortune has brought me to this strange place and where it will lead me I do not know, but I will not be taken back to bear the burden of life long slavery. Hand says he will not betray me. I have no choice but to trust him.

September 10

We left the mountain yesterday and rode down into a valley of great beauty. There is a stream of clear water here and no habitation other than the cabin of another Cherokee, called Jahlo-I or Kingfisher. Hand says the old man is a maker of powerful medicines. He instructed me to stay by the water and care for Kingfisher in his absence. He continues to find both my writing and my speech amusing.

September 12

Hand rode north this morning. I do not know where he has gone. I found that he and the old one are long acquainted. Kingfisher says we are alone here and that no whites come to this place. He was brought here by Jiya, Hand's brother. The mountain around us is capped with white rock and rises on three sides as if we are held in a pocket. He calls it the Place of the Pigeons.

September 15

We walked into the forest today. Kingfisher caught a rabbit in a snare. We climbed among the rocks and he gathered plants to make his medicine. Although he is feeble and is greatly troubled by rheumatism, he takes to his work with great enthusiasm.

September 20

I write while the thoughts are fresh. A portion of my ink was spilled in our flight and I must take care with my words. We ground corn today and caught more rabbits, which seem to be plentiful here. I am worried for Hand. If he does not return I may go on alone. I have no idea of his brother's whereabouts.

September 25

Hand returned this afternoon and seemed much fatigued. He brought meat and flour and another rifle. He told us that the Georgia Guard passed close by during his travels, but he hid from them in the woods for an entire day. He expects warrants to be issued for both him and his brother. He says we must leave this place and ride west before the first frost.

September 26
We climbed the mountain once more, and Hand shot a deer. He remained there while I returned to the valley with the meat. Kingfisher said that he goes to see about his money. I am uncertain of what he means.

September 29
Hand returned in the afternoon. He is in the darkest of moods. He says if he had some whiskey he would surely drink it all.

September 30
Kingfisher rolled the beads for Hand and they spoke for some time alone. Hand left once again and told us that he will return within the week. He went to provide for his family. He also spoke of collecting what is owed him. I hope that he can accomplish this without another fight.

October 1
I am now of the disposition to tell my story or at least as much of it as the ink will allow. This ledger was purchased solely for that purpose, and I have long concealed it in anticipation of this joyful day. May God smile on my effort.

My name is Neptune Adair. That is not my given name, but is the name I have chosen for myself. I am uncertain of the year of my birth, but feel that I am presently about thirty years of age. My birth place was the Cherokee Indian Nation in the shadow of the house of my father, Jackson Adair, a Cherokee of full blood, also called Warspeaker. My mother was Elizabeth Owens, born a slave in Carolina.

I am of two bloods, but due to the illegitimate circumstances of my birth, I was bound into slavery as was my mother, a cruel and inhuman system into which I came through no choice of my own, and under the grace of a just and Almighty God will not die. Although the course of my *life until now has brought me only obscurity, perhaps this account of my struggle for freedom will find value in a more enlightened and just society.*

Eldon shifted his weight in the chair. His back was already tightening up. After he was more comfortable, he took a pencil from the desk and began to make notes on what he was reading. First he wrote the name *Neptune Adair* and the date *1834*, connecting it with an arrow to the notation *M. Adair* and the date *1868*. He tapped the pencil on the ruled pad several times before jotting down the name "Burma Adair Williams." Adair was repeated too often here to be just a coincidence. And wasn't Paralee's mother, or was it her aunt, named Burma? "Damned fascinating," he whispered to himself.

October 2

> *Kingfisher is determined to go into the forest alone and says he will stay the night. I am unused to being alone myself and am at first uncomfortable with his proposition, but on studying the matter realize such solitude is a welcome aspect of my freedom.*
>
> *I spent my early years on the lands of my father near the Conasauga River, where he owned several thousand acres of good land and operated a ferry. At the time of my earliest memories, he accounted for twelve slaves among his properties and was considered a man of some means. We were well fed and our work though hard was not unreasonable. From my later experiences, he could be termed a good master, a condition of high status for any slave.*
>
> *My experiences until the age of six were no different from those of other boys of my station in life, other than my premature exposure to certain responsibilities expected of an adult. I fed the chickens and collected their eggs, and helped feed and otherwise tend to the livestock, but most of the time I was free to run the woods which in those times were little more than wilderness. In the course of my education upon the farm, and even before I gained any knowledge of written language, I was taught my numbers*

Mission School
Spring Place

p 53

by another slave, Henry Harris. On several occasions I caught glimpses of the master's accounts and soon discovered that I possessed a remarkable capacity for numbers, an ability that brought no end of amazement to my fellows, my master, and to my later disadvantage, his white overseer, a man of the basest instincts. Whenever he would find my sums scratched into the earth, he would whip me or shorten my mother's rations. These beatings quickly taught me the value of stealth.

My father sired two sons by his Cherokee wife. They were my unacknowledged half brothers, a fact that was sensed and shared, but never spoken. The older son was William, and the younger was Farris, whose age was about that of my own and who would become my primary playmate. At the age of eight he was sent to the Mission School at Spring Place where his education became mine, for he secretly shared his lessons with me. I soon found that my skill with words was the equal of my skill in numbers, but from long seasoning, I recognized that too overt a display of my growing knowledge would not be accepted in a system based upon the subjugation of anyone with dark skin. I concealed my literacy—content to entertain, to amuse my father and his friends by doing long sums in my head. Although publicly he gave me little credit, I began to receive subtle forms of patronage, most importantly access to his house.

October 3

The weather has cooled and there is some color on the mountain. The chestnuts will soon fall. Kingfisher has returned and he told me more of Hand. There is a story here too.

Eldon looked up from his reading. I wonder what he means by that, he thought, as his eyes turned back to the diary.

In the winter of 1816, when Farris was fourteen and his brother sixteen, Warspeaker was unexpectedly taken by a fever and died within a week, leaving his earthly affairs in much disarray. I am sure of the year, because it was the first year of which I was aware and could record in my memory.

His sons were as yet too young to direct their inheritance, a circumstance which at first brought me great sadness, but in time has led me to this place and my freedom.

The operation of the estate fell upon his wife, Usdi, a kindly woman with no inclination toward commerce, and his younger brother, John Adair, also called Bobcat. He was an erratic man, illiterate yet wise when sober, violent and unpredictable when drunk. The overseer of the farm, a vile and dishonest man named Wigley, saw in my master's death an opportunity to advance his status. Like all overseers with whom I have had acquaintance, he viewed the slaves as brutes, no better than animals, and singled me out for special mistreatment, in part because of my attitude and abilities and perhaps because he suspected my parentage. One day he beat my mother with a strap, an affront that I could not answer. Over time, determined to gain revenge, I gathered evidence of his thievery and presented it to Bobcat. Although he never thanked me, perhaps out of embarrassment, or in any other way acknowledged my revelation, Wigley was soon dismissed.

For all of Wigley's sins, the farm suffered in his absence, largely due to Bobcat's drinking. The following summer Bobcat began to sell off stock. On one such trip he took myself and another slave to Vann's Ferry on the Chattahoochee River to sell horses. Upon our arrival we once again chanced upon our mutual adversary, Wigley. It seemed he was now in the business of catching runaway slaves, an occupation well suited to his cruel and inhuman spirit. They exchanged sharp words, but Bobcat was not drinking and the slavecatcher left with the ferry.

That night Bobcat fell in with a pair of white men at the tavern, and when thoroughly drunk entered into a foolish wager—the next morning they were to race on horseback from the ferry to the crest of the first hill above the river, a distance slightly less than one mile. A small crowd gathered for the show and as was the custom at such events, the drinking continued. Although fast by the standards of Cherokee stock, Bobcat's horse was no match

for the white man's. As I watched his defeat from the bluff,
I had no notion of the implications of the wager. I soon
found that not only did he lose his string of horses, but in
a side wager he also lost me. On a drunken whim, I was
now cast into the unknown, at the mercy of two men who
seemed little better than the detestable Wigley, a world
away from my mother and all that I had ever known. Later,
as I was led across the river and toward Carolina, my new
owners laughed about their windfall and talked of money
and women. My hatred for these men and their kind was
tempered by overwhelming fear.

October 5
There is still no sign of Hand. A chill has come to the air,
but I have seen no frost. Kingfisher slept most of the day. He
appears ill, but will not tell me what is troubling him.

 I was taken directly to Augusta and sold to Weyman
Ellsworth, a prosperous banker and cotton broker. The sale
was not at auction, but was handled by an agent, privately,
and was determined entirely by my talents. When asked if I
could read and write, I replied that I could read from the
Bible and write my name, being reluctant in view of my
past experience to reveal the extent of my ability. Literate
slaves were considered by most a liability, but by the same
token, I was determined not to work as a field hand. I also
lied about my name, telling him that I was called Neptune,
a name I fancied from one of Master Farris's texts.

 My decision on this point was the correct one, and by
luck alone I found the agent had been searching for a male
slave of my age, about sixteen years, who had some facility
with words. It remains until this day the turning point in
my life, for Mr. Ellsworth meant me to enter into training
as his personal servant, and upon entering his household I
encountered a manner of living which was until now
completely foreign to me.

 I was to remain a part of his household for almost a
dozen years. During that time I was afforded great kindness
in most things, and for that reason look upon my former

owner as a beneficent and reasonable man. He was stern and exacting, and I do not mean to say I went without punishment, but he never struck me and his admonishments were consistent and appropriate under the rules he established. He taught me many things, and for the first time I was allowed to see the extent and power of the white man's society. Perhaps I would still be under his roof if events beyond my control had not intervened.

October 7

Kingfisher is troubled by a dream and begins a fast. He takes me with him to a blue water spring at the foot of the mountain where we bathe. That night he goes into the woods once more to be alone. I sense he is a powerful magician.

Mr. Ellsworth was a widower with two daughters, both of whom were by the time of my appearance, grown and married. I was put in the charge of an older slave, Gideon, who had been with Mr. Ellsworth's father before him. He in turn put me with yet another slave, Dock Thomas, who instructed me first in the care of the carriage and horses. After I mastered this task, I was brought into the house and was taught how to serve and greet visitors, and in time to assist Mr. Ellsworth whenever he deemed it appropriate. This assistance took the form of deliveries, errands, and to a limited degree the filing of household accounts. Gideon warned me from the beginning that honesty must be my byword, for in matters of money, Mr. Ellsworth had no peer and would send me to the fields without a second word should I ever fail him.

Mr. Ellsworth was said to have the finest library in Augusta, and indeed I have never seen a larger assemblage of books. The only book allowed me without restriction was the Bible, but in time the temptation grew too great, and I began to examine the books in the library in spite of this restriction. Gideon caught me there almost immediately and admonished me for my deceitfulness. Mr. Ellsworth was away at the time, but upon his return he called me to the library. His words still speak to me as if it was yesterday.

"*Gideon tells me you are quite the scholar,*" *he said. I could not answer. He rose from his desk and walked behind me. I did not move. I expected a blow at any moment, but instead he spoke into my ear as if he were telling me a secret.* "*Neptune, you are different from most of your black brothers. I saw that the first time I spoke to you. That is the reason for your being here. It is your greatest strength and at the same time your greatest weakness. You have much further to fall than the others. You are never to enter this room unless you are summoned here by myself. Do you understand me?*" *I answered forthrightly that I did.* "*In addition, you will read nothing but the Bible you were given. You will concern yourself only with your business and nothing more.*" *He raised his voice until it became painful.* "*Do you understand!*" *From that day forward I heeded his every word. I gratefully accepted the one week of half rations without the slightest word of protest.*

I did not understand the motives behind his leniency, and even at this distant date they remain so peculiar as compared to all other whites I have known, that I continue to have trouble in believing my good fortune. The reasons for his tutelage lay in his relationship with Gideon and in his own peculiar personality. (He was to later call me his experiment.) The men had been together since Mr. Ellsworth's childhood in Charleston. Their relationship as adults was such that although based on the principle of master and slave, the arrangement was so mutually agreeable that the dependence of each on the other was unique. Gideon was his eyes and ears, his confidant and spy, his advisor and sage. But Gideon was aging and Mr. Ellsworth saw an eventual need. I was meant to fill that need.

October 9
I killed a deer by the creek with Hand's gun. If the slavecatchers come I will surely use it on them. I have had much time for thought. I wonder if anyone will ever read of my struggle?

Mr. Ellsworth had frequent occasion to travel. In the fifth year of my service, Gideon was taken with dropsy, and I was allowed to accompany Mr. Ellsworth to Savannah. For this purpose, I was given two suits of new clothes. Never in my life had I felt as grand as I did at that moment.

The following year Gideon died, and I was given his room above the carriage house. Another slave was bought to fill my previous position as driver and house servant. I traveled to Savannah and Charleston at least once a year in company with Mr. Ellsworth, and with each trip my experience grew. He allowed me pen and paper, and for the first time I was able to practice my writing without resorting to secrecy. I came to understand Gideon's slavish gratitude and can now admit to feeling it myself, yet despite my advancement and relative good fortune I continued to feel a deep dissatisfaction with my lot—a secret longing that no amount of privilege could satisfy—I wanted to be free.

On the occasion of his fiftieth birthday, Mr. Ellsworth called me to his side and told me that upon his death, I could expect my freedom, a confidence which served to temporarily satisfy my impatience. However, fate would have otherwise for he soon chose to remarry. His new wife, Alice Gallman, was younger than himself by some twenty years, was widowed also, and had three young children. She let me know from the start that she did not share Master Ellsworth's dependence upon my services. She seemed jealous of my position and missed no chance to admonish me. All of the household slaves felt the weight of her new discipline.

Shortly thereafter Master Ellsworth fell ill and took to the bed with a complaint of the intestines. The doctors did not think he could survive. I was torn at this point between his promise of freedom and the hardened attitudes of his wife. I began to lose all faith in gaining my freedom by way of my owner's death, and upon that realization, I began to plan my escape.

Eldon paused here and walked to the bookshelf. From behind two thick volumes on obstetrics, he withdrew a flask and took a long swallow of Scotch whiskey. He was intrigued by what he was reading. He took a second swallow.

October 10
Kingfisher has still not returned. I thought of going to look for him, but I have no idea of where he might be found. As he predicted upon my arrival the sky is now dark with pigeons. They seem to roost in every available tree and I am kept awake at night with their chatter.

To everyone's great surprise, the master survived his grave illness and if anything, seemed invigorated by this brush with death. In the spring of this year, he announced, as was the usual, that I should prepare his affairs for travel. However, we would not be going to the coast, but rather to the west, and that much of the journey would be on horseback and that I would not need to pack the customary trunk. It seemed that he had acquired part interest in a mine in the gold region of Georgia and was intent on seeing his investment first hand. I thought to discourage him in consideration of his recent illness, but was tempered in my protest by the realization that such a journey would bring us close by the Cherokee Nation and provide me the opportunity I had so long sought.
We at first traveled by stagecoach to a frontier town called Gainesville where we hired the horses he had mentioned. We crossed the Chestatee River at a heavily used ford and continued on to Auraria, a town in the midst of the gold fields. The mine in question was close by and Mr. Ellsworth took a room in a boarding house, informing me that we would be staying several days and left me as was his custom to make my own arrangements.
The muddy town was newly built, full of rough men and their loud talk. I met another slave in the stable, and he told me that the Etowah River lay hardly a mile down the road to the west and was crossed by a sturdy bridge at that point. This river was the supposed boundary between

the Cherokees and the whites, but to my understanding this division was made of paper, and the miners dug where they pleased, much to the dismay of the Indians who had no power to stop them.

Good luck smiled upon me once again that day for in the afternoon it rained heavily, but the skies cleared toward dusk and that night brought a bright half moon. I attended to my master's baggage and was dismissed to take my supper in the stables. About midnight, assured that my master and most others were fast asleep, I gathered up my meager bag and my letter of protection, forged to resemble his own hand, and quietly left the stable, walking without haste toward the river. Above the bridge I heard men talking and turned from the road at that point and ventured into the woods. There was lantern light among the trees on the opposite bank, and I walked for some distance before finding a place to cross. The water was swift, but never rose above my waist. The far bank was low and devoid of cover, and I left it quickly, climbing a steep, barren hill on my hands and knees, making as little noise as was humanly possible. I then walked straight west as fast as safety would allow. I found no path and within the first mile my hands and trousers were torn and I was bleeding from the many briars and sharp stones. At one point I narrowly escaped certain injury after stumbling onto the brink of a deep hole used by the miners. Only the moonlight and a merciful spirit saved me.

October 12

Kingfisher finally returned and seems stronger. He read the signs and said another moon will pass before we see a frost.

At first light I reached a small stream and sat down, exhausted beyond measure. I ate a little of what I had brought and felt renewed by the food and the thought of my freedom. There was no sign of pursuit, and I began to take heart that I had succeeded. As the daylight grew, I rested, drank, and ate more from my cache. I left the stream with the rising sun at my back, and within a short distance I

*chanced upon a path which seemed to lead toward the
north and the west. I walked and ran and walked for some
miles, crossing many high ridges and more streams, always
in the deep woods with no sign of either house or farm. I
was determined to continue without rest for the remainder
of the day and reasoned that I could cover most of twenty
miles if I used all of the light. After several hours the foot
path crested a ridge, and I spied higher mountains to the
north. Deep in thought and perhaps too certain of my
safety, I ran downhill from this high place in my eagerness
to continue and in so doing passed by a large rock. As I
paused under this rock to catch my breath, a strange man
unexpectedly stepped forward and stood before me. By his
dress, his turban and his silver jewelry, I recognized him as
a Cherokee. He held a rifle across his chest. I greeted him
in his own tongue, a language I had not used in many
years. He smiled, lowered the gun, and returned my
greeting. "Good morning, black man," he said. Then he
laughed, "You move too fast for this time of day. Come and
share food with me." With the speaking of these words, I
knew that he would aid me in my journey.*

Footsteps sounded in the hallway and stopped before the door
to the study.

"Eldon, are you in there?"

"Yes, I am."

"Have you noticed the time?"

"No."

"We are supposed to be at the Cogburns by six."

Eldon glanced at the walnut-cased clock on the bookshelf. It
was 5:15. "Okay, dear, I'll be along shortly."

But I presume not to dictate in these high concerns of government, and I am fully convinced that such important matters are far above my ability; the duty and respect we owe to religion and rectitude, the most acceptable incense we offer to the Almighty, as an atonement for our negligence in the care of the present and future wellbeing of our Indian brethren, induce me to mention this matter, though perhaps of greater concernment than we generally are aware.

—William Bartram, *Travels through North & South Carolina, Georgia, East & West Florida* (1773–1778)

The Snowbird Mountains, North Carolina
July 1980

Vester Bales could spot them a mile off. Tourists just looked different; they might as well have worn badges on their sleeves. Usually the menfolk came in to ask directions—the roads around Brunt County were confusing enough even if you had lived here all your life—while the wife and kids headed for the restrooms and then hit the Coke machine. The hotter the weather, the more that old machine sang. Vester appreciated the money, but he always found it a bit amusing that people should sprint to the toilet to find relief and then just as quickly gulp down another twelve ounces of liquid. After pumping gas for eighteen years, the one thing that you learn is that it's people's nature to be peculiar. Take that man in the RV with the Arkansas plates, for example. He had no more business driving that big old thing than Vester did flying an airplane. He not only drove over the curb pulling into the station, but came real close to sideswiping Mat Pullins's new truck, and then for good measure took a good five minutes to park. If it hadn't been eleven o'clock in the morning, Vester would have sworn the man was drunk. Strange too, that unless there were other folks sleeping in the back, the fellow appeared to be alone.

Eldon Weatherford sat behind the wheel for several minutes

after cutting off the engine and consulted his map and notes. Satisfied of his present location, he climbed down out of the front seat and onto the stained asphalt, taking the time to stretch his legs and to readjust the wide concho belt around his more-than-ample midsection. The sun was bright and July hot, and he reached back inside to fetch a small Stetson to cover his bald head. Vester stood behind his shopworn desk, quietly watching Eldon's progress, trying to size him up, waiting for the inevitable advance on the office. He did not have to wait long.

Eldon opened with a "Howdy."

Vester howdied back and added, "What can I do for you?"

"Well, I need some directions."

I thought you'd never ask, Vester thought, trying to look receptive.

"I'm looking for Santeetlah Road."

Now if there was one thing Vester could do besides run a gas station, it was give directions. He demanded precision, however. "Would that be Big Santeetlah Road or Little Santeetlah Road?" he asked.

A transient look of bewilderment passed over Eldon's flushed face. He pulled a small spiral notebook from his shirt pocket, and flipped through a couple of pages. "Uh, I'm not sure—just says Santeetlah Road."

"Lookin' for any place in particular?"

"Well," Eldon paused to consider to whom he was talking, "why, yes, I'm looking for a man named Isaac Corn. Would you know of him?"

"Ike Corn? Sure I know him. Lives way out at the end of Big Santeetlah." Now he was prepared to continue. "Follow 124 West on out of town about two miles. Then turn left on Lickett Road and go about four more miles. You'll pass the ranger station on your left and then skirt around the reservoir on your right. The road will dead-end by a Baptist church—you turn right on . . ."

Eldon made notes on his pad with a Cross pen, and when Vester was finished, he repeated the directions to the letter.

"I sure thank you for your help."

"No problem."

"One more thing."

"Shoot." Vester glanced toward the pumps. A Chevrolet wagon had pulled in, and a woman and two kids rushed around the corner of the building.

"Do you have a Coke machine handy?"

"Yep. Through there in the garage," Vester said, pointing across the room, while in the same motion lifting the key to the restroom from its hook. He stepped by Eldon just in time to hand it to the woman from the Chevy who had appeared at the front door.

While simultaneously pumping gas and giving the woman's husband directions to the Bear Cove Campground, Vester continued to watch as Eldon got not one, but three sodas from the machine. Something different was going on here, he thought. That fellow just did not fit the usual tourist formula. What was he up to and why did he want to talk to that old Cherokee? He continued to watch as Eldon eased the RV from its resting place and pulled back onto the highway, headed west as directed, but never easing off on the brakes. "That guy can't drive worth a damn," Vester mumbled to himself.

Was Eldon hungry again or was he simply being deceived? The gnawing was back and the indigestion too. Maybe it was the sausage biscuit and two cups of coffee he had wolfed down in Murphy. Hungry or not, he needed to take stock. Pulling into the parking lot in front of Cagle's Hilltop Grocery, he angled the truck away from the store, out toward the highway where there was plenty of room. Why had he rented this rolling house, anyway? He would have been much more comfortable in the Buick. So much for the great adventure. After checking his supplies, he dismounted and ambled inside.

Harroldsville was too small for any chain stores, like Ingles or Piggly Wiggly, and the Hilltop was the maximum size that the town could support. Lou Cagle, the grocery's proprietor, was content with her homey operation; why, she had seen the future in one of those twenty-four-hour superstores down in Atlanta while visiting her sister, and she was certain that the future would never make it this far. Her little store stuck to the basics, plus whatever a camper or hunter might need, be it Coleman fuel or charcoal briquettes. The business was seasonal, heavy in the summer and fall before easing off come winter, and that suited her just fine. Either way she made a comfortable living and had spent February in Florida for the past five years. She tried to treat most folks the same, a hello and a smile, and she took no particular notice of Eldon until he pulled into the checkout line behind Elda Scruggs, who was buying a week's supplies for her four kids. He was an obvious outsider and looked kind of uncomfortable, physically uncomfortable, as if he were ill. He laid out a jar of peanut butter, a package of oatmeal cookies, and two Snickers bars before handing her a twenty-dollar bill. His voice was soft, not pushy at all. "Could you tell me where I might find a drugstore?" he inquired.

She noticed he was perspiring heavily, despite the fact that the air conditioner was set on a solid seventy. "Around the corner on Graham Street—on the other side of the courthouse." He looked real pale, and Lou suddenly became afraid that he might faint on her. "You doin' okay today, mister?"

"Must have been something I ate didn't agree with me."

"Well, you talk to Harry, the pharmacist. He'll fix you right up."

"Thank you, kindly." Eldon always found it a bit surprising how much people depended on their druggists. He liked it that way.

The drugstore was quiet save for an older woman at the pharmacy counter who was talking far too loud, as if she were hard of hearing. The druggist stood listening patiently to her tirade, slowly nodding his head in agreement. Although he could not see the man's name tag, Eldon guessed that this must be Harry, dressed in steel-framed glasses and a blue pharmacist's shirt, the type that buttons up the side. In spite of his distress, Eldon had no intention of interrupting. He bought four large bottles of Mylanta and paid the high school girl working the register. He asked if he could see a local phone directory, and although he found four Corns listed, none bore the name Isaac nor did they confirm the proper address. Once reestablished behind the wheel of the RV, he wasted no time in taking several large swigs of the creamy antacid. After wiping the white residue from his lips with a handkerchief, he prayed for some minor relief, but the medicine had no immediate effect. Impatient with his increasing discomfort, he decided to wait no longer, and started the engine.

Eldon drove as far as the National Forest Ranger Station, where he stopped to see if they had any maps. While reaching into the display rack, he noticed that his hand was trembling badly, and he glanced toward the counter to see if anyone was watching. The pain was no better. After confirming the gas station directions with the ranger on duty, he hurried back to the camper as best he could. He entered via the rear door and pulled a can of Coke from the refrigerator. The trembling seemed worse, and he could feel the surge of his heart in his ears. This was getting damned serious. From one of the galley cabinets, he retrieved a leather bag, the sort used as a shaving kit, and pulled out several plastic pill bottles and set them on the table. He poured the Coke over a coffee mug of ice and took an initial sip to siphon away the foam and the first inch of liquid. From yet another cabinet under the seat, he pulled a half-gallon bottle of bourbon and poured a large shot on top of the Coke. He emptied the contents of one pill bottle onto the table and quickly downed two of its white tablets. He counted the remaining tablets—twenty-eight. From a second bottle he took a single yellow tablet and swallowed it. After finishing the drink, he rearranged the gaudy orange and green floral cushions on the seat and stretched out to let the medicines work their magic.

The entry of the alcohol into his bloodstream calmed the tremor, and after a half hour or so, he felt the onset of the euphoria produced by the narcotic. The second drug began to ease the boring pain in his gut. He fell asleep and dreamed of a young woman and a chase through a forest, a scenario that when awake would make no sense. The slamming of a car door fortuitously interrupted his drugged sleep, for when he consulted his watch, he found it was fifteen minutes before two. The inside of the RV had grown unbearably hot without benefit of the air conditioner. He must get moving.

The road hugged the reservoir for several miles, rising and falling in steep curves. The lake was not full, and the remarkable blue-green water, the sort of shade Eldon associated with purity and clear air, did not reach to the trees, leaving an unsightly band of red earth to mark the shoreline. Once beyond the Otter Creek Baptist Church, the road twisted ever more tightly and Eldon passed into a deep, unbroken forest that rose precipitously to the left and fell just as quickly away from the shoulder to the right. He almost stopped at one point when he came upon two crows pulling at the flattened carcass of a rabbit, but otherwise he made steady progress. He encountered little traffic. After crossing a wide, noisy creek and its corridor of cooler air, the road straightened for a time, and soon crossed over the last thin arm of the lake. The road forked, and he took the higher one, passing by several small houses and then a sign that read "Silver Boar Lodge." Just past this sign the road began a steep ascent until it finally crested in a high gap affording a panoramic vista of a high valley rimmed by magnificent mountains. Eldon stopped here to reconnoiter and walked over to the metal guard rail, clutching a map. The entire floor of this broad basin was carpeted by a dense rain forest unbroken by any visible sign of habitation. A cool wind rose out of the valley and the map folded and fluttered in his hand. Where in all this vastness would he find the key to the puzzle of Neptune's diary?

Renewed by the spectacle in front of him, he mixed himself another drink, taking care to go lighter on the bourbon this time. He followed the drink with more of the antacid. A scattered progression of road signs confirmed his position as he descended from the gap, and he left the pavement and turned onto Slick Creek Road, which twisted sharply for two miles before crossing the stream of the same name. Big Santeetlah Road, the object of his search, appeared just before the creek and led into a narrow bottom that at intervals was broken by small pastures and an occasional frame house. He bypassed numerous pieces of rusted logging equipment, both trucks and trailers, and a newer metal building marked "Snowbird Community Center." At last he came to Santeetlah Creek, where a group of children, obviously Cherokees by their faces, were pitching stones into the water. They stopped their play as he approached and watched sullenly from the overgrown roadside as the RV eased by. Vester had been unsure of how far past the creek Ike lived, but told Eldon he thought that it was less than a mile. Soon enough, he spied a mailbox painted an unattractive beige, bearing the name Isaac Corn in hand-painted white letters, and under it, in black paint upon bare plywood was the solicitation "SMALL ENGINE REPAIR."

Any attempt to climb the narrow drive was out of the question, and Eldon maneuvered the RV onto the thin shoulder of the road, checking in the rearview mirrors to see if he had allowed enough clearance for other cars to pass. After all the hours and all the miles, he was finally here. With that singular realization, a dark fear passed over him, an uncertainty of purpose, a premonition of failure, the risk of rejection, the possibility of seeming foolish and out of his element. Eldon had never even met a Cherokee. The man might not give him the time of day. Perhaps he would be standoffish, even hostile. Did Ike receive the letter at all? Eldon reached for the pill bottle on the dash and took another of the Percocets, using the melted water from his drink to get it down. Courage, Eldon, courage, he thought—you've come this far. From yet another bottle, he took a sip of mouthwash and began to swish it about, while simultaneously picking up his hat and reaching for a thin briefcase laying on the floorboard. He cracked the door and spit the green liquid into the dust of the roadway, and then finally, mentally ready and pharmacologically fortified, he stepped down into the sunlight.

Isaac's modest house was about thirty paces off the road. It was frame, not unlike the many others Eldon had passed in this final phase of his mission, and, on closer inspection, was in need of some repair. Zinnias, marigolds, and clumps of orange daylilies encroached upon the gravel driveway, and insects buzzed about in the still air. The margins of the porch were demarcated by potted plants, ferns mostly, and the chairs were of the common kitchen variety. There was no doorbell, so Eldon tapped on the screen, at first softly, and when he got no answer, more firmly, but still he got no reply. The single open carport was empty. He cracked the screen and peeked through the glass of the door. From what he could see no one was in the front room. Should he just go in? No, waiting would be better, perhaps back in the truck, but then it was cooler here on the porch. As he considered his options, he heard something—a come-and-go, repetitive-type of sound, not unlike the strike of a hoe or shovel in soft earth. It seemed to originate in the rear of the house.

Carefully, quietly, he rounded the corner and walked through the open carport, past a large stack of firewood and several heavily scarred sawhorses, past spent tires, miscellaneous machine parts, and rusted cans of motor oil. Beyond a narrow strip of lawn, he saw a luxuriant vegetable garden. A man stood between two of the rows, slowly chopping at the dark soil with a hoe. A small branch flowed past the garden, and several baskets of bright tomatoes sat on the grass alongside an array of other hand tools. At intervals, the man would stop to rest or shift the position of his attack, at one point grasping at his flank as if stretching out a cramp. After watching him for a moment, Eldon stepped from the shadow of the house and paused on the grass. Although he could not have seen Eldon's advance or scarcely heard his footfall above the sound of the hoe, the gardener suddenly stopped and turned to face his visitor.

The man was of medium height and wore a faded red ball cap. He was dressed in worn jeans and a green khaki work shirt spotted with moisture. His midnight-black hair was cut short and flecked with gray. He did not appear startled, but stood resting part of his weight upon the handle of the hoe, as if waiting for Eldon to make the next move.

"I'm looking for Mr. Isaac Corn."

The man said nothing, but put down his hoe and walked forward. He brushed off his hands on his pants and when he reached Eldon, he extended the right one and replied, "You got him."

His hand was covered in a thin layer of dirt and was callused and strong—a hand well-accustomed to hard work. "My name is Eldon Weatherford. I wondered if you had gotten my letter?"

The dark eyes yielded to a faint smile, "So you're the doctor. Yep, I got it. Sorry, I didn't get back with you, but I ain't much on writin'. I wondered the other week if you'd turn up." His tan-brown skin was heavily lined. Eldon wondered if they might be about the same age.

Eldon felt a bit lightheaded. "Is there someplace we can sit down and talk?"

"Sure. Come on in."

The main room of the house was partitioned by either furniture or built-in cabinets into a living room, a dining room, and a kitchen. A wood heating stove was centered on the longest wall, and most of the furniture was clustered about the television set. The chrome-legged kitchenette table was covered in a blue-checked oilcloth centered upon a set of much-chipped Aunt Jemima salt and pepper shakers. Ike removed his cap and hung it on a peg by the back door. He pulled out one of the kitchen chairs and said, "Can I get you anything to drink?"

"Water would be okay."

As Ike prepared the drinks, he said, "Plenty hot out there today."

"Yes, it is. Looked like you were working up quite a sweat."

"Yeah, I'm the workhorse around here. You drive all the way from Arkansas?"

"Yes."

"That's a long way. I was through Little Rock once when I was in the army." He brought the drinks to the table, ice water and what appeared to be lemonade. "Whatever you have to say must be pretty important to bring you all that way."

Eldon put his briefcase on the table and opened it. "Well, it might not be important to some people, but it's very important to me. You see, all this trouble has to do with a hobby of mine." He pulled out a spiral-bound notebook and opened it to the first page. Ike sat watching him without comment. "In my spare time I study history, specifically Native American history."

"I thought you were a medical doctor."

"I am. As I said, I do this as a hobby." Eldon increased the seriousness of his tone. I must try to sound convincing, he thought. "Lately, I have been researching Cherokee history, specifically the Western Band, the Cherokees in Oklahoma." Ike continued to listen, taking occasional pulls on his drink. "Do they call you Isaac or Ike?"

"Just call me Ike, Doc."

"Well, Ike, I've been researching the life of a Cherokee leader named William Hand."

"Can't say as I've ever heard of him," Ike replied, taking note that the doctor's breath smelled of whiskey and mouthwash.

"That's not surprising. He died in 1844."

"I guess that explains it," he laughed. "That's a long while back."

"Yes it is. So you are not familiar in any way with Mr. Hand?"

This time shaking his head in the negative as if to emphasize the point, Ike repeated, "No, but then I've never been real good with rememberin' names."

"Are there any folks around here named Hand?"

"Naw, not that I'm aware of."

This is not going to be easy, thought Eldon. He indicated the position of Hand's name on a flow chart in the notebook, "Anyway, this Mr. Hand was originally from Georgia and . . ."

"Now, I've heard of that," Ike interrupted, breaking into a broad grin.

Eldon smiled along with him. "Well, he was from Georgia and moved to Oklahoma around 1835."

"Was he moved or shipped?"

"I don't know for sure, but I think he left of his own accord."

This caused Ike to raise his eyebrows. The simple mannerism heightened Eldon's feeling of insecurity.

"He was a man of some prominence in the Western Cherokee Nation. He owned a store and was an associate of Joseph Vann, said to be the richest Cherokee in Oklahoma. They were killed together in a steamboat explosion as a matter of fact."

"That's very interestin', but what does that have to do with me?"

"I'm not entirely sure, but in researching Mr. Hand, I discovered that he had a half brother named Jiya." Eldon watched Ike closely when he spoke this name but no response was forthcoming. "In checking on all of this, both through information obtained from the Western Band and through the rolls available through the Eastern Band, it seems that Jiya never left Georgia."

"You mean he died there?"

"Not that I can tell. In fact, in comparing rolls, in particular the Miller Roll of 1906, Jiya, or a least a man of that name, turned up in North Carolina. He is also listed as the grandfather of Mary Bird."

Ike sat back in his chair. "Mary Bird was my grandmother."

"And if that is so, Jiya was your great-great-grandfather."

"Well, I'll be darned." He laughed again. "Too bad he weren't rich like his brother."

"I doubt that he was. It is my thinking that Jiya hid from the federal troops during the removal and somehow made his way into the mountains to hide, where in time he was counted among the North Carolina Cherokees, who were protected by state law from being removed."

"Hmmm," was Ike's only response.

"Do you have any knowledge of this man Jiya? Through your mother or your grandparents, perhaps? Do you have any family records?"

Ike took on a more introspective countenance at this point. "I remember my mother and my grandmother talkin' about the family all the time, you know the stories old people tell, but they were both gone before I turned twelve years old." He picked a piece of ice from the glass with his fingers and crushed it between his teeth. "To tell you the truth, now that you mention it, I do remember seeing Jiya's name on the old rolls—my sister keeps a copy of them. Ain't it funny how you can forget things like that? In fact that reminds me of something else . . ."

He pushed back his chair and walked to a cabinet at the front of the house. He returned with a book, a Bible, an old Bible by the looks of it. Opening the thumb-worn front cover, he pointed to a list of names and dates written there. "This here is all the family tree that I know of." He pointed his finger at the top of the list.

Eldon pulled a pair of reading glasses from his front pocket and looked at the column of names. The entries were written in both Cherokee and English. "May I make a copy of this?" Eldon asked.

"Sure."

He began to jot down the names and dates inside his notebook.

Ike finished his drink and sat the empty on the kitchen counter. "Where did this fellow Jiya live in Georgia?" he asked casually.

"I'm not exactly sure," Eldon replied continuing to write, "but he is listed in an early census as having a small farm in the Armuchee Valley. His half brother owned a larger farm somewhere on Chickamauga Creek."

"Where's that?"

"In the northwestern part of Georgia, up toward Chattanooga and Lookout Mountain." Eldon finished his writing. "Would you have any more information like this?"

"No, that's about it."

"Would your sister have any more information?"

"She might. I got two sisters living in Cherokee, and a brother over in Snowbird. I can give you their addresses."

"I would sure appreciate it." From the briefcase, Eldon pulled a manila folder and a map, which he partially unfolded. "I have highlighted where Hand might have had his farm, as well as where Jiya might have had his."

Ike scrutinized the map and ran his finger along the course of Chickamauga Creek. Eldon opened the folder and placed several pieces of paper upon the map. "Would these references mean anything to you?"

On the sheet of paper was a neatly printed list of words and phrases, again in both languages. "Kingfisher, Place of the Pigeons, Lookout Town . . . ," Ike read aloud, shaking his head. "No, can't say I ever heard of any of these places."

Eldon's sense of disappointment grew with each negative. In addition, a wave of nausea rolled over him so suddenly that he wavered in his seat. Droplets of perspiration sprouted across his forehead, and he felt the color drain from his face. He covered his mouth with his hand and closed his eyes.

"You doin' okay, Doc?" Ike asked. "You're lookin' a little green."

"Not really. I think I'm coming down with the flu."

"I had it last winter—'bout killed me. Do you want to lie down?"

"No . . . , thank you." In a burst of extreme concentration, Eldon gained temporary mastery over the illness that sought to bring him down. He spoke slowly, knowing full well that he was fast approaching the end of his capabilities for that day. "Did you ever hear your mother mention a man called Neptune?"

Ike continued to shake his head. "Neptune? Funny name. No, never heard of anyone called that."

A cold sweat now streamed from Eldon's every pore, as if his body were making a final attempt to rid itself of some poison. He pulled a damp handkerchief from his seat pocket and mopped weakly at his brow. "I'm going to be staying around here a couple of days," he whispered. He cleared a silent, dyspeptic belch, which he managed to cover with the damp handkerchief. "I really must be going." He began to put away his materials. His pale hands moved as if he were in slow motion. It seemed as though even his vision was failing him.

"Do you have a restroom I might use?" Eldon asked, closing his eyes to balance himself.

"Sure. Just through the kitchen on the right."

Ike watched Eldon leave the room and then placed the doctor's half-empty glass on the counter next to his own. He heard the sound of retching through the closed door. Without making a sound, he pulled Eldon's map from the open briefcase and studied it for a moment, paying great attention to each notation. He then replaced the map and quickly flipped through the stack of papers beneath it. When he came to the list of place names, he pulled it from the stack and deftly slipped the single piece of legal paper under a cushion on the tattered sofa. He heard the sound of the toilet flushing and stepped away from the table with his hands to his side. Eldon reappeared in the kitchen, and his beefy face now appeared ashen.

"You look awful, Doc. You sure you don't want to lie down?"

"No thanks. It's just a bug. I'll just take me a little nap in the truck."

"Whatever you say."

Eldon closed his briefcase without a glance and continued, "As I was saying, I'll be here a couple of days—would you mind if I got back with you in case anything comes to mind?"

"Sure. I ain't got no phone, but I'm here most of the time, unless I'm at church or gone to town with my wife."

Before moving toward the front door, Eldon shoved a blank piece of paper across the oilcloth. "Would you mind giving me those other addresses before I go?"

Ike watched the ill man descend the entire driveway before retrieving the list from beneath the cushion. He carried it back to the cabinet containing the Bible, where he picked up a notebook and pencil left by one of his grandchildren. Finally, from a shelf above the television he took down a long wooden box and returned to the table. Before allowing himself to sit, he glanced once more out the front window. Reassured of his privacy, he worked for a time in silence, making notes while attempting to reproduce the salient points of Eldon's map. He then opened the box and removed a large manila envelope closed by a clasp. Inside was a yellowed piece of paper covered in a complex of faded lines and symbols. He placed the fragile paper next to the list and after a long period of comparison, placed both the papers back in the envelope. This was one of the few times in his life when he wished he owned a telephone.

With the envelope tucked firmly under his arm, he left the house by way of the back door. There was a certain determination in the manner of his leaving and in the way he strode past the garden and bounded across the rickety footbridge spanning the stream. He took a well-traveled path into the forest and within seconds passed from sight.

By the time Eldon reached the road, the nausea had returned. Before he could get inside to the RV's toilet, he felt a hot liquid rising in his throat and jerked away to avoid hitting the door. Gripping the handle for all he was worth, he sent a stream of vomit splattering into the middle of the road and onto his shoes and the cuffs of his trousers. It came and came again until finally, gasping, the violent contractions in his gut eased. All strength passed from his knees, and he slumped backward against the seat. "Oh, my God," he hissed through the bitter taste in his mouth. In the midst of the mess at his feet were streaks of bright red blood mixed with what appeared to be coffee grounds. The medical implications were clear.

A movement at the periphery of his vision caused him to look up. Across the narrow dirt road, not twenty yards from where he stood, was the same group of Cherokee children he had passed on the bridge. There were five of them, two older boys and three little girls, their almond eyes silently sharing his distress in unison. Before they could either move or speak, he turned away and struggled inside, slamming the door after him. He put the keys into the ignition, closed his eyes, and breathing heavily, rested his forehead against the steering wheel.

"Eldon, you damned fool, you're killing yourself," he groaned.

THE WAYBILL

"STOP THE THIEF"
Two Hundred Dollars Reward

For apprehending and bringing to conviction, a young man who calls himself Elijah Dotson . . . ; he came to this place about 12 days ago, under the pretense of commencing the Hatting business, but took his departure on the night of the 11th instant, at which time he stole from me one gray Horse, about 15 hands high, 6 years old, rather light made, no brands recollected . . . ; also at the same time robbed me of one gold and four silver watches, viz., one gold watch, double cased, the outside case considerably damaged, day of the month from the centre, Swiss plan, fly sprung, cap, gold chain and seal, which appears as if touched with mercury. One silver, double cased English, silver cap, makers name Eamer and Sons, London, No. 361 . . . The above Dotson, or Craddock, or Evans, is about 20 or 21 years of age, five feet 8 or 9 inches high, rather gross made, fair complexion, . . . The above reward will be given to any person who will apprehend and confine him in any gaol, so that he can be brought to conviction.

John M'kee
Chester Court-house, S.C.
May 13, 1815

—ADVERTISEMENT, MILLEDGEVILLE, GEORGIA, NEWSPAPER

New Orleans
April 1984

The morning's call touched the sleeper softly. Somewhere beyond the open window, a pair of solitary footfalls receded along the graveled walk. Clay awoke unclothed, lying flat on his back, half-covered by a tangle of sheets. A pleasant, soporific coolness filled the room with inertia, and from the vantage of his borrowed bed, he watched the early sun project a caricature of a French door across an expanse of faded floral wallpaper. Other than a subliminal headache, he felt amazingly well, considering the time of day and the extent of the previous night's debauch.

With some effort he managed to push himself erect, then onto the side of the bed, taking great care to avoid waking the woman next to him. The room, just for a moment, spun around him and then, just as rapidly, righted itself. He rubbed at his face and then at his left shoulder, the one with the scar, for it was stiff from his drugged sleep. Before standing, he glanced at the luminous red numerals of the bedside clock—7:50.

The wooden floor creaked under his bare feet as he crossed to the bureau, where from among a jumble of personal effects, he pulled a pair of thin-framed, horn-rimmed glasses. After some further rummaging about in a suitcase propped open in the corner, he gathered up the appropriate clothing and padded toward the kitchen. Standing before the sink, he first drank a large glass of water, followed by a similar measure of iced tea poured from a pitcher in the refrigerator. From a bottle on the sill, he added three aspirin tablets, more for prevention than for any substantive pain. He replenished the tea, added more ice, and idly drifted into the living room.

A door slammed somewhere outside, and Clay peered through a shutter onto what seemed an empty street. Satisfied that he would not find the source of the noise, he closed the louver and circled by the bookcase, punching off the overheated amplifier as he passed. Two partially filled wine glasses stood on the coffee table, surrounded by an array of discarded clothing. Rather than trying to sort it out, he finished the tea and left the empty glass by the others, using his free hand to retrieve a pair of loafers protruding from under the sofa.

He made no serious attempt at consolidated thinking until he had properly adjusted the shower, filling the bath with steam. As the stream of hot water cascaded over the crown of his head, he considered his meager responsibilities. The reunion was scheduled for ten, giving him less than two hours. Royce's punctuality was traditionally in question and the Gillios would most certainly be fifteen minutes late, meaning that he was roughly on schedule. There was no need to hurry.

He toweled dry and opened the small window for ventilation. After wiping the condensation from the mirror, he stood for a moment studying his image. He would soon be thirty-eight years old. Always an attractive man, he stood just over six feet tall and had managed to maintain his weight at around 180, give or take 5 pounds. For the past five years he had sported a mustache that he felt gave his face more character, and his thick sandy hair showed no trace of gray. His hazel eyes were as yet unlined, but the furrows across his forehead had deepened. He remained fit—the muscles of his arms and belly retained their tone—but that was a relative matter at his age, and he was well aware that he no longer possessed a schoolboy's body. He carefully shaved and then compulsively trimmed his mustache before starting to dress.

His dress shirt traveled well, still crisp and white, and he re-tied the knot in his tie several times until satisfied with the result. Returning to the bedroom, he remembered his linen sport coat tossed across the back of an armchair, but elected to leave it be until the negotiations with his hostess were completed.

The feminine topography of the bedclothes had not changed since his departure. He knelt gently before a spray of brown hair spread across the nearest pillow and whispered, "Brenda." He got no response. "Brenda," he repeated, applying gentle pressure along the curve of her hip, "wake up."

She moaned but did not stir. "What time is it?" she whispered, as if in pain.

"About nine," he said, glancing toward the door.

"Oh, my God!" she mumbled, sliding further under the quilted bedspread.

"You sound rough," he offered.

"You have no idea. I feel absolutely awful. Terrible. Shitty." She adjusted the covers. "Now please leave me alone. If you re-spect me at all you'll let me die in peace."

He measured his response. "Can I help you? How about some aspirin? Maybe some iced tea?"

"Ohhh," she groaned. "I'm not really sure what I want right now."

He persisted. "Do you want to go to Brennan's?" No reply. "You know, to meet my friends for breakfast?"

She rolled toward him and uncovered her face, squinting into the reflected sunlight. He noted that she looked good even with-out her makeup. "I forgot all about that—your college friends. When?"

"Ten o'clock."

She half-raised herself onto her elbows and looked toward the clock as if she did not believe him. Slowly she sank back onto the pillow, reclosing her eyes in the process. "Dearest Clay, I really and truly feel like hell," she said, now rubbing her temples.

"You said that. Your head?"

"Yes, that too, but more my stomach. The mere thought of food makes me nauseous."

"Ah, come on, you know a couple of Bloodies would turn you around."

"More like upside down." She would not be going. He already knew that. . . . His timing had guaranteed the desired response. "Oh Clay, I'll just have to pass," she said. "Please don't be mad at me. I don't know these people and they don't know me. All I'd do is sit there and look sickly." With that pronouncement, she disappeared once more beneath the coverlet, freeing Clay to grab his coat from the chair back and move toward the front door.

"Do you want to use my car?" she called after him. "The keys are on the bureau."

"No, thanks. I feel like taking the trolley."

As he latched the wrought-iron gate, Clay smiled at the prospect of going it alone. Actually he was quite fond of Brenda; she was nowhere near an embarrassment, but this morning was special, and she had been entirely correct in her assessment. But why the inconsistency on his part? In actuality, none existed. For several years now Clay had taken very little seriously, least of all himself, and nothing about the beginnings of this day had given him any reason to effect a sudden change. He was presently very comfortable with his lack of commitment to the opposite gender and was not interested in allowing this detachment to lapse.

The weather was a delight, a bright acute sun, the temperature in the mid-sixties, with the molasses-thick humidity of summer still many weeks away. He tossed his coat over his shoulder and walked the two blocks to St. Charles Avenue in good time. Within ten minutes he caught a downtown trolley and took one of the slatted wooden seats not far behind the driver. The car was nearly empty—the only other passengers were two elderly women dressed for church and a black teenager with a gym bag. He lowered the window to admit a welcome breeze as the car rocked its way along the shaded avenue, stopping at irregular intervals either to deliver or to admit passengers, brief noisy interludes bracketed between the jangle of bells and the clatter of change falling into the coin bin. The procession of ancient live oaks lining the street, as well as the many fine homes that they guarded, had changed little during the twelve years he had been absent from the city. Their solidity gave him a feeling of immense security, and perhaps in reaction to the peculiarities of that particular spring morning, he indulged in an uncharacteristic moment of introspection.

Clayton Chastain Hardigrew first came to New Orleans in 1970 at the age of twenty-three. Blessed with a high draft number due to the fortuitous timing of his birth, he had achieved a business degree at the University of Tennessee unhampered by the specter of military service. His availability attracted a great many job offers, the most attractive being a marketing position with a computer firm headquartered on the West Coast. The firm was heavily involved with the petroleum industry at that time, and after considerable success in Texas, its goal was to push eastward into the Gulf Coast market, a market centered on New Orleans. He arrived there in a six-year-old Plymouth and spent a portion of his first paycheck as a down payment on a used Norton motorcycle.

On the advice of an aunt, his deceased mother's sister, who was a longtime resident of that peculiar city, he found a place to stay uptown, a short walk from Audubon Park. The Victorian building was originally constructed as a private residence, but later, in more expedient times, had been partitioned into apartments, three upstairs, three down. The Deltonia, as the house was unofficially called, with its granite steps, beveled-glass entry, and dark oaken hallways, had retained an air of distinction in spite of its relegation to rental, providing its tenants with the faded impression of living in extraordinary circumstances.

His room was on the second floor to the rear of the house,

connected to the former kitchen by a forgotten staircase and over-looking an ill-kept yard walled in by ornamental bamboo gone wild. His immediate neighbor fronting on the street was a social worker in her late twenties, a New Yorker named Cynthia, memo-rable by way of her red hair, liberal bent, and considerable promis-cuity. Just across the hall and occupying the remainder of the floor were Royce and Ernie, both law students, men of contrasting styles, who in spite of their extremes, were oddly complementary.

Ernest Xavier Gillio was from Marrero, just across the river, where his father owned a busy garage. He had been an all-state safety in high school, a talent that brought him a scholarship to the state university in Baton Rouge, where he played two credi-ble seasons before injuring his neck in the second quarter of the Ole Miss game. The career-ending injury, a ruptured disc, was ultimately fortuitous, for while it allowed him to retain his schol-arship, it also granted him both a medical exemption from the military and a release from any further distractions posed by col-lege athletics. Since he was the first of his family to gain access to higher education, Ernie possessed a strong perspective on the blue-collar ethic, a point of view that fostered an extreme sensitiv-ity concerning his modest upbringing. He used his dark good looks and gregarious nature to best advantage and compensated for any intellectual deficiencies by the steady application of hard work. His consistent, goal-oriented behavior was to make him a success in the law and reward him with the prize he sought most—social position—as well as its economic corollary, money.

Ernie's roommate, Royce Compton Harris, was raised in Greenville, Mississippi. He spoke with the easy accent of the delta aristocracy, a way of speech long associated with privilege, sub-stantiated by his uncle's being a state senator and whispered talk of family money. His academic record was erratic, consistent with an unpredictability that at times obscured his superior intellect. He had gone north to Princeton for a single year, then left by choice to spend some time in Mexico, where he learned to speak passable Spanish. Upon reentry, he enrolled at the University of

Florida, having by that time reaffirmed his affinity for warm weather, and where over the next four years, he gained a degree in history, an extended tenure necessitated by two changes in his academic major.

Royce entered law school only at the pleading of his widowed mother. This represented a compromise meant to further delay the assumption of any responsibility, and afforded him a course of study broad enough not to confine him upon its completion. In addition, his enrollment guaranteed a renewal of his student deferment. His association with Ernie was by chance meeting in the student lounge, but their relationship was of mutual benefit. Although as undisciplined as his friend was determined, Royce's brute intelligence carried them both into the upper third of their class, while in return for his intellectual generosity, he profited from Ernie's aggressive, yet affable nature. Tall, thin, blond, and marked by weak blue eyes, Royce had grown philosophical under the influence of too much pot, and in his relationship with Clay, he served as a foil to his roommate's often narrow pronouncements.

In the fall after his arrival, Clay began work on his MBA by enrolling in evening classes at Tulane. This perpetuated, at least in part, his former student lifestyle, such that he shared a certain perspective with his new neighbors, and in a short time the three became the best of friends. This communal outlook was particularly beneficial to Clay for it offered him both the security of male companionship, while providing some compensation for the vague uneasiness he felt in the corporate world. Their day-to-day association was taken for granted—they lived from weekend to weekend—but like all of childhood it had to end, and as is so often the rule among boys, its demise began with the intervention of a woman.

Just before Clay received his degree, Ernie met a girl, Gwynne, a rich man's daughter from west Texas. She was blonde, almost beautiful, and undoubtedly well-bred, but possessed of an obnoxious predictable propriety that made it impossible to really like her. In weak deference to their friend, Clay and Royce concealed their mild distaste for her, a needless concession, since it was doubtful that Ernie would have noticed all but the most obvious affronts, for his attention was by now directed elsewhere. Within weeks she drew him away from their accustomed way of life at the Deltonia, a separation that was to become permanent, first by the ignorance of infatuation, then later by intent. After graduation Ernie secured a position with a substantial intown law firm, and he and Gwynne were married that September. The year was 1972.

Royce's path through life continued to be less direct. Once Ernie moved out and Clay transferred to Texas the following year, he hung onto the old ways for a while, playing in adolescent parody the professional student, taking a graduate law course here and there to no purpose. With the help of his uncle, he did a six-month stint with the National Guard over in Biloxi and then disappeared for almost a year. Abruptly, without explanation, Clay received a cryptic letter from Paris—it seemed Royce was taking some courses there, the Napoleonic Code and all; that message was followed by another year of silence before the correspondence resumed—grainy, floridly colored postcards, always moving eastward, Turkey, Afghanistan, Kashmir, Bali, pictures of obscure ruins, minarets, and smiling, golden Buddhas. Clay tried to maintain contact via letters mailed to the nearest American Express office, but he was never sure how much of his news got through.

Late one night he received an unexpected call from the Los Angeles airport and found that the prodigal Royce was home. The chatter on the line was familiar, but at the same time slightly different, and Clay wondered about the face behind the voice as he returned the receiver to its cradle. In time Royce returned to New Orleans, where he dabbled in real estate or some such—Clay was never quite sure. Occasionally during a move or while searching for something misplaced, Clay would come across a cigar box filled with those far-flung cards and think of his friend and better times. Other than a selection of letters from his mother and a few from his ex-wife, they comprised his only concession to nostalgia.

In contrast to his rare communications with Royce, cards regularly arrived from Gwynne Gillio each Christmas; usually tasteful affairs picturing the kids, ending in a series of typeset names, always with a handwritten addendum in colored ink along the margin, inquiring about his health and that of his little girl, a gaffe he excused in view of its source. The cards would sit on the mantel for a month or so as part of the seasonal decor, before being dispatched with the trash to start the new year.

A sharp turn by the trolley interrupted his daydream, reminding Clay to disembark at Canal Street. He jogged through the light traffic into the shadow of the dim storefronts and began walking toward the river. It being Sunday, the street vendors and the usual crowds were absent. He turned onto Royal, where within the measure of a few steps, he encountered the peculiar bell jar atmosphere of measured decay that characterizes the Vieux Carré, a gumbo of confined air and muted light, a mixture of smell, sound, and visual texture found nowhere else.

He crossed over at Iberville in front of the Monteleone Hotel, and doubled back in the next block to avoid a fat man washing the curbside with a hose. He slowed his pace, stopping on two occasions to stare into darkened antique shops. At the corner of Conti, in front of Manheim's Gallery, he paused to check his watch and found that he was early. Rather than window-shop and look too much the tourist, he continued on a few more feet to the pastel facade of the restaurant. The hostess, a thin woman with her hair severely confined in a bun, informed him of Mr. Harris's arrival and suggested he join him outside on the patio.

The restaurant's patio was enclosed to form an atrium. The two higher walls were of plaster over brick, the plaster missing in spots, faced to a large degree with both standing and climbing greenery. The enclosure tended to magnify sounds, echoing its feeling of intimacy, mixing the chatter of the patio with the tinkling of tableware from the dining room.

Clay quickly spotted Royce, standing near the center, engaged in conversation with an unfamiliar bearded gentleman, soon introduced as a Mr. Englehardt. The stranger appeared weathered, looking slightly out of place in a worn wool suit. As he extended his hand, Clay noted he wore a heavy bracelet of Indian silver. The stranger did not linger and excused himself to sit at a nearby table with a couple who appeared to be in their sixties.

"Who was that?"

Royce chuckled as he answered, "Another old friend. He dates from my misbegotten days in Mexico. I see him with about the same frequency as I do you. Funny how you have both turned up at the same time—such a coincidence." His voice had evolved a studied, more deliberate tone. He offered his hand a second time—still the same weak handshake. "How have you been?"

They sat down near a bank of subtropical foliage. Clay ordered a Bloody Mary, and Royce continued with a milk punch. The passage of years had produced other changes in the great thinker: shorter hair, still quite blond, exactly combed; the same boyish face, now bracketed by oversized, black-framed glasses, faintly tinted, perhaps an attempt to disguise the wearer's advanced myopia; and finally, more significantly, a bow tie, also in black, perfectly in keeping with an elegant, white linen suit in an unintended (or was it?) parody of the river culture.

"Did you walk over?" Clay asked.

"Yes. It's not far, and I'm afraid about the only form of exertion I'm subjected to these days."

"Tell me again exactly what you're doing."

Royce once more offered an easy laugh, "Renovations mostly. Some rental. The law never suited me as you know, much too confining, and when I got back from overseas I bought some apartments off Washington, then some duplexes out in east New Orleans, turned over a couple of houses—just bought and sold when it looked right. I really can't complain. I've done well."

"Tell me about the house on Esplanade."

"It's a big place, a real mess when I got it, all dark and Gothic. It suited my mood at the time. I had this idea to make it into a hotel, but . . . ," He shrugged slightly, "then I moved in. Never intended to stay." He signaled to a waiter. "How's your love life?"

"Slow, but that's come to suit me. I see some locals out of biological necessity, and a recent one down in Atlanta when my aesthetic senses need attendance."

"Aren't you staying with someone?"

"A girl I met while skiing. She lives uptown near Napoleon."

They both ordered a second drink. Clay already felt the first. His headache was mercifully past.

"And yours?"

Again the smile, this time more subtle, a device. "Off and on. I was close to someone for most of last year." A strange choice of words, thought Clay. Royce finished his drink and stared down at the ice. "She was, uh, an artist, a painter, and like most of them, frustrated at her lack of success. One night she got real down on New Orleans and me, said I was too morose or something, and I was a little loaded—actually we both were—a fight ensued, in which I informed her in no uncertain terms of her marginal ability and that she would be no better a painter in New York than she was in New Orleans, so she got understandably pissed—left for the Big Apple within the week." He swirled the last of the ice about in his glass as Mr. Englehardt's party rose and entered the dining room. "I understand that her most recent work has completely vindicated me."

"Do you see much of Ernie?"

"Usually by accident or by reason of Gwynne's hypertrophied sense of social obligation. She continues to consider me too controversial, but at the same time recognizes that I add a bit of color. They have me over to dinner once in a while, or we might meet for tennis. They're real big on their kids and their club."

"I thought you said you got no exercise."

"It isn't, the way I play." He glanced at his watch and excused himself.

Two couples had taken Mr. Englehardt's place. The women were both well dressed, but overly coiffed, while their male counterparts contrasted, one being thin and almost appropriate in a loud madras jacket, whereas the other was beefy and florid of complexion, wearing sunglasses and a formal Stetson. He wore snakeskin cowboy boots. Clay tried, but could not follow their conversation.

Royce returned with Ernie and Gwynne, having met them in the foyer. Smiling broadly, Ernie applied a perfectly firm handshake, just as Gwynne offered her perfectly smooth cheek to be kissed. Her hair was blonder than he remembered. She looked great to the smallest detail, an attribute Clay continued to resent as an unfair advantage. Rather than resuming on the patio, they were seated inside, where the Gillios' tardiness was blamed on a slack baby-sitter.

"How's business?" Ernie began.

"Great," Clay answered. "We weathered the slowdown." He would have answered the same even if it were not true.

"Aren't you in the hardware business, Clay?" Gwynne followed.

"Building materials—a family-owned business along with my brother." Clay looked toward Ernie. "And how's the lawyer?"

"I can't complain. I'm paying the bills. The firm's growing while a lot of others aren't."

Royce carefully buttered a piece of bread. "How's your father?" he interjected.

Clay appreciated the question. "He had a rough year or so following my mom's death, but he's better now—enjoying retirement."

Another round of drinks was consumed as breakfast was ordered. Ernie ordered scotch. Gwynne passed. The waiter then brought coffee and two loaves of warm French bread.

"When's the last time you had a decent po' boy?" Royce asked.

"More like a real one. Let's see . . . ," Clay talked as he broke bread, scattering shards of brown crust over the spotless white tablecloth. "Sammie's, Pass Christian, fried oyster, nineteen and, let's see, seventy one. Does the place still exist?"

"It did as of Labor Day," Ernie said.

Breakfast arrived: two eggs Benedict, one eggs Sardot, one eggs Hussard. The presentation was perfection.

"My God, it's great to be back," Clay continued.

"Who's this woman you're staying with?" Ernie asked as he cut into his portion.

"A redhead named Cynthia," Clay returned, faintly winking an aside to Royce. He was referring to Ernie's noisy liaison with their former neighbor at the bygone Deltonia.

"Does she still talk in her sleep?" Royce asked, continuing the assault.

Ernie frowned slightly at the two of them and repeated, "I'm serious." Gwynne missed the point.

"A woman I met in Colorado last winter. She works for IBM."

"Oh, for the single life," Ernie said, flashing his patented smile.

"Where were you skiing?" Gwynne followed, giving her husband a slightly disapproving glance. She was beginning to catch up.

"Vail. I met her in Vail."

"Oh, what a beautiful place. Didn't you just love it!" she gushed in response. "One of Ernie's partners has a condo there, and we just love it."

"Looks like we all love it," he agreed. "Royce, do you love it?"

"I *really* love it," Royce replied, reaching for the cream.

"How many drinks have you boys had?" Ernie asked with the slightest of frowns.

"I'll only admit to being several ahead of you," Royce replied, smoothly avoiding an apology.

The remains of the main course were taken away, and the mandatory bananas Foster were prepared before the table. Clay attempted to balance the alcohol with a third cup of coffee. They talked of old friends in new circumstances, Ernie's practice and his passion for sailing, Royce's ever-evolving renovation, Clay's fixation with running, and finally children. Clay had prepared himself for the predictable inquiry about his divorce, and the instant a lull settled over the conversation, Gwynne unleashed her wall-to-wall smile and asked, "And just how is little Lillian?"

How in the world did she remember her name? Clay thought. "She's doing well. She'll be seven in August. Joan started her in a private school, which she seems to enjoy." He took his last bite of the dessert. "Her mother has no faith in public education."

"Do you see her often?"

"Oh, every few months. Since Joan remarried and moved to Atlanta, the home environment has stabilized, making life easier on everyone."

"Are you and Joan on better terms?" Ernie inquired, referring to Clay's ex-wife and the well-known animosities stemming from the divorce.

"When necessary. We both realized our continued fighting was counterproductive and hard on Lillian, so we've entered into a truce of sorts."

"What's her new husband like?" Gwynne said, continuing to press the point.

"Nice enough. He's a factory rep—plays a lot of golf. What more can I say?" He took a sip of the lukewarm coffee. "Tell me again—how old are your kids now?" He was intent on changing the subject.

The silent covey of attendants reappeared and cleared away the dessert plates, refilling the water glasses and the coffee cups. Ernie got up to make a call. Gwynne continued to chatter, the content of which neither Clay nor Royce could remember two hours later. Ernie returned, now in a hurry, with a vague explanation about a meeting at the yacht club around one, whereupon his wife added, as if by cue, of their need to change clothes and check on the children and so on, until with handshakes all around and another bevy of kisses, they were gone. The time was 12:30. Clay and Royce watched them exit, then sat back down in momentary silence as Royce lazily bulldozed bread crumbs about the table with the handle of his spoon.

"Why do I feel relieved?" Clay asked.

"Like a weight's been lifted from your chest? Let me tell you why—you find them as tedious as I do."

"I guess. We really shouldn't be so judgmental," Clay observed. "I sort of feel sorry for Ernie."

"I'm afraid I don't possess that much restraint. It's their life to live. Don't worry about old Ernie. He's making plenty of money and there's not a door in New Orleans that's closed to him." He caught the waiter's attention and pointed at his cup. "Kahlua, please." After pushing his chair back from the table, he pulled an antique silver cigarette case from his coat. "Do you mind?"

"No. I didn't realize you still smoked."

"Only on very special occasions." The waiter came and went with a new cup. Royce took a long sip and savored it. It seemed to relax him. "Now, just how is your father?" he asked, repeating a previous question in such a way as to imply that the previous answer had been inadequate.

"All things considered, he's doing okay. As I said, he took Mom's death pretty hard, and for a while there I worried for his sanity, especially when he stepped down from running the business. But he's adapted in his own way to her being gone."

"How so?"

"Do you remember how he was always the amateur historian, the small-town scholar?"

"Very well."

"Now it approaches an obsession. He's become even more involved in the local historical society, edits their newsletter. He bought a van and fixed it up, rambles all over the place. Why, just a few weeks ago he drove up to Williamsburg for some sort of genealogical meeting."

"Sounds therapeutic. His health's okay then?"

"Basically, yes. He's got a bad hip that an orthopedist in Chattanooga says will have to be replaced, but he plans to put it off as long as he can."

"How old is he now?"

"He'll be seventy next month. In fact that reminds me, I meant to look for a gift while I was here."

Royce exhaled a thin column of smoke. "What did you have in mind?"

"I don't exactly know. What would a seventy-year-old widower enjoy? He received two pairs of bedroom slippers last Christmas." The man in the Stetson walked by their table, his face now crimson from the effects of his meal. "Actually, I thought I might find something for his collection."

"Does he still collect clocks?" Royce was calling on memories from his single visit to Mathis Ford over ten years before.

Clay laughed at the question. "That too has gotten out of hand. It may sound strange to you, but I'm not sure exactly what he collects now—seems to be anything and everything. He's filled up half the house. Old farm implements, tools, household items, books, letters, odd pieces of furniture—anything remotely connected with local history. 'Portals to Our Past,' he calls them. More than once he's confided in me that he hopes it will serve as the nucleus of the presently nonexistent Wilmot County Museum."

"Interesting. Almost eccentric. I like it." Royce sat his cup back in its saucer and lay his palms flat upon the table. "I might be able to help you. Do you have any plans for the rest of the day?"

Clay thought of Brenda for the first time since climbing on the trolley. "No, not really. Or at least not for a few hours."

"Neither do I. I happen to have a friend here in the Quarter who handles unusual items. Let me give him a call." He hurried away.

During his absence Clay let his mind turn over slowly. Something about his friend had changed. He seemed more controlled, less outspoken, but it was not that simple, like an affect that had always been present in part, but was now more apparent.

He never finished the thought. Royce stood by the table. "We're in luck. He's not enjoying good health—recovering from surgery I believe—but says he feels well enough for a little company."

Upon leaving the restaurant, they crossed in front of the Royal Orleans Hotel onto Chartres Street, walking by the storefronts with hardly a glance. Royce set a good pace.

"Is this friend of yours in the antique business?"

"Not exactly—more of a collector. He's a bit hard to categorize . . . ," was the abbreviated reply.

The sun had risen above the roof lines, and at Jackson Square they left the shade afforded by the sidewalk and stepped into the bright sunshine before the cathedral. Clay loosened his tie. The levee was in plain view beyond the stained equestrian statue, and he could smell the passage of the great unseen river. Against the iron fence surrounding the park, the street artists were setting up for the day. Royce paused to speak with one of them, a graying gentleman sporting a beret, who from the scope of his exhibit seemed to specialize in portraiture. There was the briefest of introductions to which Clay only half-listened, preferring instead to watch a pair of plumpish, middle-aged women compare two portraits of Elvis Presley. The smaller of the paintings depicted a darkly handsome young man, dressed entirely in black; the larger, costing one hundred dollars more, the image of the King later in life, before his fall, costumed in a garish, sequined expanse of white. They walked on before the women came to a decision.

Beyond Saint Ann the Quarter assumed a different character. It became quieter, and the still air grew heavier. There were fewer shops and less clutter, and the pedestrians became scattered and more seasoned. They passed several buildings in disrepair, more than one faced with scaffolding. Royce, in contrast to the first portion of their walk, became considerably more vocal, but whether as a consequence of the previous evening, or the effects of the breakfast, or merely a simple lack of concentration, Clay heard very little of what his friend had to say. Indeed, later he would find it difficult to retrace the exact course of their journey.

They walked as far as the Ursuline Convent, then somewhere

before reaching Esplanade made a turn, stopping after a half block or so in front of a substantial two-story building with tightly shuttered windows. Clay was to recall that the front door of the house was actually a door within a door, a much larger door, presumably intended as a carriageway. Both had once been painted a shade of green, now faded and flaking from the cracked, sun-bleached wood. Royce rang the bell, mounted loosely beneath a small metal grill and a tarnished brass nameplate. The plate read:

M. Oro

Antiquities

As they stood waiting in the direct noonday sunlight, a surly woman in a shapeless print dress watched them from a stoop several doors away. She was drinking a can of beer. A ragged cat nosed its way along the curb. Clay turned his back on the woman's stare. Beads of sweat appeared along his brow, prompting him to further loosen his tie. Nothing happened at the door. Royce rang a second time. Behind the grill, a speaker came to life, admitting a burst of scratchy, low-fidelity static, followed by an almost unintelligible "Yes?"

"It's Royce Harris." An unpleasant buzzing signified both recognition and the release of an electronic lock, providing them entry into the guarded interior of the house.

The transition between the street and the arched passageway was dramatic, one extremity sealed behind them by the closure of the door, the other directly ahead, illuminated by light reflecting from the damp brick floor under their feet. Standing in the half-light under the archway was a large, muscular man with his arms folded across his chest. He was wearing tight jeans and a faded Saints T-shirt. His hair was tightly bound by a blue scarf. Only on approaching did Clay realize he was black.

"Good morning, Raphael."

"Good morning, Mr. Harris. Mr. Oro wanted you to wait in the front rooms."

The house was constructed in the classic style about a rectangular central courtyard, the longer dimension extending toward the rear. A balcony encircled this space at the level of the second floor, its rows of doors and windows closed and silent. Within this space grew a garden profuse with ferns, philodendron, and ornamental palms, all moist and vibrant as if encased within a hothouse. The plant life was confined to a progression of radially spaced planters, walled in by raised stonework and separated by walkways of mossy brick, surrounding at the center, an elevated, circular pool done in Moorish tile. A wavering stream of water issued from the arms of a young boy, a green copper statue standing to one side of the pool. The water fell onto a bed of lilies blooming yellow and lavender, and the soft, tinkling echo of its impact radiated throughout the compound. There was nothing new or polished about this secret place. The overall effect gave one the impression of aged, perpetual intimacy.

The aesthetic appeal of this private garden proved irresistible. The unpleasant sensory state that Clay experienced while standing in the street left him the moment he stepped inside the carriageway. Rather than feeling stagnant and overheated, he now felt comfortably at ease. An unseen cure had touched him, clearing his mind, creating an acute awareness of every detail within the range of his senses, as if having received the benefit of some profound stimulant, an ambivalent drug that while producing invigoration simultaneously left him oddly out of sync. Rather than finding these inconsistencies unsettling, he was overwhelmed by a sense of satisfaction, the same elation one experiences when viewing an object of great beauty. The black attendant, whose dramatic posture in other circumstances could have been interpreted as threatening, along with the rest of the house, and even the unseen Mr. Oro, had become animated curiosities.

They were escorted to a sitting room in the main, or front, portion of the house. The furniture was austere and entirely antique. Two large windows, unframed by curtains, extended symmetrically from the polished wooden floor, contributing to the impression of restraint, and gave those inside a framed view of the garden. The only extravagance present was a marble bust of Franklin Delano Roosevelt centered atop a Doric pedestal standing exactly between the two windows.

"I believe Mr. Oro was acquainted with Mr. Roosevelt," Royce commented, anticipating Clay's question.

"Was he in politics?"

"Sometime, at least peripherally, during the war. I'm unsure of the circumstances."

Precluding any further comment, the room's second door opened to admit a thin, older man dressed in wrinkled canvas bermudas and wearing sandals. Clay noticed his offered hand was badly scarred and missing a portion of the ring finger.

"Welcome back to New Orleans, Mr. Hardigrew. I am Maurice Oro."

Their host was of indeterminate age and origin. His complexion was dark and his narrow face centered upon a prominent, faintly Semitic nose. His hair was silver and combed straight to the back of his head. He gave the impression of reserve, the wisdom of age, though he looked no more than sixty. His pattern of speech was polite and urbane, and was affected with the slightest of accents, European, perhaps German, although that would not fit his surname. From his casual use of English, his familiarity with Americanese was a long one.

"Would you like a glass of wine—or perhaps something lighter?" he offered. Clay accepted out of politeness rather than need. Mr. Oro stepped into the hall and spoke a few words, evidently to Raphael, who appeared a short time later with three glasses of red wine and to the side, a small silver tray containing three tablets, one light green, the other two white, somewhat larger than an aspirin.

"So you and Royce date back to your student days?"

"Yes, we were once neighbors."

"Ah, for the student life." He raised his glass in salute. "And how long ago was that?"

"Twelve years now."

"Time enough for change." Mr. Oro said, accentuating this observation by tossing down two of the pills and chasing them with half a glass of wine taken in a single swallow. The wine seemed to deepen and enrich his voice, an auditory effect magnified by a slight reverberation inherent to the room. "Do you find the city different?"

"Of course. Mostly small things."

"I hardly notice anymore." He paused and unexpectedly raised his glass. His hand trembled. "To our magnificent and prolonged decline!" Clay wondered if the man might not already be drunk. "Forgive my histrionics. Do you find it warm?" Without waiting for a reply, he rose and turned on a ceiling fan high above their heads. The motor squeaked faintly as it turned.

Once he was reseated, Clay offered, "Royce thinks you might be able to help me."

"With a gift for your father?"

"Yes, for his seventieth birthday."

"A fine age to be. What exactly did you have in mind?"

Clay found himself drinking more than he had planned. The wine was excellent. "I'm not entirely sure." He cleared his throat. "You see, he is an amateur historian of sorts and has quite an extensive collection of, uh," he was searching for words, "items of minor historical significance."

"I see very clearly. What in particular does he collect?"

"Again that's difficult to answer." He was trying hard not to sound ridiculous.

"He's an eclectic?"

"You might say that."

"He likes Americana—especially of the southern frontier period. Some would call his tastes unconventional," interjected Royce as he placed his empty glass on the side table.

"I have some familiarity with the word."

Royce continued after allowing the faintest of smiles, "His collection follows the same lines as yours, only far more modest."

"Thank you." Mr. Oro gathered up the final pill and swallowed it along with the last of his wine. "Let us have a look."

The three skirted the garden, walking in single file toward the rear of the courtyard. Mr. Oro's sandals slapped gently against the brickwork in syncopation with the falling water, and from somewhere inside Clay caught a wisp of a feminine voice.

They entered an enclosed stairwell illuminated by a single sooty skylight and ascended a creaking set of wooden stairs to the second floor. Exiting to the left, they circled above the courtyard along the balcony, walking past a series of identical panel doors. Each was deadbolted and bore a faded oval at its center as if they had once been numbered. Mr. Oro stopped before one of these and withdrew a knot of keys from the pocket of his baggy shorts.

The interior of the room was darkened, and its few windows were both barred and shuttered. It was also pleasingly cool, air-conditioned, yet it retained the musty aroma of untreated air. Mr. Oro touched a switch beyond the door, illuminating a series of four crystal chandeliers that cast a yellowed patina of dusty incandescence over a room of considerable size. It extended in both directions, and the fourteen-foot ceiling, demarcated by an elaborate crown molding, magnified the feeling of spaciousness. The walls were covered in an archaic fabric wallpaper depicting an idyllic European landscape, a feature that more than any other imparted a sense of lost grandeur.

About the walls was a progression of identical glass-fronted cabinets, each with its own interior lighting. After closing and re-locking the door, Mr. Oro led them to the nearest of the cabinets. It was filled with an array of scientific and navigational apparatus, a brass microscope and sextant, a hand lens and two nautical telescopes, an open box filled with medieval-looking medical instruments, a telegraph key and an early telephone, apothecary bottles labeled in Latin, several glass vials containing, on close inspection, biological materials, such as teeth and locks of hair, and on the bottom shelf a number of leather-bound books, the largest of which approached the size of a portfolio. Most of the items were identified by discrete adhesive labels, each bearing a four-digit number, handwritten in ink.

"Mr. Hardigrew, few of the items you see here are unique in and of themselves, but more importantly, at least to my eye, each is a rarity by way of its association with some small bit of history. For example, this first pair of spectacles once belonged to Louis Pasteur, and here," he said, strolling to an adjacent cabinet, "is an inkwell used by Mark Twain."

His monologue continued as they viewed each cabinet in turn. He talked easily, using his hands to frame each point, and for the first time his manner struck Clay as slightly effeminate. They strolled past displays of musical instruments and articles of clothing, including a turban and a bishop's miter; a scattering of firearms, swords, and knives; an entire case of dolls and antique toys, aboriginal masks and handwoven baskets, and row upon row of campaign buttons and ribbons; a cabinet of miniature porcelains, along with another largely devoted to erotic statuary; a complete Confederate officer's uniform and other Civil War memorabilia; a shelf filled with scarabs, another with snuffboxes; and so on, cabinet after cabinet, until Clayton was rendered effectively mute.

"Well, Mr. Oro, I find all of this a little overwhelming," Clay replied weakly. "With all due apology, are we viewing merchandise for sale or is this your private collection?"

From his expression, Maurice Oro, for the first time, seemed to acknowledge some insight into his guest's bewilderment. He prefaced his explanation with a glance of admonition toward Royce. "My dear Clayton, I have been a collector all of my adult life. Although not always my sole livelihood, there have been extended periods when at least a majority of my subsistence was derived from the buying and selling of collectibles, or in many cases their procurement for other collectors. In the past few years, I have not encouraged the mercenary side of my passion, but have chosen instead to let the disease run its course. Ironically, my physician has recently informed me that I am stricken with a more legitimate illness, unfortunately a much less benign malady that is progressive and for which there is no cure—the end of my long and full life is drawing close.

"Compounding this dilemma is the fact that I have no heir and am faced with the proposition that all of this," a point emphasized by a broad sweep of his deformed hand, "will end up willy nilly upon the auction block. To avoid such an ignoble end to my novelties, I have taken to giving and selling bits and pieces, primarily to friends and worthwhile referrals. Nothing gives me greater pleasure than to see one of my small prizes received by someone who appreciates its significance. I am certain there is something here that will brighten your father's declining years. Do you indeed see nothing that he would fancy?"

Although Mr. Oro had left much unsaid, Clay's confusion gave way to a compassion for this odd little man. He saw both too little and too much. He felt an obligation to select something. "I apologize for my lack of decisiveness, but until this moment I must admit to having given my decision little thought. Then you expose me to all of this and . . . I never meant to impose."

"Nonsense. I would never have invited you here if it were an imposition. You must feel no obligation to me by your being here." He looked away for a moment, toward the window, and then back again, now bonding Clay's stare to his. "But you, young man, must come to a decision. You must be taken by inspiration. Can you think of nothing in particular? I have considerably more."

Royce laughed out loud. "I'm glad you're not given to understatement." Mr. Oro ignored him.

"I have a considerable assemblage of documents, including some noteworthy signatures. Also maps." He watched Clay's eyes for any sign of interest. "What of silverware and jewelry? I would suggest coins, but most of what I have retained are of investment quality and are held elsewhere."

"Well," Clay mumbled, now looking at the floor. His mind was drifting blankly, when from somewhere in its recesses came the words, "He does, or rather did, collect clocks, and as I mentioned before, is most interested in the frontier history."

Mr. Oro smiled broadly, "I knew it was there. You give us a direction. Your home is in Tennessee, I believe?"

"Yes, eastern Tennessee, between the Cumberland Plateau and the Appalachian Mountains."

Mr. Oro pursed his lips and turned away, bowing his head in contemplation. He walked half the length of the room before turning on his heel to face them. "I will make your decision for you. I have the gift you seek." He raised one finger into the air as if he meant to jab it into the ceiling. "Yes, a most unusual acquisition. Come along."

They once again circled along the balcony. Somewhere below a telephone began to ring, and Clay caught a glimpse of a woman rushing past the fountain. Although her face remained hidden, her grace of movement betrayed her youth. Her skin and long hair were dark, Latin perhaps, contrasting with a white featureless dress that flickered among the greenery like a moth. Their guide made no mention of her passing, and within the space of a few steps the ringing ceased.

The second room was far smaller than the first, almost cozy. A cluster of three light bulbs hung above a bare pine table, and four oak cabinets thick with dust were centered on each of the walls. A pair of English grandfather clocks stood silently in one corner, but otherwise the room was empty. The cabinets were all of the same unusual dimensions, about the height of a file cabinet, while much broader, and divided into a series of narrow, shelflike drawers running the entire breadth of each.

On top of the nearest cabinet was a ledger that Mr. Oro immediately consulted, apologizing for his memory as he read. For several minutes he studied a series of lists before announcing, "Here it is," and walking to the third cabinet, second drawer.

After producing yet another key, he partially opened the

drawer. "Royce, could you help me?" They carried the drawer to the table. Its broad floor was covered in blue velvet, worn thin in spots. Arrayed across the fabric was a row of pillboxes, another of thimbles, another of cigarette holders, and to one side, several pocket watches. Without further hesitation he selected a gold watch from among them and double-checked its number before holding it forward in the palm of his left hand.

Mr. Oro assumed a more didactic tone while exhibiting the watch, "This handsome piece is French, single-cased in gold, early nineteenth century. Interestingly, it is an excellent copy of contemporary watches of the period by the French master, Brequet. Its first owner was André Junot, who at that time was a prominent citizen of New Orleans and a brother-in-law of the last French governor of Louisiana. I fear it is prohibitively expensive."

Without awaiting a reply, he replaced the gold watch and chose another. "This second watch is from the same period, 1809 by the hallmark. It is British-made, double-cased in silver. The construction is not the best, since it was originally an inexpensive watch intended for the colonial market. Its value is minimal with the exception of the damage done to its case," he said, pointing to an obvious linear defect splitting the case at about two o'clock. "This crease was made by the passage of a musket ball at the Battle of New Orleans. Unfortunately, the same bullet ended the life of the owner, a Major Thomas Barkham."

Clay leaned forward. "May I see it?"

"Certainly."

He turned the damaged case toward the light. "How much?"

Mr. Oro laughed loudly, "It's not for sale."

Clay frowned and handed the watch back. "Please don't be angry. It's only a small joke," Mr. Oro offered in response. "Perhaps if I show you your gift, you will forgive me. I feel that your father would find it the most intriguing of the three."

With a deliberateness bordering on ceremony, he removed a modest wooden box from the back corner of the drawer. "This box is made of cherry," he said, removing the unhinged top. "Notice the interesting feather motif at the edge," pointing to the series of chevrons carved along the lid's margins.

From the interior of the box, which seemed to hold a collection of papers, he withdrew a leather pouch, which in turn produced yet another watch. He removed the outer case completely, and then opened the inner case, swinging the crystal and works forward on a single hinge to expose the interior. "This watch is very similar to the last watch—English, inexpensive, double-cased in sterling. The uniqueness here is in the inscribed case, very unusual for a watch before 1840, as well as the nature and location of the inscription." From a drawer beneath the table, he retrieved a hand lens, handing it to Clay so that he might examine the inscription inside the inner case.

The face was porcelain, barely chipped, bordered with Roman numerals. The framework supporting the mechanism was brass, only slightly tarnished, and was worked into elaborate scrollwork that whirled about the flywheel in minute waves. The maker's name, E. Dolworth, was plainly visible without the lens, as was the serial number, 1014. The interior silver was smooth, as if polished by the motion of the mechanism, and was interrupted by three distinct sets of features: the hole to admit the key when winding the watch, the various hallmarks, haphazardly applied to the sterling about the center of the case, and lastly, along the edge, a single line of indecipherable characters bracketing the graphic rendering of an open hand. Not only were the characters faintly engraved, but they were of variable size, as one would expect to see in native, or handwrought silver, suggesting, certainly when compared to the uniformity of the hallmarks, their addition at a later date. Some of the characters seemed to be modified from the Roman alphabet while others were completely alien.

"Do you have any idea what this means?"

"No more than you. It's written in the Cherokee language."

"Cherokee Indian?"

"Yes, or so I was told at the time of purchase. After many years of ownership I have never taken time to secure a translation. Most unusual, wouldn't you say?"

"When was it manufactured?

"Let's see," he said, consulting his reference, "1817 by the hallmark, I believe. However, the Cherokee syllabary was not introduced until 1820 or so, and considering the useful life of such a watch, I would hazard to guess the inscription was added prior to 1830."

"Where did you find it?" Royce asked.

"From a dealer in Tulsa, who had in turn purchased it from an estate in eastern Oklahoma. I have no history on the watch other than what I have told you."

Royce raised the watch close to his face and focused it beneath the lens, "An odd place for an inscription."

Mr. Oro whispered his reply, implying the disclosure of information long held in confidence, "As if the owner was accustomed to secrecy."

— · — · — · —

Clay critiqued each of the female flight attendants in turn. He noted the location of the emergency exits and leafed through the airline magazine tucked into the seat back. He tried to nap, but could not. He munched on complimentary peanuts while sipping a ginger ale and watched through the double thickness of glass as at first Lake Pontchartrain and then the pine forests of the upper Mississippi delta receded under him, until, somewhere over Montgomery he began to rummage about in his carryall. After faint hesitation, he bypassed the thick paperback brought along with all good intentions as well as the day-old newspaper, in favor of the simple carved box wrapped in tissue paper and concealed beneath his camera. He lifted the small treasure from its hiding place and sat it upon his lap. It was a meaningless gesture meant to reassure himself of its safety, when in reality he merely sought to renew the satisfaction of temporary ownership.

The bearded man sitting at his elbow was heavyset and dressed in a checked shirt and unmatching tartan tie. Before him was an open briefcase, crammed with notebooks, folders, and papers. At intervals he consulted an intimidating portable calculator, pausing to enter the results on a yellow legal pad. The man had shown not the slightest penchant for polite conversation, but upon the appearance of the watch, he stopped his work.

After watching in silence for several minutes, he shifted his considerable weight in Clay's direction and asked, "How old is it?"

"About one hundred and fifty years. It's an English watch."

"Do you collect them?" the man continued. His breath smelled of coffee.

"No, this is actually a gift for my father."

Unable to suppress his curiosity any longer, the man asked, "Do you mind if I see it?"

As Clay handed it to him, he said, "Notice the inscription inside the back of the case."

By tilting the exposed works back and forth, the man peered into the complex of gears, wheels, and springs, admitting to his innate concern for all things mechanical. "Is it key-wound?"

"Yes."

"Well, I'll be darned," he mumbled.

After a moment he began to search for the inscription, readjusting both the overhead reading light as well as his glasses. "What language is this?"

"I don't know," Clay lied, unable to overcome his initial bias toward his fellow passenger.

"At first I thought it was Russian, you know—Cyrillic letters, but the more I look at it the more it looks like Greek. . . ." He continued squinting at the tiny letters and added, "But some of these characters are oddly drawn. Maybe it's a dialect or something."

"You really think so?" replied Clay, raising his eyebrows in mock interest.

After checking one last time, the fat man handed the watch

back to Clay. He then declared with considerable authority, "Yes, most definitely Greek," he pronounced. "You should have it translated—probably the owner's name."

"Oh, probably," Clay agreed, returning the watch to its box. Once more he turned his attention to the landscape passing under the wing, a rolling deciduous forest extending to the horizon.

My friends, how desperately do we need
to be loved and to love.

—CHIEF DAN GEORGE

Mathis Ford, Tennessee
July 1985

Clay's adolescent romance with the automobile ended when he was transferred from New Orleans to Texas in 1973. In his new position, driving was forced upon him as part of his livelihood, and in time his car was reduced to an object of simple utility, a machine like other machines, no longer viewed as an extension of his male psyche. Other than convenience and necessity, he lacked enthusiasm for facing the next few hundred miles of sagebrush and mesquite, or after another promotion two years later, the eternal snarl of the Los Angeles freeways. Upon his return to Mathis Ford, he was forced to develop a renewed tolerance for motoring, especially in light of his obligatory trips to Atlanta. Three, sometimes four, times a year, he made the lengthy round-trip, dutifully, without protest, in order to spend time with his only child, Lillian.

Clay came to look upon the open road as a form of meditation, and found he did some of his best and most creative thinking behind the wheel. Of his two vehicles, he preferred the red Dodge pickup for interstate travel; it rode high and wide, and with the cassette going and a thermos of coffee at his side, the toil of the highway passed with little fanfare. The drive to Atlanta took a little over four hours, door to door.

As divorces go, Clay's was neither sordid nor noteworthy, and while in no way should it be used to take measure of the man, he considered it the most pivotal circumstance of his life up to that point. At the time of their separation, he held no great animosity toward his ex-wife, Joan, but contrary to the usual way of such things, his dislike for her had grown with the years. The reasons for this were complex, in part due to the frail state of his mental health at the time of the proceedings, but more due to the change of direction his life had taken since that time. This chronic animosity was compounded by the undeniable fact that his former wife was a selfish woman, bent on indulgence, whose personality demanded a low-grade war of attrition against whomever crossed her. Joan was unforgiving in her intolerance, and could not be nice when it did not suit her. The word *truce* was foreign to her vocabulary.

Their marriage had been a mistake, they both knew it, and each passing year made it only more apparent. But she could not let it go—could not keep from reminding Clay that she considered the temporary union something entirely foolhardy, an act somewhere beyond the rash, as if the mere reminder of her liaison with him was a never-ending embarrassment. So apparent was her revulsion that she had taken to communicating with Clay through others, her housekeeper, or now even Lillian herself, and when direct communication was unavoidable, she kept it short and not sweet.

Pulling his truck into the driveway of Joan's expensive home, attired in faded jeans, a ball cap, and a work shirt, gave Clay a particular satisfaction, equivalent to thumbing his nose at all of her misplaced values. Early in this particular phase of the exchange program, he had quite by accident hit upon an elegant, if not graphic, means of aggravation, one that explained why he never made the trip without one of his dogs, usually a black lab named Tar, short for Tar Baby.

When the animal was young, hardly ten months old, Clay had on the purest whim chosen to take the dog with him, and upon arrival at Joan's house, found she was not at home. At the time he had thought it just as well, and had helped the housekeeper in preparing Lillian for the trip. Predictably, the little girl thought the dog was delightful, and spent the last few minutes before leaving chasing him around the lawn, an immaculate rectangle of flawless zoysia, irrigated, fertilized, and sprayed according to a timetable. Joan's house was a restrained contemporary perched on a high bluff overlooking the Chattahoochee River. Clay thought little of their play, after all, that was what front yards were for, but then a spotless black Mercedes pulled onto the false cobbles of the driveway.

Joan exited the car, dressed in a blue-on-white tennis outfit and oversized sunglasses. She paused at the edge of the drive with one hand on her hip, the other gripping a large, well-stuffed equipment bag. Clay noted that as usual, her nails and lipstick were perfectly coordinated. No sooner had the words "Lillian, you know you're not supposed to play on the grass" left her mouth, when Tar Baby, charged with playfulness, took notice of the unfamiliar voice and turned toward her at full speed. She froze as he approached, until, at the last second, she uttered a short cry and brandished the bag in a vain effort to fend off his innocent charge. The dog mistook her actions as more play and snatched the bag from her hand, taking off across the grass like some misguided tailback, spilling fluorescent green tennis balls in his wake. His charge left her pressed against the rear door of the car, sunglasses clinging to the tip of her surgically correct nose with the hem of her skirt turned back, revealing the line of her panties. Within seconds she had regained her composure and repaired the damage, other than the road grime smeared across her shapely rump. Without any further consideration of the ill-mannered dog and his prize, she stormed around the bed of the truck and confronted Clay at the edge of the drive. He smiled, unable as yet to allow himself a laugh.

"Is that your dog?" she growled.

"Sorry, Joan. He doesn't know any better. You can see he's still just a pup."

She did not immediately reply, taking the moment to glance at Lillian, who was now trying unsuccessfully to retrieve the stolen bag. Tar managed to stay just beyond her grasp, shaking the bag to and fro as a taunt, sending several wads of clothing flying into the air.

"I might have known." She flashed a sarcastic smile in return. "The dog is just as big an asshole as his master." She turned on her heel and called Lillian to her side. She stooped before her, spoke a few words, gave her a hug and a kiss, and strode into the house without ever giving Clay another glance.

Clay and Lillian cleaned up the yard, and he placed the tennis bag back on the front seat of the Mercedes rather than return it to the house and risk further condemnation. As they drove down the street in leaving, he remarked, "I'm sorry old Tar scared your mom."

Lillian looked down at the dog, who now was curled up on the floorboard and gave a small shrug, "I guess she's not used to dogs." She then looked up at Clay and, with mischief in her eyes, produced a tennis ball from the pocket of her baggy trousers, and said, "But it was still kind of funny." They both began to giggle.

— ▪ — ▪ — ▪ —

Clay's marriage and its dissolution had both occurred while he was living on the West Coast. Personal economics forced him to relinquish the fragile security of his life in New Orleans for a new life as a corporate vagabond, peddling esoteric computer software, primarily to banks and insurance companies. The company had at first sent him to Chicago for three months' training, then on to Dallas, where he enjoyed a company car and a two-bedroom apartment with a fireplace. For the first time in his life he had some degree of discretionary income, and he took to waterskiing in the summer and flying to Colorado in the winter, and getting laid without regard to season. Thanks to the surge in oil prices, his business excelled, and after two years he was promoted to the Los Angeles office. He took a place out in Manhattan Beach and with the additional salary purchased a slightly used Z-car and a two-thousand-dollar sound system. The year was 1975, Vietnam was over, and the global boom was starting. Clay was twenty-eight years of age and was supremely confident of his continuing success, so confident in fact that he chose to ignore the first symptoms of his illness, although in all honesty, no amount of introspection could have saved him.

From the moment of his arrival in California, he had felt a bit off balance, slightly askew. He at first attributed this to his workplace, a bigger office, where his performance, which had previously been monitored only quarterly, was subject to daily analysis. Although superficially casual in accordance with his expectations, it was, just beneath the surface, a rigid and highly competitive place, filled with legions of smiling, laid-back sharks. The few friends he managed to make were distant ones, and he counted none of them as allies. The pace and feel of the place were all wrong. In the only correct decision of this dark period and in adherence to the rules governing the disgruntled and upwardly mobile, he began to consider alternatives, a lateral move of some kind, perhaps something with the old autonomy. Beginning with résumés and clandestine phone calls, he began the search for a way out, but in spite of all good intentions, he failed to use enough speed, for in the midst of these inquiries, he fell in love with Joan.

The opposite sex had never been a particular problem for Clay, and indeed, most women found him physically attractive. His appearance was aided by the fact that he enjoyed the company of females almost as much as they seemed to enjoy his. He tempered his success with restraint; he was never the sexual predator, never came on too strong, preferring instead serial monogamy whenever possible. Socially, in contrast to work, he was more at ease in California, and until that point in his life he had been relatively immune to the prospect of marriage. He had considered it once when he was a senior in college—a green-eyed brunette from Memphis—but the woman's sexual allure had waned just in time for graduation. He met Joan, his wife-to-be, at a promotion party held for one of his peers. Her most striking features were her legs and a mane of honey-blond hair. A year older than himself, she had been married once before to some fellow peripherally involved in motion pictures. Her father had been a career Air Force officer, a life that left her without roots, although when asked, she claimed Virginia as home. No matter her origins, she was good-looking and intelligent, and she knew it. She moved in after the second month, and after a fast twelve they were married.

The honeymoon, which began in Hawaii, lasted about eighteen months, or until Joan became pregnant. Lillian was a diaphragm baby, born to a mother who could never accept the fact that she was unable to control the exact moment of conception. She remained with Clay until the week before the child's second birthday, when, in an unexpected announcement delivered across an evening meal of pasta and steamed broccoli, she revealed her intention to leave him.

"I can't tell you exactly why. It's a lot of little things," she offered. "There isn't anyone else—it's not that simple. I just don't love you anymore, and can't see living out my life with somebody for whom I no longer feel affection."

Clay was totally unprepared for her outburst. Preoccupied with self, he had failed to detect any signs of her growing dissatisfaction. During the preliminaries leading to any divorce, one of the combatants is usually at an emotional disadvantage, but in this instance, due to his failure to anticipate her sudden declaration, compounded by his preexisting melancholia, the negotiations were a measure of no contest. To Joan's credit, there was no other man, and for the last time she would exhibit a little mercy. The terms were reasonable and straightforward; she wanted out as cleanly and as rapidly as possible. She retained custody of the child, who was as yet too young to appreciate the undoing of her parentage—that would come later. There would be reasonable child support with the omission of alimony. Visitation was liberal, fifty-fifty weekends and holidays, as long as the parents lived in the same city. Joan kept the Volvo, most of the furniture, and her bank account. Within the year, mother and child had gone back East, taking with them the final vestige of Clay's sanity.

By the time of Joan's departure, Clay had drifted dangerously close to immobility. He haunted a one-bedroom apartment in Glendale filled with rented furniture. His work habits flirted with the inexcusable, and his performance was repeatedly brought into question. He was on antidepressants for a while without effect. He quit going out all together and began to drink nightly. He could not sleep without medication. Suicidal thoughts came and went, until his luck, if that is what you call it, changed. One evening, not two months after Joan and Lillian left town, he was driving home, having stopped for a burger and more than a few beers in a local pub, when he was broadsided at a stop sign by a drunk whose blood alcohol level was fortunately far higher than his own.

His Toyota bounced over the curb and ended up with the driver's side pancaked against a utility pole. Clay lost consciousness at the instant of impact and woke up eighteen hours later in the intensive care unit, having spent four hours in surgery. His left shoulder and chest had absorbed the brunt of the trauma, breaking five ribs and collapsing a lung. He suffered a fracture and dislocation of his left shoulder and collarbone, which required surgical repair and ultimately extensive rehabilitation. Through the haze of Demerol, he remembered little else of those first two days other than the damned catheter in his bladder.

Clay would spend a total of sixteen days in the hospital. As his mind cleared and the allure of daytime television passed, he was allowed considerable time for self-examination. The first thing he realized from the beginning of this forced confinement was that he was terribly alone. A handful of people from work stopped by, and he received a few cards, but they offered him little solace. Joan did consent to call him a couple of times, but having just moved from coast to coast, she had plenty of excuses for not getting on an airplane. She did not even put Lillian on the phone. Not until his brother, John, arrived from Tennessee did Clay feel any comfort beyond the obligatory interest of the hospital personnel.

"Looks like you had a close call," John said after their initial greeting. Clay noticed the gray at John's temples for the first time. He was reminded that he had not seen his older brother in four years.

"I guess this means I'm not immortal."

"I guess so." John sat down and glanced toward the hall. "How are they treating you here?"

"Fine. Everybody's very nice. Dr. Corallo seems to know what he's doing."

"When does he think you can return to work?"

"He hasn't said, and I haven't asked."

"Sounds like you're not too anxious to get back."

"If you want to know the truth of the matter, I'm not. I'll get paid subsistence wages as long as I'm laid up, and I was considering a move anyway."

"Because of the divorce?"

"In part. But I was unhappy with work before that."

"Any ideas about what you want to do?"

"No, but I've been giving it a lot of thought."

"Lauren said she would fly out if you needed her." He referred to their sister who was living in Washington, D.C., with her husband and two children.

"She told me. I said it wasn't necessary. The plane fare's not exactly cheap."

John reached over and took a peppermint from the bedside stand. The cellophane crinkled in his fingers as he untwisted it. "Have you ever thought about coming back home?" He put the candy in his mouth and before Clay could answer, continued, "You know, to recuperate. No pressure. Anyway, I could use some help in the Yard," their nickname for the family business, Tricounty Hardware and Supply.

"What would Dad say?" Clay said, sounding none too enthusiastic about his prospects.

"Nothing. He wanted to come with me, you know, but he's just getting over a bout of bronchitis."

"That's what he said on the phone."

"Anyway, he's not a factor at the Yard anymore. He could care less. I think he would welcome you back."

"As long as he knew you were still the boss?" Clay replied, his voice edged with cynicism.

John smiled and tossed the wad of cellophane in Clay's general direction. "What he doesn't know won't hurt him. Besides we could use a second baseman on the softball team."

Clay laughed and tried to lift his arm, "There'll be no ball anytime soon for this shoulder." He repositioned himself in bed before continuing. "Look, John, I wish I shared your optimism. I appreciate the offer, but with all that's happened to me lately, I'm really not sure right now where I'm going—but I'll certainly give it some thought."

"Enough said," John answered. He stood up and reached into the inside pocket of his coat. "I almost forgot," he said. "I brought you some pictures of the kids." They talked for another hour, and John left the next afternoon, not forty-eight hours after his arrival.

The most curious aspect of Clay's recovery was the abrupt resolution of his previous depression. It was as if the blow on the head had served as some sort of shock treatment. Whereas his previous apathy had been founded upon hopelessness, his more recent indifference was centered upon a newfound cynicism, compounded by the length of his hospitalization. He realized that he had experienced a very close call in the accident. He could claim no out-of-body experiences, but death had certainly stalked him. He was frustrated by his continuing emotional indecisiveness and at the same time sobered by what had happened to him. As he lay there day after day, he resolved to make some changes. First, he would quit his job and leave the California scene—that would be the easy part. But what next? There was a time when he would have bet all his worldly possessions against the prospects of ever returning home to Mathis Ford, but now, whenever he considered his bleak alternatives, his mind kept returning to his brother's offer. Finally, on the morning of his discharge, despite all misgivings, he called his brother on impulse.

"John, I just don't know how long it will last."

"Don't worry about it, Clay. When do you want to start?"

"I can't say that either. I need to cut the cord here, and then I thought I might go down to Mexico for a couple of weeks."

"No problem. I'll see you when you get here."

It took Clay two weeks to arrange his affairs. He canceled his lease and boxed whatever possessions he could not carry and shipped them to Tennessee. He let his lawyer know roughly where he was going and bought a one-way ticket to Mexico City. He would be out of the country for over two months. During this odyssey, he grew a beard and began running in earnest. This increased exercise, along with a case of dysentery he contracted in Oaxaca, led to the loss of fifteen pounds. He worked diligently on his shoulder and steadily increased its range of motion. In retrospect he could never remember exactly when he made his decision to return home, but in early May he called his brother from Costa Rica. It was a bad connection.

"You're where?"

"In San José—it's the capital city."

"Great. When are you coming home?"

"Next week most probably. I'll call you back with the flight number."

John met him at the airport in Knoxville ten days later. They embraced, and Clay, for once tanned, lean, fit, and sober, wiped tears from his eyes as the import of the homecoming swept over him. He had been away for nine years. The reasons for his leaving seemed distant and unimportant now, even childish in retrospect, and his genuine satisfaction in John's heartfelt greeting seemed part of the logical progression toward a new norm. They collected Clay's pack and tattered field bag and walked out to John's conversion van.

"How's Dad doing?" Clay asked.

"Well enough. His hip's bothering him a bit, but he doesn't complain about it. Seems to stay busy."

"So you said he doesn't visit the Yard much anymore?"

"Now and again, but it's largely social. He'll just show up out of the blue and spend half the morning standing out at the main counter, drinking coffee and shootin' the bull with Buddy and Dorine and anybody else that will listen. It's kind of funny, but he really doesn't seem to care about the business side any more—seems content to leave that entirely up to me. Considering all the years he put in there, along with his usual take-charge temperament . . . ," John shook his head in disbelief. "What I mean is, I find it very hard to adjust to his lack of interest."

"Sure doesn't sound like Dad. I can't imagine him missing a chance to meddle, but then again at his age, maybe he's finally taking the healthier approach."

"Maybe." John lowered the volume of the radio. Crystal Gayle was singing. He continued, "And so, Mr. World Traveler, what do you plan to do with yourself?"

Clay stared out the window at the passing countryside, the fields of corn and uncut hay and the distant blue-green hills. "I'm not real sure, John. I was hoping you could help me with that."

Clay had every intention of this being a short stay; a time to take account and get more serious about the future, but as it turned out, he never left, living out the first two months in his brother's basement before moving to a rental house close in to town. By mutual agreement, he paid his way by helping out at Tricounty Supply, dividing his time between the front counter and the storage yard. In the wake of their father's retirement, John had assumed full charge of the business, but his skills lay primarily in management and many of the details had gone lacking. The brothers quickly assumed complementary roles, since Clay had no interest in being in charge of anything. Instead he preferred the subordinate role, the nuts and bolts minutiae of the hardware trade in which John had no interest. For the first time in memory, Clay did not mind going to work. He was completely comfortable in what he was doing. The stress level was ridiculously low, and there were no theatrics or secondary agendas. Everything was up front and on the level.

As he familiarized himself with the daily operations of the place, several areas of need became glaringly apparent. The unofficial comptroller-bookkeeper of Tricounty was Mr. Boxfelder, a man soon to be seventy years of age. He was competent, honest to a fault, and thirty years behind the times. Computers were still an instrument of the devil in his way of doing things. John had long recognized the need for a change, but since Mr. Boxfelder was a protégé of his father's and refused to hear of retirement, he kept the old man on out of an obligation foreign to his otherwise solid business sense. Clay became the instrument of change.

Clay quickly junked the little-used and inadequate computer already in place in favor of a more appropriate system. He computerized the inventory, payroll, and billing operations within the first year, and supervised an overall evaluation of their entire operation. Efficiency and productivity improved immediately. To everyone's surprise, Mr. Boxfelder did not leave, but reversed his attitudes entirely and became one of the system's biggest proponents. Billings were up 20 percent that first year, and Clay received most of the credit for the improvement. He assumed the title of vice-president at the close of the second year.

In contrast to his previous way of living, Clay needed little and wanted for nothing. His expenses, save child support, were minimal. He renewed some old friendships, in particular Dewayne Morris, a high school buddy and now the town's busiest lawyer. He played softball on the company team, attended the weekly Rotary meetings, and he and Dewayne trained for and ran a half-marathon down in Huntsville. As his salary and his savings rose, he recognized a need to have his own place, both as a tax deduction and as an outlet for his creative energies. With this in mind, he began a search for land.

■ ■— ■— ■ ■—

The turnoff to the Hollifield place was exactly seven miles east of the last stoplight in Mathis Ford. Clay remembered Theron Hollifield from his childhood as a large, gruff man in bib overalls who on occasion had visited his father's business and had finally caused quite a stir at the White House Cafe on Main Street when he served up a cardiac arrest after a second piece of lemon icebox pie. The doctor said it was a clogged artery to the heart, and everyone later agreed that the man had carried way too much weight. Anyway, his widow had died the year prior to Clay's return, and the two daughters had no need of the family farm since the older one lived in Charlotte and the other one somewhere out west, where her husband was in the service. The place needed a lot of work, the price had been twice reduced, and the negotiations were brief. They accepted his first offer without a quibble.

The farm totaled eighty-two acres, divided sixty-forty between timber and pasture. The large frame house was shabby, with a tin roof smeared by rust and its last coat of white paint a distant memory. In spite of its cosmetic shortcomings, it remained structurally sound, wedged between two fieldstone chimneys, and had managed to hold on to a certain amount of character inherent in houses that show their age while continuing to remain functional. Its most salient feature was a broad front porch, shaded by a pair of immense black walnut trees, where on clear days, out across a small pond, and a ratty clutch of apple trees, one could view along the eastern horizon a distant procession of silent blue mountains. Stooped and worn by sixty thousand millennia of wind and water, this council of wise old men became Clay's confidants and touchstones, his confessors and his judges, the nucleus around which his consciousness rotated. He moved in the day the contract was signed.

———————

Clay pulled the truck into the gravel turnaround to one side of the house. The driver side door burst open, and the nine-year-old girl and the black dog burst across the sparse grass before the porch in a mad sprint to celebrate the end of their confinement. A second dog, a fat, mongrel bitch approaching middle age, appeared from around the corner of the house and uttered a single warning yelp before joining in the frolic. Clay set Lillian's luggage upon the front steps as the gang of three danced around him. He sat down and motioned for Lillian to join him.

He put one arm around her. "I have a secret," he said.

Her light blue eyes widened, and she smiled, "What?"

He tried to act nonchalant, but could not help smiling along with her. He petted at the dogs with his free hand. "Well, it's really more of a surprise."

She read his mind. "For me?"

He took both her hands. She was bounding up and down with anticipation. "Yes, honey, it's for you."

"What is it?" she said in a whisper.

"Go see for yourself." He pointed across the pond. "It's in the front pasture."

"Oh, Daddy!" she cried, hugging him around the neck before racing off down the hill, the two dogs in hot pursuit. By the time he caught up, she was sitting astride the top rung of the fence. Standing some thirty yards away, surrounded by acres of uneven fescue, was a light brown saddle horse. It stopped its grazing and looked toward them, ears erect.

"What do you think?"

"What's his name?"

"It's a she."

"How old is she?"

"Six years."

Lillian jumped down from the fence and hugged her father again, this time around the waist. "Oh, Daddy, I can't believe it. She's beautiful." She opened her mouth to speak, but no words appeared.

"Do you want to know her name?"

"Oh, yes," she responded as if he had completed a question she had meant to ask.

"Bonnie."

She stooped and grabbed a handful of uncut grass and extended it toward the animal. "Here, Bonnie. Here, girl." She clucked her tongue against the roof of her mouth and waved the intended fodder back and forth. The horse slowly walked toward her. Clay folded his arms across his chest and watched them with satisfaction.

— · — · — · —

During the years away from Mathis Ford, Clay had had little to do with Vernon Hardigrew, his father. The reasons for this relative estrangement were many: the matter of their separate geography, certain political and philosophical differences, the sort that crop up during a young man's college years, but more than anything, it evolved through the usual lack of insight, the breakdown in communication, common to misunderstandings between the generations. These conflicts were aggravated in turn by the nature of each man, Clay's determination to make his own way in life, to do it himself, to make his mark, compounded by his father's overbearing and highly focused personality.

Vernon was a Yankee by birth, but just barely so, having grown up in the hill country of southern Indiana, a circumstance often blamed for the peculiarities of his thinking. He was trained as a civil engineer in the midst of the Great Depression and took his first job with Roosevelt's boys building the great dams of the Tennessee Valley. His lot was decided when he fell in love with a local girl, Elizabeth Baker, an elementary school teacher working in Maryville, and in the spring of 1939, after a brief courtship, they were married. John, their first child, came two years later, but by then the war had intervened, sending Vernon off to France to build the bridges that would deliver destruction and defeat upon the Germans. In his absence, Elizabeth moved back to her parents' home in Mathis Ford, where her daddy ran two sawmills and operated the town's single hardware store. Mr. Baker began to suffer with his heart shortly after Vernon's return, and his son-in-law, in what was to have been a temporary show of good faith, agreed to help out with the business until the older man was back on his feet. But as things turned out, Mr. Baker became increasingly incapacitated and Vernon never returned to engineering. He stayed on at the mill and directed its growth into a factory producing hardwood flooring for the construction boom that swept across America in the wake of the war.

Vernon was a studious and industrious man and was quick to apply the logistical experience that he had learned in the military. He sold the flooring factory at its peak and used the money to expand retail stock, moving into all areas of building supplies, and as the infusion of money that began with the TVA and later Oak Ridge continued, Vernon directly or indirectly profited from almost every government contract. Mr. Baker died in 1948, and having no sons of his own, the permanent responsibility for the business fell upon his closest son-in-law. Within a decade Tricounty Supply, as it was now called, would become one of the biggest suppliers of building materials in eastern Tennessee, and along the way Clayton and his older sister, Lauren were born. "The Yard," lay at the center of their family universe and until he left for college, Clay could not have imagined his life without it.

During childhood the Hardigrew children were continually about the place, and as they grew older, found summer jobs there. Each benefited from this benign nepotism—in particular John, who would eventually take charge of the operation, and Clay, who for so long thought he might never see the place again. Lauren's present involvement was more detached, but despite living in suburban Washington with her husband and children, she made certain she visited the Yard whenever she returned to Mathis Ford for a visit, usually in the middle of summer, to stand around out by the front counter, catching up on the news, watching her two youngsters run up and down between the rows of nails and paints and caulks and riding mowers, just as she and her brothers had done in their youth.

Their father's involvement with the business had ended gradually, but this withdrawal began under sudden and tragic circumstances while Clay was living in New Orleans. In February 1972, Elizabeth Hardigrew and an old girl friend were returning home from a college reunion in Nashville when their station wagon was struck head on by a drunk in a pickup. The women died on the spot, their murderer the next day. Her death was a trauma like no other. It rolled through the close-knit household like malignant thunder, shaking everyone to the core, leaving them speechless, sightless, and without use of their limbs. Lauren, who was in graduate school in Boston at the time, along with Clay, flew home the day following the accident. They found their father shaken, but consistent with his usual take-charge attitude, he was fully able to handle the funeral arrangements. His strong facade was of course purely compensatory, meant to hide a mood so dark, so bleak, that John, the only sibling left upon the departure of the others, would later come to doubt his father's sanity.

Vernon had, since anyone could remember, always opened the Yard at 6:30 sharp. He now became erratic in this customary schedule, sometimes showing up as late as nine or on occasion not showing up at all. When asked about his well-being, he would either ignore the questioner or grumble something about having the flu. After six months he withdrew even further, choosing to defer most inquiries on the operation of the business to John, preferring instead to spend most of each day just sitting in his office with the door closed. He took to not shaving every day and quit wearing a tie to work. He was losing weight. He was not himself. He was very sick.

Dovie Medlock, the Hardigrews' housekeeper for over twenty years, confirmed the symptoms. "He ain't eatin' enough to keep a bird alive," she declared. She also described his disappearing into his study for hours with the door locked. "He ain't drinkin' in there 'cause I could smell it on him. I'm afraid he's gonna do somethin' real crazy—you know he's got a pistol."

People began to talk, and several of Vernon's best friends approached John. Alvin Prather, the banker, summed it up with a shake of his bald head, "John, your daddy needs some help, and I mean right now, and it's up to you to find it for him."

In collusion with Dovie and Vernon's minister, Reverend Kimble, John confronted his father with the evidence. It occurred in Vernon's study with Dovie standing within earshot in the hallway. There was hard talk and tears and in the end, embraces, and agreement on the diagnosis, but not on the treatment. "Dad, you have to help yourself, and if you don't, you can be forced to. It's for your own good. I talked to Dewayne about this, and I know what it takes to commit somebody."

Vernon flinched at the word commitment. "Hellfire, I don't need a shrink. I'm not crazy," he quipped. But then he admitted, "I know I'm depressed, and dammit I have every right to be. You just can't understand what a trauma it is to lose someone that's shared a lifetime with you."

"I know, Dad. We all miss Mom in our own way, but you have to understand that life goes on for the living."

The very next morning John set into motion his own form of psychotherapy. He picked Vernon up at six o'clock and drove down to the Beeline Truck Stop for breakfast. This ritual was to be repeated every day for several months and sporadically thereafter. He saw to it that Vernon was presentable in appearance and was informed about the operations of the business. He continued to make the major decisions, but took the time to give his father special projects, each with an equally specific deadline. Reverend Kimble saw to it that Vernon attended church, and John made it mandatory that he make the Rotary meeting and go out at least once a week with friends. Dovie badgered him at home and kept him involved in the maintenance of the household. This combined effort, applied over a period of months, did indeed work a cure, but not in the way that John had foreseen. Vernon, whose driving, authoritarian nature was part of the lifeblood of the Hardigrew family, and indeed of the entire town of Mathis Ford, began to change in an entirely unexpected way.

His retreat from the business world continued, until by his

sixty-third birthday, he quit coming in all together, except to gossip or to check the mail. Fortunately, his loss of interest did not extend beyond The Yard, and he chose to apply his rapidly returning energies to other things. "I'm tired of the routine," he announced to John. "Everybody knows who's doing all the work around here, and it's high time you got the recognition you deserve." With this declaration, he bought a brand new van and left Mathis Ford for four months, traveling mostly out west and into Canada.

"I'm just dropped out for a little while," he later said. "Got the idea from reading *Travels with Charley.*" When he returned home, he cleaned out his shop and began the first of several courses on woodworking. He expanded his collection of wall clocks and began to dabble in genealogy. No estate sale, flea market, or craft show passed within a day's drive without Vernon in attendance. The house on Sevier Avenue began to fill up with his "projects."

"He's got to be the messiest man alive," Dovie lamented.

John continued to be concerned, but not for the same reasons as before. Vernon seemed happy enough. In fact, John found their time together more enjoyable without the pressures of the business, but the younger man had difficulty relating to his father's new persona.

"Oh, he's just getting a little eccentric in his old age," John's wife, Katherine, would say. "You should at least allow him that." John was not so sure.

In keeping with these growing avocations, Vernon became very involved with a group for which he had formerly shown little interest, the Wilmot County Historical Society. He served first as secretary-treasurer, then as president, and finally as a semipermanent member of the board of directors. This sort of mainstream activity leant a certain respectability to his increasingly maverick behavior. Avis Carden, the wife of the retired high school principal, approached him as a collaborator on no less than a formal history of the county, a project for which he was to write a chapter or perhaps two on the natural history of the region as well as a brief outline of its earliest history, meaning early man and their descendants, the American Indians. He took to the research like a demon, traveling to several university libraries and to the state archives. He established correspondence with several notable authorities, and the mailman became accustomed to delivering books and official-looking envelopes. By the time of Clay's return, Vernon had almost finished this initial research and had constructed an outline of what he intended to say. Mrs. Carden was in full agreement with his concept, and he went so far as to "borrow" a word processor from the Yard.

Once he was able to view the situation firsthand, Clay agreed with John's observations on the changes wrought in their father's personality. Vernon was a new man all right, bright, upbeat, quick to smile, confident in his new role as a minor academician. The prodigal son did not as yet share the spirit of what his father was doing, and in the name of unenlightened self-interest, he made no real attempt to understand Vernon's new passions, choosing instead to compromise, substituting words of enthusiasm and similar useless gestures of support in an attempt to humor the old man. It seemed the least that he could do.

■ ▬ ■ ▬ ▬ ■ ▬

Clay did not get around to checking his answering machine until the Sunday night following Lillian's return to Atlanta. One of the messages was from his father, nothing in particular, just a simple request to return the call. Still feeling the effects of the long drive, he made no calls that night, choosing instead to turn in early. Vernon found him the next morning. Clay was supervising the unloading of a truckload of plywood when he was paged over the outside speaker. They never did that unless the call was important. He walked into Warehouse One and picked up the wall phone.

"Let me treat you to supper," Vernon said, choosing to ignore the fact that Clay had not returned his call. The offer was not an unusual one since they shared a meal with some frequency.

"What's the occasion?"

"It's Monday."

"Seriously."

"Oh, nothing in particular. Just got a little something I want to show you."

"You're being mighty secretive."

"Not really. How about picking me up around seven?" Since cataract surgery, Vernon no longer liked to drive at night unless he was forced into it.

"Okay."

Whenever Clay transported a second party he took his second car, a four-door Ford Galaxie. In contrast to the truck, he kept it parked under the cover of an open garage and made sporadic attempts to keep the back seat clear of debris. Vernon was habitually attentive to automobiles and usually began the evening with some sort of comment aimed in that direction.

"How are you liking this car?" He asked this despite the fact that Clay had owned the vehicle for three years.

"So far so good." Unlike Vernon, he had absolutely no interest in cars. He changed the subject. "How's the hip feeling?" He was referring to Vernon's arthritic right hip. It seemed to him that his father was limping a little more than usual.

"Well, that damned orthopedist says I ought to have it replaced. Says to let pain be my guide. Well, I'm going to put it off as long as I can stand it." Clay knew that he meant just that. They had discussed the hip on many occasions, and Clay was well aware of what the doctor had counseled.

They drove out to Briscoe's, a steak and seafood house on the Simpsonville Road. The place was a local standard dating from the 1940s. In the beginning it was little more than a roadhouse, a rough place where one was as likely to find a fight as a meal. Indeed, the original Mr. Briscoe himself got stabbed in the leg in the parking lot in an argument over a gambling debt, and after that the sheriff made him clean the place up. The old man was long dead now, and the present proprietors, Oscar and Betty Coleman, ran a nice, family-style restaurant serving steaks, fried shrimp and catfish platters, and were well known locally for their Sunday buffet. The walls were pine-paneled, stained deeply by many years of exposure to smoke, and were covered with wrinkled photos of men bearing outrageous strings of fish or arrays of field-dressed bucks draped across the fenders of antique cars, all scattered among odd pieces of taxidermy and dusty rural landscapes. Clay and Vernon took a booth up front, away from the kitchen. They both ordered T-bone steaks, baked potatoes, and iced tea.

Vernon resumed. "Well, how you been?"

"Pretty good."

Vernon squeezed lemon into his tea and took a sip. "You sound a little down in the mouth to me."

"You know me too well." The tea was served country-style— far too sweet for Clay's taste. "I have been a little down lately."

"About what?"

Clay looked down at the silverware. "I always get like this after Lillian leaves. I just can't seem to get used to her being gone."

"Be careful, son. In your situation those kinds of thoughts just aren't profitable."

"I know it. Let's move on. What is it you wanted to tell me?"

Vernon unfolded his napkin. "Well, sir, I don't know exactly how to begin and not keep it from sounding crazy." He took another sip of tea and set it aside. "Remember that box and watch that you brought me from New Orleans?"

"Of course I do."

"Well, then, besides the watch, the box contained some other items, some old letters in particular."

"Yes. I remember some papers, but not the particulars."

"The other month I finally got around to looking through them, and I found something in one of the envelopes that was very curious, so curious in fact that it sat around for a couple of weeks waiting for me to recognize its significance."

Living in freedom in the forest, the North American Indian was wretched but felt himself inferior to no man; as soon as he wants to penetrate the social hierarchy of the white man, he can only occupy the lowest rank therein, for he comes as a poor and ignorant man into a society where knowledge and wealth prevail.

—ALEXIS DE TOCQUEVILLE, *DEMOCRACY IN AMERICA*

Vernon had completed the house on Sevier Avenue in 1956. At his wife's request it was traditional in style, the exterior being faced in red brick, the roofline punctuated by three dormers. It was both attractive and comfortable, but far from commanding. The main entry was formal, its floor covered in black and white tiles with the staircase to the second story beginning on the right. Beyond the stairway was the doorway to the living room and opposite it on the left side of the room was the entrance to Vernon's study. The entry's furniture consisted of a marble-topped table done in the Federalist style flanked by two Queen Anne chairs centered upon a large, ornately framed mirror, and standing against the rear wall, beneath the curve of the stairs, an early American grandfather clock.

As a child Clay could never remember the door to the study being locked, but that did not change the rules of entry. All of the children knew that no one entered Dad's room without permission. This conditional right of passage left a distinct air in his memory, the scent of clandestine privilege, full of a man's business, full of adult secrets. Tonight the house was silent, and the sound of the two men's footfalls against the polished tiles faced no competition other than from the mechanism of the clock. Clay threw his coat across the banister and followed Vernon into the hallway.

"Do you want a drink?" Vernon asked.

Clay's better judgment advised caution. He hesitated before

answering, "I'll have one if you are. How about a weak bourbon and water?"

They stood at the kitchen counter as Vernon poured the drinks. The room was spotless, devoid of the customary clutter.

"Looks like Dovie stays on top of things."

"She doesn't miss much. Couldn't do without her."

Vernon proceeded back down the hallway to his study. He closed the door after them, in spite of the fact that the house seemed otherwise empty. The floor here, in contrast to the entry, was heavily carpeted, and oak bookshelves rose to the ceiling on opposite sides of the room. The faint echo common to the kitchen and hallway disappeared, to be replaced by the comforting sounds of two German wall clocks. At the center of the room was a plain country table littered with papers and several short stacks of books. The table was new in Clay's memory.

With audible effort, Vernon dropped to his knees and opened a cabinet below the bookshelves. From the middle of a six-inch stack of papers, he extracted a manila folder and, using the cabinet and the adjacent desk as supports, rose once more to his feet and transferred the folder to the central table. He switched on a standing lamp to provide additional illumination. The folder contained a single sheet of white paper that appeared to be of the sort produced by a copier.

"It's a copy, of course."

"Where's the original?"

"In a safe-deposit box."

As Clay looked at the paper, he observed, "Going a little heavy on the security, aren't you?"

"Can't be too careful."

Clay tried to adopt a serious demeanor as he positioned the paper under the light. He stared at the assortment of angles and curves that were scattered across the page. "I guess it could be a map."

"It's undoubtedly a map."

"What makes you say that?"

Vernon began to point at the various symbols and lines. "These three words here are written in the Cherokee syllabary. I had them checked by someone who should know. The first symbol, the one to the right, means 'pigeon.' The second one is a number, 'one,' as well as the last, which is 'two.' That's about all I can be certain of, but I do have strong suspicions about the meaning of several of the symbols."

"Could be. What about the dots?"

"Again I'm not sure, but they may be a reference point of some sort. Notice the arrow. It could represent north. That would give an overall orientation to the entire map."

"Do you have any thoughts on the scale of this thing?"

"No. Only guesses. The dots might well represent distance—miles, feet, paces. Who can say?"

"Could the one be a scale of some kind?"

"Your guess is as good as mine."

"This appears to be a tree."

"I agree."

"What do you make of this? It looks like a sideways tepee."

"It's funny you should say that. I had the same thought, but unfortunately, the Cherokees didn't use them. It probably means something else."

"And this is surely a snake."

"Once again I think you're right, but I haven't been able to speculate on its significance."

"Assuming that you're right," Clay said, "how do you know the map has anything to do with treasure? Do you have any idea about what piece of geography these symbols might be referring to? You don't even know how old it is."

"Well, you have me there. I certainly haven't had it carbon–14 dated, but one of the letters in the box is dated 1878. It could be at least that old."

Clay raised his eyebrows. "At least." He picked up his drink. He was not wild about bourbon, in spite of his upbringing, but rather hoped that its taste would deter him from drinking anything beyond a token amount. "Dad, this is really very interesting, but why are you telling me all this?"

Vernon reached for another folder already lying on the table. "I'm not finished yet. Take a look at this." He handed Clay several more sheets of paper.

"Looks like engraving on the watch case."

"That's right. A blowup."

"And?"

"Look to the next page."

Listed down the left column were small renderings of the symbols stamped into the silver of the watch case and following each was a short explanation. First was the maker's name, "E. Dolworth, 1014," plainly etched into the brass frame supporting the works. This came as no surprise, since Clay recalled this mark of identification from the time of purchase. The other symbols were new to him, as were their corresponding descriptions.

"What are these?"

"Assay marks. They testify to the integrity of the silver. The lion certifies it as genuine sterling. The leopard's head means that it was manufactured in London, and the small-case *d* indicates that the date of manufacture was 1819."

"So we have the maker and the date and place of manufacture."

"Very good. You're catching on."

Clay ignored the sarcasm and pointed to the English name engraved in the sterling. "What do you know about 'W. Hand'?"

"The Cherokee words written below the name mean 'strong hand,' which logic would tell us was Mr. Hand's Cherokee name. Notice that the likeness of the hand appears to be a left hand. It makes one wonder of Mr. Hand's handedness."

"How do you know all this?"

"We're just getting started."

Vernon then produced a short stack of letters and arrayed them before Clay. "There's a lot of material here, so take your time."

Sylvia Hanson Green
346 Camp Street
Sibley, Georgia 30623

Certified Genealogist
706-555-4723

March 12, 1984

Mr. Vernon L. Hardigrew
3187 Sevier Avenue
Mathis Ford, Tennessee 37784

Dear Mr. Hardigrew:

As mentioned in our telephone conversation of last week, I have located several references to W. Hand, or William Hand. In addition to the simplifications offered below, I have enclosed facsimiles of the actual entries. They are listed chronologically.

Mr. Hand is listed in the 1835 Cherokee census as a head of household. That would imply that he also owned property. The entry reads as follows:

Chickamauga Creek

William Hand Two half breeds, four quarterbloods, and two full bloods, 1 reader of English and 2 readers of Cherokee, two farms, 3 farmers, 1 weaver, 1 spinster (spinner).

The location of Chickamauga Creek is to the immediate east of Lookout Mountain and the National Battlefield of the same name, flowing to the northeast until it empties into the Tennessee River in the vicinity of Chattanooga. The stream is composed of two major branches, the confluence of which is about ten miles south of the river, and as to where along the creek (a distance of some thirty miles by my maps) Mr. Hand may have farmed I cannot say. However, since he would seem to be bilingual, he must have been one of the half-breeds mentioned, and the four quarter-breeds may well represent his children. The genealogy presented in the Miller Roll to follow serves to confirm this assumption. I could not find his name in the next official census (1848). If we are to believe the date of death listed in the applications to follow, then he was deceased by the time of this census.

At least two applications in this roll refer to Hand, numbers 5828 and 19,534. I will summarize these applications below. Once again refer to the copies for the format under which these applications are stored. The genealogical data as presented in originals can be confusing, so I have organized the information into a form useful for computer data entry.

Both of the applications were filed during the 1905–1910 period. The first of the applications (5828) which was accepted, was filed in Staton, Oklahoma, by Lucia Ann Crenshaw. Where the gender of a name is in doubt and should the roll list it, I have placed the known gender in parentheses to avoid confusion. And lastly, the open dates of death indicate that the individual was alive at the time the poll was taken.

Hand, Wm. (born Cherokee Nation, Georgia) ? –1844 (wife not listed).

Four children -	Sallie	? –1862
	Ward	? –1888
	Robert	? –1872
	Rose	1830–

Rose married Crenshaw, Arthur.

Five children –	Lucia Ann	1859–
	Mitchell	1856–
	Lee (M)	1854–1896
	Ola	? –1865
	Elias	? –1850 (?)

Applicant 19,534 is Orval G. Parks (birthdate 1852). The application was filed in Fort Smith, Arkansas. It was also accepted. As you can see he does list William Hand's (his grandfather) wife as Nancy Falling (no dates listed). He was Lucia's first cousin, his mother being Sallie Hand, who married Sterling Parks. His three siblings were Fannie, Artis, and Lilia, with only Fannie living at the time of the application.

The list of applications is enormous and searching through the National Archives is a laborious task in light of the curious fact that no applications are listed under the surname Hand. I am in the process of researching other sources and will be forwarding any further information that may become available. Specific information such as you have requested is even more difficult to locate, and I would suggest, should you be so inclined, that you try to locate descendants of the two individuals listed above in hopes they can provide you with the material that you are seeking.

The question of the exact location of William Hand's property may be particularly difficult to document. As you know the primary land lottery records make no reference to a grant's Cherokee occupants. Let me point out that county records in general are of little use concerning land ownership or occupation prior to incorporation, but in my experience field work in a county-by-county fashion can reveal information obtainable in no other way. I am planning a trip to Atlanta in a few weeks and will check some of the readily available sources at the State Archives.

Finally, I am sorry but I found no reference to Hand's Cherokee name, but again I will keep you informed. Good hunting!

Sincerely,

Sylvia Hanson Green

Clay shook his head as he finished reading. "How did you find this woman?"

"Through one of the periodicals I receive. She specializes in Georgia-based genealogy and is something of an expert on researching Cherokee-white ancestries."

"I'm confused by a lot of this. What does she mean by rolls?"

"She's referring to the various Indian rolls. They were a special census used by the federal government to determine exactly who was an Indian. That wasn't necessarily important until Oklahoma became a state and the land was titled and distributed for the first time. As you can imagine. that got to be quite an expensive proposition, and a lot of chicanery went on. Anyway, to get your land entitlement, you had to prove you were an Indian. Because of that, and despite all the intermarriage with whites, the genealogy of the five civilized tribes, the Cherokees included, is pretty well laid out."

"Sounds pretty complicated, so I'll have to take your word for it." Clay walked around the table and rescanned the letter. "So you've established the existence of William Hand and have an approximation of where he lived in 1835. In addition, you have the names of several people who were directly related to him as of 1910. Where do you go from here?"

"Well, this letter is only the first of several from Mrs. Green. Here, look at this."

May 5, 1984

Dear Mr. Hardigrew:

My most recent efforts are bearing fruit! Using a cross-index of surnames developed by an associate of mine, I found several references to Mr. Hand and have enclosed a bibliography should you want to continue on your own.

This is a reproduction taken from a letter dated November 2, 1834. It is a communication between Colonel Wilson Bishop, at that time commander of the Georgia Guard, and Governor Wilson Lumpkin.

Sir,

The country hereabouts is all quietness and submission, and our reception, from the lower mines to the upper, if not welcome, has been, at least, friendly and respectful. I trust that their presence will continue them in a course thus conducive to their happiness and their welfare. The dutiful performance and energetic conduct of the command has contributed greatly to this desirable result, in spite of the incessant agitations of Chief Ross and his fellow conspirators.

I would relate a singular act of lawlessness perpetrated against a detachment of Col. Nelson's men on the evening of October 22. Ten members of The Guard were returning along the Federal Road, seeking to serve a warrant against a Cherokee, John Davies, for the theft of two oxen. As the hour was late, rather than camp at the side of the road, Col. Nelson ordered his men to march on, intending to spend the night in the open ground surrounding the home of Lemuel Rogers, a known cohort of The Ridge and Chief Ross, and a man of the most servile nature. While arriving after dark, they chanced upon three or four Cherokees seen leaving the residence of Rogers, who upon seeing The Guard attempted to flee. One of them discharged a weapon which struck Sgt. Perry's horse, killing it outright, and throwing its rider to the ground. Fortunately, although knocked senseless, Sgt. Perry suffered no grievous injury, but his assailants escaped in the confusion and the darkness. Whatever these desperate wretches were up to remains in question for the occupants of the house, indeed Mr. Rogers himself, would not reveal their purpose under the most restrained questioning other than to say it was a matter of money. He denied knowing their names other than that of their leader, a half breed called William Hand, whom I have found to be already wanted for assault and who was reported by some to have fled into Tennessee.

Yet even with this insult, The Guard maintained a respectful deportment, which has been my constant aim, and I hope your Excellency will believe that nothing has been done which the good of the country did not imperiously demand. The search continues for these depraved villains, and I trust their prosecution, with full exercise of all authority, will soon follow.

This letter is to be found in Governor Lumpkin's Papers at the University of Georgia Library in Athens. I found no reference to a previous warrant against Mr. Hand. He sounds like a lawless (!) character, but considering the context of the letter that may not have been the case.

In the 1831 list of Legislative Appropriations located in the State Archives is a single payment to W. Hand of $300 to cover the cost of transporting supplies from Augusta to provision Federal troops encamped near the gold fields.

And from Cherokee Letters, page 566, held in the Georgia Archives, dated April 12, 1836, Elijah Crissom writes from Murray County, Georgia, that William Hand's improvements had been occupied by a drawer of the land (a land lottery winner), who unfortunately is not named. Interestingly, this letter was written prior to the forced removal of 1838. Murray County as of 1832 occupied the entire northwest corner of the state, including the course of Chickamauga Creek. I can find no reference to anything more specific.

From this data, we can extrapolate several scenarios. Firstly, he was at one time engaged in lawful enterprise (1831) and was a property owner (prior to 1835). He subsequently had several scrapes with the law (1832), but we can find no reference to his actual arrest or conviction. We know that he was married, had children, of whom several survived in Oklahoma and left descendants (1910) who still identified with the Cherokee culture. We also have a date for his death (1844) which we can assume was in Oklahoma also, although his condition at that time remains unknown.

I am currently corresponding with a contemporary in Oklahoma and hope to hear something from him in a few weeks. I have enclosed a bill for my time to date including an itemized list of travel expenses.

Sincerely,
Sylvia Hanson Green

"Here, check this one out," Vernon said.

"This is a hell of a lot of material," Clay complained, swirling the ice in his glass.

"You can't say I didn't warn you."

August 22, 1984

Dear Mr. Hardigrew:

I apologize for the delay, but my summer has been quite busy. I trust you received the material on Hand's wife, Nancy Falling. My associate in Oklahoma, Mr. Adel Gunter, has completed his work, and I have enclosed the results. I think you will be pleased.

He found no record of Mr. Hand in the Cherokee Emigration Rolls prior to 1835, thus he was not one of the "Old Settlers." Strangely, I have been unable to find any reference to either Hand or his family in the 1838 enrollment or to his property in the 1838 (*Cherokee and Creek Indians. Returns of Property Left in Tennessee and Georgia 1838, volume #64*). It would seem he left for the West of his own accord between these two dates. Perhaps the aforementioned warrants had something to do with his seemingly silent departure.

I have forwarded a bibliography of Mr. Gunter's sources as well as a copy of his letter. The first direct reference he discovered relates that Mr. Hand was operating a general mercantile in Webber Falls nearby the Arkansas River in 1840. Property records show that he built a home there and owned two slaves. This was a time of great upheaval for the Western Cherokees, but there is no record of his having been involved in tribal government despite his position of relative affluence.

The most intriguing fact that Mr. Gunter uncovered is the account of William Hand's death. It might have gone entirely unnoticed had he not been in such prominent company. Joseph Vann, one of the richest men in the Cherokee Nation, often called "Rich Joe Vann," and son of the infamous Chief James Vann, also lived near Webber Falls, where he constructed a large home on the plan of his father's well-known house in Georgia. Although his exact relationship with Hand is uncertain at this time, it seems that they died together, a circumstance which implies either a close friendship or a certain business arrangement. It appears that among other things, Joe Vann operated a steamboat line after his displacement to the Indian Territory, and being an intemperate man not unlike his father, drinking and poor judgment lead to his death.

Mr. Gunter's account is incomplete, but I will expand upon it from other sources. In October, 1844, Vann was in command of his fastest steamboat, the *Lucy Walker*, cruising on the Ohio River near Lexington, Kentucky. While there, he consented to a race with another boat, an endeavor upon which he wagered a considerable sum of money. Midway through the race the other boat pulled ahead. Vann, who by all accounts was intoxicated at the time, ordered the slaves stoking the boiler to add fatback to the fire to produce more steam. An argument ensued when the boss slave declared that the boilers could take no more pressure and refused to add more fuel. Under threats from the enraged Vann, the man jumped overboard and swam clear of the racing boat. Vann then supervised the application of the fatback himself and within minutes the boilers did indeed explode, killing Vann, two blacks, and a number of passengers. The full account of the tragedy in the Lexington newspaper that very week lists one of the dead passengers as William Hand. No further details have been forthcoming.

I realize that there is much left to know about Mr. Hand, but I must admit that I am rapidly reaching an end to the available reference sources to which I have ready access. Should you not be satisfied with our progress to date, or if you have any questions on the material I have sent you, please let me know. Most certainly any additional material would be anecdotal at best, however, these are often the most satisfying.

I have enclosed Mr. Gunter's charges as well as my own covering the time spent researching the above. I think our effort has been productive and hope that it has satisfied your curiosity concerning Mr. Hand. Let me know if I can be of any further assistance.

Sincerely,
Sylvia Hanson Green

"Well, what do you think?"

Clay looked up and said, "I think saying that I am overwhelmed would be an understatement."

"And I've only shown you the meat of it."

"Really?"

"I was even able to contact a couple of the people, or at least their children, listed in the Miller Roll. I called the office of the Western Band of Cherokees and had them send me the current enrollment. It was really much easier than I had expected. Unfortunately the descendants I talked to knew much less about William Hand than I do."

Clay crunched on a piece of ice. "Again, I am much impressed with all of this research, but you still haven't told me why I'm in on this."

Vernon looked him squarely in the eye. "Because I need your help."

"How so?"

"I have done as much as I can over the phone and by mail. I need to go out into the field, to get away from my desk and run this thing down."

"By *thing*, you are referring to the map?"

"Of course."

"Pardon my skepticism, but . . . ," he had decided to pull the trigger, "don't you think you're jumping to a few conclusions? A little innocent genealogy is a far cry from treasure hunting. I mean even after all this data is digested, you have given me nothing to prove that this so-called map is anything more than a bunch of meaningless scribble."

Vernon kept his cool. He continued in low tones, "Son, I have asked very little of you since your return. I don't think I'm asking that much now. I realize this sounds far-fetched, perhaps even a little insane, but I'm only asking that you to indulge me in this small thing. It shouldn't demand too much of your time. Is that too much to ask?"

Clay took a mental step backwards. "I don't guess so."

"What I am asking may also change your mind."

"Make me a believer?"

"Perhaps."

"What do you want me to do?"

"I want you to go with me to talk to a man I know. He's one of the first people I called when I found the map and he's the one who suggested it might be a treasure map. He spoke of it as a waybill, which is a term new to me. Of all the people I know, he is the only one who might help us."

"How'd you find out about him?"

"You might remember him, Lanny Potts. He was a tool peddler. Used to call on the store until he developed heart trouble."

"What does that have to do with Indians?"

"He was a pothunter on the side."

"When do you want to go?"

"How about this Saturday?"

Clay considered his schedule for a moment before answering, "Okay, you're on."

"Thanks, son. You won't be disappointed," he said, patting Clay on the back, "and one more thing."

"Only one?"

"Could you check with your buddy in New Orleans and see what you can find out about the fellow that sold you the box."

While driving home, Clay noted that the right headlight was misaligned. "Probably happened while I was loading firewood," he thought as the darkened countryside slipped past. His mind drifted to less immediate concerns, "What have I gotten myself into?" he asked himself, sighing and thinking sympathetically of his father. In a rally of positive thinking, he said out loud, "You didn't have anything else to do anyway, you creep. You owe it to him." He braked and turned onto the gravel marking the beginning of the long driveway leading to his house. Somewhere at the front of the vehicle, one of the brake pads squealed in pain.

I wish to become rich, so that I can instruct the people and glorify honest poverty a little, like those kind-hearted, fat, benevolent people do.

—MARK TWAIN

By the following Saturday morning, Vernon and Clay were in western North Carolina, entering a deep wide valley in the shadow of the Tusquitee Mountains. At Vernon's direction, Clay pulled off the main route, and after a series of turns they found themselves on a well-maintained gravel road.

"It's supposed to be the second mailbox after this iron bridge."

The house was white frame, one-story, L-shaped, and sat well back from the road among some large trees. It was flanked on both sides by mirror-image pastures, each several acres in size, tinted a verdant green by intermittent rain. They parked in a swatch of gravel and walked to the front porch. The rain had stopped, but drops continued to fall from the trees and the edges of the roof. The interior of the house was dark and showed no sign of human presence. Curiously the interior door was ajar, covered by an exterior screen door, patched in several places with squares of new silvery screening. Vernon rapped on the door frame. Nothing. He tried it again.

With the second attempt, a small dog began yapping inside. The commotion drew closer until it stopped just inside the darkness beyond the screen. They both detected a larger glimpse of movement. It was an old woman, a very old woman. She stood there for a moment staring in their direction and abruptly disappeared without uttering the first word. The irritating barking continued without let up, the sort of sound that causes people to kick dogs. Vernon looked at Clay and shrugged.

"I don't know who she is. He's not married, to my knowledge. I thought he lived by himself."

Suddenly someone inside said, "Oh, shut up, Brownie." The barking ceased immediately. The screen opened, and Lanny stepped outside to shake hands with Vernon. He was much as Clay remembered him, a stout man wearing gold wire-rimmed glasses. Every line in his face seemed rounded, and his thin gray hair was combed straight to the back of his head. His handshake was firm, the grip of a lifelong salesman. He reminded Clay of a caricature of Herbert Hoover.

"Good to see the both of you," he smiled. "Y'all come on in." He had a high, thin voice and a thick mountain accent.

The only light in the front room of the house came from the shaded windows. It was almost noon. The furniture was aged, and the sofa and two armchairs were covered by dusty sheets. They were led into a short, dark hallway, past several closed doors. The dog was nowhere to be seen. Lanny opened the door at the end of the hall, and a sudden wave of sound and smell impacted upon Clay's senses.

The kitchen was filled with a bright fluorescent light. The air was heavy and much too warm, and was saturated with the pungent smell of overcooked greens. A greasy standup fan produced a loud whirring sound that shook the overheated air. Before the stove stood the old crone, who totally ignored their entrance, preferring instead to stir the contents of a large, dented aluminum pot with a long wooden spoon. As if for their examination, she lifted up a steaming mass of dangling vegetation on the spoon, a gesture that Clay found entirely unnecessary. He had disliked both the odor and taste of collards since childhood.

"This is my aunt, Opal. She's a bit hard of hearing, and," he said, touching the side of his head with his finger, "has lost a little up here." From the tone and volume of his voice, Lanny obviously saw no danger in causing her offense.

Clay moved to the distant end of the single kitchen table, as far from the stove as the room would allow. The air was no better there.

"Y'all want something to drink?" Lanny offered. "We got either iced tea or Hawaiian Punch. Take your pick."

"No thanks," the Hardigrews said in unison. "Just ate lunch," Vernon added with a straight face.

Lanny poured himself a large glass of tea and led them further past the kitchen. Aunt Opal never looked up from her business of cooking. Clay wondered where she slept.

"Y'all will have to excuse the mess. I've never been much good at keepin' things straight."

Clay couldn't be sure if the room they were in was a bedroom, an office, or both. Indeed there was a bed, neatly made, but other than that there was very little order to the room. The two windows were shaded as in the living room, giving the impression that the muted sunlight beyond the shades was fighting its way through a cloud of dust. Lanny sat down in front of an open roll-top desk, and switched on the desk lamp.

"Do you think we could get a little more light in here?" Vernon inquired.

"Oh, sure, hit that switch by the door." The multibulb overhead fixture did help.

Vernon took the material he wished to show Lanny from a black leather grip. Lanny placed them under the light and pulled another piece of paper from a cubbyhole in the desk. It appeared to be another copy of the map. He began to examine Vernon's copy with a reading lens.

"You know I must've looked at this damn thing a hundred times since you sent it to me, and I know I asked you a lot of questions on the telephone, but let me refresh my memory—you say you found this in a box of letters?"

"Basically, yes. Clay tell him about the box."

"Well, I was in New Orleans a couple of years ago visiting with friends. One of these friends introduced me to a man by the name of Oro, who was some sort of antique broker. Anyway, he showed me this box, after I told him of Dad's interests. Frankly, he focused most of his attention on the watch, especially the engraving, which he already knew was in Cherokee. The box seemed to him to be only a minor curiosity, an afterthought."

"Tell me about the watch," Lanny said, without turning his attention from the map.

"From what I can remember, it was originally an inexpensive watch made in England. It dates from around 1820." Clay looked for confirmation to Vernon, who nodded in response. "He emphasized that the inscription on the inside of the case is unusual. There is the name William Hand in English and below it in Cherokee is the inscription 'Strong Hand.'"

"I recall that. Probably his Cherokee name," Lanny observed offhandedly.

"That's what we thought, too." To Clay's surprise, his father reached once more into the grip and pulled out the box itself. "I'd say it was pretty nondescript. The sides are done in pine. The lid's cherry. What do you think of the carving?"

"Pretty straightforward—the so-called feather motif." Lanny emphasized the word *motif* as if it were alien to his vocabulary. He rotated the box clockwise and then opened the lid. "No secret compartments, eh?" he chuckled, peering into the now-empty interior.

"Not that I could find."

Lanny leaned back in his chair and looked up. "You know, this is already interestin' as hell, even if it don't mean a thing." He took a big swallow of tea. "What about the letters you found in the box?"

"I didn't bring the originals, but here are the facsimiles. The oldest dated letter is 1878. Most are without their envelopes, which makes it more difficult. Two are addressed to Sallie, a name given to one of Hand's daughters."

"How many letters are there?"

"Six."

"And the map was folded up with one of the letters?"

"Not exactly. It was in a blank envelope, folded upon itself."

Lanny thumbed through the letters, but quickly returned to the map. "Clay, do you know anything more about this fellow in New Orleans?"

"Only that he died last year. I spoke to my friend yesterday about it."

"And Vernon, nothin' in the letters makes a reference to the map?"

"Not that I can see. You can look for yourself."

Lanny did not seem to listen, but continued staring intently at the map. From somewhere on the desk he produced a legal pad and a pencil and began to sketch the figures drawn on the map. He was left-handed.

"These Cherokee characters stand for one, two, and pigeon, you said."

"That's what my source over in Cherokee said."

"Who'd you use?"

"A woman that teaches at the high school, Mary Thomas."

"She ought to know," said Lanny, as he drew. In a moment he was finished and swiveled sideways in his chair.

"Vernon, I ain't never seen anything exactly like this." He shook his head. "I did see a waybill once, or at least that's what it was supposed to be. It belonged to some pothunter down in Georgia—Gainesville, I think it was. Anyway that must've been fifteen years ago. As I recall it was not as well drawn as this and the man, damn, his name just won't come to me, turned out to be a no good after all, and to tell you the truth I never made much of him after that." He turned toward the desk and began to retrace his sketches. "But that don't mean waybills don't exist or that this one ain't genuine. I've certainly heard tell of plenty of them, and I've heard of some being offered for legitimate sale, but this one somehow seems to be a little more on the level." He opened a manila folder lying among the clutter of the desktop and handed Vernon a piece of paper. It was another copy, this time of a newspaper clipping. Written across the top in blue ink was the notation "Atlanta Journal, November 22, 1932."

INDIAN GOLD UNCOVERED IN FORSYTH COUNTY

This past week in Forsyth County Mr. Roy Tilley of Hog Mountain uncovered a jar containing thirty-eight pounds of raw gold. Mr. Tilley is said to have found the buried treasure by interpreting mysterious symbols carved on a large rock near his farm. Local authorities feel this cache was left behind by the Cherokee Indians before they were moved to Oklahoma on the Trail of Tears. Its discovery serves to confirm stories of Indian gold which have circulated within the county for many years. The gold has been valued at over $16,000, and is now being held in the vault in the Bank of Forsyth County in Cumming.

Vernon handed the article to Clay. "Interesting," he said. "Are you aware of any more discoveries like this one?"

"Not exactly, but I did hear tell of a group of Cherokees that came back to the same area from out west around 1900. They camped out on a creek not twenty miles from this fellow Tilley's place. The locals said they dug all sorts of pits out in the middle of the woods, but nobody saw 'em find anything. About two weeks later they packed up and left in the middle of the night and were never seen again. I talked to a fellow who saw the holes in the ground himself. He also said those woods were full of sign trees."

"What are sign trees?"

"Beech trees. The Indians carved messages on them. They're the only tree that holds a cut. You carve something on a beech tree and it'll stay there 'til the tree dies."

"So what you're telling us is that the Cherokees did bury treasure before they left," Clay said.

Lanny turned in his swivel chair to face them. "All I know is what I've told you. People love to talk about buried treasure, and no matter where you go in this country there is always somebody ready to spin a tale about a lost gold train, or a lost gold mine, or a lost chest of gold at the bottom of some damn river," he laughed. "You name it and I can tell you a treasure story, but . . . ," he paused to adjust his glasses, "but I will tell you this. Whatever this is strikes me different than anything else I've ever run across. I don't know exactly what it says, but I'd be willing to bet it's genuine. It ain't no fake or setup. Now where it will lead, I just don't know." He turned back to the desk. "You say this man William Hand was a half-breed who got shipped out to Oklahoma?"

"I've got good documentation on all of that," Vernon said, "But I can't really tie him to this map, only the watch with his name on it."

"Yeah, looks like we gotta make a few assumptions," Lanny commented.

"You're not kidding," Clay said.

Lanny scratched at his chin before continuing. "I think we can all agree that this is a map of some kind. It's written in a way that's hard to make out so the maker must not have wanted anybody else to be able to read it. It's got Cherokee figures on it, so we know it had somethin' to do with their history. That tells me that it's meant to show a hidin' place of some kind, like for people or for money." He placed his hands behind his head and stretched. "And that's the facts of it. Everything else we got is, well, let's say, pure guesswork."

"At best," Clay added, prompting a sidelong glance from Vernon.

"Now if we assume all of that is the gospel truth, which looks to be about all we can do unless we want to just forget it, then we have to take it for granted that the owner of the watch was the maker of the map. If we do that, then we can say the map represents someplace in the Cherokee Indian Nation or thereabouts. True enough?"

Clay and Vernon mumbled in agreement. Clay thought Lanny was beginning to talk like a lawyer. The rain had begun to patter against the roof once more. Clay glanced toward the high ceiling as if expecting a leak.

"Now Vernon, according to the story you told me, this feller Hand was a bit on the left-hand side of the law, and that bein' the case, he may have had somethin' or somebody, like himself or his family, that he wanted to hide. Right?"

"Sounds reasonable."

"Now if you look at history, it's much more likely he would need secrecy in Georgia rather than out West."

"How can you say that?" Clay challenged.

Lanny's tone sharpened, "For one thing, you told me he seemed to live as a pretty normal citizen once he got to Oklahoma."

"At least as far as we can tell."

"So in Georgia he was in trouble with the authorities, and he didn't ship out with most of the other Cherokees. And he seemed to be a man of some means. How much we don't know. There was a lot of infightin' among the Cherokees during the Civil War, which might've made such a map necessary, but he didn't live that long, based on what you've told me. I just got this hunch that this map ties in with his situation before he took off."

"Sounds reasonable enough," Clay admitted, surprising even himself.

"Let's look at this thing together," Lanny said, starting to check off the characters. "The words are words. As you said, Vernon, the arrow gives us a direction. This wavy line is probably a stream. This triangle could be a mountain or a rock. The straight line, and for that matter, all the lines must be some significant feature, a boundary, a road, or a fence."

"You can't see a boundary," Clay noted.

"Well, just remember, this map's based on things that represent other things—symbols. In fact this map is chock-full of symbols. That's what's gonna make understandin' it tough. I mean, don't take what I'm sayin' as the voice of some authority. It's only *my* opinion, but then again it's free." That brought another small laugh. "Look here, just for example, these overlapping humps could be most anything, but I think they look like rocks."

"I vote for breasts," Vernon added. That provoked an even bigger laugh.

"This symbol here is probably a tree. A sign tree maybe like I said before." Lanny took another swallow of tea. "Over here on the left it confuses me. This eyeball could be a line of sight, or, . . ." he paused and continued, "a place to stop and get your bearings."

"It may also tell us the overall direction of travel in the map—right to left rather than the other way around," Vernon said.

"Which would mean east to west," Clay said, expanding on the point.

"That's good," Lanny continued. "Now, this collection of lines could be all sorts of things, but here is another wavy line next to one of them, perhaps another stream."

"What about the snake?"

Lanny squinted into the paper using the lens. "That's the most interestin' thing on the whole damn paper. Sure looks like a snake, don't it. But look here on its sides, these little triangles almost look like wings, like it's a flying snake. A monster snake."

"Oh boy! The treasure is guarded by a giant monster snake!" Clay howled.

Lanny never looked around. "You may think that sounds funny, but it could be an Uktena, a monster from Cherokee mythology. As I recall, it was said to hide in the high mountains, in dark places, under rocks, in caves, sometimes in deep rivers, anywhere the sun didn't much shine. Heck, more than any of the other signs or words, it tells me that this piece of paper is on the level. Now, what it means is somethin' else entirely. It's just not the sort of thing a forger, especially if he was a white man, would think of."

Clay responded with a low, incredulous whistle. "Cool it," Vernon admonished.

Lanny continued, "I don't know what these two other little triangles are for, maybe a rock outcrop, or somethin'? The dots are also mysterious. I agree with you, Vernon, they may be some kind of measurement, relatin' back to the 'one'. I get the feelin' that the scale of this map is pretty big, like the dots are miles, or at least hundreds of paces."

"Lanny, I agree with most everything you've said, but what we really need is some orientation for the map. We need to tie it down to some real geography."

"Where'd you say Hand had his farm?"

"Somewhere along Chickamauga Creek."

"And that doesn't mean that's where he buried his gold," Clay said.

"No, it don't."

"Where do you think we ought to go from here?" Vernon asked.

"It ain't likely that any more pokin' around in some library is goin' to help you. You're gonna need to get out in the woods, or wherever. I'd start in northwest Georgia and spiral out. Go to the courthouses, talk to the old-timers." Lanny wheeled about in his swivel chair once more and winked at Vernon with that remark. "I wish I could go with you," he said, tapping on his chest. He got up from the desk. "Can I keep my notes? I might put a little more thought into them."

"Sure."

Lanny moved toward the kitchen, but stopped midway as if struck by another thought. He was standing by an outside door and turned to glance into the side yard. "You know, I got somethin' that could come in handy. As a matter of fact, it might help you get some work out of this here son of yours." He never looked at them as he was talking. "Come on."

He stepped out into the light rain and followed a grass and gravel path around the rear of the house. At the back of the property, tucked up against the forest was a small, unpainted barn. It was dry inside, and the heavy air smelled of hay and manure. Lanny switched on a bare overhead bulb and walked to the back, opening yet another door into a small storage room. Seconds later he was back. "Dammit, can't see a thing."

From a metal cabinet, he found a working flashlight, and re-entered the dark storage room. He soon returned carrying several pieces of equipment.

"Is that a metal detector?"

"Good eye, Vernon. I bet you I haven't used it a dozen times. It's a good one, a Garrett manually adjusted VLF. I got it used and still paid a couple of hundred bucks for it. The battery was okay the last time I used it, but you might need a new one." He handed the detector and its earphones to Clay and returned to the storage room. "Got an instruction book here somewhere," he said over his shoulder.

Lanny followed them to Clay's truck. "Sorry we didn't get to see your collection," Vernon said.

"No apologies needed," Lanny replied. "My collection, such as it was, is long gone."

"How come?"

"Had to get rid of it when I got sick. Needed the money. I sure can't work no more. Can't take being on the road."

"So you don't want to join us on this wild goose chase?"

"As I said, I wish that I could, but the old heart won't take that much excitement."

They shook hands all around.

"Thanks a million for the help. When do you want me to get this detector back to you?" Vernon offered.

"Oh, anytime. I'm sure not gonna be needin' it. Just consider it a permanent loan. If you decide to keep it, just send me a check for whatever you think it's worth."

"Well, thanks again. I'll make it up to you. Now you'd better get inside before you get all wet."

They watched him slowly climb the steps of the porch. A small brown dog pushed by the screen, and he picked it up. He cradled the little animal in his arm and turned to wave a farewell to them. His image blurred through the glass as Clay turned on the wiper.

"Well?" Clay asked.

"He confirmed what I believe about the map."

"I'll admit what he said sounded plausible, but," he grimaced slightly as he finished the sentence, "that whole scene back there was a little far-fetched."

Vernon reserved his reply for a moment. "Clay, I am well aware that this whole affair seems silly to you. I've known for a long time that Lanny was an odd duck, but that doesn't make what he had to say any less credible. He may be a ways out of the mainstream, but that's what it's going to take to solve this puzzle. Now I appreciate your driving me down here in this weather and putting up with my crazy interest in this map business, but I'm getting damned tired of your smart-ass remarks. I mean, is it so hard to humor me or to humor poor old Lanny? If you spent half as much time worrying about other people as you do yourself, you and the rest of the world would be a whole lot better off."

This outburst caught Clay off guard. He had not realized that he had struck such a nerve. He gave an "aw shucks" kind of expression and said, "Look, I'm sorry. I really hadn't meant to cause insult to you or Lanny. All this is just a little hard for me to accept at face value."

Vernon looked him in the eye. "I'm sure you meant no real harm in what you said. You're just skeptical. Loosen up, boy. Let's play make-believe. It's fun. Fantasy and fact can be one in the same and no harm will come of it. Take it from this old man, there may come a day when you find that fantasy is all you have left."

Vernon's admonishment was followed by a prolonged period of silence between the two men. As they crested the Copper Basin heading back toward Tennessee, Vernon remarked, "I've been thinking about that newspaper article Lanny showed us."

"The one about the jar of gold?"

"Yes. The value of the gold was listed as sixteen thousand dollars."

"That's a lot of money even today," Clay said, trying to be agreeable.

"That's my point. Those were 1932 prices—when the price of gold was fixed at thirty-five dollars an ounce. That same thirty-some-odd pounds today would be worth close to a couple of hundred thousand dollars. And who knows, maybe Hand's treasure amounted to more than that."

"Could be," Clay said. "Could be."

Send forth the hunter into the wilderness,
Send him forth into the mind's prairie,
To seek the quarry that shall not grow less
Though he grow lean and weary.

—BYRON HERBERT REECE,
"SEND FORTH THE HUNTER"

October 1985

Vernon did not concern Clay with the waybill for several months following their return from Lanny's. They continued to associate on a regular basis as was their custom, but the topic of the map did not come up, other than Clay's making polite, but terse, inquiries and Vernon's responding with equally appropriate, but brief, replies. Clay hoped that in time his father's interest would falter and move on to more fertile areas of research, but one Sunday night, not fifteen minutes after he returned from a weekend softball tournament in Memphis, he received a phone call.

"Did y'all win it all?" Vernon asked.

"Came in third," was Clay's impatient answer.

"How'd Buster do?" Vernon said, referring to Tricounty's premier player.

"Fair. Hit four homers."

There came an ominous pause. "What're you doing next Friday?"

Uh-oh, here it comes, Clay thought. "Working I guess," he said.

"Why don't you take the day off? I need you to help me with some leads."

Clay took a deep breath before framing a series of answers, "The waybill?"

"Of course. I've just been laying low while I planned my next step. I need to drive down to Georgia and visit a couple of courthouses. I've already done a lot by telephone, but you could sure speed things up by going along."

"Well, Dad, you know I took this past Friday off. John's going to get pretty irritated if I ask for the next Friday too."

"Now, don't you worry about John. You've got that damn place set on autopilot anyway. He can certainly spare you."

Clay was had. Using the time-off ploy was a mistake. He had no additional excuse other than the onset of a life-threatening disease. "I guess you got me," he said weakly.

"Don't take it so hard. We'll have fun," Vernon said confidently, acknowledging his victory. "I'll let you go now. You must be tired from your trip. I'll call you later in the week with the details."

"Okay." Clay slammed down the receiver and fumed, "Thanks for the consideration."

They left Friday morning after once again enjoying a breakfast at the Beeline Truck Stop. Beth, their usual waitress, fixed two coffees to go. Clay had sidestepped the issue of another day off by telling his brother that the request was by order of their father, which at Tricounty was tantamount to a royal decree. John smiled and said, "Sure," without the slightest bit of hesitation. They headed south once more, using Clay's usual route to Atlanta, but veered west when they passed through Rossville, just south of Chattanooga. Vernon outlined his progress, or lack of it, since their last trip, and told Clay of the preliminaries leading to this excursion.

"I have narrowed the area of the search to five Georgia counties, Dale, Wainright, Walton, Chatuge, and Coosa. I realize all of this is a mighty big assumption, but if the map is real, taking into account the known location of Hand's farm and the historical context of his departure, then we should look here first," he explained, pointing to a road map he had annotated with a fluorescent pink highlighter. "I've written to all the county courthouses and local historical societies in hopes of finding someone with the additional facts we need."

"What sort of input are you anticipating?"

"I won't know till I hear it." Vernon returned to his original line of thought. "I followed up the letters with phone calls wherever the replies seemed promising. I asked for your help so I can take those calls one step further. I would have tried it myself since your feelings concerning this matter are apparent, but I'm afraid the remaining mileage on this hip of mine is growing short."

He's playing on my sympathy, thought Clay, but then in the same breath, a second thought intruded, don't be a jerk—he's sincere about this. Just stick to the driving.

The cut-rate carpet and fireworks stores lining the interstate gave way to a more mundane country landscape, farms and fields and stretches of woodland punctuated by the occasional mom-and-pop store. Both men pursued their own thoughts for a time until Vernon continued, "Anyway, I thought we could get started by your dropping me off in Talbot at the courthouse. There's a woman there in the commissioner's office that sounded as if she could be helpful. She's holding some copies for me and is putting me in touch with the town's resident historian . . . ," he checked his notebook, "a Mr. Dill."

"There must be more."

"Oh, yes. While I'm involved there I wanted you to drive down to DeWeese. It's not more than twenty-five miles. There's a fellow there, the county clerk—by the name of," again consulting his notes, "Weyman Bledsoe. He seemed very knowledgeable on the phone, but informed me that the courthouse burned down in the 1920s, destroying all the early records. However, he was going to get together a list of folks thereabouts who might be of more help. I thought that you could talk to him, mention Hand, his farm, you know in a general sort of way, and see what he had to say. Also if any of the local sources sounded promising, you could maybe give 'em a call, feel 'em out."

Clay shook his head, "Dad, this is getting pretty abstract. What in the world am I supposed to tell these people we're looking for?"

Vernon laughed and said, "Tell 'em you're writing a book. I don't know. Make something up. Use your imagination."

As discussed, Clay dropped Vernon off in front of the yellow brick courthouse. He followed the sign at the stoplight and headed south toward DeWeese. This whole scenario was becoming far more complex than Clay ever imagined possible. The accumulation of secrecy, the fabrications, the little white lies, the willingness to strike out into unknown territories, and the map itself, had led them into a netherworld of mythology. "Heaven help me," he whispered to himself.

Abruptly, rising precipitously from the flat countryside to the west of Talbotville, was an eight-hundred-foot wall of rock known as Marker Mountain. Awash in the colors of the season, red and yellow and orange along with swatches of residual green, its location signified the dramatic eastern margin of the ridge and valley region. Geologically distinct from the crystalline bedrock of the Appalachians and the Piedmont, it was composed of ancient sediments, shales, limestones, and sandstones, rocks susceptible to the action of water. Broad valleys paved with the softer limestone were partitioned by flat topped ridges, some rising vertically as much as twelve hundred feet, capped by the more resistant sandstones. Fertile farms covered the valley floors, while the mountains themselves remained heavily forested in hardwoods and a dappling of conifers. Carbonic acid-laden water still worked at the rock, but most of its effects went unseen, as it dripped and ate its way through the limestone, forever extending the vast array of caverns which honeycombed the ridges. Surface water was sparse and when present often appeared in the form of clear limestone springs.

The highway toward DeWeese climbed the mountain in a series of broad switchbacks, flattening for a half mile as one crossed the top of the ridge, only to descend once again by the same series of sudden twists and turns.

As is so often the case, Clay's destination was named for a long-dead regional politician rather than its founder, and was constructed alongside a shallow creek which was prone to flood. The courthouse was built in 1924 of local limestone. Its style, four columns in the front, and a windowed cupola on the top, escaped Clay, but then he had never been interested in architectural history. He parked the truck to one side of the building, fed some coins into the meter, and slowly climbed the worn granite steps. Upon entering the building, he found himself in a shallow entry giving way to a long central hallway with a twelve-foot ceiling. A country fellow in overalls passed him as he studied the directory. The clerk's office appeared to be on this floor, number one hundred eight. The wooden floor creaked underfoot as he walked down the hallway, checking the sequential numbers on the frosted glass panels. About midway along the hallway, he found it. The front office was narrow, much too small to be a productive work place, and had but a single window. The room was too hot and smelled of coffee. Facing him, with her back to the sunshine, sat the secretary. A wooden nameplate with brass letters announced her as Mrs. Mavich. She was a heavyset woman, about forty-five, who wore her heavily sprayed hair in a modern variation of the bouffant. As Clay entered she was raising a coffee mug the size of a large beer stein to her lips.

"Good morning," he said, using his most charmingly boyish affect.

She was unmoved. She sat the mug aside and replied in the standard bureaucratic monotone, "Good morning. Can I help you?"

"I'm looking for Mr. Bledsoe."

"Do you have an appointment?"

"I believe so. My father, Vernon Hardigrew, spoke with him last week."

"Just a minute."

Hoisting herself to her feet, she went to a door to her right and knocked once. So great was the energy she seemed to expend in this effort, Clay wondered why she did not invest in an intercom. She went inside, but Clay could not make out what was said. Her head reappeared in the doorway, "Are you Mr. Hardigrew's son?"

"Yes. That's Clay Hardigrew." Maybe I should have written it down, he thought.

She swung the door wide, "Come on in."

Weyman Bledsoe sat in the midst of a forest of file cabinets, the tools of his trade. The only break in the institutional green of the cabinets was a pair of barred windows and, curiously, a walk-in vault. He rose from his swivel chair and offered his hand. His handshake was weak, but he smiled easily. He was a small man, hardly five-six, bespectacled, and appeared to be in his fifties. He combed his heavily oiled graying hair into a miniature pompadour. Clay wondered if he and his secretary shared hairdressers.

"Glad to meet you, Mr. Hardigrew. Let me get the materials your father asked about." He stepped to one of the cabinets from which he extracted a pile of documents. After shuffling these about for a moment, he settled on a two-inch stack and carried it back to his desk. "As your father might have told you, the first two courthouses in this county burned, so that any records before 1920 are spotty at best. The tax records, births and deaths, and the like were all lost, that is unless they were duplicated elsewhere." He spoke in a very precise and exacting fashion using a shrill nasal voice that resonated against the plaster walls like the twang of a banjo string.

"Yes, he mentioned that—a real tragedy," replied Clay, attempting to maintain an air of fastidious politeness.

"These copies pertain to information on the first settlers in this area. Much of this material is held in the state archives in Atlanta, and your father may already have it in hand, but if he doesn't, all the better." He raised his eyebrows and smiled. The thick lenses of his glasses magnified his gray eyes into crystalline half dollars.

Clay was beginning to like this little man in spite of his bizarre appearance. He seemed to know his business. "I wouldn't know, but he's grateful for every little bit of information. It all adds up."

"Yes, it does. I believe he said he was writing a book?"

"Why, uh, yes. On the Indians, the Cherokees, you know, the Trail of Tears and all."

"Certainly, I'm familiar with those times. I am somewhat of a history buff myself. It is truly sad what happened to them."

"So you didn't turn up any information specifically on William Hand, the Cherokee gentleman my father was most interested in?"

"No, I didn't. Sorry." Suddenly, Weyman caught himself and stared straight ahead as if in a trance. Before Clay could offer a response, he resumed, "That's funny, I said no, but your asking me about that name rang a bell." He opened yet another drawer, and produced several stacks of business cards, all bound in rubber bands. Each was labeled with a year. "Seems like it was four or five years ago," he said, thinking out loud.

"I beg your pardon?"

"Someone else asked about that name once. A man, a doctor. . . ." He selected several of the stacks and began flipping through the scores of cards. "Said he was writing a book too. Please, bear with me." Clay sat in silence perusing the information handed him. Several minutes passed. Then Weyman stopped, held up a single ivory-colored card, and turned it to the back, reading what was printed there. "See there! I was right. I seldom forget a name." Beaming with self-satisfaction, he handed the business card to Clay. It read, "Eldon H. Weatherford, M.D., General Practice." "Turn it over," Weyman said. There printed neatly in ink was the message, "7/80. Seeks information on Cherokee brothers William Hand and Jiya, or John Otter. Owned farms in area in 1830s?"

"Did this man actually come by here?" Clay asked.

"Yes, he did. Sat in the very chair you're sitting in. Nice fellow. We had a long talk, but I never heard from him again."

"You said he was writing a book?"

"That's what he said. He asked all sorts of questions about the nature of this area before the white man. I can't remember much of it, but he was real interested in Indian names."

"How so?"

"The names of places, streams, mountains, so forth. You know—natural features."

"Didn't he have maps?"

"I guess so. Really didn't think about it."

"Did he talk to anyone else?"

"I really can't say," Weyman said.

The possibility that someone else was interested in Hand aroused Clay's curiosity. Could this be more than coincidence? "Could I get a copy of this card?"

"Sure." Weyman rounded the desk. "Hilda, could you copy this card front and back for Mr. Hardigrew?"

Hilda disappeared, presumably to find a copy machine. She returned with the card and handed it to Clay. "That'll be six dollars and eighty cents." Clay looked mystified. She pointed at the copies on Weyman's desk. "Eight cents per page. That's the standard charge."

As she made change from petty cash, Weyman extended his hand in farewell. "It's been my pleasure," the little man remarked.

Clay sat at the curbside for several minutes again thumbing through the papers he had just purchased. I've a good mind to charge Vernon twenty-five cents a copy, he said to himself. He returned to the business card several times, unable to accept it as a meaningful piece of evidence.

Clay arrived back at the Talbotville Courthouse shortly after four o'clock. He saw no sign of his father, so he parked the truck and started down the sidewalk. Before he could take a decent look around, Vernon hailed him from across the street, then jaywalked to meet him, heavily favoring his bad leg.

"How'd you do?"

"I'm not sure yet," Clay replied.

"Did you find out anything at all?"

"I got one good lead. Let's get on the road, and I'll tell you about it." He related his conversation with Weyman Bledsoe and pointed out the copy of Eldon Weatherford's card.

"What did you tell this Bledsoe we were up to?"

"I told him we were writing a book."

"Good enough. Let's stick to that. So this Doctor Weatherford was also looking for information on William Hand?"

"That's the story. Said he was also interested in Indian place names."

"And he's heard nothing else from him since 1980?"

"Evidently not. It was a one-time meeting. I was amazed that he could remember it at all."

"Well, maybe it was our day after all. This could be the break we've been looking for—who's to say?" Vernon began to examine the remaining papers. "Anything else?"

"Only what you have in your hands," Clay said, as he backed the truck from its parking spot and headed north. "How'd it go with you?"

"No one at the courthouse was much help. I did talk to the Dills fellow—he runs the feed store—knows a hell of a lot about local history, but couldn't help me specifically. I did mention, in vague terms of course, the stories of Cherokee gold and he knew all about them. He even claimed he knew the location of a couple of sign trees."

"Everybody's got an angle," Clay remarked.

"Like Lanny said, there are a lot of stories out there," Vernon said softly as he stared intently at Eldon Weatherford's business card. "And it will be up to us to find the one that's true."

NEPTUNE'S
ACCOUNT

Knowledge is of two kinds. We know a subject ourselves, or we know where we can find information upon it.

—SAMUEL JOHNSON

November 1985

Vernon wasted no time in attempting to contact Eldon Weatherford, M.D. His initial efforts were unsuccessful, since the number listed on the card was no longer in service and information for Pyott, Arkansas, contained no other reference to a Dr. Weatherford. After thinking about the problem, he redialed the operator and said, "Hello, my name is Vernon Hardigrew. I have just received word that a dear aunt of mine has fallen ill and I need to find out the number of the hospital in Pyott."

In turn, the operator at the hospital tried her best to be helpful, and, fortunately for Vernon, was a longtime employee. "Dr. Weatherford used to be on the staff here, but, I'm very sorry, he died three or four years ago."

Vernon was not prepared for this. "That's most unfortunate," he offered, as he stalled for time. "Do you know if the good doctor has any family remaining there in Pyott?"

"I know his wife still lives here, and if I'm not mistaken, one of his sons also. I think he's a lawyer."

"Would you happen to have her number handy? You've been so kind, and it would save me another call."

Although he had never met the man, the news of Eldon's

death was crushing. Vernon's confidence in accomplishing a breakthrough evaporated as he returned the receiver to its carriage. He considered how he might best approach the widow. He began to dial once more. There was no answer, no answering machine, nothing. He would try again in the evening. The waiting was intolerable, so he grabbed his cane from the back of chair and limped out of the house. He climbed into his car and drove slowly to the Yard.

Vernon spotted Clay outside, his back to the office, talking to one of the warehousemen who was sitting on an idling forklift. The noise of the machine prevented normal conversation, so rather than hail him by voice, Vernon stood at the door waving his cane. The man on the lift tapped Clay on the arm and pointed toward Vernon who continued the motion until Clay showed some sign of recognition. He shouted some final instructions to the driver and walked toward the main building. They left the open yard and went into Clay's office.

"Did you call Arkansas?"

"Yes, I did," answered Vernon, wearing a look of dejection.

"What happened?"

"Would you believe that Eldon Weatherford's dead?"

"Oh man, you've got to be kidding me," Clay groaned.

"I wish I was. I really thought we had it this time."

"Were you able to find out anything else about him?"

"Yes. His widow evidently still lives in town, as does a son. I thought I would call her first. She might be easier to deal with."

"Maybe. You never know. What are you going to tell her?"

"My version of the truth."

"You had better polish that silver tongue of yours."

The intercom came alive and a female voice said, "Mr. Hardigrew, Harold needs for you to take a look at the damage to that truckful of cedar siding."

"Okay." Clay punched the off button and said, "Look, I've got to get back. A good quarter of this shipment is not up to grade. Give me a call if you reach her. I'm curious to hear what you find out."

"You seem more interested in all this than you were last week."

Clay smiled. "I am. Let's just say I've had a change of heart."

Vernon called the Weatherford home each night for three nights. On the fourth day he called the son, or at least the man he thought might be the son, the only Weatherford in the directory listed as an attorney.

"I'm sorry, but he's in court up in Fayetteville," the secretary responded.

"I am an old friend of the family and have been trying to reach his mother."

"I might be mistaken, but I think she's in Florida. She always goes to Florida this time of year."

"Do you have any idea when she might be back?"

"I wouldn't know that either, but to my memory she's always back for Thanksgiving."

"Thank you," Vernon said.

"Would you like me to have him call you back?'

"Oh, no. I'll just keep trying." He hung up the phone and began to pace about the room. "Great, just great," he hissed under his breath. He was forced to exercise great patience, waiting the two full weeks before he tried again. At last, a woman answered.

"Is this the Weatherford residence?"

"Yes, it is."

"Would this be Mrs. Weatherford?"

"Yes."

He had used the weeks to plan and even practice his line, and now, over a distance of hundreds of miles, he placed it into motion. "Mrs. Weatherford, you do not know me. My name is Vernon Hardigrew. I am writing a book about the Cherokee Indians, and in the course of my research I ran across your husband's name. In trying to reach you I was saddened to find that he was dead. Having lost a wife myself in the recent past, I do not wish to rekindle any unpleasant memories, but I have good reason to believe your husband and myself shared very similar interests. Would you possibly have any knowledge of this?"

"So you are a writer?"

"After a fashion. I'm actually a retired businessman with a full-time hobby. I have been working on this project for several years. It's become . . . ," he gave a dramatic pause, "very important to me."

"Mr., did you say Hardigree?"

"No, it's Hardi*grew*, Vernon Hardigrew."

"As you might expect, this comes as a great surprise after all these years." She composed herself. "I apologize in saying that I did not share my husband's interest in the Indians, but I would like to help you, and would be the first to admit that I am some-what less than an authority on the subject. I was unaware of his specific interest in the Cherokees, although for a time he did col-lect a wealth of information on herbal and folk medicine. He had also intended to have the material published, but fell ill before finishing it." In truth, she had displayed little sympathy for her late husband's efforts, having been hardened over the years by his never-ending procrastination and his drinking.

"Again, I'm very sorry," he said, and, misreading her true feel-ings, continued, "It sounds as if he and I were more alike than I had imagined."

Her tone remained businesslike, "Are you also interested in folk medicine?"

"In part. My primary concerns are biographical, but when one delves into Native American culture, their belief system becomes of central importance."

His scholarly tone found a receptive ear. "Oh, really," she re-plied. He could sense that she was warming up.

Vernon tried to picture her over the phone. She sounded middle-aged, maybe fifty-five to sixty-five—hard to say. "Do you know what became of his research materials?"

"Why, as far as I know, they are all still here. In his study. My sons and I attempted to go through it all after his death, but there is so much of it, and since we were wholly ignorant of what he was up to, we simply gave up. I had thought of giving it to the university or some such, but have not really explored that possibility."

He decided to pop the big question. "Mrs. Weatherford, please understand that I do not mean this as an imposition, but it just so happens that I will be traveling to Tulsa in a few days and had hoped, should his papers still be available, that you would allow me to review them. Of course, I would copy nothing without your permission."

She hesitated for a moment. She was obviously not prepared to deal with his request. "Well, uhm, I guess that would be all right."

"Again, I do not mean to intrude. Would you like a few days to think it over? I won't be leaving for a week or so."

"No, that will not be necessary. Could you please be more definite as to your arrival time?"

"Of course, I will call you back when I know my itinerary. Also, would you mind giving me your address?"

She complied and then asked, "Where are you now?"

He laughed, "I apologize. I live in east Tennessee in a small town south of Knoxville."

"Will you be flying?"

"I had planned to. I'll let you know, and thank you so much for your gracious consent." Vernon wondered if he was not being a bit too ingratiating. She did not seem to notice.

He called his travel agent the very next morning. Just after making the reservations, he called Clay at work.

"So she said you could go through his papers?"

"That's what she said."

"Did you ask her specifically about Hand?"

"We really didn't go into much detail."

"When are you leaving?"

"Monday morning. I was wondering if you could drive me to the airport?"

"Sure. No problem."

Since the discovery of Eldon Weatherford's interest in William Hand, Clay's attitude toward his father's obsession with the waybill had undergone a change. The prospect of a considerable monetary reward for their efforts had become much more of a possibility, while the eccentric nature of the search appealed to his oddball sensibilities, and he was forced to admit to a grudging fascination for the growing web of historical circumstance. His skepticism, although still present, had softened. He realized that it was insane to harbor any real hope of success, but the possibility that somehow it would work out, that something would come of this, had begun to intrigue him as if he might be holding the winning ticket in a lottery. By nature Clay was not a collector of details and minutiae, nor was he a great reader, but he possessed a facility with numbers and puzzles, and after his sobering fall from grace in California, he had come to appreciate the value of patience. He no longer viewed his father's requests as intrusions and mused over the possibilities presented by the trip.

Vernon flew to Little Rock and picked up a rental car rather than switch planes to Fayetteville or Fort Smith and be subjected to a layover. He looked forward to the drive; after all he had a full day, having written Sara Weatherford that he would not be arriving until Tuesday. He took Interstate 40 west, intending to leave it after a few hours and spend most of his time touring the Ozarks. It was clear and cold and the gray-brown of early winter covered the landscape. He had somehow expected these mountains to resemble the familiar ones of east Tennessee, but they did not. They were smaller, more gradual in their ascents, and the vegetation, even at this time of year, was less luxuriant. He passed through several towns and stopped at an overlook above the Buffalo River where he snapped a picture. The driving made him hungry and he pulled into a convenience store and bought an ice cream sandwich.

"How far to Pyott?" he asked the clerk behind the yellow Formica counter.

The man was in the process of spraying some sort of medication into his nose which delayed an immediate answer. "Sorry, I got me one heck of a cold." After the apology he continued, "That's up near Fayetteville, ain't it?"

"Yes, I believe so."

"'Bout an hour and a half, I guess."

Vernon arrived in Pyott around 4:30 and drove around the square. He noted three motels and arbitrarily selected the one that appeared to be the most reputable. The desk clerk was Indian, Asian Indian, who introduced himself as Mr. Patel. A faint smell of curry permeated the small office.

"Is there a phone in the room?" Vernon inquired.

"Yes," answered Mr. Patel, while handing him a stack of clean towels and an extra blanket.

"Is there a good restaurant close by?"

"Certainly. The Wagon Wheel," he said, in heavily accented English, while pointing across the parking lot. "About a mile down on the right."

The motel was constructed in three wings of ten rooms each, roughly centered on a small, forlorn swimming pool surrounded by a low chain-link fence. Vernon counted only four other cars besides his own, a pickup, a van, and two sedans. His assigned room, number nine, was to the left as he stepped from the office. It was predictably Spartan, but clean. He threw his bag on the extra bed and turned on the television to see if it was functional. As a picture flickered into view, he unloaded his shaving kit and switched on the light in the bath. Once again the fixtures were worn, but functional. After slipping off his shoes he took a pill to cover the aching in his hip and closed his eyes.

Vernon awoke around 6:30, washed his face, and decided to eat. It was dark when he left the restaurant, and he spent the next half hour idly driving about the town, which in a distant way reminded him of home. He found the Weatherford house without any difficulty and observed the lights in its windows, wondering all the while if the answers he sought were inside. Cruising around the block, he slowed this time, but not enough to attract attention, and having stored a picture of the layout in his head, drove back to the motel. Tomorrow would be a big day. He must have his rest.

Vernon awoke early the next morning, showered, put on a coat and tie, and went to eat in a café on the town square. He refrained from calling Sara Weatherford until 9:30.

"Mrs. Weatherford, this is Vernon Hardigrew."

"Are you in town?"

"Yes, I arrived late last night. I'm staying at the Greenleaf Motel."

"I trust you found it satisfactory. Pyott doesn't offer much in the way of accommodations."

"It was more than adequate." He cleared his throat. "I wondered what time might be convenient for my visit."

"I was hoping that you might join me for lunch."

"Are you sure that's not too much trouble?"

"Oh, no. I insist." He listened patiently to her directions without once hinting that he knew full well where she lived. They were to meet at 11:30, two more hours of waiting. He switched on the television and began to review his notes.

The Weatherford house was a spacious white Victorian situated on a street lined with similar homes. The yard was at one time shaded by three large American elms, but the blight had taken them, and only their wide stumps remained. The lawn was meticulously kept, even in the cold months, thanks to the efforts of Mrs. Weatherford and a chorus of yardmen, and the house was likewise, painted every five years whether it needed it or not. Vernon picked up his satchel, took one deep breath, and limped to the front door. He elected to use his cane in the belief that it might evoke some sympathy, besides, he had become dependent on it. He tried the weathered brass knocker and waited.

Sara Weatherford was a handsome woman. She was dressed in a subtly spotted silk dress, which accented her still girlish figure, and a single strand of pearls. Her gray-white hair was pulled back into a bun. She gracefully offered Vernon her hand and invited him inside.

She led him into an oak-paneled den at the rear of the house. It had the look and feel of a later addition and was adjacent to the kitchen. Vernon caught a glimpse of another woman preparing food. Somewhere, at the other end of the house perhaps, he could hear the muffled yelping of a dog. Before sitting down he accepted her offer of lemonade over coffee, which the woman in the kitchen brought on a heavy sterling tray.

"Now tell me more about yourself," she began. He offered a brief biographical sketch using all the material he thought safe. "And you told me you are a widower?"

"My wife died several years ago in a automobile accident." He diverted his eyes away from Sara.

"I'm so sorry." Her voice was touched with genuine empathy.

"Yes, as you know, losing one's mate is a very hard thing to adjust to," he said sincerely, but quickly returned to the business at hand, "Did your husband die suddenly?"

"He was ill for six months. Cancer of the stomach."

Vernon once more offered his condolences. "You said he was interested in herbal medicine."

"Yes. As I told you, I don't know much about it, and frankly, Mr. Hardigrew, he didn't choose to share it with me. He collaborated, I guess that's the best word, with a local black man, an herbalist of some sort, but then the man died some years ago, and Eldon seemed to lose heart in the project. He put it aside for the longest time, and then, starting about a year prior to his death, he renewed his interest and began to talk once more about publishing his work."

"Fascinating."

"Tell me again how you came across his name." She knew perfectly well Vernon had not mentioned it.

"I received it from a county clerk in Georgia. Evidently your husband had stopped by the courthouse seeking information just as I had."

"And when was this?"

"My visit or your husband's?"

"My husband's."

Vernon opened his satchel and produced his notebook. Although he knew the exact date by heart, he made a show of consulting his notes. "He met with the clerk in July of 1980."

She appeared to do a little mental arithmetic. "He did take a trip back east that summer. To do research, he said. I hadn't thought of that until you mentioned it. He went by himself. I offered to go, but he said I would not enjoy myself. He became sick while he was traveling." She sighed. "He was very excited about it as I recall, but his illness cut the trip short. They thought it was just an ulcer, but the biopsy showed cancer."

Vernon went on, "He asked this clerk about a specific person, a Cherokee named William Hand."

She again shook her head in the negative, "I wouldn't know anything about it."

They ate the noon meal in the dining room under an ornate crystal chandelier. The housekeeper, a stout country woman dressed in a plain gray dress, served them an excellent tuna salad along with sliced tomatoes and cucumbers. They talked about their children, Sara's annual trip to Florida, Vernon's life in Mathis Ford, and by the end of the meal were on a first-name basis. As people of their age do, they discussed their mutual health as well as that of their family and even a few friends. "How long have you needed a cane?" she inquired.

"Just lately," he replied in truth. "The orthopedist says I need a new hip joint, but leave it to me being hard-headed, I plan to put it off as long as possible."

"Good for you," she agreed, but added, "But don't wait too long."

They were served homemade chocolate pie for dessert, one of Vernon's favorites. They shared some coffee in the den and returned to the topic of Eldon's papers.

"I'm afraid you will think I'm keeping some sort of shrine to his memory," she said.

"How so?"

"Well, I haven't really done anything to his study since his passing. Oh, Sally dusts and vacuums in there, but I've no real use for the room, and I can't bear the thought of throwing anything away."

Vernon's heart soared. "You're making me impatient."

She laughed and got up, "Come along. We might as well have a look at it."

As they both stood Vernon reached out and picked up one of the numerous photographs adorning every horizontal surface in the den. The majority were of the grandchildren, but this one in particular caught his eye. It was a portrait of the Weatherford family taken in the front yard of the house. The elm trees still stood guard, and the rotund, balding man at the center of the group was obviously the father. He possessed a kind face, a face that did not show his age. Sara looked to be about thirty-five, the two boys were not yet in their teens.

"That's Eldon."

Vernon smiled. "I guessed that. How long ago was this taken?"

She accepted the wooden frame and stared at the photo for a moment. "The boys look to be about eight and ten. That would make it twenty five years ago."

Sara placed the picture back in its place and exited the room. They turned down a darkened hallway where she stopped to open the door that led to Eldon's study. Old-style, broad-blade Venetian blinds covered the single double window that faced the front of the house. Despite Sally's attention, Vernon noted that the blades were covered with dust as Sara opened them. All sides of the room were covered by bookshelves, and additional stacks and boxes of materials were pushed into three of the corners. One of the boxes held an assemblage of Ziploc bags that appeared to contain plant specimens. "Sure looks like I've got my work cut out for me," he observed. In contrast to the rest of the room, the small English mahogany desk with the green leather top was swept clear. She switched on the desk lamp and then, stepping back to the doorway, the overhead light.

"Yes, I really don't know how you are going to make any sense of this mess."

"Oh, I'll manage," he mumbled, now becoming preoccupied with the task ahead.

"Pardon?"

"I said, don't worry, I'll find a way. I'm sure there's more order here than meets the eye."

"I'll leave that up to you. Would you like more coffee?"

"That would be nice. Thank you."

She left him for the moment. Vernon placed his satchel on the long unused desk and hung his cane from one of the bookshelves. Where to begin? He pulled the chair after him and began with the nearest pile of papers. Two hours later he was still at it. Sara came and went and then came again, finally stopping to help him sort a portion of the material. Their joint effort was an attempt to introduce some sort of system to the mishmash of notes, books, and periodicals. Vernon was now at his most compulsive, but no matter how hard he scrutinized the material presented him, he found not the first reference to William Hand, or in fact, any other Cherokee. As Sara had predicted, Eldon's vast trove of information seemed composed entirely of data relating to folk and herbal medicine. There seemed to be no exception, no reading between the lines, no double entendre. There had to be something here that Vernon was missing.

He sat up in an attempt to stretch his aching spine. He glanced at his watch and said, "Time just gets away from me when I get involved with this sort of thing."

"Oh, don't worry about the time. Nothing out of the ordinary happens around here very often, and a visit such as yours is most enjoyable."

"Perhaps I had better leave this with you for now. I don't want to wear out my welcome."

"Nonsense. Stay as long as you like."

As she spoke, Vernon quickly scanned the surrounding shelves and thought to himself, if it's not here in the open, then he must have hidden it. Eldon would not have driven all the way to Georgia for nothing, he reasoned. "Did your husband have a partner in his practice?" he asked suddenly.

"Why, no, he didn't. Against my wishes, he insisted on remaining a solo practitioner. I sold his records to a colleague as part of the estate settlement."

"Then his office is closed?"

"Oh, yes. I sold the property too. It's now occupied by an insurance agency."

Then it can't be at the office, he thought. There could be a safe-deposit box, but it's more likely to be somewhere in this house, most likely in this very room. He tried to put himself inside Eldon's mind. But why did he not tell anyone, a confidant, his own wife? It's all so strange, so very strange. From the pattern of her responses, Vernon had the impression that Sara and her deceased husband had shared few interests. He rose from the cramped posture of the chair. "Perhaps I could stop by tomorrow for a few hours. Just getting all of this organized has about worn me out."

"Well, I would be delighted to have you back."

He gathered up his notes and said, "About the same time?"

"That would be fine. Come by earlier if you like. I'm usually up by seven myself."

"I'll call before I leave the motel." He trudged back to his car, exhausted by the anticipation and intensity of the search.

Vernon called the next morning at nine o'clock and was back in Eldon's study by 9:30. His conversation with Sara was polite, but to the point, and he set himself hard at work reviewing the material they had sorted the previous day. As soon as she left the room, he tried to open a gray file cabinet that sat in one corner, but it was locked. Next he went through the desk. The search turned up nothing, but the two drawers at floor level were locked. He then sat down at the desk and made a show of taking notes, a ploy meant to convince Sara that his interest in Eldon's work was genuine. He worked at top speed, peering through his bifocals at the exhaustive lists of native plants and their uses. A considerable amount was of an eclectic nature, articles clipped from newspapers, a folder full of correspondence from a botanist at the University of Arkansas, and just before noon, he chanced upon the first reference to Shine, quotes and accounts of their trips to the field. There was also a brief essay on the history of Sula, the African-American community in Pyott. He was reading the essay when Sara walked into the study and announced, "Vernon, I'm sorry, but I have to step out for a couple of hours—a garden club luncheon. I hope you don't mind. If you need anything, Sally will be here. I asked her to fix you some lunch."

"I'm not too hungry at present. Could you ask her to wait about an hour or so? And by the way, would you mind my looking through that file cabinet?"

"Why no."

"Out of curiosity I tried one of the drawers, but it seems to be locked."

"And of course we need the key." She looked puzzled. "I'll have to think where that could be. Did you look in the desk?"

"No," he said innocently.

She opened the central drawer, and they both rummaged through its contents. No key was found.

"I just don't know where it could be. My son might know. Perhaps I'll give him a call."

Vernon was not sure that he liked that idea, but if it produced the key, he would think of something. As soon as her car pulled from the driveway, he quietly closed the study door to a narrow crack. Rather than close it completely and turn the lock, he pushed a stack of books against it. Anyone attempting to enter would not suspect his need for privacy, and he would be better able to hear their approach. He pulled a small divan to the first shelf and began to methodically unload the books stored there, starting with the highest shelf, flipping through the pages of each book in turn, before checking behind them for anything that might be concealed. His examination of the first two shelves revealed nothing. Exhausted from the effort of reaching over his head, he stopped to rest and reconsider his plan.

He scooted the divan across the carpet to the shelves closest by the desk. On removing the top row of books, mostly thick texts on medicine, he came upon a half-empty bottle of vodka and a dust-filled glass—how curious! Next to the bottle was something wrapped in a white cotton rag. It was heavy, a pistol, a Browning nine-millimeter automatic along with a fully loaded clip. Although not what he was looking for, the discoveries confirmed that Eldon was no stranger to secrecy. Vernon attacked the books with renewed enthusiasm, and by one o'clock he was almost finished. Oblivious to the time, he was startled by the sound of Sally's approach and hurriedly stepped down from his perch, almost falling in the process.

"Yes?" Vernon said, in response to the soft rap on the door.

"Lunch is ready, Mr. Hardigrew."

"I'll be right there," he answered calmly.

She lead him to the kitchen. "I hope you like bacon, lettuce, and tomato."

"It's one of my favorites," he admitted truthfully. While he sat eating his sandwich and chips, Sally busied herself around the kitchen.

"How long have you worked here, Sally?"

"About six or seven years now. I came about two years before Doctor Weatherford passed on."

"Did you know him well?"

"Not real well. He kept to himself a lot when he was around the house, but then he wasn't around that much. You know the boys were gone, and he seemed to work all the time. People would never leave him alone. If you ask me, I think he worked himself to death."

"Sara said he had cancer."

"Well, that's what finished him off, but that work had already worn him to a frazzle."

"Did he spent most of his free time in the study?"

"Yes, or watching the television. He liked sports a lot. Sometimes he would bang around down in his basement workshop. Seems he always had some project going." She paused at this point, as if his questions had helped her resolve something. "He was a good man. His patients thought the world of him."

"I'm sure they did."

Vernon asked for a cup of hot tea, and Sally gladly complied. He was able to finish searching the last of the bookshelves before Sara returned. Other than the pistol and the forbidden liquor, the search had turned up nothing. He sat on the corner of the desk and stared out the window. A few spent leaves blew across the dormant grass, and he watched a Federal Express truck deliver a package at the house across the street. What am I looking for? he asked himself. Where could it be? Could it be somewhere else in the house, the workshop, a closet, a secret compartment? He glanced once again at the locked drawers, about the only obvious place in the room he had not searched. He went through more of the papers, not bothering to take notes now, and found only more of the same. It was 2:30. He heard the approach of Sara's Oldsmobile in the drive. Overcome by fatigue and frustration, he sat at the desk in silence and waited for his hostess to enter the room.

"How was your luncheon?"

"It was very nice. Did Sally take care of you?"

"She certainly did. Her food gave me the energy to finish my review, but, I am sorry to say, I haven't been able to find what I was looking for."

"You told me that the man who gave you Eldon's name said that Eldon was asking about a particular individual?"

"A very specific individual, a man named William Hand, and I have found absolutely no reference to either Mr. Hand or anyone associated with him."

"Vernon, I just don't know what to say."

Grasping for any possible break, Vernon said, "Did you ask your son about the key?"

She looked distraught. "Oh, I'm so sorry. I don't know what's become of my memory. I'll go and call him right now." The study had no phone.

In her absence Vernon once more stared at the double window, then on impulse raised one of the blinds. The window frame was screwed shut as a security measure. He studied the situation for a moment: the window was not more than five feet off the ground, the approach hidden behind shrubbery, the latch was a simple one, and he had seen no alarm pads or decals anywhere in the house. Quickly, he fumbled in his satchel and produced a Swiss Army knife, a big one, the kind with multiple tools, including a Phillips head screwdriver. Working against time, he backed the screws from their holes and using a handkerchief opened the latch. Grasping the two shallow handles, he attempted to open the window. It would not budge, perhaps it was painted shut, but the desk also prevented him from exerting his best effort. While positioning himself for another attempt, he heard Sara's footfall. He was lowering the blind as she reentered the room.

"Your yard is beautiful," he said. "How in the world do you manage?"

"Thank you. It's my primary obsession, I'm afraid, but I must admit to having plenty of good help."

"Did you find out anything?"

"He said he could not remember offhand where the keys were. He remembered going through both the file and the desk after Eldon's death, but couldn't recall exactly what was in them other than papers relating to finances and his practice." That much was true. He really did not know where the keys were, but he had also cautioned his mother in giving free access to a stranger. He had suggested that he meet Vernon also. Taking this under advisement, she suggested, "He was most interested in your work and would enjoy meeting you. Perhaps we could have dinner together."

Vernon's fears were now realized; that the son would use less restraint than his mother and would begin to ask probing questions rather than accepting all of his story at face value. Gaining control of his apprehension, he steadied his resolve, after all, he in fact had nothing to hide. His actual motive was something they could not imagine even if confronted with most of the facts. He flashed his most genuine smile and replied, "Of course. That would be wonderful. I would love to meet him. Do you think we could go out tonight? I know it's on such short notice, but as I was going to tell you, I have to be in Tulsa tomorrow and will be leaving in the morning."

"I'm certain we can work out something. I'll call him right back."

Sara's son Jack was, like his father, a pillar of the Pyott community. He was the county's best-known young lawyer, a sober, hard-working sort, blessed with the down-to-earth charisma of someone with political aspirations. They met at Sara's house at seven and drove some forty minutes to reach a country club in the Fayetteville suburbs.

Vernon noticed that Jack drank soda water while he and Sara enjoyed highballs. He gave his inquisitor the same consistent story, laced with a few more historical facts, many of which dealt with William Hand and the Cherokee situation in Georgia in the 1830s. They spoke of Mathis Ford and their mutual families. Vernon inquired of his host's situation in Pyott and the health of his wife and three young children, but the questioning kept returning to Vernon.

"You said that this fellow Hand was killed in the explosion of a boiler on a steamboat?" Jack asked.

"Yes, on the Ohio River in 1844."

"How interesting. And you have no idea why my father was interested in him. You have found no reference to him in all those stacks of papers?"

"Not a one."

"And you've found no connection between my father's interest in folk medicine and Mr. Hand?" Jack asked.

Vernon felt the pressure building. "No obvious link, but then there may be one of which I am not aware." He tried to deflect any additional questioning along those lines by asking, "Do you know much about where he went on his trip back East?"

Sara reminisced, "I remember that he was very excited about it. He planned the trip for months—rented one of those big motor homes and all. I know he called me from Tennessee and Georgia and somehow ended up in North Carolina. That's where he became ill."

Jack could add nothing to her testimony. He was studying for the bar at the time and could hardly remember the trip at all. They finished their meal and drove back to Pyott, adding to the same small talk that had ended their dinner conversation. Jack and Vernon shook hands, and Jack and his mother watched Vernon drive away.

Later that night Sara sat on the edge of her bed thinking, trying to recall the facts of five years before, straining to interpret the actions of a dead man, an unhappy man who drank too much, a man who by nature and vocation kept his feelings buried too deeply inside. She switched out the light and gathered her nightgown around her and lay down. She lay there for the longest time, unable to sleep, thinking about the past, when suddenly a vague memory floated into her consciousness. She threw the covers back, switched on the light, and put on her blue satin slippers. She crossed the hallway to the room of her eldest son, who worked for a bank in St. Louis. In one corner of the room was a bookshelf filled with the neglected books of a boy's childhood, and there, lying on its side because it was too tall to fit in the shelves, was a much-used Rand McNally Road Atlas.

Eldon had often used this book when planning family trips and had always marked out their route beforehand. The maps of the states were arranged alphabetically, and she quickly found her way to Tennessee. Using a green highlighter, someone had traced a route across the length of the state via Nashville, turning south to Chattanooga. The green line continued into Georgia, where in the upper left corner, the northwest corner of the state, and in several other spots across the northern half of the state, the same person, presumably Eldon, using the same transparent marker, had accented the names of close to a dozen counties.

As she rearranged the heavy book in her lap, a folded piece of legal paper, long compressed by the weight of the book, slipped from between the pages and fluttered to the carpet. Before continuing in her search through the states, she stooped to gather up the fallen paper and upon unfolding it, instantly recognized Eldon's handwriting. An unexpected surge of emotion rose into her chest and gripped her by the throat. Water welled in her eyes and she wiped it away with the sleeve of her gown. She was grateful that she was alone.

Written at the top of the sheet in large printed letters were the words, "Make Itinerary," underlined twice. Below it was a list of things to do, such as "buy groceries," and "buy extra batteries." In the right margin were a series of doodles, the squares and lines one makes while passing time. Mixed up in this collection of off-hand geometrics were two words. The letters of these were embellished and had been traced over many times, darkening them, accentuating them, as if Eldon had singled them out for his special attention. The words were "Neptune" and next to it, "Hand." They were connected by parallel arrows pointing in opposite directions, symbols that could only be interpreted as implying an association of the two words. Whatever this notation meant was an absolute mystery to Sara, but their appearance, at least the one, had given instant credibility to Vernon. She shook the atlas to see if any more pieces of paper had been left behind, but nothing fell. Taking the single sheet to her room, she set her alarm for six o'clock, and returned to bed. She fell asleep thinking of what to tell her son.

Vernon awoke uncertain of his next move, but his indecisiveness evaporated with Sara's early morning phone call. He quickly shaved, slapped on some cologne, and drove directly to her house without giving a thought to his customary cup of coffee.

"Are you sure this is Eldon's handwriting?"

"As if it were my own."

Damn, Vernon thought. This was the verification that he had been seeking all along; the tangible evidence that Eldon knew something of William Hand, a knowledge the doctor seemed to have shared with no one else. But what was the meaning of Neptune?

Vernon thumbed through the atlas. The number of towns where Eldon might have gone on his trip would take a long time to run down.

"And how long did you say he was gone?"

"Roughly two weeks."

"And he got sick in North Carolina?"

"Yes."

"Do you recall exactly where?"

"No."

Vernon noted that the Cherokee Reservation along with several other towns in western North Carolina were carefully underlined, this time in black ink. The range of possibilities grew. "Sara, you have been most helpful, and I am grateful for all of your assistance and kindness. This convinces me that Eldon and I were on similar paths, but whatever material he collected on the subject is just not here, unless he kept it all in his head." Vernon at that moment decided to become more overt in his questioning. "Would there be any other spot where it might be hidden? A safe-deposit box or somewhere else in the house?"

"It's definitely not at the bank. Sally and I could take a closer look around the house. Could I reach you at a later date? Perhaps next week."

"As I told you, I have appointments to keep, but I should be finished with those by the weekend. Why don't I give you a call before I fly home?"

"That would be wonderful," she said.

Vernon paused. "Do you mind if I take this paper and copy it? I can mail the original to you, or, if I'm back in town, drop it by the house." He stood up. "Oh by the way, what did your son have to say?"

It was her turn to hesitate. She chose her words carefully, "He had no objection to your looking in the cabinet, but to his recollection, there was nothing there pertaining to the Cherokees. He said he would look for the keys himself, or if necessary call a locksmith, but he would like to go through the cabinet and desk himself before we give you access."

A nice way of putting me off, he thought. He probably thinks that will be the last of it. She offered her hand in parting, and he said, "I hope it won't come to that. I will call you in a few days." She held his hand a little longer than was customary.

"I will look forward to hearing from you," she said.

The weather had clouded over and turned colder and the wind came in fits and starts. By the time Vernon got to his car, his hip was aching mightily. He cursed his luck and started to drive, uncertain of what to do next. Without a firm plan in mind, he drove to Fayetteville and checked into the Holiday Inn. He bought a newspaper and checked the movie section. It was now three o'clock, four Eastern Standard Time. He removed his travel papers from their packet and sat down by the phone. He had come to another decision. After calling his travel agent in Knoxville, he charged a round-trip ticket as well as an additional return fare. Rather than disturb Clay at work, he would wait and call him at home, and in the interim, Vernon would go to a movie and enjoy a leisurely supper, taking the time to sharpen his powers of persuasion. He would be asking a lot of his son this time, much more than in the past, but Clay was his last hope for success.

I will tremble for my country when I reflect that God is just, that his justice cannot sleep forever. Commerce between master and slave is despotism. Nothing is more certainly written in the book of fate than that these people are to be free.

—THOMAS JEFFERSON

Vernon called Sara back a couple of days later. "How was your trip to Tulsa?" she inquired.

"Only mildly productive, I'm afraid. I finished earlier than I had anticipated."

"I'm sorry."

"Has your son found out anything about the file cabinet?" he asked, hoping that an easy solution was in the offing.

"I haven't heard from him. He's been out of town off and on, and there's no telling when he'll get around to it."

I'm sure it's right up there on his priority list, Vernon thought. "I'm about finished here and was hoping I might get to see you again. Maybe tomorrow night for dinner?"

She picked up on his lead. "Why, what a nice invitation. Tomorrow night would be fine."

"I'll call when I arrive, probably in the late afternoon."

She almost offered him a place to stay, but propriety, and her son's potential displeasure, dictated otherwise. Immediately upon hanging up, she walked to the closet and began flipping through the clothes hanging there, her heart as light as a schoolgirl's.

Prior to Clay's arrival, Vernon visited several hardware stores. At the first, he bought a pocket-sized flashlight, a hammer, a pair of pliers, and some masking tape. At the second he purchased a crowbar, a chisel, and assorted screwdrivers. At his last stop, he went into a Wal-Mart and picked up a cheap canvas athletic bag and a small stepladder before driving on to the airport.

Clay was glum and, strangely enough, asked few questions. As they left the parking lot, Vernon asked, "Did you get the keys?"

"Of course."

"Did Buddy do any good on the file cabinet?"

"He picked out a couple of keys that he said would probably work." Clay turned to look at Vernon, "But he added, 'Don't worry about it, because the thing is easy to jimmy open.'"

"Great," said Vernon, looking straight ahead. He then proceeded to tell Clay about his visit with Sara, followed by detailed instructions for Clay while he and Sara were at dinner.

A look of pain spread over Clay's already dour face. "I knew it. You're trying to get me arrested. Shitfire, you've completely lost your mind."

Vernon was unmoved by the protest. "We know that Eldon knew something of Hand. We have a map. All we need in addition is a single specific geographic point to which we can relate the map, and we're home. I looked everywhere in that study and found nothing. If a terminally ill man went to all the trouble to plan an entire trip around a single reference to a long-dead and very obscure person, a person that no one else seems to have any knowledge of, then whatever he saw in William Hand must have been very intriguing. Unless he buried his information in the yard, he must have hidden it in the house. His office was cleaned out without anything coming to light, and he seems to have centered all of his work on his study."

"I can't disagree with any of that, but why don't we just call the son again?"

"He's a suspicious bastard. If I call, it will only make him more so. We need to do this quietly and get on out of here."

"Quietly, presuming I don't get caught."

"I'm telling you it's a piece of cake. The window's hidden from the street and I opened the latch," Vernon answered, as he began to chuckle. "And the house will be empty. I'll see to that."

Clay viewed this guarantee as neither comical nor reassuring. He no longer protested his involvement in the plan and rationalized the impending theft as an amoral act, unworthy of guilt or punishment. He likened it to stealing watermelons as a kid. In spite of his checkered past, Clay was, like his father, an upright sort, but he also was increasingly perplexed by the mystery of the map. His skepticism steadily eroded with each new clue, and the latest plan seemed only slightly more outrageous than their previous forays. Clay had gone so far as to add refinements of his own such as a dark sweater, a blue knit cap, and a pair of brown cotton gloves. If all went well, he reasoned, he should not be in the house more than an hour.

The morning before Clay's arrival, Vernon had gotten a haircut and had his sport coat, slacks, and shirt cleaned and pressed.

"You're either thinking about marriage or you're going to a funeral," Clay observed.

"Take your pick," Vernon said.

Vernon picked Sara up at seven. They had a drink in the den and were gone before eight. Clay watched them from a second rental car parked down the street, waiting for Vernon to pump his brake lights three times as a signal that the house was empty. As soon as they were out of sight, he pulled into the driveway and parked in the rear of the house, turning the car toward the street in case he needed to leave in a hurry. Other than a light in the kitchen, the interior of the house was dark. The single outside spotlight illuminated only the front driveway, meaning his approach to the study window would be in deep shadow. He crept around the far end of the house and slid behind the high shrubbery, wiping cobwebs out of his face with his free hand, carrying both the gym bag as well as the short folding ladder with the other. After reaching out to touch the sill, he realized that the target window was just high enough above the ground to preclude unassisted climbing. The ladder would be a necessity. Vernon had planned well.

The screen came free easily, and Clay propped it gently

against the side of the house. The window indeed seemed to have been painted shut. By using the screwdriver and an occasional light tap from the hammer, he soon removed a line of paint along the margin of the window opening. After stopping momentarily to allow a car to pass on the street below, he carefully wedged the end of the crowbar under the sash and, using the sill as a fulcrum, tore the window free. By pushing upward with both arms, he raised the sash an additional eighteen inches, but not without making a horrible racket—a piercing, metal-on-unoiled-metal sound that caused him to hold his breath. Clay was fully prepared to run, but after what seemed an eternity, the street remained silent. He felt the nape of his neck grow damp with perspiration.

Clay placed the bag through the opening and followed with relative ease by using the desk to catch himself. He dared not shut the window, but closed the blinds so that he might use his handlight. He walked quietly to the closed door and punched the lock, and with the almost inaudible click, triggered a paroxysm of frenzied barking on the opposite side of the door. So sudden and startling was the dog's uproar that Clay gave a visible start and dropped the makeshift burglar's bag to the floor. Shit, dammit— Vernon didn't say anything about a goddamned dog, he thought. The barking continued unabated, but was unaccompanied by any human sounds. Clay rushed to the desk without pause and pulled a ring of keys from the bag. His hands were visibly shaking. The fourth key on the ring opened both drawers as if made specifically for that purpose. He searched them in sequence, but found nothing other than miscellaneous check stubs, business papers, medication samples, and an unopened bottle of vodka. He stopped as another car passed the house, turning his attention to the file cabinet once its lights had faded. The obnoxious barking continued at the same multidecibel level. The cabinet's lock proved more resistant, and he used most of the keys on both rings before he found one that worked. It turned easily, and the lock tab snapped open.

The drawers were filled with hanging files, most of which were labeled in alphabetical order. There were income tax returns, medical licenses, and every other imaginable form of personal documentation, but in taking each drawer one by one, Clay found nothing that pertained to his search. Something about the bottom file seemed different however, and when he pulled the hanging files to the front, he found underneath them a spiral-bound notebook and a fat manila folder both squeezed into the space between the cardboard files and the bottom of the metal drawer. He opened the notebook and on the first page found several references to William Hand. The name also appeared on several of the papers in the folder.

By now the dog had begun to hurl itself against the door, adding a new dimension to the unnerving effect its racket had upon Clay. He was certainly not about to go beyond this room. Whether this was all of it or not, he would have to take what he had and run. He frantically crammed the folder and the notebook inside the bag and gathered up his tools. Almost as an afterthought he shined the narrow beam of the light into the file drawer a last time before he relocked it, and in doing so noticed something that he had missed. Standing on its edge at the back of the drawer was a package wrapped in what appeared to be green and red Christmas paper bound by brittle Scotch tape that had long ago lost its adhesiveness. Clay peeled open the paper to find an untitled leather-bound book. Turning to the first page of the book, he stared for the briefest second at the multiple signatures of Neptune Adair. Without another thought he pushed the book into the bag on top of the other discoveries and shoved the drawer closed with his foot.

Clay unlocked the study door without opening it and replaced everything as he had found it. The shriek made on closing the window was just as shrill as its opening, and he wasted no time in returning to the car. He switched on the headlights as he turned into the street and glanced at the clock on the dash. His time in the house was thirty-four minutes.

Clay drove around town for another half hour after leaving

the burgled house, unsure of himself, simultaneously flushed with success and at the same time terror-stricken by the thought of discovery. He was having difficulty believing that he had actually pulled it off. In spite of his fear, the theft would never really fit his notion of a crime, but more resembled a college prank tempered by a liberal dose of imagination. After all, Sara Weatherford was wholly ignorant of Eldon's obsession with William Hand and would not have known what to do with the information in the file cabinet even if she had known of its existence. Certainly, if he and his father did not find and use the knowledge contained in the lost notes, then no one would. The same rationale that led him to commit the felony in the first place now allowed him to feel fulfillment upon its completion.

On the outskirts of Pyott, he stopped at a convenience store and bought a cheap Styrofoam cooler, a bag of ice, and a six-pack of beer. The ritual of drinking, rather than the alcohol, seemed to calm him, and he returned to the motel. After twice securing the door and adjusting the curtains to his liking, he punched on the television and removed his sneakers. Now ensconced upon the bed, comfortable in his stocking feet, he began a haphazard examination of the stolen notes. He assumed his father might not return for some hours.

Clay started with the journal, since it seemed the most accessible of the materials, once more opening to the first page. The bedside light, when compared to the trembling beam used in the darkened study, was more than adequate, and the ink, although faded, was now easily legible. Just as in Eldon Weatherford's case over seven years before, the series of signatures and first page of text reached out and touched him with their peculiar allure, causing him to pause for a long moment before moving to the third page. He read the next few entries carefully, studiously, and he noted the initial reference to Hand. A diary perhaps? Instead of pushing deeper into Neptune's story, he opted, perhaps out of deference to Vernon, to put the journal aside, and continued with the stack of papers held in the manila folder. Besides, the journal entries appeared lengthy and would resist any sort of cursory examination.

Gripping the papers en masse, Clay spread them across the bed. His initial perusal of the notes seemed as discouraging as his glance at the journal. He glanced at his watch, just after ten o'clock, and wondered once again when his father might return. The television remained on, the news, but the volume was so low that it provided only background noise. He passively watched the ball scores, took a last long swallow of lukewarm beer, and sent the empty can flying across the room to ricochet against the rim of the trash can before falling from sight. Silently he raised three fingers into the air, drew them back again, and took up the first sheet of ruled paper.

Eldon's notes were exacting and to the point. It seemed that he had consulted a genealogist, a man based in Oklahoma City, and the sum of their correspondence, some five letters each way, was neatly held together by a lightly corroded paper clip. Bound along with these letters, written in the doctor's now-familiar free-flowing hand, were two pages summarizing this exchange. In comparing the biographical facts presented there with his recollection of Vernon's material, Clay surmised that Eldon's research on William Hand was every bit as complete and accurate as his father's. Many of the other notes seemed more speculative, filled with flow diagrams much like his own and hypothetical maps, all with comments written along the margins, many enclosed within quotation marks, a key detail as yet unappreciated by Clay. There were several pages of seemingly unrelated paragraphs, short references to unfamiliar people and places, odd dates and even several contemporary names and phone numbers. One page in particular, headed "Paralee Williams," appeared to be a family tree. He studied it for a moment before moving on. The names hanging from the uneven branches remained a mystery to him. Sitting cross-legged, hunched over his cache, he tried to place the many and varied pieces into some sort of order, trying to cross-reference as much as he could from memory. Frustrated, he leaned over and pulled another beer from the cooler, now conveniently wedged between the twin beds. Uncrossing his legs, he leaned back on the pillows and watched ten minutes of David Letterman. Midnight had come and gone, but sleep seemed out of the question.

At the bottom of the folder, overlooked under the stack covering it, was a second spiral-bound notebook. Written across its front cover in black Magic Marker was the name *Neptune*. The name was often repeated in the notes and Clay's thoughts wandered back to the journal. The notebook seemed to contain an outline, and the left margin was defined by a series of numbers in sequence. The first entry read

> 2 – 9/8 – *Reference to crossing the Etowah River (September 1, 1834?).*
> 9/10 – *A valley (to the west?). First mention of "an old man, Kingfisher."*
> 9/12 – "Hand and Jiya have gone north." Mountain on three sides, exposed rock. "Place of the Pigeons."

As in a chess game, when a path to victory is suddenly focused within the mind's eye, Clay made the pivotal connection needed to understand, or at least begin to understand, the method in Eldon's work. He picked up the journal once more, reopened it to the second page and saw that the numbers along the margin of the notebook corresponded to unnumbered pages of the journal, and that the notations emphasized key points, in particular the geographic and temporal relationships mentioned in Neptune's dialogue. All at once Clay was seized by the insight that Eldon and Vernon were working toward the same as yet undefined end point. Paradoxically, despite moving from opposite points of reference, the two men, without knowing it, were reaching for the same focus, trying to solve the same forgotten, obscure mystery, and what each man lacked was now undeniably apparent; the springboards, the origins of their mutual obsessions, the Cherokee waybill and the escaped slave's journal, were now, for the first time, joined as one.

A tide of excitement swept over Clay as he covered each line of Eldon's interpretation of the journal. He was certain, beyond the reach of any doubt, that the key to the meaning of the waybill lay in the journal, that the other dates and persons and places contained within the notes were interesting and gave substance to what he was reading, but the point of the matter lay here. As he began to read the core of Neptune's autobiography, another emotion took hold of him, a more subtle form of zeal, a creeping fascination, the same wonderment once felt by Eldon now flowed into him, as the power of the words made their impact. Whether this mad search ever took him one inch beyond the cinderblock walls of this motel, the power of Neptune's account stood on its own. More than any clue to a treasure hunt, more than any mere historical document, it was the shared passion of one man's search for freedom and recognition. The individuals in this story, until now only symbols on a detached page, took on a real and intimately tangible human form, audible words came from their mouths, tactile emotions circulated within the palpable pulse of their hearts, and they acted out their lives in real time. Within the course of a dozen pages, Clay ignored Eldon's notebook altogether, not out of disinterest or because of its sudden unimportance, but as a result of his growing involvement in the original prose. He first read of Neptune's early life, his escape through the gold fields, and his initial encounter with Hand and Jiya. The story continued.

October 13

> Hand returned today. He was in an agitated state and announced that he would be leaving the Nation and going west to beyond the Mississippi River the following day. He brought two additional horses with him and asked if Kingfisher and I wanted to ride with him. The magician declared that he was too old to undertake such a journey and would remain. I inquired of the attitude toward Negroes in these western lands and Hand replied that he did not know. I agreed to go with him since I reasoned that it would indeed carry me a good distance from my original

condition and that by doing so I could continue to enjoy his patronage. I asked him of his brother and he said that Jiya did not see the same danger in the whites as he did and would not leave his house. He thought this attitude foolish and said that the whites would not be stopped by good intentions. I asked of his family and he replied with some sadness that they would be staying for the time being.

The memories of my first encounter with Jiya remain vivid in my mind. He kindly shared food with me and asked me often about myself, but since I was as yet unsure of his intentions, my answers were both vague and wanting of the truth. Although he never directly threatened my life, his gun held me close, and I knew I could not hope to continue my flight until after nightfall. That same afternoon Hand returned from his unspoken business. He seemed from the first to be a strong and secretive man, and the workings of his mind, often as now, are a mystery to me. He talked and dressed like a white man, yet in his manner he seemed not different from his brother. In all matters, Jiya minded the words of Hand and I soon realized that a decision concerning myself would soon be made. I prayed that God would soften their feelings toward me.

We wasted no time in leaving the camp under the rock and rode several miles further west and north and did not make stop again until after dark. We arose at first light the next morning and continued as before, descending in the late afternoon along a stream of uncommonly clear water. The path was rocky and seemed little traveled and Hand directed us to pause by the water and rest while he rode ahead to scout. We did not make a fire, but sat with the horses until he returned. As before, Jiya and Hand held council in private, and afterwards I was told that a turnpike was not far from this place, and that we would wait until dusk before continuing. I was given no reason for such stealth and did not ask it.

We ate sparingly and continued our journey, crossing a well traveled road within a few miles of our resting place only to reenter the forest on the other side, following a path so obscure that for a time I was sure of our being lost. Within the hour we came onto the grounds of a large two-story house, according to Jiya, the home of a rich Cherokee named Rogers. Down a low hill from the house was a fine spring which flowed from between the rocks. The turnpike was just beyond the trees, and it seemed that the spring was well known to travelers in these parts. We stopped here to water our horses, and Hand directed Jiya and myself to wait for him in the barn which lay some few hundred paces from the house. He walked to the house alone. It was about two hours past the sunset.

Not long after we dismounted, we heard the approach of many horses, and Jiya displayed great alarm. He walked forward in the shadow of the barn to see what was amiss, when a single shot was heard, followed by much loud shouting and the sounds of general confusion. Without awaiting the fate of his brother, Jiya ran past and called for me to follow. So blind was our flight that I lost complete control of my horse and am alive today only because the frightened animal followed Jiya's desperate lead. We rode for many hours in such a reckless manner, crossing countless miles of desolate country with seemingly little concern for the welfare of either ourselves or the horses. We paused only twice to rest, but never long enough to sleep. At dawn we climbed a steep ridge and stopped upon its crest inside a wide clearing marked by the circles of many fires. To my everlasting astonishment, we were greeted by Hand, who, without warning or explanation, stepped forward from a place of concealment.

So dark was the night and so rapid our progress that I lost all notion of direction and can say little more about this portion of my adventure. Hand told me later of a confrontation with the militia and admitted that it was he who fired the shot in order to make good his escape. Jiya spoke little of the matter. I remain uncertain as to the reason for their troubles, but tend to believe that this *episode was not the first of Hand's problems with the authorities. By now I realized that I had fallen in with desperate and lawless men, but in reconsidering my plight, saw that their condition was little different from my own.*

Clay removed his dusty glasses and wiped them on his shirt tail. He then laughed and said aloud, "You seem to attract desperate men, Mr. Neptune."

October 14

This morning we bid farewell to Kingfisher. Hand took him aside, and they spoke for some minutes. Then we mounted and rode west up the mountain through the break in the cliffs that was by now familiar to me. The path beyond the crest was narrow but well traveled and soon passed between a number of large rocks of many odd and wonderful shapes. Late in the afternoon we came to a junction of trails which was situated in a shallow hollow, centered within a grove of heavily scored trees. He said the marks were messages and that he had hunted here often in years past. After leaving this place we came upon the edge of a deep precipice and were afforded the view of a great chasm with a broad valley and still other mountains beyond. We rode down from this high place as the sun was setting and made camp in the forest near a rocky stream. We had ridden the entire day and had seen no other travelers.

October 17

We have now been two days in Lookout Town, a Cherokee town in a valley between two long mountains. I was told that Hand's mother was born here, and we are among her kinsmen. There are no whites here or anywhere abouts and there is much strong feeling against them. For the first time I feel I am beyond the reach of the slave catchers. The circumstances of the past several days are so peculiar that I feel compelled to describe them although Hand continues to conceal his purposes from me. His shoulder, injured during our secretive journey, was set back in place by two men and considerable whiskey, and I think we will remain here until he is able to ride again. I will now relate what happened to us.

Three days ago we left the camp by the stream and continued riding into the forest. There was no path to lead us but Hand was sure of the way. We passed over much rough ground and were finally forced to dismount and lead our horses by the reins, climbing past many large rocks until we encountered a heavily used trail. For a time we enjoyed level country and rode peacefully for several hours. We stopped at a shallow spring muddied by horses. Hand pointed to another scored tree and asked me if I could read the marks carved upon it. I could not, a response which he found amusing. We then left the path once more, this time riding toward the north.

Rain and clouds had come in the night, and the sky was dark, and we soon descended into a deep canyon filled with the roar of water. Hand told me that it was a place of great magic and that he and Kingfisher had gathered eagle feathers nearby when he was a boy. After a time and much hardship we came upon a rock shelter darkened by fire. Hand instructed for me to stay under the rock while he took candles and a rope from the packs. He then left me alone. The rain fell ever harder in his absence and there was much thunder, and the horses were afraid, and after some hours of it I became afraid also.

Finally Hand returned, but his shirt was torn, and he appeared in a bad way. He said that he had taken a fall and as a result had lost the use of his arm. In all my association with him I had never witnessed him in such a state. He was insistent that I follow him and return to the site of his fall. The rain continued falling heavily, but I did not dare deny his request. I followed him without question, and we climbed for such a distance that I thought the fall must have rendered him mad. When almost all breath had left me we passed between several large boulders and came to a low cliff face where scattered among the rocks were a vast number of coins. At his instruction, I retrieved these coins *and placed them in a box broken open by his fall. He told me to carry this heavy box back to the rock shelter while he followed close behind carrying a pair of saddle bags. The footing below the cliff was unsure, and I fell on several occasions, at one point breaking my spectacles.*

At long last we reached the horses, and Hand, being in no condition to travel, indicated that we would spend the night here. He had me count the coins in front of him, over four hundred Spanish dollars, along with a number of gold coins, Napoleons and Reed coins, he called them. He never explained himself, rather he admonished me with his knife and frightened me so with his threats that I would have forsaken him other than I was by now lost in this unknown country and held no hope of escaping to the west without his help. I reassured him of my honesty, but slept little that night.

We came to Lookout Town the following day. He had me unload the horses and lay the packs close by his bed so that he might always watch them. From the weight of the saddle bags, they must have also contained money, but I did not directly look at their contents. I now suspect that the coins were part of a cache assembled by Hand and his brother for the purpose of leaving the Nation and that his mysterious and secretive nature is in great part based upon the need to conceal his purpose in this matter.

October 20

Hand's condition is much improved. His shoulder remains bound, but none of his wounds have festered. I have been well treated and feel no urgency to travel, but the weather may change soon, and who can predict what lies ahead for us. There is a man here who has been to the Indian territory and says that winter comes earlier to those parts.

October 23

We will leave for the West tomorrow, being well provisioned, and the horses are rested. The sky remains clear.

October 25

We have traveled two full days and Hand is in good spirits. He says we will reach the Mississippi River within the week. He talks of going first to New Orleans by boat, but I cannot tell if he is indeed serious on this matter.

October 27

We rode over forty miles today by my estimation. The land has turned flat and seems to be entirely covered in trees. We have encountered few other travelers. When asked by others, Hand has identified me as his personal servant, an unofficial arrangement that serves me well for the time being.

October 30

It has rained since last night, and we camped without the benefit of a fire. I was very cold and would have suffered greatly without a blanket.

November 2

We have reached the Natchez road and Hand has indeed decided to go south. He is determined to be at our destination before the first snow and says that we can reach the Indian Territory by water and save a good week of travel. How that will help us I am not certain.

November 4

This road is much traveled and we are little noticed among the multitude of wagons and riders.

November 7

We have reached Natchez and are boarded for the present in a stable close by the river. The river is as large as I might have imagined. I purchased a pair of peddler's spectacles and am glad for it. Hand obtained heavy coats for the both of us. He thinks we will need them soon. I have no money left for ink.

November 9

Hand got drunk last night and told me that he planned to open a store when he gets to the western lands. He said that I could help in this endeavor, but must never give him reason to doubt my loyalty. I think he is alone in this. He has secured us passage on the Star of Canaan, which is to leave at first light.

November 14

I am told that we are now on the Arkansas River and will be put ashore tomorrow. There are a number of other Cherokees aboard, and Hand has sought other company for the present. I have never before been on such a boat and have found the trip to be most interesting. I have found no difficulty in playing the role of a slave since it has for so long suited me, but cannot help but wonder about the future.

November 18

The land here is drier than I have seen. We travel with another Cherokee, a man called Oliga, and his family. The wagon slows us down, but Hand seems in no hurry since we left the river.

November 21

Rain.

November 25

We have stopped at the intersection of two rivers. Oliga knows the land, having scouted it several years before, and left us to go north along the second river which is called Illinois. There are many Cherokee houses and farms here, and Hand plans to stay the winter before claiming land of his own.

December 4

Snow.

The chronology abruptly ended with this entry. The remaining twenty pages of the ledger seemed to be partially filled with more random entries. Many were not dated. There were two pages of figures, a debit sheet of sorts, which appeared to concern itself with the operation of a household or farm, and columns dealing with the purchase of materials, feed, and animals.

He scanned most of this latter material, looking for names or dates that might be useful. Several notations were of interest.

*Traveled with Hand to New Orleans to buy for store.
Bought five books—seven dollars.*

August 8, 1839

Neptune Adair married Bernice Lackey.

Then the debits began. They were dated May, June, and July of 1839. At their conclusion was a single entry.

Received $25 for doing accounts. Bought horse and good saddle.

At that point a renewed series of personal entries began.

February, 1840

*Boy child died. God bless.
Received $50. J. Vann for accounts.*

March, 1841

*Girl child died.
Eighty acres. R. Blair. Illinois Valley.
Hand goes down Arkansas with Vann. Paper and ink—$12.
J. Vann—cotton gin. $100. Gone to Ohio.*

October 6, 1843

*Manus Adair is born.
$20. Simon Gilkey account.*

And then came the most interesting entry of the lot.

October 3, 1844

Hand killed in steamboat explosion. I told his wife how it was. That drunkard Vann is gone too. Some say he put fatback on the boilers to try and win the race. Only God knows. Both buried in Kentucky. And I got burned pretty good too.

Steamboat explosion? Where had he heard that before? And who was this Vann character?

June, 1845

Bought 160 acres on Sula Creek. Good water. Need wagon.

November 22, 1846

Silkie Adair is born.

And then the last entry.

December 8, 1846

Bernice Adair died of fever. May God bless her soul.

As Clay turned the last page, he felt a difference and saw that two pages were missing. They were cut from the book so cleanly and close to the binding that their absence could have easily gone unnoticed.

Clay returned to the diary and reread the final pages to see if he had somehow overlooked anything because of fatigue, but nothing came to light, and he laid the book to one side. Then he thought for a moment and picked it up again. By thumbing through the pages, he found what he was looking for.

"He had me count the coins for him, over four hundred Spanish dollars along with a number of gold coins, Napoleons and Reed coins, he called them," he read out loud. Clay then reached far back in his memory to a shoe box hidden on the shelf of a little boy's closet, to his own modest collection of coins, and to a thin red book that named and valued them. "Reed coins," he repeated. "Well, I'll be damned. I'll bet he's got it wrong. He means Reid coins, Templeton Reid coins. . . ."

Clay shook his head in wonderment. His eyelids felt swollen, and his eyes themselves burned. Moving to sit on the edge of the bed, he looked once more to his watch. "Where in the world is he?" he mumbled aloud.

No sooner had the words left his mouth than the telephone rang. Clay answered before a third ring.

"Hello?"

"Did you find anything?" It was Vernon. His voice was clear, even though he was whispering.

"Yes, I found something. Where in the hell are you?"

"I can't talk. She's in the bathroom."

"Are you at her house?"

"Dammit, yes, and it looks like I'll be here all night."

Clay began to laugh. "Why, if it ain't the old bull himself. If I'd known what you were up to I wouldn't have risked life and limb."

"Cut the clowning. What did you find?"

"It's a diary of sorts, written by an escaped slave. He knew William Hand. You're not going to believe it."

"Great. I've got to go. See you in the morning."

Clay sat on the bed for a moment, stunned by what he had read and heard. Slowly he slipped out of his jeans and shirt and switched out the light. Unable to sleep in spite of his exhaustion, a flood of images rushed by his mind's eye until finally he crossed into a troubled sleep filled with vivid dreams, the most vivid one filled with dark, cold water and distant fire.

— · — · — · —

The Ohio River near Lexington, Kentucky
October 1844

A pall of smoke and cinder spread across the expanse of brown, silt-laden water as the lead boat swung across the river to follow the channel. Within the span of a minute, the *Lucy Walker* entered this black curtain and the clusters of passengers lining the upper deck turned away from the choking cloud. Only Joseph Vann, the owner of the riverboat, did not turn, but instead gripped the railing and leaned into the wind as if the gesture might somehow increase the speed of his failing effort. There was no denying his losing and his reddened, whiskey-soaked eyes saw all too clearly the extent of his predicament. He let loose of the railing and pounded the wood with his fist.

Curling his full lips away from his teeth, he screamed in anger, "Goddammit, we've got to have more speed!"

He stuck his head into the pilot house and shouted to the captain, "Try to cut him off. Take all the shallow water we can stand." The man at the wheel nodded and began to adjust their bearing. Vann left him and bounded down the stairs to the first deck. He entered the double door leading to the boiler room and stood for a moment with his hands on his hips. A half dozen black roustabouts labored in the intolerable heat radiated by the twin boilers. The hiss of steam and the surge of the pistons filled the air with such noise that normal speech was impossible. Immediately in front of him a chain of men, working in pairs, struggled toward the firebox carrying four-foot lengths of hardwood. Stepping forward into the worst of the heat, Joe Vann grabbed the head man by his sweat-soaked shirt and dragged him bodily back to the relative quiet of the deck.

Pointing in the general direction of the opposition, he shouted to be heard, "Nathan, we've got to have more steam. I want every piece of wood we have put on those boilers."

The black man's face glistened with moisture, and deep creases appeared about his eyes as he squinted downriver. "Masta Vann, we's makin' 'bout all the steam them boilers can handle."

Without warning, Vann whirled about and cuffed the black man in the ear with his open hand. "Dammit, don't you tell me how to run this boat! I said we need more steam, and more steam we're going to have. Now get back in there and do as you're told."

The roustabout crouched in pain, holding his hand to the damaged ear. He offered no acknowledgment other than a grimace. His silence served as further provocation to the irrational owner, who raised his hand to strike the cowering slave once more. But Nathan saw this blow coming and ducked onto the decking. Vann drew back his foot as if to kick the fallen man, but then had other thoughts. "I've wasted enough damn time on you," he spat.

Vann removed his coat, threw it at the prostrate Negro, and turned on his heel to reenter the engine room. Once inside the inferno, he grabbed an ax hanging close by the door and struck a barrel lashed against the wall, sending a cascade of animal fat sliding across the floor. He screamed at the two nearest men and threatened them with the ax.

"I want this fatback thrown on the fire. I want those boilers as hot as hell itself."

The terrified laborers complied, tossing the strips of dripping fat onto the tightly packed masses of roaring oak and hickory. Nathan slipped to the doorway, watching his crew stoke the fires. The *Lucy Walker* was by now no more than two hundred yards off the north shore—the captain was taking Vann at his word. The entire mass of the boat vibrated with the effort of the pursuit.

Nathan mumbled something to himself and reached a decision. Barefoot and hatless, he mounted the rail and without hesitation jumped feet first into the swirling water, swimming quickly away from the side of the boat in an effort to escape the turbulence from the starboard paddle wheel. Once clear of the wake, he stopped and treaded water, watching the progress of the boat as it sped away from him. So intent were the passengers on watching the progress of the race, that not a single spectator among those on the upper deck saw Nathan abandon ship.

Neptune Adair and William Hand stood by the pilot house along with another passenger, a stout white man with a thick salt and pepper beard, dressed in buckskin breeches. "Looks like Rich Joe is gonna lose a little money," the bearded man said.

"He isn't the only one," Hand replied.

Suddenly a gust of wind passed over the boat. It caught the rim of Hand's hat and blew it from his head. It tumbled across the bright red planks until it caught against a post supporting the banister of the rear stairway.

Neptune was the closest to the errant hat, and he quickly left the other two and walked toward the stern of the boat. He bent from the waist to retrieve the hat and as he rose again caught sight of a man in the water. He waved his arm, but the swimmer did not respond. He walked back to Hand.

"One of the Negroes down below fell in the water," Neptune said.

Hand took the offered hat, placed it upon his head, and began adjusting the brim. "I sure hope he can swim, because I doubt that we'll be stopping any time soon to pick him up."

"It'll teach him to be more careful," the other man said.

Neptune stared at the bearded man for a moment and then said to Hand, "I'm going downstairs."

Hand answered with a shrug and turned away to watch the progress of the race. Just as Neptune reached the stairwell once again, he heard what sounded to be a shout. The sound drew him to the railing and he looked down just in time to see two more of the stokers leap into the water. What was going on here? he thought. He was on the third step when the first boiler blew.

Although the details of the next few seconds would be lost forever, Neptune would recall being lifted into the air by the concussion. His back was turned to the blast, so that he did not see the explosion itself, only the brown of the river and the blue of the sky and the green-yellow of the trees lining the shore. He also forgot the exact moment of impact, but his submersion into the water with its cold and its lack of air and its screaming panic would remain vivid in his mind. He fought his way to the surface and thrashed about in an attempt to stay afloat. One of his shoes was missing, and he somehow, by floating on his back, managed to remove the other along with his heavy, sodden coat that pulled at his arms like an anchor. Pieces of debris lay all around him, and he managed to find one, a broken door, that would support his weight.

Neptune's makeshift raft was now abreast of the *Lucy Walker*. The blast had temporarily abolished his hearing, and he floated by the wreck surrounded by the silence of a dream. There were no shouts or other human sounds. He watched frantic figures running along the tilted decks and saw others splashing about in the water. The riverboat was still afloat, her funnels gone, her hull broken partly in two, listing steeply at both ends. Columns of silent flame leapt through her windows, and billows of acrid smoke swirled about her. She would not last long.

He could not help them now. The flames and the screams and the smoke were snuffed beneath the surface of the mindless current. She was going down now, settling into the ancient mud of the river's bottom, sinking until only the projections of her upper deck were visible. The silence was no longer artificial. The moving water was all around him and Neptune was finally and completely alone.

The commercial development of the United States was in its infancy at the beginning of the nineteenth century. Little, if any, specie was available, but not much was needed to meet commercial needs. All but the more heavily populated areas conducted either a subsistence farming or a quasi-barter economy. This was especially true of the backward frontier area of Southern Appalachia.

—DONALD H. KAGIN, *PRIVATE GOLD COINS AND PATTERNS OF THE UNITED STATES*

May 1986

Clay and Vernon left Mathis Ford Friday afternoon as they had for the past two weekends. They took the Dodge pickup. Vernon had scarcely taken his seat before he asked, "Did you bring the letter?"

"See for yourself," Clay replied, referring to a piece of correspondence he had received only that afternoon. "It's on top of the folder."

Vernon pulled the letter from the open envelope and began reading:

American Numismatic Association
P.O. Box 2366
Colorado Springs, Colorado 80901
May 14, 1986

Dear Mr. Hardigrew:

Concerning your inquiry on Templeton Reid, I have enclosed a copy of an article published in *The Numismatic News* in August 1982. I hope that it answers most of your questions.

If we can be of any further help please feel free to contact us. I have enclosed a membership form should you wish to join our organization.

Sincerely yours,
Martin C. Hamilton
Assistant Editor

Vernon wiped off his glasses and leafed to the article.

THE MYSTERIOUS TEMPLETON REID

In spite of the historical significance placed on the Templeton Reid gold pieces, their creator remains one of the most enigmatic figures in American numismatics. He was born in Greene County, Georgia, in 1789. Little is known of his developmental years, but he left home as a young man and by 1816 had established himself in Milledgeville, at that time the state capital, as a metal worker, maker of cotton gins, watchmaker, and later (1824), according to his advertisements in the local newspaper, as a gunsmith and jeweler. He seems to have been mechanically gifted, perhaps a bit eccentric, a minor innovator and inventor, and an entrepreneur of little lasting success. As far as we know, he never married.

In July of 1830, a notice appeared in the Milledgeville Recorder announcing that "our ingenious townsman, Templeton Reid" had begun to issue the first in a series of privately minted gold coins in the amounts of $2.50, $5.00, and $10.00. How he came about this idea no one knows, but it is certain that the seed for his endeavor was the discovery of gold in northern Georgia in 1828, and the nourishment for its implementation was undoubtedly the continuing shortage of viable coinage (there was less than one circulating coin per capita in 1830). His reception was at first positive, and within a few weeks he had moved his coin press and dies to Gainesville, then a boomtown at the edge of the Georgia gold fields. Over the next three months, he would produce an estimated one thousand five hundred coins in the various denominations, a meager output that would provoke considerable controversy as to his honesty and would bring into question a previously unchallenged point of Constitutional law.

Within a month of the first Reid coins' reaching circulation, a letter from an anonymous writer to an Augusta newspaper accused Reid of extracting an unreasonable profit of 7 percent. This initiated a series of public letters pitting Reid against his unknown accuser (who titled himself "No Assayer"). Although no third party intervened to settle this dispute, the argument in and of itself damaged public confidence in the Reid coinage. Adding to Reid's woes were additional accusations by "No Assayer," who this time was joined by other parties, that his privately minted coins were a violation of at least the spirit of the Federal Constitution, which bans the States from coining money (Article I, Section 10) but neglects to specifically exclude individuals. These persons, who in fact were accusing Reid of breaking the law, assumed that whatever was prohibited the States must certainly be prohibited the individual citizen.

This growing hue and cry against Reid quickly forced him to cease his operation, and over the subsequent two years the Reid gold pieces were systematically removed from circulation by the United States Mint. Interestingly, an exact assay of his coins at that time gave an average value of $9.58 for the $10.00 gold piece, an actual profit of 4.4 percent, which may not have been so unreasonable after all. On the question of the legality of his idea, strict interpretation of the Constitution seems to have prevailed in several New York and Washington editorials, which viewed the issue as one of omission rather than commission. Evidently, the Federal authorities thought likewise for no charges were ever mentioned against Reid.

Upon leaving the gold fields, Mr. Reid returned to Milledgeville and shortly thereafter moved on to Columbus, another frontier town, this time at the extreme western edge of Georgia on the banks of the Chattahoochee River. For the balance of his life, he continued as a maker and inventor of cotton gins, a vocation that brought him mixed success. He died in 1851 at the age of sixty-two years. His obituary mentioned that his body was found at the bottom of a steep bluff alongside the river, and the writer theorized that he slipped there and being feeble from rheumatism was unable to seek help. He evidently died of exposure.

Although Reid was a failure as an assayer, his idea remained viable and his coins are now viewed by numismatic historians as the first of the so-called Pioneer Gold Issues. In his wake numerous gold coins were issued by dozens of private mints, primarily in California, and their presence became a primary stimulus for the Federal government to establish branch mints throughout the nation. The most accurate estimate of the number of his surviving coins is thirty-nine. They are among the rarest and most valuable of all American coins. A $5 Templeton Reid gold piece was sold at auction in 1979 for $200,000.

"This is amazing," Vernon said, shaking his head. "If any of these Reid coins somehow remained hidden, this ups the waybill's ante considerably."

"That's an understatement," Clay agreed. "If you'll remember, the diary spoke of *coins* in the plural. Can you imagine finding more than one of them? They could bring $250,000 each, depending on their condition."

"Whoa, boy," Vernon laughed. "Keep your feet on the ground. This isn't some Spanish galleon we're looking for."

They speculated without pause for the next two hours, until they made their first stop at a gas station about twenty-five miles west of Interstate 75. Clay parked the truck, bug-splattered and replete with a new camper top, to the side of the station, close by the air and water hoses, under the imperfect shade of a red oak tree. He visited the restroom and bought his standard road snack, a package of cheese crackers and a Coke. Vernon sat in the cab with an area map spread out across the front seat, marked here and there with red ink.

"You want a cracker?" Clay asked.

"No thanks, I'm not hungry." Vernon repositioned the map. "Look at this. I think we ought to drive down here again," he said, indicating a particular spot on the map, "Toward Cedar Hill."

"Sounds good to me."

They were well into the countryside now, where the roads narrowed and the traffic thinned out and the houses sat back from the pavement and barbed wire replaced picket. They passed a man riding a horse along the shoulder and Vernon waved as they sped past him. This and similar highways were becoming all too familiar in their continuing effort to locate the site of Kingfisher's camp. The journal was a critical step in their search, but had not proven to be as valuable as they had at first hoped, for assuming Neptune's descriptions were accurate, the lack of modern place names made locating the exact route of his journey more formidable than they ever imagined.

The mention of Lookout Town, the site of Hand's recuperation, was a key reference, for it was the one secure point of it all, the anchor for at least a portion of the story. The site of this former Cherokee town was well known and lay just west of the mountain of the same name, situated in a broad, well-watered valley as described in the journal. However, considering the inexact nature of Neptune's dialogue and the fact that he and Hand were on horseback, the radius of the search could easily be expanded from a minimum of twenty to a maximum of sixty miles, depending on degree of interpretation. Since the two had ridden from the east, Vernon had concentrated his efforts on Lookout Mountain itself as well as some of the surrounding ridges. Unfortunately, and in keeping with Neptune's impressions, the region's most salient geological features were its hundreds of miles of linear limestone-based ridges, many faced with broken cliffs, and after all these many weekends of driving and talking, talking and driving, one mountain or one valley was beginning to look much like the next.

Cedar Hill was located at the intersection of two obscure state highways. It was unincorporated and seemed to consist entirely of a single store and two gas pumps. The name of the store, Cedar Hill General Merchandise, flanked by circular Coke emblems, was in keeping with the building itself, frame, painted white, appearing to be at least fifty years old, conforming to the regional style familiar to such places of business. Broad wooden steps led up to a roofed front porch and the entrance was covered with double screened doors advertising Wonder Bread. The ceiling of the interior was at least fifteen feet high, and the floor was wooden and groaned underfoot. To Clay's surprise the inside was air-conditioned, but the lighting was archaic and seeing one's way around without stumbling was more dependent on the sunlight coming through the front windows than the weak illumination coming from overhead. To one side, opposite the cash register, was a caged and petitioned window that served as a U.S. Post Office, and spanning the difference between the two was an open circle of several benches, former church pews by the looks of them, and an assortment of cane-bottomed chairs. This varied seating arrangement centered upon a woodstove, one of the squat energy-efficient types. Seated on the pews were three men, all wearing ball caps, two appearing in excess of seventy years, the third wearing a black beard mixed with gray, maybe fifty years of age. The proprietor was a portly fellow wearing thick glasses who stood unmoved behind the counter.

In anticipation of engaging in conversation with whomever, Vernon instructed Clay to buy some gas, even though they did not need any, since the owner of a business is always more likely to talk when you are about to buy something. As Clay stood by the truck, Vernon went inside, hailed everyone present, and picked up a couple of candy bars and sodas. As he placed the merchandise on the cool marble of the countertop and waited for Clay, he began his pitch.

"How y'all doin'?" he said.

"All right, how 'bout you?" the proprietor returned.

"Not bad. Me and my boy are plannin' on doin' a little campin'."

"It's a good time for it. This weather's supposed to hold through the weekend. Where are y'all goin'?"

Vernon signaled direction with a jerk of his head, "Up to the state park." He then pulled a twenty-dollar bill from his pocket and laid it down on the counter. "This oughta cover the food and the gas." He then picked up an orange soda and walked over to one of the chairs. "Y'all mind if I sit down?"

One of the older men spoke up, "Naw, go right ahead."

About that time, Clay walked in and walked to the register. "Twelve dollars and fifty cents, plus a quart of this 10W-40."

Vernon continued, "Y'all had much rain?"

"Not enough," the same man replied.

"You put in a garden?"

The man smiled, glanced to his fellows, and rolled some snuff around with his tongue, "You might say that."

"My friend, you are talkin' to about the best gardener around these parts," the other retiree added.

Vernon acknowledged the man's skill with a nod and continued, "Well, we could certainly use you up our way. It's been as dry as a cob."

Clay took the change, picked up a Payday bar and tore open the wrapper. His appetite was unfazed by the crackers. He hung back, eating slowly, watching his father work the men.

"Yeah, I think we're in for another bad one," remarked the youngest of the three, adjusting the bill of his cap, referring to the ongoing drought.

"I'd give it up," said Vernon, "if I could live without tomatoes."

That comment brought a chuckle from around the circle.

"Where you boys from?"

"Tennessee, Mathis Ford, south of Oak Ridge."

"I got a nephew lives in Oak Ridge," the man with the snuff said, pausing to spit the overflow into a handy paper cup. "Works at that aluminum plant."

Vernon sat quietly for a moment. Clay was half-finished with the bar and popped the top on a Cherry Coke. It was time to get down to the meat of the exchange,

"First time we camped out down this way," Vernon offered. He paused and took a sip of soda. No one responded. He continued, unfazed by the silence, "We camp out a lot. All over as a matter of fact. We're into huntin' Indian artifacts."

"You mean points?"

"Yeah, those, and pots too, and whatever else turns up." Once again there was no further immediate response to this lead, so he persisted, "Anything like that ever turn up around here?"

The gardener, who was turning out to be the most talkative of the three, said, "I used to turn up arrowheads with the plowin', but I ain't seen none in years."

The younger man added, "I used to pick 'em up by the bagful

down at the Bagbys'. You know, down by the creek," he said, looking to the two older men for agreement.

"What creek would that be?" Vernon asked.

"Hard Weather Creek."

"That's an unusual name," Clay noted.

The snuff man laughed, "Yeah, that's cause it won't stay put. Tends to get outta hand when it rains."

The proprietor, who until now had been silent, walked to a glass display case, and opened the back. "Tell me what you think of this," he said, holding up a perfectly formed flint point, perhaps six inches long.

Vernon stood up and walked over to him. He put down his drink and turned the point in the light. He gave a low whistle and observed, "This is a nice one. Where did you get it?"

"From a fellow who lives hereabouts. What do you think it's worth?"

"Forty or fifty dollars, I'd think," Vernon said, not entirely sure of what he was talking about.

"Ha, guess I came out all right on that one. I swapped him a case of beer for it." Once the laughter had passed, he remarked, "You know, he had a pot with him too."

"You don't say. What did it look like?"

"Hard to say. It was in a couple of pieces, and he had it wrapped up in a newspaper."

"And what did you say that fellow's name was?"

"I didn't," said the owner abruptly.

"Sorry," he said. "Just asking."

The man relented. "His name's Garland Humphries. Used to work over at the White Rock Farm."

"Still does . . . ," added the bearded man, "when he's sober."

Vernon handed the point back to the proprietor. "You want to sell it?"

"How much?"

"Well, I told you what I thought it was worth."

"Fifty."

"How about forty-five?"

The man smiled and handed the piece of flint back to Vernon. "Mister, you got yourself a deal."

Vernon handed him two more twenties. "Now tell me where to find this fellow Humphries."

The old man spit once more and added with the faintest frown, "My friend, are you entirely sure you want to find him?"

CAROLINA ROSE

There is something to me very softening in the presence of a woman, some strange influence, even if one is not in love with them.

The main house of White Rock Farm sat in a grove of hardwoods at the foot of Johns Ridge, a spur of Lookout Mountain. The oldest portion, with its modest portico, dated from the 1870s and was constructed of blocks of native limestone. To the left was a low wing of a different style, unobtrusive clapboard, painted gray, obviously added at some later date. Overall it worked, for as one climbed the long drive and pulled into the wide concrete turnaround below the front steps, the impression was one of restraint and genteel age.

"By the way, let's hold off mentioning this fellow Humphries. I got the feeling he's somewhat of a bad actor," Vernon said as they pulled to a stop.

"You don't say."

"Also, we ought to leave our hats here. These folks look like they might be more uptown."

Clay complied, ran his fingers through his hair, and wiped off his glasses with a handkerchief. "How about we use the book angle again? Nobody's questioned it yet." This particular come-on had become their mainstay.

"Who's writing it this time?" Vernon asked.

"I'll give you the honor."

Vernon grunted up the steps, leaning heavily on his cane. Before Clay pressed the button to the bell, he pointed to the name plate above the ornate brass knocker. It read "Rose."

They rang once and waited. Clay turned briefly and looked across the shaded lawn to the wide pastures and cluster of concrete silos beyond the highway. Somewhere in the distance, a couplet of shotgun fire rolled across the landscape. "Dove hunters?" he commented.

"Not this time of year. Maybe skeet."

A middle-aged woman came to the door, dressed in a plain print dress. She appeared at first glance to be a domestic, but Vernon, rather than cause offense, took an indirect approach.

"Good morning, madam," he said bowing slightly from the waist and presenting his card. "My name is Vernon Hardigrew, and this is my son Clay. We are collectors of Indian artifacts and were told by some men at the Cedar Hill Store that such things turn up from time to time on your farm."

The woman eyed the card, which listed only his name and address, and hesitated in answering. She was trying to decide if they were salesmen. "I wouldn't know anything about that," she replied. Glancing over one shoulder, she went on, "Let me go see if Mr. Rose is here."

She did not ask them in, nor did she close the door. Cool air flowed from the doorway as they waited on her to return. After a short time a man appeared at the door. He was in his early thirties, dressed in faded designer jeans and a pink polo shirt, and stood several inches over six feet. He was a handsome fellow, broad in the face, with wavy brown hair. He extended his hand and said, "Hello, I'm Charlie Rose. Can I help you?"

Vernon applied his best handshake, as did Clay. "I don't know, Mr. Rose, if you can help us or not, and we certainly apologize for disturbing your Saturday unannounced like this, but in our business if something turns up, we like to follow up on it." Rather than wait for a response, he continued, "We are amateur collectors of Indian artifacts and heard at the Cedar Hill Store that such things have been found on this farm in the past. I am presently editing a catalog of Indian sites in the Southeast and wondered if I might ask you a few questions? I assure you we won't take up much of your time."

Charlie glanced at the card in hand, flashed a reserved smile, and replied, "I'm really not sure I can help you."

"We would be appreciative of any information that you might have. Sometimes the smallest findings can turn out to have the greatest importance," Clay added.

The weight of Vernon's insistence had its effect as the master of the house pursed his lips and replied, "It's not a topic that I deal with regularly, but I'll tell you what little I know. Come on in."

He led them into a sitting room in the front of the house. It was tastefully furnished with antiques and the heart pine floor was covered with a red-on-blue oriental carpet.

"So you're writing a book?"

"Of sorts. I'm actually collaborating with several other people. My responsibility in the project is northern Georgia, Alabama, and eastern Tennessee."

"Are you a writer by profession?"

"Oh, no," Vernon laughed in truth. "I'm retired from the building materials business. Clay's in charge of that now." Clay made no attempt to correct him.

Charlie looked at the business card for a second time. "Isn't Mathis Ford south of Knoxville?"

"Yes, about forty-five miles."

"So, the fellows over at Cedar Hill told you about me?"

"Not you in particular, but one of the older men, I didn't catch his name, mentioned that a number of arrowheads and even a few pots had been found at White Rock Farm." Vernon then became more direct. "Is that true?"

"I won't deny that. I've lived here off and on my entire life, and we have always found arrowheads when we plowed, but then so has everybody in the valley. As for pots, I've never seen anything beyond a few pottery shards."

"Has your family owned this land for some time?"

"My great-grandfather bought the site of this house shortly after the Civil War. He built this part of the house from stone quarried on the land."

"That's very interesting. If you don't mind my asking, how much land do you have?" Clay interjected.

"Presently, about five thousand acres."

"Well, you certainly have a nice place here," Clay replied, realizing almost as soon as the words left his mouth how inane the comment must have sounded.

Vernon said, "Is there any particular location on the farm where you remember finding the broken pottery?"

"As I recall, most everything was found in the fields alongside the creek."

Having previously consulted the map in the truck, Vernon asked for confirmation, "I believe they call that Hard Weather Creek."

"Yes."

"Would you have happened to have saved any of the shards?"

Charlie thought for a moment, "I can't say right off. I've got a box of that stuff somewhere around here." He stood up. "Let's go have a look."

He directed them down a hallway into the newer portion of the house. "Would y'all like something to drink?" he asked.

"Sure," Clay replied, more out of politeness than any thirst.

Charlie turned left and led them into the kitchen. The color scheme of the room was a basic white and blue, and the matching appliances appeared spotless. The woman who met them at the door was busy chopping celery. "I believe y'all met Doris, didn't you?" She acknowledged their entry with a nod, but avoided eye contact. "What'll you have?"

As he stood in the doorway, attempting to formulate a response, Clay's memory leapfrogged back to another time and another kitchen and the pungent smell of overcooked greens. "Do you have some iced tea?" he blurted out, not knowing why he had accepted Charlie's offer in the first place.

Vernon raised his hand in a sign of refusal, "Not for me. I'm fine."

As they stood waiting for the housekeeper to prepare the

drink, Vernon remarked effusively, "Is this portion of the house part of the original, Mr. Rose?"

"No. It was added in the early fifties by my father. And please call me Charlie." He then turned and asked, "Doris, would you know where that old box of arrowheads might be?"

She never looked up, but replied, "In the closet of your old room."

A long bank of windows lined one side of the kitchen. Looking past the white cotton curtains, Clay could see a flagstone patio, an off-white beach umbrella and beyond that, the aquamarine water of a swimming pool. Through the glass he could make out the sounds splashing and a child's unrestrained laughter. As he took the glass from the housekeeper, the squeals of delight grew louder, and a door crashed open. Around the corner of the kitchen entry, a little boy ran into view. He appeared to be about eight years old and wore baggy red swimming trunks. His wet feet slipped on the tile, but before he could fall, Doris stepped forward, quick as a snake, and snatched hold of his arm. Just as she made her lightning grab, another woman, presumably the child's pursuer, appeared from around the corner, half-colliding with the struggling prey and his irritable captor.

The second woman was similarly barefoot and was clothed in the briefest of black bikinis. Tall, deeply tanned, and without obvious flaw in her well-defined physique, she too almost slipped to the floor in an effort to recover from the collision. Her dark hair was pulled away from her handsome face by a pair of tortoise-shell barrettes, and matching sunglasses concealed the surprise in her eyes. She quickly regained her balance, adopted her most rigidly correct posture, and gracefully pushed the glasses back to their proper position. Both Clay and Vernon immediately assumed this must be Charlie's wife.

For those few seconds, everyone in the room stood stock still, other than the child who wiggled like a fish in an unforgiving trap. Then, without the slightest hesitation or sign of embarrassment, the scantily clad woman stepped forward and unexpectedly offered her hand to Clay. He savored the warm pool water on her hand. She smelled of sun and chlorine. She was not wearing a ring. He could not help but notice the chill spreading across her exposed skin any more than he could control the rapture in his gaze.

She did not falter in her greeting, "My brother is not much on introductions, and as you can see, I was not prepared to receive company. My name is Carolina Rose."

— · — · — · —

It was Wednesday and Clay was running the Sanger Road loop, a distance of about six miles. Dewayne usually went with him on Tuesdays and Thursdays, but he was scheduled in court all afternoon, so Clay did it alone in forty-nine minutes, just over his usual time. He cooled down by walking up the drive to his house and sat on the front steps, catching his breath while enjoying the company of the dogs. He considered at length what he should have for dinner, and no matter how he figured it, the menu featured spaghetti; after all, he never tired of it and more important, the dish was readily available, for he had frozen several containers worth of sauce the previous week. He put the pasta on to boil and climbed into the shower.

As he was toweling off, the telephone rang. It was Vernon. "We got a bite."

"How do you mean?"

"That nudist woman called me."

"Who are you talking about?" Clay answered, having some notion of what might come next.

"That Rose woman we met at White Rock Farm. The one in the bikini."

Clay cradled the phone in the crook of his shoulder while he patted his torso dry. "Really. What did she have to say?" he continued, trying to temper his enthusiasm. In truth, this turn of events pleased him immensely for he had found himself infatuated by her memory. Unable to conjure up a convincing line, he had hesitated to contact her, but the advent of this call saved him the trouble.

"She basically said that she would like to help. That she had some family information she would like to share with us."

I wouldn't mind sharing something with her either, Clay mused. "She must have been more specific than that," he said.

"Not really. She also asked for your number."

Clay attempted to sound unimpressed. "Do you have hers?"

Vernon answered as if he was not listening. "You know, I got the feeling your number is what she wanted all along."

"I can think of worse requests. As I said, if you have her number, I'll call her back tonight."

"Well, that's another funny thing."

"How so?"

"She made a point of saying that *she* intended to call you rather than the other way around."

As Clay replaced the receiver, the voice of reason counseled for restraint. He carefully combed his hair and put on a pair of clean briefs. Clean, comfortable, and confident, he ambled down the hall to check the progress of the evening meal, determined to wait her out.

For whatever reason she delayed in calling until the following evening. Her voice on the telephone seemed less confident than he remembered it.

"Do you live in Mathis Ford also?" she asked.

From his perspective it was a foolish question. She could easily have assumed that information from the area code and the exchange—it was identical to his father's. "Outside of town a few miles. I own some land."

"My brother said you operate a hardware store."

"You might say that. It's a family business—along with my brother."

"Do you have a large family?" she continued.

"My brother, who is here of course, and an older sister who lives in Washington."

"State?"

"No. D.C." He waited patiently for the next question.

"Do you have a family of your own?" she inquired.

"I'm divorced," he said. Reading her mind, he continued. "My only daughter, who's nine, lives in Atlanta with her mother."

"I can sympathize," she said. "My divorce became final last year—in New York."

"Were you living there?"

"Unfortunately." He detected an audible sigh. "I don't know about your experience, but the entire process was upsetting to me. I came back home for a rest and haven't summoned the energy to leave."

"Do you have any children?"

"No, I don't."

"So, that was your brother's little boy we met?"

"Yes." She paused here for a moment. He's anticipating me, she thought—I'd best get to the point. "As your father may have mentioned, I have access to some family history that Charlie, my brother, takes little interest in, and, uh, thought you might find it useful and wondered if we might get together and discuss it." The sentence almost made her breathless. She closed her eyes and bit her lip—why was she so damn nervous?

"What did you have in mind?" Clay answered smoothly, leaving the initiative in her hands.

"I know it's a drive for you, and my time is my own, so perhaps we ought to discuss your schedule first."

"It's highly flexible." This is too easy, he thought.

"How about this weekend, say Saturday?"

"Sounds good to me. When and where?"

"Could you possibly be down here by eleven? That would give us the entire afternoon."

"At your farm?"

She responded without hesitation, "Not the farm. I had a little hike in mind, an adult field trip, so to speak. It's not more than a few miles up the mountain. And don't worry about lunch, I'll take care of that. Now let me give you the directions."

As he lay in bed that night, Clay's curiosity concerning Carolina grew. Why in the world had she asked to meet him in a church parking lot rather than at her brother's home? Although he felt a strong physical attraction to this mysterious woman, there was more than a sexual allure here, something peculiar, something special. She became his recurrent daydream for the balance of the week.

Saturday morning he left Mathis Ford at eight o'clock, knowing full well he would arrive at the rendezvous before eleven. The church in question, the Mount Nebo Primitive Baptist, was about twelve miles west of the Cedar Hill Store in the same general direction as White Rock Farm. It was a compact brick building with a propane tank to one side and permanent tables of rough-sawn lumber constructed under the trees to its rear. The nearest house was a convenient quarter-mile down the road. Carolina appeared five minutes late, driving a much-used Jeep Wagoneer. She pulled into the graveled parking lot going a good ten miles an hour too fast and rather than attempt a full stop, she rolled by, waved hello, and then shouted through the billows of dust, "Follow me."

By the time he got his car started and moving she was well ahead and showed no inclination to wait. They raced along for several miles before turning right onto an unmarked gravel road. A mountain loomed over them, and as the road began to climb its flank, Carolina pulled the jeep to one side and climbed out. Again she had on sunglasses, this time white-framed, accented by a white and green bicycle cap. She wore snappy khaki shorts (her legs were even better than he remembered) and a T-shirt bearing a logo for some bar on Martha's Vineyard. She strode forward and offered her hand.

"Good to see you again," she said in a businesslike tone. Her grip was much firmer than he remembered.

"I'm glad you called," Clay returned. He glanced toward the mountain. "Where are we?"

She smiled. "This is called the Flint Ridge. The road, if that's what you want to call it, forks around the corner and the real climb begins. Why don't you leave your car here?" He had brought the sedan.

As he climbed into the Wagoneer, he noticed a fully loaded day pack sitting in the middle of the back seat. Before they proceeded, Carolina switched into four-wheel drive. Her assessment of the road soon proved all too accurate. From a point just beyond the predicted intersection, it climbed virtually straight up the hill without benefit of a single switchback. Erosion, along with off-road traffic, had combined to gouge deep ruts in the roadbed, and at several locations their ascent flirted with the impassable. To the right, a deep gorge appeared, and above the roar of the engine, Clay caught the sound of water. After a half mile or so, the road suddenly leveled off and abruptly ended in a small field covered in knee-high grass. A low metal gate blocked further access by the road which beyond the gate became choked with blackberry bushes.

"This is the beginning of the state's land," she remarked as she opened the door.

Shouldering the pack, she led him up a slow incline under a line of trees, where, after a few hundred yards, they encountered a series of rolling pastures also covered in high grass, mostly broomsedge. Just ahead of them, crowning the summit of a low hill, stood a solitary fieldstone chimney, but no other trace of a house was visible. A half dozen twisted and diseased apple trees stood close by the house site. All around this open place, defining its limits, enclosing it within three high green walls, was the mountain itself, forming a delightfully intimate pocket, bounded as if something had taken a bite from the mountain during its formation. It was a wondrous and unexpected geological quirk.

"This is beautiful!" Clay exclaimed.

"Yes, it's nice, isn't it," Carolina agreed. "You would never suspect it was up here from down below. We're lucky that no one else took the trouble today." She continued across a field bordered by masses of yellow daisies, finally stopping under a grove of second-growth oaks where the grass thinned. "Time for lunch," she announced.

From within the pack, she removed a linen tablecloth that flashed blazing white in the hot sunlight. Over it she arrayed a variety of freshly cut vegetables, two roast beef sandwiches on onion rolls, an unopened bag of ripple potato chips, a Tupperware container of deviled eggs, a Ziploc bag full of chocolate chip cookies, along with several bottles of soda as well as two bottles of wine, one Chardonnay and one Beaujolais. "Red or white?" she asked.

"White," he replied, and she handed him the bottle along with a collapsible corkscrew. As he worked on the cork, she prepared two paper plates and when finished, removed two plastic wine glasses from the pack. He poured. She touched her glass to his, and said, "Come what may."

The implication of the toast was perfectly clear to Clay. It both excited and unsettled him, for he uncharacteristically could not come up with an appropriate response. He took a second swallow of the wine and let its oaken vapors fill his head. "You set quite a table."

Carolina accepted her wine and stretched out on the grass and began to munch on a carrot stick. "This spread isn't exactly low cholesterol, but I just couldn't help myself." She took another sip of the wine. "So, tell me about the Indians."

"I hope you don't mistake me for an expert. My father is the one who got me into this."

"Are y'all close?"

"We are now."

She seemed not to hear him. Facing into the sun, propped up on one elbow, she removed her cap. Her black hair came free and fell about her shoulders, and for the first time since he had met her she removed her dark glasses. Turning toward him, she said abruptly, "Well then, let's talk about something else."

Her eyes suddenly became her best feature, a light, airy, almost colorless blue, contrasting dramatically with her dark hair and complexion. Clay for the first time was able to critique her face as a whole; she was more handsome than beautiful, patrician by her fine features, but at the same time comfortable here in the unforgiving sunlight. The way she moved, the way she handled herself, the strength of her pose, hinted at an innate athleticism. He was by now totally, irrevocably, taken by her.

Clay moved closer to her. "Let's talk about you," he said, taking another swallow of wine to clear the dryness from his throat. The sun was hot on his exposed neck.

She lay back to consider the question, crossing her legs and placing her hands behind her head. The light cotton of her shirt stretched tightly across her breasts. "Shoot."

"How'd you get your name?"

"It was given to me by my mother. She was from North Carolina—Bryson City, the mountains."

"And?"

"My life story?"

"Why not?"

She closed her eyes. "I was born at White Rock Farm. I am almost thirty-four years old." She lazily waved at an insect with the back of her hand. "I was considered a tomboy as a child, so much so that my mother sent me off to Chattanooga to a boarding school when I was twelve years old. She died of a brain tumor when I was sixteen. It was the single most tragic event of my life." She opened her eyes wide as if to release some unpleasant thought and turned toward him. "I was never very close to my father. He seemed to always favor his namesake, Little Charlie, and by the time I was out of high school, we had essentially quit communicating. I was already pretty wild. Anyway, perhaps that explains some of the differences between my brother and myself. Big Charlie, that's what everybody called him, died in a plane crash while I was at the University of Pennsylvania.

"I majored in Spanish, and after school I lived in Barcelona for two years, working for a steamship company. After that I traveled a while, you know, got the wanderlust out of my system, and when the urge had passed I came back, first to Boston where I worked as a management trainee for the phone company, but got tired of that after a year or so, took a couple of years off and lived in Oregon and Aspen, where I worked as a waitress, then moved back east to New York. I got a job with a brokerage firm and lived in Manhattan, which is how I met my husband. In retrospect—I guess everybody says that—I don't know why in the hell I married him. He was an Italian from the City, and we really didn't have that much in common, and we ended up fighting for most of our five years together. He was a liar and womanizer, and frankly I was no saint. It was a total dead end. I came back here about a year ago and have not done much of anything since. I run and walk at least twenty miles a week, tutor Spanish once in a while, I've read all the best-sellers, and have become a general torment to my brother."

Perhaps that explained why she chose to meet him at the church. "Why don't y'all get along?" Clay asked.

"Part of it's hereditary and part of it's financial, at least from his point of view. Our father left me half the farm, which means that in theory I have as much to say about its operation as Charlie, but he doesn't quite see it that way."

"Do you and his wife get along?"

"He's divorced too. He married this cute little redneck right out of high school and that lasted about a year. Frankly, I'm not even sure where she is right now."

"So he's got custody of the boy?"

"It was never a contest. She was a real no-goodnick." Sitting up, she looked away and continued, "So that's my book. Now how about yours?"

Clay then related his abbreviated autobiography, omitting most of the unflattering details. He captured her complete attention.

"So what sort of relationship do you have with your ex?"

"We're barely civil."

"How often do you see your daughter?" she asked.

"Select weekends, holidays, and a month in the summer."

He poured them both a second glass of wine. He felt the first one going to his head. She took out a wide-mouth plastic bottle full of ice cubes and dropped one into her glass. She then looked directly at him, fixing his attention with her gaze. Her eyes were hypnotic.

"I assume that you guessed I didn't call you up to talk solely about Indians."

"I suspected that," he admitted.

She smiled and put her wine aside. Getting to her feet, she brushed the adherent leaves from her bottom, and said, "Finish your drink. I want to show you something."

She rummaged about in the pack and pulled out a metal Sierra cup, wedged it into her belt, and struck off into the trees, following a faint path winding through the luxuriant undergrowth. In her wake, he watched the calves of her muscular legs flexing as she climbed. She spoke little as she walked, remarking only that she had come here often as a young girl, and recalled when the ruined house was inhabited. After a walk of some fifteen minutes across the mountain's wooded face, they entered into a narrow clearing before a moss-covered outcrop of gray-white stone. At its base was a pool of deep, blue water fed by a spring issuing from the rocky face. Other than the shafts of stippled sunlight breaking through the leaves overhead, they stood in cool, moist shade. The spring head had been modified by man at some much earlier date, for it was defined by blocks of finely cut limestone fitted along its margins and a lintel of the same rock spanned its crystalline outflow.

"Another surprise," Clay remarked.

"They call it Bluebird Spring."

"Who built it?"

"I don't know," she replied. "It's been like this as long as I can remember."

She then removed her boots and socks and sat down on the

stone bridge, dangling her bare feet into the cold water. He followed her lead, sitting down close beside her. She dipped the cup into the pure water and shared it with him. Its taste was beyond comparison, sweet and ultimately pure, filtered through a thousand feet of porous rock. Their faces drew close together as they drank, and he captured her scent, and in a mutual understanding of the eyes, joined her in a delicate kiss, a long, warm kiss, tasting of spring water, the faint salt of perspiration, and the fading aroma of wine. They gently embraced and kissed once more.

As they finally drew apart, she said, "I haven't been touched by anyone in over a year." She then lowered her eyes. "I feel foolish."

"Well, you shouldn't. But why me?"

She looked up and began to stroke his face. "I don't know. Fate, hormones, who can say?" She shrugged and then smiled. "I guess I just liked your looks." She initiated another long kiss.

She then suddenly stood up and without warning disrobed in front of him. She slipped so easily from her shorts that her action appeared to have been choreographed, and just as neatly she peeled her shirt from over her head. As he sat in awe of her taut body, she stepped down into the spring and held out a beckoning hand.

"I presume we won't be disturbed?" he asked as he removed his shirt, unable to accept the enormity of his good fortune and her seeming lack of any inhibition.

"They won't—but, if they do . . . ," and with this she smiled, "it will certainly be a hike they will never forget."

Clay removed the rest of his clothing. As he stepped down into the chilly water, Carolina picked up the metal cup, refilled it to the brim, and then ceremoniously poured its contents through her hair. The water rushed over her in a single, clear cascade and then, agitated by a shiver and the immiscibility of the oil covering her skin, coalesced into a thousand liquid lenses. It was an act of overpowering eroticism.

"Don't you think I look better wet?" she asked.

He gently cupped her submissive face in his hands and

whispered, "Wet or dry doesn't matter—you're a mystery to me either way."

Her ice-blue stare bore into him as she ran her hands over the light brown hair covering his belly. "Be careful," she said, "and never forget, the beauty of a rose hides many thorns."

Before marriage a Creek girl enjoyed considerable sexual freedom, and any sexual relationships she had with unmarried men were not considered adulterous. But after she was married she was expected to be faithful. If caught in adultery she was likely to be beaten by her husband's relatives, with or without his consent, and in some cases they would take a knife—sometimes a dull knife—and cut off the ears of the woman and her lover. . . . But the Cherokees were far different. A Cherokee woman, whether married or single, could more or less go to bed with whomever she chose, and her husband could do little or nothing about it. The Cherokee woman had the same sexual freedom that a Cherokee man had.

—CHARLES HUDSON, *THE SOUTHEASTERN INDIANS*

Six Days Later

Carolina entered the office of the gas station and asked the attendant for two dollars in change. She walked to the pay phone and took a folded piece of paper from her shirt pocket. After consulting the operator, she deposited the correct amount and waited for the switchboard to answer. "Could I speak to Mr. Hardigrew, please?" she inquired.

As she stood waiting, with her back turned away from traffic, a pickup truck rounded the corner and slowed as it passed her.

"Ain't that Carolina?" asked the driver, a stocky man wearing a black T-shirt.

His passenger, a huge, rounded fellow with a scraggly brown beard, turned and looked back through the rear window. "Sure looks like," he agreed.

"Let's see what she's up to," the driver said, changing direction to round the block. He followed this maneuver by parking alongside the curb so as to have full vantage of the phone and its user without being seen. She talked for two minutes by the clock, hung up, climbed in her jeep, and pulled away from the station, taking the highway north toward Chattanooga. The two men did not follow her, but continued in the opposite direction.

They did not drive up to the main house of White Rock Farm, but drove on to the barn, where they began to unload a newly repaired air compressor. While they were closing the tailgate, another pickup turned off the highway and pulled into the barnyard. Charlie Rose, the big boss, got out. "Well, Bait, is it fixed?"

"It oughta be," the stocky man answered, lighting up a Marlboro. "It sure took 'em long a damn 'nough." He handed Charlie the bill. "Saw Miss Carolina in town."

"So?"

"She was talkin' on the pay phone at the Union station."

"It's not against the law to talk on the phone," Charlie answered, studying the figures.

"Then she took off toward Chattanooga."

"She said she was going shopping. She's got a lot of girlfriends up there from school."

Bait displayed an apologetic smile and glanced once toward the big man, who was attempting to move the compressor by himself. "Yeah, there probably wasn't much to it. Just thought you might like to know."

Charlie frowned ever so slightly and walked past the two workmen and through the gaping front door of the barn. He stood there for a minute with his hands on his hips, then turned back to the door. "Bait, come in here a minute," he yelled.

The stocky man appeared at his side without delay, and they stepped further into the shade.

"You must've thought something unusual was going on, or you wouldn't have mentioned it," Charlie said.

Bait adopted a sheepish look, "I didn't mean no harm, Mr. Rose. It just struck me as funny, you know. We weren't snoopin' or nuthin'. There she was, right out in the open, but she was standin' kinda like she didn't want nobody to see her, you know? And, uh, you did tell us to keep an eye on her and all."

Charlie clinched his fists and then relaxed them. "Yeah, I want you to keep an eye on the goddamned pillhead, all right. You did okay, Bait. I'm not pissed at you. It's just that she knows too much of my business already." He slapped his man on the shoulder good-naturedly and continued, "Keep it up. If you see anything even the least bit suspicious you let me know. Okay?"

"You got it, Mr. Rose."

— ∙ — ∙ — ∙ —

"Well?" Vernon asked.

"Well what?" Clay replied, continuing to bang away at the keyboard of the computer.

"You know what I mean. How did it go?"

Clay stopped. Having evaded the question for several days, he saw that further resistance was futile. "It went fine. Great, as a matter of fact." Then he lowered his voice. "But we didn't talk much about the Cherokees."

"Dammit, that's what I thought."

"Look, don't give me a hard time. The truth of the matter is that her offer was really a pretext for seeing me again. Frankly, I don't think she has much of an interest in Indians at all, but you can relax, I didn't completely lose my head." In an attempt at pacification, Clay offered the one bit of information Carolina had given him that in the least way pertained to the search. "She did happen to mention an aunt of hers that had a lot of information on the family and the farm."

"Now, how is that going to help us?"

"I don't know. She just mentioned it—that's all."

A look of exasperation swept over Vernon's face. He turned away and tapped on the floor with his cane. "You got any time this weekend?"

Clay braced himself for the explosion. "I'm seeing *her* this weekend."

Vernon slowly turned back in order to face his son. In contrast to moments before, his expression was now a picture of composure. He adjusted his glasses and spoke quietly.

"Clay, I understand your attraction to her, and I appreciate all of your help, and should you find the time in your busy weekend to question her further about her aunt, please do so. As you know we've made progress based on lesser leads." He moved toward the door. "Have a good time and call me when you get back."

After Vernon had limped from the office, Clay sat staring at the screen for several minutes. He could not help but feel guilty for enjoying himself. The enthusiasm he had experienced upon reading Neptune's journal was now directed toward this woman whom he hardly knew. He could not help it if Carolina found him attractive. It just happened.

This morose introspection was abruptly broken by crackling of the intercom on his desk, "Call on line four, Mr. Hardigrew." By the time the receiver touched his ear, and he heard her say hello, all remorse had passed. He went over the final directions to his house and listened patiently as she repeated them.

The balance of the week became insufferable. His father's disappointment, combined with Clay's growing anticipation over Carolina's visit, made it impossible for him to concentrate. By Friday afternoon he had become entirely detached from his work. Shortly after lunch, he leaned back in his swivel chair and studied the clock on the wall. She should be there by 4:30. "Oh, man, have you got it bad," he said aloud, and glanced over his shoulder to make sure no one had overheard him. He punched the intercom and said, "Sharon, what's going on the rest of the afternoon?"

"Well," she was checking the appointment book. "Nothing that I can see."

"Good. I'm leaving for the day. Have a nice weekend." He switched off the terminal, checked over his desk, throwing a paper or two into his briefcase before latching it, and left by the side entrance. His icemaker was on the blink, so he stopped by the store and picked up some extra, as well as some more beer and a pint of half and half. He was not planning on running that day, so he was in no hurry, but still got home before three o'clock, straightened up the house once more, fed the dogs and Lillian's horse, and stacked charcoal in the grill. He took his second shower of the day and was sitting on the front steps reading the sports page as Carolina drove up the drive and parked under one of the twin walnut trees.

He had warned her over the phone that no plans had been made for that evening, which was indeed fortunate since they were in the bed within fifteen minutes of her arrival.

"You didn't even give me a chance to get my bag out of the car," she offered in mock complaint.

"First things first," was his simple reply.

When they had finished, the sun was failing, and the tricks of the oncoming twilight played across the beamed ceiling. He lay against her, and she stroked his back as the confluent shadows of true darkness made their way into the room.

"Where did you get this bed?"

"Bought it from a widow lady in town—tiger eye maple. Her grandfather made it, she said."

"Why in the world did she sell it?"

"She was in ill health and her kids had moved off. I don't think they got along, and I just happened by when she was in the mood to sell it."

"It's noisy."

"I call it local color."

A softer noise joined them as a thin yellow cat leapt onto the bed cloths.

"Meet Kitty."

She laughed. "Very original."

He smiled and began to massage her tight rump.

"Well, are you planning to keep me captive in this bed all weekend or are you going to feed me?"

"All in good time, little girl."

She pushed him away and climbed on top of him. "Many women blame it on hypoglycemia, but I'm just plain bitchy when I'm hungry."

"Okay, okay, I'm moving."

He turned on some music, mixed them both gin and tonics,

started some potatoes in the microwave, put her in charge of the salad, and went to work on the steaks. They ate by candlelight on his only table and drank a bottle of wine between the two of them.

"I know not to drink this much. It makes me sick," she said.

"We'll run it off in the morning."

"You are going to make me run after all of this?"

"Moderation in all things," Clay said philosophically. "I used to drink too much at times—still do when the situation warrants it, but I've learned to draw the line when I need to. I finally came to the realization that alcohol is an imperfect drug for the everyday pain of living."

She sat back from the table and wiped at her mouth. "I had a problem once," she said softly.

"Booze?" And what have I got here? he thought.

"No. It wasn't that simple. I was guilty of polypharmacy—all sorts of things—mostly prescription drugs, uppers and downers, you know," she answered nonchalantly.

"After the divorce?"

"Some before, but it only reached crisis proportions after. I was pretty crazy for a while."

"I think I can understand that. Did you seek treatment?"

"Yes and no." She stared down at the food on her plate. "But that's really why I came home—to dry out so to speak."

"Has it worked?"

"Maybe," she said enigmatically. "That wine we drank last week was the first I have had in over eight months."

He stood up and said, "And just look what happened to you." He walked around the table and stood behind her and placed his hands on her and began to knead the muscles of her shoulders. "You won't resort to such things when you're happy with your life."

"I'm sure you're right, but happiness has always eluded me."

"Well, I'm certainly no authority on happiness, but maybe our meeting is a first step," he said. She stood up, they kissed, and then, on impulse, he swept her off her feet and carried her back to the bedroom. "Damn, you're heavy, Carolina."

"I've got thick bones," she said dryly.

"Tonight it's pleasure, but tomorrow we'll suffer. Six miles, minimum."

"I hope it's hilly," she whispered, drawing him close to her.

The following morning her admonition would prove accurate. Clay led her down Tucker Road and up the hill behind the Hendshaws', where from the crest, one could see the primary western ranges of the Appalachians. The ascent was not a steep one, at least not until the last few hundred yards, but there the hill became mean. She hung at his shoulder until the last and both were laboring as they reached the top. He walked to a small rock outcrop which afforded the best views, where he bent from the waist trying to catch his breath. "Damn, if she isn't strong, too."

As he stood up at her approach, she gave him a solid, but not telling blow to the stomach, which caused him to audibly wince, and then dancing lightly out of his weak reach, she retorted, "And don't you forget it, wimp."

He walked, still hitched over, to the rock and sat down. "I see why your brother has such love for his sister."

The day was especially clear, free of the customary summer haze, and huge columns of cumulus cloud were building over the distant mountains. Below them in the trees, someone was running a chainsaw.

They sat without talking while their breathing slowed in unison. "Nice place," Carolina remarked.

"It is, isn't it? I run up here at least once a week."

She fully extended her legs in the early sun. "By the way," she offered, without the benefit of any prompting, "I talked to my great aunt the other day."

"How's that?" he asked.

"My great aunt Eleda called the other day."

"Who is she?"

"You know—my father's sister, the one I mentioned that knows all about the family."

"Oh, yes. I had forgotten." This was only a half-truth. His father's directive had been lurking in the back of his mind most of the morning.

"What I mean is I didn't call her, which is not unusual. She's psychic in a way—always seems to know when I'm thinking about her. Anyway, we were very close when I was little. We played mutual favorites until I went away to school, but then, as is so often the case, we lost a lot of that personal contact, although we maintained a strong correspondence. Well, as I said, she called and told me she was rummaging through a box of old photographs and suddenly thought of me and said she was very disappointed that I hadn't been to see her in several months. Then I told her about you and your interest in Indians."

"I hope you didn't scare her off. Where does she live?"

"A little place called Aerie, Alabama."

"Never heard of it."

"I'm not surprised. It's sort of an art colony, mixed with some summer places—more a collection of houses than a formal town."

"You're getting warm," he remarked, as he noted the perspiration beading along her brow. Clay was not sure exactly how enthusiastic he should be. In spite of Vernon's wishes, the chances were one in a million that this elderly aunt living in another state would have any knowledge, either consciously or unconsciously, relating to William Hand's legacy if indeed it still existed. The many months of fruitless searching had taken their toll, and his old skepticism was reemerging, especially in light of his competing interest in Carolina.

"Don't give me a hard time." She stood up and began pacing in front of him. "To return to the original topic, I'm not much on geography, but I can read a map." She placed one hand on the ground and began stretching her calves. "My brother's going away on a fishing trip to Florida over Labor Day. Why don't you come down? We could go see Eleda if you want and have the farm completely to ourselves."

"Sure," he grunted as he stood up also. "Sounds like fun."

"Let me warn you, my aunt is a different sort of woman." Carolina laughed. "She's really wild—simply wild." The affection in her voice was contagious.

"So she's the black sheep?"

Carolina began stretching the alternate leg. "Oh, not really. More like eccentric. She's just always done things her way."

"What does she do now?"

"She's outlived two husbands. The last one was wealthy and did well by her, but you would never know it. I guess you could say she's retired, but she's always been artsy—ceramics and pottery mostly, and still dabbles some with that. You never can tell with Aunt E."

"Labor Day, it is," he confirmed.

"Great, I'll call her first thing." She walked toward the path of descent. "Come on, let's go before we cool off any more."

━ ∙ ━ ∙ ━ ∙ ━

Charlie Rose left with his son and Howard Samples, the local sheriff, along with Woodrow Howell, his insurance man, on the Thursday morning before the Labor Day weekend. Buddie Howell, one of the county commissioners, begged off at the last minute due to family commitments. The four of them flew out of the White Rock Farm airstrip with Charlie as the pilot, headed for Crystal River, Florida. They did not plan to return until the following Tuesday. Clay arrived Friday about noon and parked his car behind the main house next to Carolina's jeep. She had given the help the holiday weekend off.

The following day, they left in midmorning for the one-hour drive to Aerie. As Carolina drove, Clay read a story she had fished out of the console. "It's an article from *Southern Living*, I think," she said. "My aunt sent it to me a while back."

The historic community of Aerie was founded in 1876 by a displaced Frenchman, Claude Lacombe. While traveling through Alabama on his way to visit relatives in Louisiana, he was taken to a mineral spring by a local planter, whereupon a remarkable cure took place. A lifelong sufferer from asthma and other unspecified respiratory ailments, Mr. Lacombe, after partaking of the waters from this obscure spring, was for the first time in memory rendered symptom-free. Upon arriving in the humid climes of the lower Mississippi Valley, his bronchial tubes were once again provoked to seizure, so much so that he was given up for dead by the attending physician. Rather than forfeit his life so easily, he hired a wagon with the last of his funds and ordered the skeptical driver to transport him back to the miraculous spring with all possible speed. Upon his return, his powers of respiration were once again restored, and he vowed to all the saints and spirits to never again leave the curative air and water of this magical place.

Formerly a successful entrepreneur in his native country, he used his talents in business, along with a series of impassioned testimonials by both himself and other visitors, to develop a modest spa later known throughout the Tennessee Valley. Mr. Lacombe died in 1888 of pneumonia, and in 1890, his heirs build a grand hotel close to the springs. For the next twenty-five years, Aerie thrived and prospered and during this time came to attract visitors from throughout the eastern United States. With the beginnings of the continental war and the increasing availability of the automobile, the popularity of spas in general and Aerie in particular suffered, so that by the onset of the Great Depression, the hotel was already on precarious financial footing and soon closed for good. For a generation the town became a backwater within a backwater, visited only by the few families that maintained second homes on the mountain.

In the early 1950s a New York mystic-turned-artist by the name of Sybil Perlman happened upon Aerie and was taken by the charm of its decayed Victorian cottages and was also convinced of the healing powers of the spring. She bought one of the houses on the spot, restored it, and over the years attracted a handful of individuals who shared her unconventional views. She also, in 1962, founded the annual Aerie Arts and Crafts Festival, which propitiously coincides with the vernal equinox.

He looked up from his reading. "Are you sure your aunt is ready for us?"

"I don't think there is anything that she can't handle," Carolina replied.

They made the steep climb up to the town itself and passed by the old hotel, which was enclosed at one end by a huge lattice of scaffolding. Most of the windows were boarded up, and a gang of men were walking around on the roof.

"They've got their work cut out for them," Clay said.

"Some rich fellow from Birmingham has his heart set on restoring it. Eleda says he's already spent a half-million dollars."

"No doubt."

They pulled past the hotel and Carolina indicated that they should stop in a small graveled parking lot. A neatly routed sign read, "Lacombe Spring, 75 Yards." Clay followed her down a broad set of steps to the springhouse made of native stone. They were not the only ones there, for in one corner five or six people sat surrounded by what appeared to be many dozens of plastic milk jugs. A woman, heavyset and dressed in a man's work shirt, stooped by the spring itself, a small rivulet of water that flowed from under a large rock that formed most of the rear wall. As they appeared, she snatched up her jug, and said, "Y'all go ahead, I got all day."

"No, no," said Carolina. "We're just looking."

"What are you doing?" Clay asked the woman.

"Collectin' water," she said.

An elderly black lady with her hair tied up in a blue bandana piped up, "There ain't nothing like this water, mister."

"It's the cure for what ails you," the fat woman added. A murmur of agreement swept through the little throng.

"Like what?" Clay continued.

"Rheumatism, dizziness, weakness, the grippe, breathin' problems—you name it."

"Specially breathin' problems," someone emphasized.

"Your nature—that's the ticket. Ain't nuthin' like it," said a white-bearded black man surrounded by a small mountain of jugs. That comment brought a chorus of chuckles from the women.

"Well, well, I could use about a gallon. Who'll sell me a bottle?" The older black woman rushed forward. "How much?"

"A dollar and a half."

Clay gave her the money, took the container, and they walked back to the car. "Why did you do that? You could have taken the water for free."

"I paid her for her time and the jug. Besides, maybe the stuff works," he said, giving her a large wink. Her response was to pinch him on the behind.

"Careful, I might drink the whole thing for lunch."

Eleda did not live in the town proper, but about two miles north. They turned onto a well-maintained dirt road and within a few hundred yards encountered a sign that read, "Eleda Jane Birdsong, Potter." The small front yard contained two birdbaths, a concrete garden pagoda, and several pieces of abstract metal sculpture. A black Toyota truck sat in the drive. The house itself was faced with the same brown fieldstone as the springhouse and was placed right at the brow of the mountain, affording a sweeping and unobstructed view of the valley below. Its roof was of metal, painted a deep red. A well-tended vegetable garden was growing to one side, and the front of the house was all but hidden by an equally effusive flower garden. Another building, frame, smaller, perhaps a workshop, sat to the other side shaded by a clump of stunted and wind-twisted pines. As Clay pushed on the parking brake, the front door of the main house opened and two women stepped into the yard. Carolina ran up the walk to embrace the taller of the women for a long ten seconds. They separated, and the hostess stepped forward and offered her hand to Clay.

"Clay, I am forever in your debt for bringing my dear Carolina to see me." She appeared to be in her midsixties, but Carolina would later confide that she was ten years beyond that. Her white hair was trimmed in a short, businesslike fashion, and she was dressed in loose-fitting cotton shorts and a white smock with sleeves cut to the elbow. She wore no makeup and was barefoot.

Her fingers were exceptionally long and they cut circles in the air as she talked. She possessed a warm smile and exuded welcome, and Clay liked her from the very first moment.

"This is Mrs. Huffstetler, a good friend and neighbor." The second woman was an obese, cheery woman dressed in a vast floral muu-muu. Her rose-tinted glasses rested comfortably on her bosom, tethered there by a gold chain looped around her neck. Her speech approached a falsetto and twittered like a wren, "So pleased to meet the both of you. I've heard so much about you, Carolina." Then she said, looking to Clay, "And you have brought with you such a handsome young man." Clay stifled a blush. "Well, I really must be going. I know y'all have all sorts of things to talk about." With that she turned to Eleda, clasped her hands to her chest and bowed slightly from the waist as if it were a stylized farewell, "Good health, and I'll call you." Clay followed the slap of her thongs long after she turned onto the road.

The floor plan of the house was U-shaped with an interior that was surprisingly spacious, much like a large studio, and looked onto an asymmetrical patio built at the very edge of a cliff. The rear of the house faced northwest, and the afternoon sun flooded through a series of large picture windows onto a stone floor covered by a patchwork of rugs in various styles. The ceiling of the great room was tongue-and-groove pine, and the furniture went beyond eclectic, being a mixture of Spanish, oriental, and American primitive, along with a dash of Moroccan leather. Works of art, ranging from the mainstream to the bizarre, filled every corner and adorned every wall.

She bunked them in the small guest bedroom, which overlooked the patio. The topic of separate bedrooms was never discussed. The walls were paneled, also in pine, and the panes of its single window were full of minute bubbles and displayed a wavy, handcrafted texture. Eleda pushed on the coverlet of the bed, sending a faint ripple to the other side. She looked to her guests and winked, "It's a water bed," and then raising one finger to her lips, "Very quiet."

"Thank goodness," Carolina answered, but Clay remained silent, other than to mumble his thanks. Eleda then conducted them on a leisurely tour of the remainder of the house and grounds.

The walls of the kitchen were made of wormy chestnut, and the breakfast nook overlooked a small water garden filled with yellow and magenta lilies. An overfed gray cat sat unmoving by the water. It appeared to study something in the water, perhaps a fish.

Her workshop was not contiguous with the house, but was connected to it by a covered walkway. She pointed out how it was unwise to place the kilns under the same roof as her own and left them browsing in her modest showroom while she went to fix sandwiches. Her talent seemed to lie in the crafting of large urns, some several feet tall. Clay picked up a smaller one for examination.

They ate lunch on the patio. "It wouldn't pay to have a fear of heights living here," Clay noted.

"Believe me you get used to it," Eleda replied. "I couldn't imagine living anywhere else."

"Did you design the house?"

"Yes, I did. I moved to Aerie after the death of my second husband."

For want of something better to say, Clay said, "Tell me about the furnishings."

"That would waste our weekend. I will admit to having traveled off and on, and on two occasions lived overseas—in India and Tunisia, but that was a long time ago." She took a bite from a dill pickle. "Now, tell me about yourself." Clay briefly obliged her.

"So you happened to meet by chance?" she asked.

"Yes."

"Carolina tells me that you are interested in Native American culture."

For what seemed like the hundredth time, Clay explained, "I

have a passing interest only. My father is quite the scholar, and I help him with some of the legwork. I find it very interesting."

"I would think so. So how did this take you to White Rock Farm?"

Clay related the encounter with the men at the Cedar Hill Store, ending in his unexpected meeting with Carolina in the kitchen.

"Oh, we used to turn up spadefuls of arrowheads all the time when I was a little girl," she said. "I wonder what happened to them all?"

This turn in the conversation forced Clay to remember the reason, Vernon's reason, for his being there. He found it unexpectedly difficult to adopt the necessary frame of mind when confronted by Eleda's honesty. He wanted no part of manipulation and deception today, but almost without thinking he found himself asking, "And when was that?"

She chuckled and looked to Carolina. "The next thing you know, he'll be asking my age."

"Oh, no, that's not what I meant," he apologized.

She laughed aloud at making him uncomfortable and rose from her chair. "Let me show you something." A few minutes later she returned with several large boxes filled with photos as well as one which was framed. This sepia-colored photo was a family portrait done on the steps of the White Rock Farm house. She handed the picture to Clay. "This is my father and mother, Carolina's father, who was my older brother, and myself and my two sisters. My mother, Dorothy, was actually his second wife. His first wife died in childbirth."

"When was this picture taken?"

"Well, I look to be about five or six years old, so that would make it 1916 or '17."

"And he's the man that built the house?"

"Yes, I am uncertain of the exact year, but I believe he started it in 1882 or 1883. I just can't remember dates anymore."

"How did he get the land?"

Eleda adopted a more academic tone. "He bought it from a man named Gill, who as I remember got the original land lot when they moved the Cherokees out. That part would be easy to confirm."

"Do you know anything else about this man Gill?"

"Nothing specific, I'm afraid."

"Were there any stories from your childhood that mentioned the Cherokees?"

"Well, there was an old cabin down by the creek when I was young. My father said that it was built by the Cherokees, not Mr. Gill, and that the Indians once had a big camp there by the creek, which would explain all the arrowheads that turned up. The roof of the cabin was about gone even when I was small. Big Charlie, that's Carolina's daddy, used to frighten me by saying it was haunted. I believed him with all of my heart, and then one night, I couldn't have been ten years old, he and I saw lights down there, at least we thought we did, and from that time on its haunting was a fact in our minds. "

"Do you ever remember finding any pots or other Indian signs?"

"Nothing intact, but I do remember some of the field hands turning up pieces of broken pottery."

"Carolina's brother mentioned that also."

Then she paused as if something had suddenly stimulated additional memories. "Oh, yes, I do remember, it's all very vague now—one time, when I was very small, maybe about the time of this picture, a man named Pete who worked for us turned up some bones while digging a ditch along the edge of one of the fields."

"What sort of bones?"

"I don't know, I was too young. But I do remember a big discussion over whether they were human or animal bones. It went on for years. My father said they were the bones of a bear, but he may have told us that so that we wouldn't be frightened anymore than we already were."

Carolina poured them more lemonade. "I was looking through

these old pictures the other week, when I thought of Carolina. Someone will need to look after these when I am gone." She began to file through the pictures. The faces interested Clay, for they told a story of a family and its fortunes. There were pictures of reunions, picnics, trips to the beach, old motor cars, men in uniform, children, and animals. At one point she flipped past a faded photo of two men standing by a team of mules. In the background were two large rounded rocks which seemed to be in the midst of a field. Something about the picture attracted Clay's attention.

"Where was this taken?"

She looked for some minutes with a quizzical look and then raised one finger. "This was taken down in the big field just beyond where the barn is now. These rocks used to be at the far corner. We often played on them. Big Charlie called them the turtle rocks."

Clay sat upright in his chair and spoke carefully, "And why did he call them that?"

"Oh, I don't know. Because of their shapes most probably." She pointed to the picture. "Use a little boy's imagination."

"You said they *used* to be in the field?"

"That's right. The men used to have to plow around them, then one day somebody broke a plow and that made Daddy real mad. He got some men to come out from town with dynamite and blow them up. I remember the explosion because it broke a couple of windows in the barn."

"So you can't see the rocks anymore?"

"I guess not."

"Could you place them today if you had to?"

"Approximately."

"Could you describe their location to Carolina?"

"Of course." She frowned. "But why are you so interested in these particular rocks?"

He cleared his throat as he sought a believable answer that would discourage any suspicion as to his motives. He began with a short laugh. "I can't really say. My father has a copy of a map from the removal period, and it has a reference to a turtle-shaped rock." He cleared his throat and took a swallow of lemonade. "It's probably just a coincidence."

As he spoke, he was picturing the cluster of symbols drawn at the eastern extreme, the beginning, of the waybill's journey. He and Vernon had always assumed them to be, at least since the discovery of the Neptune's journal, near Kingfisher's camp, the Place of the Pigeons. By some stretch of his imagination Clay could make them appear to be a turtle.

"Since the rocks are now gone, this picture could represent an interesting piece of information." Clay hoped that his response would sound plausible. Eleda seemed to accept it.

"Well, I'll let you thumb through these while we clean up," she said, looking to Carolina.

The two women went back into the house and left Clay to rummage through the pictures. He soon encountered another equally worn photo showing the same field from a much more distant perspective. The rocks in question were plainly apparent behind a row of low bushes. What must have been the creek was in the background and served as the one potentially consistent landmark. He tried to imagine the present topography of the farm, and could not; but then his memories at this point did not matter, for the rocks, at least in their original form, were now obliterated, and this picture was all that remained. The longer he stared at the seventy-year-old image, the more he was convinced that these rocks bore an uncanny resemblance to the symbol on the waybill. Checking the doorway, he slipped both pictures into his hip pocket and packed the rest of the photos back into the boxes. He then walked out front and got his own camera out of the car, pausing just long enough to slide the purloined photos under the seat. Whereas he had experienced considerable indecision on burglarizing Sara Weatherford's home, he did not give a second thought to this minor bit of larceny.

He took three snapshots of the house and garden and then stepped back inside. "Let's take some pictures," he announced.

He took three more of Carolina and her aunt before explaining to Eleda the workings of the camera, which allowed her to take several of Carolina and Clay. He then sat the camera on the table, aimed it carefully, and adjusted the self-timer to take two pictures of the three of them. The gray cat joined in and Clay snapped it sunning on the wall of the patio. "I'm almost out of film," he explained, returning the camera to its case. "Better save some for tomorrow."

They spent the balance of the afternoon eating and talking. Carolina and Eleda told many old stories about the family, none of which helped Clay, other than as passing anecdotes. Eleda took Clay back to the workshop, and he watched her turn an urn on the potter's wheel. He examined a completed urn as she worked, and when she was finished, she said, "Take it."

"No, I can't."

"I insist," she said leaving the matter closed. "You know it is bad luck to refuse a gift."

About four o'clock, Eleda directed Carolina and Clay into the garden to pick vegetables for the evening meal. As he was picking pole beans, Clay noted a pair of tall bushy plants growing behind the string lattice that supported the bean vines. Upon closer inspection his suspicions were confirmed. "Damn, Carolina, look at this. Isn't that marijuana?"

"I know."

"What do you mean 'you know'?"

"She's had a few plants around for years."

"Does she use it?"

"Only in her cooking, or so she says. As an herb, I guess."

"Jesus, isn't she afraid she'll get caught?"

"I asked her that once, and she said she wasn't. My aunt is pretty well known and well thought of around here. If someone blew the whistle on her, she could simply plead ignorance. After all, it's just a weed."

"If you say so," Clay said, unconvinced.

About five o'clock they began cocktails. Eleda drank gin and tonic. A light wind blew across the patio and activated a copper wind chime hanging from the eve. A large thunderhead appeared from the west, completely hiding the sunset, and caused them to retreat indoors. Clay had finished two beers before Carolina appeared with the first of the hors d'oeuvres, a platter of artichokes and a curry dip.

They had pasta for dinner. It seemed Eleda was largely a vegetarian. She lit a covey of pleasantly scented candles and turned on a cassette tape, a light, nonvocal, heavily synthesized sound with the overtones of a religious chant. When they were seated, Eleda reached out for each of them, forming a small circle of clasped hands.

She offered a short prayer, "Oh, great Creator of the heavens and the earth, bless this food which comes from your bounty. Bless our visitors and grant them safe passage home, and may they grow in your knowledge while they are here in your special place. Amen."

The entrée was excellent, as was the salad, and the red wine, though inexpensive, was adequate. "Do you grow most of your own vegetables?" Clay inquired.

"Mostly, and I freeze the extra for the lean months."

Clay was suddenly more aware of the music. It filled the room with its vibration, and the candle flames seemed to resonate to its melody. In the background a light rain pattered against the metal roof. He felt relaxed and at peace with himself. Carolina was correct in her assessment of Eleda; she was indeed a special person.

"I am very impressed with both Aerie and your lovely home," he said.

"Thank you, Clay. Perhaps you'll come back again."

Carolina reached under the table and touched Clay's leg. He placed his left hand upon hers and squeezed it. For dessert, Eleda had prepared a German chocolate cake so irresistible that Clay had difficulty limiting himself to only seconds. He helped them clear the table and then poured himself another half glass of wine. The women made kitchen sounds as he stepped onto the patio.

His uneasiness with the height of the cliff had vanished. The rain had passed and cleared the air and the stone underfoot glistened with wetness. He took a deep breath and felt invigorated. Far below were the lights of other houses. Another pair of lights raced along a highway, and Clay stared at the progress of the car until Carolina crept up behind him and embraced him from the rear, pressing her body warmly against his. "Eleda has gone to bed," she whispered.

Deep in the night, Clay was privy once again to the most vivid of dreams. He walked in the White Rock Valley, but there was no sign of the farm, no fences, no evidence of cultivation, and in time he came upon the rocks he had found in the pictures. They were silvery and smooth and appeared to be more metal than stone. A man whose face he could not see stood on top of the largest of them with his arms spread wide apart as if he were mimicking a bird. He was nude. They faced one another in silence, until the man rose soundlessly into the air as if weightless. Clay then climbed onto the rock to take the stranger's place, and that was the last of the dream that he would remember.

Carolina and Clay arrived back at the farm early Sunday afternoon. It was oppressively hot, and they took a swim and some sun, and then showered together. Since awakening that morning, Clay, instead of bearing the burden of the previous evening's overindulgence, had been blessed with a special lucidity of mind that he could not entirely explain. In addition, throughout the drive home and even while laying by the pool, he found himself absorbed with Eleda's photos and their potential link to the waybill. The preoccupation that he had experienced when reading Neptune's story had returned.

"You doing okay?" Carolina inquired.

"Sure. Why do you ask?"

"I don't know. You just seem a little detached today."

"Don't worry. I'm just very happy," he said as he kissed her. In truth he was having a great deal of trouble determining his priorities. After they had dressed, he casually suggested a tour of the grounds.

They walked down the drive toward the cluster of buildings that centered on the large gray barn. As they strolled along, talking quietly, Clay for the first time could enjoy the expansiveness of the farm without fear of recrimination. It extended from the barn to the north and to the east. Beyond the farm buildings were vast pastures, mostly planted in corn and hay, divided by windbreaks of trees. Confining the areas of cultivation was the mountain itself, curling around the property across a distance of several miles, a semicontinuous wall of ancient sedimentary rock, once the floor of a long-forgotten ocean, now covered completely by air-breathing trees. At intervals along the crest, the cap rock broke through the green covering, showing its tan-white face to the earth's weather. They walked by sheds full of equipment, several tractors and a single combine, and on past the barn and its attendant silos.

"Show me the creek," Clay said.

They continued straight ahead following a fence line and within a quarter of a mile came to the creek. At this point it flowed through a grove of trees and was hardly more than a yard across. Deep hoof prints fouled its banks amid uncut clumps of fescue.

"This is it," Carolina announced.

"Not much to look at. Do you think you could show me where the turtle shaped rocks might have been?"

"If I understood Aunt E. correctly they would have been over there," she said, pointing to the other side of the barbed wire. Rather than walk back to a crossing, they helped each other over the wire and walked along the outer edge of a corn row. They hugged the margin of the corn for approximately two hundred yards, crossed another fence and entered an even larger field covered in grass and innumerable piles of manure. At the far edge of the field, lying in the shade of some large trees, Clay could make out several black Angus cattle. They seemed to take no notice of their approach. About midway to the trees, Carolina stopped and looked around. She walked toward the creek for twenty yards and stopped again. There were no outward signs in the grass or from the lay of the land that blasted rock lay hidden somewhere beneath the feet. "I think this would be about it—as best I can tell."

Clay walked over next to her and turned a complete circle. In his mind he went over all of the available information: the waybill, the journal, the topo maps, the hearsay, the conjecture, and the photos. There was the mountain on roughly three sides, there was the creek within earshot, and if the stones were here, he should now turn about thirty degrees from the north and look for—and there it was, right where it should be—the break in the cliff, a small discontinuity, nothing obvious, the sort of thing you could look at a thousand times and never guess what you were looking at. You could never see it from the road or the house or even from that next line of trees. You had to be standing right here.

"Damn," he muttered under his breath, continuing to stare up at the mountain.

"What did you say?"

He pointed toward the break and said, "Have you ever been up there?"

"Where?"

"There," he repeated, pulling her to him and sighting her eye along his arm.

"Yes, but not in some time. There used to be a trail up there—it's been years, though."

"Come on," he said, dragging her after him. "I want you to show it to me."

"What?" she complained, digging in her heels. "Why in the world do you want to go up there? We'll never get back down by dark."

He turned and gave her the first hard look of their relationship. "Carolina, I know it sounds weird, but I *need* to go up there. Don't ask me why right now. Let's just say it has to do with the

Cherokees—take my word for it, that it's very, very important to me."

So insistent was his tone that she abandoned her resistance and joined him. They walked a blistering pace, crossing several open fields and then the highway. Beyond the road was a small pasture of uncut hay that ended against the base of the mountain. They waded a diagonal through the middle of hay and climbed yet another fence before stopping. The cultivation ended here. They were now standing in forest within the shadow cast by the mountain.

"Do you remember where the path started?"

"Not exactly," she said sharply. "Somewhere along the edge of this pasture is all I remember."

"You go that way, and I'll go this way."

They separated, and he found the path within two minutes. He shouted her name and listened for an answer. "Carolina, over here," he repeated. As he stood waiting, he noticed a decayed line of barbed wire some twenty feet beyond the one bordering the field. Two shriveled hardwood posts and a pair of rusted hinges marked the passage of the path through this older fence, but there was no sign of the gate. From the width of the opening, it had been constructed for more than the exit of livestock.

Carolina reappeared, breathing heavily, "Oh, goody, you found it," she said sarcastically.

"Come on," he said, unsympathetically. "The last one to the top is a smoker."

The path was unmistakable. It started as a wagon track and narrowed to single file as it climbed in broad switchbacks up the precipitous slope. This forest was mature and unmarked, oak, hickory, basswood, sweet gum, dogwood, and redbud, intertwined with creeper and trumpet vine, silent other than the singular chuck of a gray squirrel and toward the top, the rustling of a larger, unseen animal, perhaps a deer. Clay walked like a madman, staring straight ahead, hardly mindful of Carolina, who struggled along in his footsteps. Pushed beyond the limits of her patience, she finally cried out, "Clay, would you please slow down!"

Her protest was so urgent that it broke his single-mindedness for an instant, and he stopped as if jerked from a daze. "What the hell has gotten into you?" she snapped upon finally catching him.

"I'm sorry," he said. "I was just hoping to use all of the available light."

"Well, if you're so concerned about the light, maybe you should have brought a flashlight," she retorted, storming past him. He let her lead the rest of the way and offered nothing further in the way of conversation.

Their destination gave them no warning. The parallel cliffs began where the forest ended and climbed vertically, well above the tallest trees. The path cut straight between them via a passage some twenty feet wide, no more. The funnel of stone was thick with leaves and a few fallen branches, but within minutes they had scrambled easily through the break in the cliff and stood panting on the completely level mountain top. They looked across the valley to where the linear shadow of the mountain was beginning to climb the far wall.

"It's a great view," Carolina offered. "I hope you find it satisfactory."

"You have no idea," he said, awed by an immense sense of accomplishment. The view from their perch was secondary to his concern as his eye followed the path to the west—into the forest and toward the rapidly setting sun.

"Do you know where this path leads?"

"How about Kansas," she hissed, choosing that moment to lay down flat on the ground.

He sat down next to her and stroked her forehead. "Carolina, I have been looking for this place a long time. I cannot describe to you the feelings I am feeling right now. It's overwhelming."

"I'm so happy you decided to share it with me. I'll let you scratch my chiggers for me." He gave no immediate reply. She adopted a more supportive tone. "Why this place?"

He chose his words carefully. "This place, as you call it, may be what brought my dad and I to your house that first day. It's been the central focus in his life for years now. . . . It's what's kept him going."

"Well, perhaps I could be more tolerant if you would please explain its exact significance."

"My father found, years ago, a sort of map, an Indian symbol map. It had to do with the removal of the Cherokees, you know, the Trail of Tears. We knew who drew it and about when it was drawn, but we, at least until now, have never known where or why, and yesterday, beginning with your aunt's pictures and today with the tracing of this path, I have taken the first step in answering those questions." He now leaned over and kissed the tip of her nose. "Now, before it's completely dark and we have to roll down this mountain, do you know where this trail leads?"

"Solomon's Temple," she said without hesitation.

"How far is that?"

"A few miles, I guess. We used to ride horses over there for picnics."

"How many people live there?" he asked.

"None." She started to laugh.

"What's so funny?"

"It isn't a town, silly. It's just a bunch of rocks. A collection of rock formations would be a more accurate description."

"Would you describe them as oddly shaped?"

"Yes, you could say that. It's a big area of weathered boulders sitting right out in the middle of the woods. It's like a labyrinth."

"This is too much," Clay said, lying back in the leaves. "That cinches it."

"You mean Solomon's Temple is on the map too?"

"In a manner of speaking," Clay answered, deciding at that point that he had revealed enough.

"No wonder you've had such a time of it," she said rising to her feet. He joined her. "I've never seen you so excited about anything," she said, wrapping her arm around his waist. "Not even me."

Man can be driven by love or by the passion to destroy; in each case he satisfies one of his existential needs: The need to "effect," or to move something, to "make a dent."

—ERICH FROMM, *THE ANATOMY OF HUMAN DESTRUCTIVENESS*

September 1986

There were some folks, white and black alike, who would swear even today that Garland "Baitfish" Humphries was the best football player to ever come out of Coosa County. He went both ways, as fullback and linebacker, which was not unusual in those days of rural Class-A ball, and terrorized the opposition in both directions. Unusually fast for a white boy, he was as strong as an ox, and wrote the book on toughness. He also possessed the essential ingredient needed to excel in contact sports; some called it competitiveness, others called it heart, but in the final analysis he just liked hurting the other guy. He loved dishing it out and could take all the other side could give and then some.

Bait was bestowed with his unusual nickname after the homecoming game his sophomore year, where after scoring two touchdowns and making twelve solo tackles, he swallowed a dozen live minnows on a bet. His physical size, five feet ten inches, 190 pounds, caused many of the big schools to overlook him, and his poor grades dismayed even the most lenient of athletic programs. If the truth be known, he made one of the lowest SAT scores ever recorded in a state renowned for such scores, and later was heard bragging about his lack of test-day prowess. Although he never officially graduated, someone managed to get him into a junior college in Texas where he scored touchdowns at will and developed a wicked taste for alcohol.

Bait had never been a steady drinker, but when he drank, he was transformed into something that was less than human. One Friday night while horsing around in the dorm he broke a teammate's jaw during an assault that, along with his three F's and a D, got him dismissed from school. The year was 1965, Vietnam was heating up, and he decided at that point he wanted to be a Marine. Of all his past and later pursuits, he excelled most as a soldier. His inborn aggression was somehow directed and controlled, and he responded surprisingly well to a new authority. In combat, he was the personification of hostility and won two silver stars. Unfortunately, with only two months remaining in his tour, he was shot point-blank in the face during a night assault. He strangled his assailant with his bare hands and held his station until the last shot was fired, but the damage was done. The high-velocity bullet carried away his right cheek and eye, and despite a half dozen surgeries intended to put his face right, it never was quite the same.

Bait had never been physically down in his life, so the medical evacuation and the six months in a VA hospital, two in San Francisco and then four in Atlanta, took their toll. First addicted to narcotics and then back to alcohol when he ran out of prescription medications, Bait came home a shell of his former self. By returning to his rural, southern roots, he avoided the hostility and alienation encountered by many veterans, but there were problems all the same. He quickly found that he could not live on the disability checks alone. He lacked job skills and discovered that steady employment was hard to find. Fortunately, a former high school classmate and member of the same Coosa Cougars team took pity on Bait and gave him a job. That benefactor was Charlie Rose, the son of one of the county's wealthier men. He made Bait shape up and dry out and kept him busy around the farm, and in time the broken down, one-eyed ex-fullback would become his right-hand man, the fellow he went to when he wanted something done, the overseer of the farm and all of its dirty business, a man that, in the hard times, could keep his mouth shut when necessary.

Bait lived in the barn on a bed in the tack room for two years. Charlie liked it that way; Bait was always around and could be watched. Bait bought himself a set of weights and for the first time in his life made some attempt to improve his health rather than destroy it. With his drinking under some control and under the salutary influence of manual labor, Bait's strength returned and there ceased to be any more snide comments about the scarring and his glass eye.

When Charlie promoted him to foreman, Bait moved out, into a trailer closer to town. Within the year he met a woman, a divorcee by the name of DeAnn, who was every bit as mean as he was. Their fights became notorious throughout the county, but somehow they stuck it out for five years and the birth of two children. Their fighting usually involved the excessive intake of alcohol by either one or both parties, and after she swore out a warrant concerning her broken nose, Bait learned to leave the premises rather than give her her due.

This particular Labor Day Saturday night, Bait had gone over to the VFW Post with some of his buddies to play cards. He had a couple of beers and got home about nine, having completely forgotten that he had promised to take DeAnn to the movies over in Calhoun. When he showed up, she pitched a fit and started throwing things. Rather than weather the storm, he left, taking an open fifth with him, and sneaked back to his old room in the barn to spend the night. He drank all of the liquor and passed out well after midnight, awakening in the late morning with a terrific headache. He downed two Tylenol with codeine from a stash in his footlocker, and fell back into bed.

Hours later, partially recovered from his stupor, he was awakened by voices outside the barn. He sat up, rubbed his temples, and mumbled "Jesus" under his breath. His badly scratched Timex told him it was almost four o'clock. Was it his imagination talking? He roused himself out of bed and walked to the small window—no one could be seen. There they were again, receding in the distance, and one of them was female. The voice was not that of his wife. What's going on here? he thought. He slipped on his boots, moved quietly into the main room of the barn, and crept up to the front door. Still no one could be seen. Cautiously, he stuck his head around the corner, just in time to see Clay and Carolina stopping by the creek. "While the cat's away . . . ," he chuckled to himself. He waited for them to cross the fence and disappear behind the head-high corn before making any attempt to follow. Who is that guy and what in the hell are they up to? He slipped between the corn rows while maintaining a half crouch, catching a word now and then, knowing full well they would either cross the next fence into the cow pasture or turn away from him and jump the creek. Just ahead, maybe forty yards, he could see the fence in question and when he was within twenty yards or so of the open field, he dropped to his belly and slunk forward, marine-style.

There they were—just standing in the middle of the field. The stranger is pointing up at the mountain. He wants to go, and she doesn't. They're crossing the pasture headed toward whatever he was pointing at. Can't follow them up there—it's way too open. Bait eased backward, sprang to his feet and trotted back down the corn row, headed for the main house with all the speed he could muster. The throbbing pain in his temples was subsiding.

——— · ——— · ——— · ———

Two days later Bait met with Charlie Rose in his study. "You mean to tell me that she was here half the weekend with some man that you've never seen before?" Charlie asked.

"I ain't sure how long they were here. I picked up on 'em Sunday, and he took off early Monday," Bait replied, while pulling at a pack of cigarettes from his T-shirt pocket.

"And you say he was driving a Dodge truck with Tennessee plates?"

"That there's the license."

"I bet you it was that same slick guy who came snooping around here with his father."

"I wouldn't know about that."

Charlie shook his head and said, "Okay, Bait, it's no big deal. You did a good job. I may want you to follow up on this, but I want to talk to a few people first. You can go now."

"Right, Mr. Rose."

"And, Bait, one more thing."

"What's that?"

"If you see this guy around again, you let me know."

"You got it."

Charlie swiveled about in his chair for a few moments considering the situation. He had not entirely believed the two of them from the first, something did not smell right, but the old man talked a good line and seemed harmless enough. Now where had he put that card? He opened the drawer of the desk and looked in the back right corner where he usually put such things. It was not there. He closed the drawer and leaned forward on his elbows. What was their name, Hardy? or something like that. Anyway, he did remember Mathis Ford. Sure of his few facts, he picked up the phone and dialed the number from memory.

"Let me speak to Sheriff Suggs, please. This is Charlie Rose."

He waited. "Howdy, Charlie, what's goin' on?"

"Not much, Howard. You eat up all them fish yet?"

"Not by a long shot."

"Look, I got a little something I'd like you to look into for me."

"And what's that?"

"Couple of the boys saw a strange truck around here while we were out of town, and I wondered if you would run a license plate check for me?"

"Anything wrong?"

"Naw, just suspicious is all."

"Go ahead."

Charlie gave him the number. "And Howard, uh, one more thing."

"What's that?"

"If you turn up any other info on this guy, I would be most appreciative."

"We'll see what we can find out, Charlie."

He hung up the phone, pulled a legal pad from the top drawer, and jotted down a series of words and figures. He tore the page loose from its backing and walked to a heavily carved oak cabinet standing against the far wall. Inside the cabinet squatted a small safe, which he stooped to open, spinning the dial right and left out of habit. Once the paper was secure, he stepped from the house and drove down to double-check the runway lights on the airstrip.

■ ▪ ■ ▪ ■ ▪ ■

The topographical map was pinioned to the table at its four corners by three books and a glass paperweight. A lamp had been brought over from the desk to provide better illumination. Clay stood by the table wielding a number-four lead pencil.

"The turtle-shaped rocks were about here, and the break in the cliffs shows here. The path through the break then headed off about in this direction, and she said that the boulder field was several miles further to the southwest. That would place them about here," Clay said.

"I don't understand why they aren't marked on this map."

"It's sure made things a lot harder."

"I don't know that we would have noticed them anyway." Vernon walked around the table, holding a copy of the waybill in his hand. He looked up at Clay and gave a broad smile. "I'll be damned, Clay, if it doesn't all fit. You may have found the key we've been looking for."

"Well, let's not count our chickens." Clay addressed the map again, "And if my guess is right, this dirt road right along here comes to within a mile or so of the rocks' approximate location."

"When can we leave?"

"I can't go this weekend. John's not happy with the numbers and we're doing another inventory. How about Friday week?"

"It's going to hurt me having to wait that long. Have you got an extra sleeping bag?"

"I'll find one."

Vernon then raised his eyebrows a half inch, then asked, "Did you tell that Rose woman we were coming down?"

"Her name is Carolina," Clay replied. "Anyway, the answer is no. I'll think of something. Maybe I'll be going to Atlanta to see Lillian."

They left Friday week as planned and took the most direct route possible. Carolina accepted Clay's lame excuse, but the disappointment in her voice was obvious. They topped off the gas and purchased a few last-minute supplies at the Cedar Hill Store and talked weather with the man who had sold them the spear point. As they pulled out onto the highway, this same man watched them pull away from the pumps and then picked up the telephone and began to dial.

They found the road pictured on the map without a problem, but the condition of its surface was another matter. It was in fair shape during the ascent of the mountain, but quickly deteriorated thereafter. Once on top, the mountain did not look like a mountain at all. Relatively flat, it was like a western mesa. Although heavily wooded, the vegetation here was less vigorous than that in the valleys surrounding the mountain, for there was relatively little ground water to nourish it. Whatever fell from the sky quickly drained into one of the numerous sinkholes or the myriad fissures hidden below the thin topsoil. There was no sign of either farming or pasture, only an occasional overgrown logging road disappearing into the trees.

They bounced along for about four miles, watching the odometer closely, and, at about the predicted distance, came upon a cleared area to one side of the road. Several large oaks towered over the spot as if to mark the site of an old house, but there was no visible trace of it. A profusion of litter, beer cans and plastic bottles mostly, was scattered about in the undergrowth. Clay got out and poked about, quickly finding the trace of another road, also walled with litter, and generally headed in the right direction. "I bet this is it," he speculated and eased the truck down the side road in question.

They drove no more than a hundred yards before they came upon an earthen barrier, evidently pushed up by someone to impede further motorized traffic. Clay got out and said to Vernon, "Wait here, and I'll go check it out." He jogged up the trail at half speed. In less than a half hour, he returned, perspiring heavily. "You were right," he reported back, and they began to unload the camper.

Because of his arthritic hip, Vernon carried only his sleeping bag and a few clothes. Clay let his father set the pace, following patiently at the rear carrying his own backpack, the tent, and most of the cooking gear and food. He packed only enough for the one night, having left the balance in the truck. Before leaving he twice checked the cab and camper to make them secure.

The light wind blowing over the forest carried no sound other than the rattle of the dying leaves overhead and the staccato of the men's isolated conversation. A path gently rose and fell for about one mile beyond the truck, and they made steady progress, although what had taken Clay ten minutes to cover by himself, took more than twice that in tandem. The final approach led them up a low hill, and there, for no apparent reason out of the many thousands of acres of forest covering the top of the plateau, loomed the first sentinel of Solomon's Temple, a sandstone boulder as large as a house. As they approached it, they saw that this monolith was only one of a varied collection covering some 160 acres, the remnants of a band of soluble sedimentary rock that overlay a more resistant layer of limestone and shale. The rocks were highly weathered, twisted and eroded into an assortment of fantastic shapes, and scattered throughout this nondescript patch of woods as if cast aside on the whimsy of a passing giant. The boulders did not displace the forest, but merely provided another foundation for it, as trees of all sizes made their home among the rocks, forming a curious geobotanical labyrinth.

The path doglegged between a roughly parallel column of boulders before entering a courtyard formed of stone, surrounded completely by still larger boulders, some reaching twenty feet in height. The sandstone ranged in color from pink to brown, the colors swirling together as if they had once been liquid. The ground itself was entirely covered by a carpet of golden poplar leaves, the first casualties of the impending fall, accented here and there with the brilliant cardinal red of the maple. The only exceptions to the leaf color were several old fire circles filled with smudges of charcoal and burned-out cans. "Let's stop here and get our bearings," Vernon said wearily.

"I happened upon a better place just ahead. It's more enclosed, and I have a feeling this wind may pick up tonight," Clay answered.

They walked up a narrow, single-file corridor and entered a second roofless room a fraction the size of the first. It seemed to have no outlet other than the one that had admitted them. Clay pitched his external frame tent at the center of this enclosure and began gathering kindling for a fire. Vernon spread the sleeping bags out in the tent and began puffing on his air mattress. They had perhaps two hours of good sun left.

"We need more wood, and I want to look around," Clay said. "How are you doing?"

"I feel fine," Vernon replied, "but I'm going to leave the initial exploring up to you. I need to rest. We have all day tomorrow."

Clay satisfied his impatience by first climbing the most accessible of the boulders, the one that separated them from the other clearing. The climb was an easy scramble, and he found the top of the rock relatively level, pockmarked with shallow holes, many filled with algae-laden rainwater. As he looked about, his perspective of the boulder field changed, for now he was elevated fifteen feet above the ground. He could clearly see the approach path and most of the interior of the larger stone courtyard, as well as the tops of dozens of other boulders, all separated by deep cracks and crevices ranging from a few inches wide to more than a dozen feet, many sprouting sizable trees and taller bushes. By leaping the narrower of these cracks, he could easily travel on another plane relative to the ground and could envision the underlying maze of passageways. He walked to the edge of the courtyard and noticed a large circle of rocks, unnatural, manmade, another fire circle by the looks of it, but a curious place for one, since the stony surface underfoot was certainly not level enough to provide comfortable sleeping. To the side of the cold circle was a simple rock cairn of uncertain purpose. Someone had expended considerable effort in the building of the two, which, taken together, had all the looks of a religious site, a crude altar of sorts.

Vernon spread out a green nylon ground cloth and sat down, pouring himself a cup of water as he did so. "See anything of interest?" he shouted up to Clay.

"Not yet," was the answer.

After a few moments of rest and a second cup of water, Vernon dragged his knapsack to within arm's reach and began to rearrange its contents. He pulled out his shaving kit and a woolen sweater, which he carefully unfolded to reveal a .25-caliber automatic pistol. After ejecting the clip from the gun and checking the magazine to be sure it was empty, he placed both inside the sweater and stashed them in the tent next to his sleeping bag. Again satisfied with the situation, he stretched out on the ground and closed his eyes as a gust of wind passed over the camp.

Clay crossed the tops of several of the boulders, at one point having to leap a crack five feet in width. Due to the topography of the ground and the intervening trees, he could not tell the exact extent of the boulder field nor could he see more than one hundred yards in any direction. One stretch of rock was particularly expansive and open, and from its middle he spied the highest point he had yet encountered, a minaret of sandstone rising well above the others. He was not able to approach it directly, but had to descend to the ground once more and wind his way along the passageways below. Although his objective was relatively close at hand, he became confused at one junction, and indeed had to backtrack several times until he reached the base of the blunt spire of rock. Its ascent was much easier than expected, since one facet of the pinnacle was gently sloped and offered many hand-holds. Once on the top, Clay stood above most of the nearest trees and extended his view of Solomon's Temple considerably. From some distance away, presumably on the access road, he caught the unmistakable sound of an automobile's engine.

Clay took a plastic-encased compass from his pocket and re-established his sense of direction. He could picture Hand and Neptune riding from the east, probably passing to the south of the rocks from which point Neptune took his all too brief description. The symbol on the waybill pictured two rocks leaning toward one another, formed into the rough semblance of a portal. Whether this was a true representation of a pair of existing rocks or merely an arbitrary symbol for all of Solomon's Temple, neither Clay, nor Vernon, could say. Clay sighted east and south, while to his right, the first red glow of the approaching night was spreading across the horizon. Knowing that his time was limited, he descended from the lookout, and using the compass, walked south as directly as the massive stones would allow. He zigged and zagged at first, but the stones opened up once again after five minutes or so and he quickly walked to what appeared to be their southern extremity. Here he found a particularly interesting stone, standing alone, eroded until it was shaped into a gigantic tan-brown wedge with its base now smaller than its top. Clay circled it, noting the remains of another campfire under its protective overhang. A large Virginia creeper clung to one side of the rock and, should it be strong enough, seemed the only possible route to the top.

His curiosity satisfied, he walked eastward again, skirting the largest stones, hoping to circle back to the campsite once again.

As he was walking, he spotted still another stone standing off to itself, and, in drawing closer, realized that this single stone was in reality two very similar stones, standing side by side. He moved past them to the south and then turned back. Just as in the way-bill, the two lobular pillars of rock leaned against one another, creating at their separate bases a low door that appeared to give entry to Solomon's Temple itself. He clinched his teeth and banged one fist into his open palm and kicked a burst of leaves into the air.

Rather than waste any more time in celebration, for the light was failing fast, he turned away from the stone door and walked further into the woods. Not one hundred feet to the south, he crossed a faint, linear groove indenting the floor of the forest. Although filled with fallen leaves, it was plainly seen, and meandered east to southeast, disappearing among the trees in both directions. There was no doubt in his mind that this was a path, a very old and well-traveled path by the depth of it. He now felt confident this was the path mentioned in the journal, and on turning once more to face the imagined doorway, the symbol pictured on William Hand's map became reality. The pieces fit as snugly as if cut to order by a machine. He took a bearing on the path before placing the compass back into the pocket of his jacket and then started back to bring Vernon the good news.

When Clay arrived his father was trying to understand the intricacies of the camp stove.

"How do you pressurize this damn thing?" Vernon asked.

"I found it."

Vernon stopped what he was doing and looked up. He raised one eyebrow in reply.

"I found the rocks pictured on the map, and the path mentioned by Neptune," Clay said matter-of-factly.

Vernon got to his feet. "Where?"

"On the south side of these rocks just as we expected." He pointed over the rocks that encircled them. "Over there, not one quarter mile."

"Are you certain?"

"Ha! I'll bet my half of the treasure."

Vernon said, "Do you think I can make it?"

"I would say so, if you take it easy, but let's wait until in the morning."

Vernon took a flask out of his pack and laughed. "I brought some Wild Turkey just in case we hit pay dirt. Hot damn, we did it!" They shook hands twice, mixed shots of the bourbon with water from the canteen, and congratulated one another over and over. Clay got the stove going and began to boil water. They spread several topo maps out on the ground cloth and plotted their further strategy.

"Say the path approximates the direction and distance shown on the map, then it should descend the western side of the mountain somewhere in here," Vernon pointed out.

"Yeah, if it went much further south it would have to cross the Little River Canyon, but that may not have anything to do with where Hand cached the money. Remember they went down the mountain, camped that night in the valley. The following day, the day of Hand's injury, they ascended again before finally descending into the canyon. On horseback, a day's ride could have taken them a long way."

"You're exactly right, but I think, and you're certainly welcome to correct me, that they rode back into one of these two canyons." His index finger traced the outline of two deep indentations into the flank of Lookout Mountain.

Playing the devil's advocate, Clay said, "Say they rode west to Fox or maybe even Sand Mountain." He tapped on the map. "If you take the waybill's directions as correct, the second mountain climbed was to the west of here."

Vernon withdrew his hand and said, "That's an unfortunate possibility. This eyeball, or lookout point, or whatever it is, is certainly facing west. If that were true, it would expand the circle of possibilities considerably. If we could find this initial marker tree, we might have a better chance of finding where they descended the mountain on the first day."

"Unless the old path can be followed over a distance, our

chances of finding a single tree out of the tens of millions covering the top of this mountain are slim. Anyway, I would doubt the original tree would still be standing."

"I can't argue that." Vernon moved his finger over the map. "What do you think the numbers mean?"

"I still think they're some sort of measurement—a unit of some kind. A mile or an hour or maybe a day's ride."

They drank a second shot and ate their chili and rice as the last glow of the sunlight disappeared. One by one the stars took their assigned places. The wind that Clay had predicted appeared and then brought down a thin cascade of leaves before taking the warmth of day with it. Clay used the last of the hot water to make a mug of tea and sipped on it as he cleaned the dinner plates with a Brillo pad, taking care to conserve water, since during his walk he had encountered no springs or streams. He had neglected to gather wood during his search and therefore they did without a campfire. They talked for an hour or so by the feeble light of a candle lantern, pausing at intervals to consider the stars, and by nine o'clock made their way toward the sleeping bags.

As always when spending his first night outside after a long time, Clay could not go to sleep. Long after his father was snoring, he was still awake, listening to the wind. The last time he looked at his watch, the time was five minutes after eleven, and then he must have dropped off to sleep. Sometime around two, he was awakened by a pain. He had broken a primary rule of camping— whiskey and tea at bedtime make for a full bladder in the deep night. For thirty minutes he just lay there, unwilling to leave the warmth of the sleeping bag, to put on his boots and brave the chill and relieve himself, but ultimately necessity ruled otherwise.

The sky was clear with impending winter, and while Clay had slept, a bright half moon had risen. Once past the shock of exposure, he found the chill of the night air stimulating. As he began to manipulate his zipper, an impulse struck him that rather than urinate in the clearing and despoil their campsite, he would scramble up the rock to enjoy Solomon's Temple by starlight.

From that vantage the silent shapes and moonlight-generated

shadows of the rock formation spread out around him like the score of a midnight fantasy. He was grateful for his present sobriety and its attendant frame of mind. As he stood relieving himself on the rock, enjoying the majesty of this view, something very peculiar caught his eye.

He could barely make it out at first, and whatever it was seemed to wax and wane, to come and go like some faintly red, coldly luminous firefly. So intriguing was this minute point of light, that when finished with his primary business, he carefully slipped forward toward the edge of the boulder, the dropoff overlooking the larger clearing, trying to make some sense of this phenomenon. Squinting into the darkness, his eyes slowly adjusted to the low light, and then, in the same place as before, the faint light appeared once more. It grew brighter for a moment, then faded, swept downward suddenly and disappeared.

It's someone smoking a damned cigarette! The realization that someone else was out here in the middle of this cold nowhere at two-a-damn-clock in the morning struck him with all the force of a closed fist. Clay had seen no signs of other campers, and to his knowledge there was not a house or farm for miles. Anyway, any normal camper would be asleep, or at least covered up, that is unless he needed to take a piss, but a piss is a piss and people just don't get up in the middle of the night because they want to smoke a cigarette.

Silently, using as much stealth as possible, he squatted close to the rock and then moved forward onto all fours. What to do now? His hands grew numb against the cold rock. The light came and went again. When the cigarette is finished, I won't be able to see him at all, he thought. He judged the distance at maybe thirty to forty paces—hard to say. Creeping backward, he again found the cairn and began running both hands over the collection of stones until his right hand found one about the size of a baseball. Slowly rising to his feet, he stood motionless waiting for the glow to reappear. There it was! Taking one measured step forward, using the practiced leverage of his entire body weight, he sent the stone hurtling into the darkness.

Whenever a culture exists for many generations in conditions of chronic insecurity, it develops an ethic that exalts war above work, force above reason, and men above women. This pattern developed on the borders of Great Britain, and was carried to the American backcountry, where it was reinforced by the hostile environment and tempered by evangelical Christianity.

—David Hackett Fischer, *Albion's Seed*

A Few Hours Earlier

Bait was repacking the wheel bearings on one of the utility trailers when the phone in the barn began to ring.

"Heah, Leon, how's 'bout grabbin' that phone," he shouted.

A few minutes later, Leon came to the door of the barn and said, "It's Dewitt Partain over at the Cedar Hill Store. Says he needs to talk at you real quick."

Bait jumped up and ran to the phone, "Yo, Dewitt, what you got?"

"That young fellow and his father that you told me to look out for was just in here."

"They've left?"

"Yeah. They was in a red Dodge pickup, maybe an '80 or '81, with a camper top and Tennessee plates. I didn't catch the number, but believe me it was them."

"What'd they want?"

"Nuthin' really. Bought a couple of gallons of gas and some food, you know like they was goin' to camp out. They made small talk and then took off."

"They didn't ask directions?"

"Not this time. They didn't waste no words."

"Did you see where they went?"

"Sure," Dewitt said, sounding slightly indignant. "They took off down 143 headed in your direction."

"Thanks, Dewitt, I owe you one."

Bait slammed the phone down. "Get your shit together, Leon, and let's go!"

"Go where?" the big man said, laying down his wrench.

"I'll tell you once we're on the road."

Bait was letting the possibilities roll through his mind. Clay and Vernon, by taking Highway 143 had limited themselves to three basic routes within the first ten miles beyond the store. The first was to turn onto Ajax Road, which led toward the farm, meaning that they would soon pass Bait and Leon going in the opposite direction. The second would be to turn north on route 317 toward Ashkelon, which, to Bait's thinking, would take them away from the store and the farm. The best bet, he thought, was for them to continue west on 143.

"Hell damn fire, Bait," Leon drawled, "You're sure pushin' it." Bait was toying around with seventy five miles per hour.

"Yeah, just keep your britches on. Mr. Rose wanted us to look out for a couple of fellows been snoopin' around, and Dewitt just called to tell me they was just in his store."

"And we're tryin' to head 'em off?"

"You got it, Einstein."

Bait rocketed north, then turned west onto 143. Less than fifteen minutes had passed since he had hung up the phone. Within a few miles, they passed a small frame house with a herd of concrete deer in the front yard. An elderly man, almost feeble, was attempting to rake leaves from amongst this inanimate menagerie. Seeing no sign of their quarry, Bait braked hard onto the shoulder, just past where the old man was at work. He jumped down from the truck and ran into the yard.

"Yo, Julian!"

The man stopped and looked up. He displayed no sign of recognizing Bait for several seconds, then replied slowly, "Why, hello, Bait, what're you doin' over this way?"

Bait spoke loudly since he knew the man was hard of hearing. "I'm lookin' for a couple of buddies of mine, and I think they might be lost."

"Lost?" the old man repeated.

"Yeah, they ain't from around here." He moved a step closer. "They would be in a red Dodge camper pickup, and they mighta been by here not ten minutes ago."

The old man did not hesitate. "Yeah, they went by here." He then stepped by Bait and pointed across a distant field with the handle of the rake. "They slowed down and turned up on Rim Rock Road."

"How do you know that?" Bait asked, knowing full well that Rim Rock Road was around two curves and beyond a half mile of trees and could not be seen or heard, much less by Julian, from this front yard.

"Well, they was goin' slow, ridin' their brakes, lookin' up toward the mountain, and another car passed 'em right here in front of the house and then later, I saw dust comin' up over the trees." He pointed once again. "It coulda been somebody else comin' from the other direction goin' up there, I guess, but I kinda think it was your friends."

"I betcha it was them," Bait said, his crooked mouth erupting in a smile. "We was thinkin' about doin' a little huntin' up there. Thanks, Julian. See you around." The old man watched them drive away, following their trail of dust as it billowed up from beyond the treeline. "I wonder what the hell that bunch is up to?" he said out loud, as he began once more to pull at the meager pile of leaves.

Bait slowed his driving. He was now in no hurry. Rim Rock Road was named that for a reason and climbed up and over the mountain for a good fifteen miles without a meaningful tributary.

"What'd they go up here for?" Leon asked.

"You got me, big boy, but we're sure gonna find out. Are there any shells in the gun?" he said, jerking his head to one side to indicate a battered twenty-gauge pump shotgun cradled in the gun rack to his back.

"There's supposed to be some in the toolbox."

"Well, get 'em out."

Bait stopped at the crest to listen for the lead truck. There was no other machine sound other than that of Leon sliding several shells into the gun. Bait checked his watch and calculated the thirty-five minutes since he had spoken to Dewitt at the store.

"What are we waitin' on?" Leon asked.

"I want to give 'em a little line to play with. They can't make much time up here, and I'll betcha they're lookin' for something, and I want 'em to have all the time they need to find it."

Twenty minutes passed before they resumed the search. They drove past the faint clearing marking the trailhead leading down to Owen's Cave, but it was empty. They crept along, with Bait stopping now and again to listen. In time they came to the Solomon's Temple trail and spotted Clay's truck sitting quietly among the trees. Unbeknownst to them, Vernon still sat in the passenger seat, but Bait had no intention of stopping just yet. He continued on past for another half mile and turned the truck around and shut off the engine.

"What now?"

"We wait a bit. Here have a cigarette." They both lit up, and sat quietly as the white tobacco smoke drifted through the open windows and dissipated in the clear air.

"Shit, man, it's Friday, I oughta be half-drunk by now," Leon said mournfully.

"Aw, you ain't missin' a damn thing, Leon. I guarantee you that we're gonna have us some fun before this night's over." They sat in the truck until dusk was well under way, and then Bait all but coasted back toward Clay's truck. "They're settled in for the night. It's too late for 'em to move on." He picked up speed and continued back the way they had come.

"Where are we goin' now?"

"We're goin' back to the farm to plan a little surprise party. What's your brother doin' tonight?"

"I don't know."

"Think he's at home?"

"Probably."

"I want you to call him and to ask him if he wants to raise a little hell and make a little money too."

"What in the world are you plannin' to do, Bait?"

"I want to find out what those folks are up to, and we might want to give 'em a little scare in the process."

Leon smiled. He manipulated his upper plate, which he always did when he was nervous or excited, making a faint clicking sound. "Okay, I could go for that—as long as I get me a bottle beforehand."

"I'll let you take care of that. Just hunt up your brother, show up half sober, and meet me back at the farm at midnight. I'll take care of everything else."

— · — · — · —

Leon's brother Horace was a pig farmer and was the bigger of the two, standing about six-four and weighing well over 260 pounds. Generally sober, he had five kids and was always short of money. Bait knew the lure of payment would be more than he could resist. Leon smelled of cheap whiskey and cigarettes, but seemed steady enough as he walked over to Bait's truck.

"We'll all ride together," Bait said. He pulled a tarp over the back of the truck and fastened it with shock cords. They crested the mountain by one A.M. and rode the last mile without the headlights. Bait stopped short of Clay's truck and turned his around in order to facilitate their getaway. He left the keys in the ignition.

"Now, Leon, I want you and Horace to be the point men so to speak—ease down the trail toward the big rocks real quietlike, but don't get in among 'em 'cause I don't want you to wake nobody up—yet. While y'all are watchin' out, I'm gonna get into their truck and see what I can find."

"What if they cause trouble?" Leon said.

"Well, don't shoot nobody, but I don't care what you do short of that. If anything happens just holler and get on back here."

Bait handed Leon the twenty-gauge, and Horace a twelve-gauge Remington automatic along with a pocketful of shells. As Leon started down the road toward Clay's truck, he turned on a flashlight. Its white spot of light temporarily blinded Bait.

"Goddammit, turn off the fuckin' light!" The light went off. "You stupid shit, why don't you just send 'em a damn telegram? No talk—no lights, understand?"

"We got it," said Horace in a low baritone. The two of them headed off into the darkness as Bait began to rifle the truck. He wore a pair of horse-hide work gloves and deftly slipped a piece of metal between the driver's side window and the door panel. By working the makeshift tool up and down, he popped open the door lock with ease. He entered the truck with all speed in order to limit the amount of time the inside light was on. Using the light from the glove box, he began searching the cab. He found nothing of interest other than the registration and a few road maps. He jotted down the name and address, which confirmed ownership, and opened several of the maps. The Georgia road map was marked with ink. Without looking any further, he slipped it into the pocket of his jacket.

The lock on the camper proved more resistant than the truck itself. Only by bending the aluminum frame of the door was he able to pull the tailgate open. He climbed inside and went through the piles of clothing and extra camping gear. Once again he found little to nothing that could help him explain Clay and Vernon's reason for being here. He was reclosing the tailgate when he heard the deep, echoing report of the twenty-gauge. He passed his hand across the pistol tucked into his other pocket and started down the path at a slow trot.

Horace and Leon stopped short of the first boulders as ordered and situated themselves to each side of the path. The woods
were completely silent. There was no sign of life whatsoever, no
smoke, no light, no sound, no hint of where Clay and Vernon
might be camped. After a few minutes of this fruitless waiting,
Horace signaled for Leon to stay put, then crept forward and
peered into the first clearing, a place familiar to him from his ado-
lescence. Leon hung back, cold, nervous, and sleepy. He wanted
a cigarette badly. As his brother went ahead he put his gun aside
by leaning it against a tree and squatted low to light a match. The
cigarette calmed him and after the first few drags he began to feel
more alert. He picked the gun back up and lightly fingered the
trigger. He clicked the safety to and fro between drags.

Just as Leon began to relax, leaning back against the tree
while trying to pick out his brother's form from among the gray
and black shadows, the rock thrown by Clay smacked into a large
branch not five feet over his head. The sound had the same solid,
woodsy sound of a Louisville Slugger connecting with a solidly hit
ball to the center field fence, and so startled Leon that he dropped
his cigarette and swung the gun into firing position, reflexively
pushing the safety in the same motion. As he did so he stepped
backward, catching his boot between two unseen roots, throwing
him off balance. As he fell back, he blindly groped into the dark
in a belated attempt to somehow break his fall, but instead
slammed the butt of the gun's stock hard into the ground. In a
brilliant flash of light and sound, a circle of number-six birdshot
roared skyward, ripping a hole through the foliage overhead.

Clay, standing atop the boulder, in anticipation of a reply,
dropped to one knee as he let the rock fly, never expecting a shotgun blast in return. He crawled backward in retreat as fast as was
humanly possible and fairly bounced down the incline in a mad
scramble for cover. Horace, momentarily frozen by the sound of the
gun to his back, ran down the path in a half crouch, only to find
Leon rolling about on the ground, groaning with a twisted ankle.

"What in the hell are you tryin' to do," he hissed.

"Ah, come on, Horace, I didn't mean to, now help me up. I'm hurt."

Vernon had been awake when Clay left the tent. He had long ago adapted to the sleep habits of the elderly, easy to achieve, hard to maintain. He lay quietly in the snugness of his bag, listening to his son climbing up the rock, the last sound he had heard for some minutes. The gunshot arrived out of nowhere, prompting him to sit straight up and immediately reach for the hidden pistol and its clip. Ignoring his shoes, he climbed outside in his sock feet only to meet Clay sliding down the rock by the seat of his pants.

"What's going on?" he asked in a loud whisper.

"Damned if I know," Clay said. "I was pissing and saw somebody in the woods smoking a cigarette. I figured they might be up to no good and threw a rock in that general direction and the next thing I know they started shooting."

Vernon inched into the passageway leading to the clearing and slipped the clip into the pistol. He sensed no further sign of intrusion.

"Is that a gun?" Clay asked, the panic rising in his voice.

"Yes."

"Listen, I think we ought to sit tight," Clay counseled. "Maybe they were just hunting, and I simply scared 'em."

"Maybe," Vernon answered. "But we sure aren't going to be getting any sleep anytime soon. Why don't you crawl back up on that rock and keep an eye out. Keep low. If you hear anything, throw a pebble down."

At the periphery of the rocks, Bait ran into Horace who was now carrying both shotguns. Leon limped along behind a few paces behind him.

"What happened?"

"Oh, Leon claims somebody threw a rock at him, and he tripped, and his gun went off. He's done hurt his ankle too."

Bait emitted a low growl and said, "You guys are just too fuckin' much. Did you see anything before you fell on your butt, shithead?"

"No, I didn't see nuthin'."

"Okay, sissy, why don't you just have yourself a little seat. Horace, you come with me. We ain't finished with these assholes yet." They left Leon sitting by the path and within minutes had crept back into the shadows of the rocks.

"Did you see into the clearing?" Bait whispered.

"Naw, I didn't get that far."

"You stay right here, and don't do no shootin' unless you're shot at—savvy?" Horace grunted in the affirmative. "And for God sakes don't shoot me."

Bait went forward, staying right in the middle of the path, away from the dry leaves that might give him away. In spite of these precautions, his advance was not silent. Clay caught the sound of a snapping twig as Bait stepped to the edge of the clearing, still in the black on black shadow of the approach. He flipped a pebble down to his father, alerting Vernon, who edged into the passageway, where he crouched on both knees and waited.

Suddenly, Bait spoke out, using a loud and pseudo-friendly voice, "Hello, in there. You boys up to throwin' any more rocks?"

Clay did not move, but answered, "And who wants to know?"

"Just some old coon hunters," Bait said cutely. "We didn't mean no harm. We just don't like people throwin' rocks at us. Somebody's liable to get hurt."

"Sorry about that," Clay said, "I didn't know anybody was out there."

Bait thought a moment and stepped forward into the moonlight. Clay could see the outline of his silhouette plainly. "You wouldn't mind if we camp here, would you? I think we done scared off all the game."

"Camp where you want," Clay said, "it's a free country. But it's gettin' a little crowded around here, especially with y'all carryin' guns."

Bait had zeroed in on the direction of the voice—across the clearing, up on the top somewhere, no way to get at him. His depth of field was bad enough in daylight but in the dark his single eye was even more of a liability. He wondered if they had more than rocks to throw. Deciding his position was untenable, he stepped back into the darkness.

"Well, that sure ain't very neighborly, but we don't want to stay where we ain't wanted." He took another step back and lowered himself to one knee. "Y'all have a good evenin'," he said cheerfully and then raised the Remington. He watched for movement, but none was forthcoming. Without the slightest warning, he squeezed off two rounds, deliberately aiming over Clay's presumed location. Clay reflexively closed his eyes and hugged the rock like a lizard as the cascade of lead pellets rattled into the forest behind him.

Vernon's response was immediate. He stood up and pulled off three quick shots, aiming at the afterimage of the muzzle flash. One of them would probably have hit Bait, if he had not aimed directly at the powder flash, but all three passed in front of the target, ricocheting from the rocks in all directions. Bait did not flinch, but instead swung calmly toward Vernon and fired two accurate shots in reply. Most of the birdshot bounced harmlessly from the rock, but the central portion of the second pattern funneled down the passageway, scattering from side to side, wasting much of its velocity. In spite of the scatter, two of these many missiles managed to strike Vernon in the upper leg, causing him to recoil to one side, falling heavily onto his right hip. A deep-seated, nauseating crack reverberated through the entirety of his skeleton, and he yelped in pain. Bait heard the shout and figured that he had struck home and rather than wait for a report, turned and ran for all he was worth. To his back, there sounded several more gunshots, but he never slowed, flying past his two accomplices, who were already in headlong retreat. He didn't stop until he was crouched behind the relative safety of Clay's truck. Skeptical of any pursuit and while waiting for his cohorts to catch up, Bait pulled out a pocketknife. With a firm pressure and considerable relish, he stuck the blade through the sidewall of the nearest tire and listened in silence as the rubber-scented air hissed from the slit.

Clay edged backward as soon as Vernon started shooting, and

as the echoes of the reports died, heard his father's shout of pain. He ignored the possibility of additional return fire and jumped to the ground, where he found Vernon prostrate on his back, unmoving and moaning in quiet pain. Vernon held the pistol out and said, "Take it, there should be six or seven more rounds."

"Are you hit?"

"No, or not bad, but I think I've broken my hip," he groaned.

Clay turned to face the crashing sound of Bait's indiscriminate retreat. He stepped forward and blindly fired three quick shots into the darkness and then, grabbing his father under the arms, dragged him around the corner. "You say it's your hip?"

"Oh, yes. It has to be. Can you believe it? I've gone and broken my goddamn hip," was the cruel reply.

—·—·—·—

A white Ford pickup with the White Rock Farm logo on the door pulled into the turnaround at the rear of the house. Bait climbed out and knocked at the kitchen door. Doris, the housekeeper, appeared behind the screen.

"Mr. Rose is expectin' me," he said.

She cracked the door. "He's back in his study. Mind your boots."

Bait wiped his soles on the mat several times and removed his hat. She led him into the hall and stopped before the door of the study. She knocked lightly and announced the expected visitor. Bait did not care for Doris and the feeling was reciprocated. He was certain that she subjected him to this minor formality just to cause him aggravation.

Charlie was sitting behind his desk. "Have a seat, Bait." The request made Bait nervous.

"What happened?"

Bait cleared his throat and began his side of the story.

"So you were in the man's truck when Leon's gun went off?"

Bait shook his head and mumbled in the affirmative. "Then I went to see what was going on."

"Did you find anything to make all this unpleasantness worthwhile?"

"Just this map." He handed the marked road map over to Charlie, who unfolded it across the desktop.

He studied the map for a full minute, rubbing his chin as he followed the tangle of ink lines. "All I can say is it looks like they've covered most of this part of the state." He looked up calmly. "Was there anything in the back of the truck?"

"Just some clothes and extra camping gear and some tools."

"Burglary tools?"

"Naw, nuthin' like that. Just a shovel and . . . ," suddenly a mental image appeared to Bait, something he noticed at the moment of the first gunshot. "Uh, there was something else too, a, uh," he was searching for the word. "You know, like a mine detector." The words came to him, "A metal detector, that's what it was."

"What in the hell were they doing on the top of that mountain in the middle of the night with a metal detector?"

Bait smiled, "You got me. I knew a boy over in Tryon used one to hunt minie balls. You know, Civil War stuff. Had pretty good luck as I recall."

Charlie was stumped. "And you said that they fired at you first?"

"Yeah, I told them not to worry none 'cause we wasn't shootin' at them and then they opened up on me."

"And you of course returned their fire."

Bait found the question mildly irritating. He did not like the insinuation that he had lacked restraint in the manner. "I fired up in the trees. Just two shots. I didn't hit nobody. I was scared they might hit one of us if we didn't make 'em keep their heads down."

"And they were hidden in the rocks?"

"Yeah. Somewhere beyond that first clearing where everybody camps."

"And they couldn't see enough of you to make an identification?"

"No way."

Charlie stood up, signaling the beginning of the end to the conversation. "I'm not sure what to make of all this. Are you sure you didn't see anything else in the truck, radio gear or anything?"

"No. There wasn't nuthin' like that unless it was hidden real good."

"Well, just be more careful in the future. I want you to keep an eye out, but for Christ sake don't do anything in a hurry, especially if somebody could get hurt. I expect you to consult me first. Understand?"

"Sure, I understand," Bait repeated. I can understand damn English, he thought, while rotating his cap nervously in his hands. He turned for the door and was gone.

Charlie leaned across the map and studied it further. There seemed to be no pattern to the towns and roads marked, other than they were confined to a five- or six-county area. They could not be hunting Civil War artifacts because there had been no activity in this area beyond Chickamauga and the battlefields leading to Atlanta. Metal detectors detect metal, not arrowheads and pots. What in the world were these two nuts up to? They were armed and ready to defend themselves, but who knows what kind of provocation Bait may have given them. They could not be the law, state or federal, for the sheriff made sure of that. On paper they were just who they claimed to be, but a nagging inconsistency remained. Even if they had not the slightest interest in Charlie Rose, they might, with their snooping around, find out more of his business than he could afford. Damn, Carolina! She was more trouble than she was worth. He wished that he could pay her off and be done with it, but the money was just not there. If she were at all trustworthy, he could at least present her with the facts, but with her track record she could not be relied upon. He put the map into the safe with the rest of the information and returned to the phone. He dialed the sheriff's number from memory.

My people, like the Hindoos and the Scotch Highlanders, have the faculty of dealing with the occult, of seeing and hearing that which is withheld from more highly educated minds. Always there is some souvenir of the spirit-world in a nook of a mountaineer's brain. He is unwilling to accept it, never believes all that it seems to imply. Still, there it is.

—ACCOUNT FROM A MOUNTAIN WOMAN, IN DAVID HACKETT FISCHER, *ALBION'S SEED*

18

For some reason, perhaps because he had felt the distance to the paved road was too great, Bait had chosen to puncture only a single tire. This simple act of uncharacteristic charity probably saved Vernon's life. Clay waited until first light before he tried to move his father, and spent those long dark hours trying to figure out how he was going to do it. The hip was broken, all right, easily diagnosed by the extreme, unnatural rotation of the foot. He could not carry Vernon bodily all the way to the truck, for the pain would be too great, especially since they would often be forced to rest. A crutch was out of the question for the same reason—Vernon could not support the weight of the leg alone. At last Clay settled on the construction of a litter, which proved to be easier than he had anticipated.

Luckily, he had brought along a compact cross-cut saw for cutting firewood, and with it dropped two small saplings. He measured the width of the passage leading from their campsite so that adequate clearance was possible and then lashed the crosspieces in place with short pieces of nylon cord and covered them, first with the ground cloth and then with his self-inflating air mattresses. After folding the tent and loading his own pack, he tied his father's belongings to the foot of the litter.

Calling on the dim memories of his scout days and by using yet another small tree cut for the purpose, Clay lashed a crude splint along the length of Vernon's leg, anchoring it at the left knee, and then, above the fracture site, around his waist. The acute pain of the first hour had subsided, but the pain accompanying any movement approached it in severity. After many starts and stops, Vernon was secured on the litter and covered with a sleeping bag, which was in turn tied in place along with the patient. At long last, Clay hoisted the business end of his construction and began the long, slow march back toward the truck.

The first few hundred yards beyond the boulders was not too bad, but Clay's thighs began to burn as he pulled the first of several gentle grades. Also, from time to time he would encounter some minor obstruction that would temporarily impede their progress, and each time he was forced to unshoulder the litter, he lost some of his shrinking reserve of strength. He finally became so fatigued that he dropped his pack by the trail and went to the extreme of offloading Vernon's few items, all in the name of weight. The narrow cord that he had used as a harness pressed into his flesh, and by the halfway point his hands and waistline were painfully abraded. Vernon would grunt on the major bumps and groan on the minor ones, but otherwise tolerated the trip in silence. In spite of all obstacles, Clay staggered back to the truck in slightly under two hours. He lowered the litter to the ground for the last time and in doing so noted the flat tire and the forced entry into the camper, but at this point in the ordeal these problems seemed minor. By lowering the tailgate, he was able to use it as a fulcrum and push his father, litter and all, into the bed of the truck.

"I'm thirsty as hell," Vernon croaked.

Clay left him a full canteen and started back for the pack, moving as fast as his trembling legs would allow. He returned in a relatively short time and found his father mumbling to himself. The canteen lay to one side and most of its contents had spilled into the bedding. Clay felt Vernon's pulse and judged its quantity to be adequate. He then crawled into the camper and picked up the canteen. "Did you drink any of this?" he asked.

Vernon looked at him. His eyes seemed disconnected from Clay. "You found the door?"

"Jesus, Dad, what are you talking about? Here drink some of this."

Clay forced Vernon to drink the balance of the water. The confusion was frightening, but further first aid was futile. Clay had no options other than to get the two of them down off this mountain as quickly as possible. He quickly set about changing the tire. He padded the litter as best he could, but the ride over the first few miles of the road were tough. He stopped as they began the descent and called into the back, "How you doing?"

"I'm still thirsty," was the weak reply.

Clay considered stopping at the nearest phone and trying to call an ambulance, but he reasoned by the time the transfer was made he could be many miles up the road. By noon they were in the emergency room in Chattanooga, intravenous fluids were started, and the necessary x-rays taken. Clay was shocked at how pale and ill and old his father looked. The vigor, the love of life was not there; it was as if part of his soul had already departed. It shocked him beyond anything in memory.

When they were alone for a moment, Vernon, his voice slurred by an initial dose of Demerol, whispered, "Don't tell 'em exactly how this happened."

Clay took his hand and squeezed it and said, "Don't worry, Dad. Everything's going to be all right."

Clay looked over the orthopedist's shoulder as he reviewed the films. "He's been told he needed the left one replaced."

The orthopedist, a vigorous man in his early forties, nodded in agreement. "I'm surprised he has put up with it for this long." He then pointed to a pair of opaque circular densities overlying the muscle of the right upper leg. "Looks like a couple of the bird-shot got him. You said this was an accident?"

Without the slightest pause and inflected with the appropriate amount of remorse, Clay answered, "Yes. We were breaking camp when I brushed the gun which I had stupidly leaned against a tree. I thought it was unloaded, but it went off as you can see.

Some of the shot ricocheted and as my dad jumped back, he tripped and fell onto his hip."

The doctor shook his head, "Too bad, but it may work out for the best yet." He began to point at the view box once again. "Your father has advanced degenerative arthritis in both hips. At some point he would have needed a hip replacement, probably on both sides, and the nature of this fracture lends itself to replacement. We can replace this one now, and if all goes well, and he's amenable to it, fix the other one in a few weeks."

"That's up to him," Clay said. As the doctor turned away to reenter Vernon's examination room, he added, "How long do artificial hips last?"

"It's highly variable. I've seen 'em last ten years or longer if the patient is relatively inactive. It's a wear-and-tear thing much like the original problem."

■ ▬ ▪ ▬ ▪ ▬ ▪ ▬

Vernon spent the next five weeks in the hospital, having both hips replaced in sequence. He would have gotten out a week or two earlier, but developed a minor wound infection that responded to antibiotics. Clay's sister, Lauren, flew down from Washington and helped out, and Clay and John developed an informal shuttle service between Mathis Ford and Chattanooga. During his convalescence, Vernon renewed his acquaintance with Carolina, who managed over time to charm him much as she had his son. She in turn met Lillian, who had ridden from Atlanta with Clay to cheer up her grandfather. All of these family visits worked the desired effect, for Vernon's spirits, which had reached a new low following the first surgery, improved steadily. At the one-month mark, he was up and about, having discarded the walker in favor of his familiar cane, and he talked of being home for Thanksgiving.

One weekday evening, as Clay was getting ready to leave and make the long drive home, Vernon, for the first time since his injury, wanted to talk about what happened. "We'll never know who that guy was."

"It's doubtful, especially since you and he and I are the only ones that know the truth of it, and I seriously doubt that he will be coming forward anytime soon."

"I am having trouble convincing myself that what happened that night was all pure coincidence."

"Well, we have no evidence to the contrary."

"You don't sound so sure of it yourself," Vernon said.

"I have to admit I'm uneasy also, but, uh, there was one thing—I hated to mention it before, because it seemed so trivial, and I didn't want it to slow down your recovery."

"Well?"

"It was such a small thing that I wouldn't have even noticed it if the things in the glove box hadn't been scrambled up."

"Come on. Out with it," Vernon snapped impatiently.

"One of the road maps was missing."

"Map? Which map?"

"The Georgia map."

"And that's all?"

"I've been through the truck twice, and I'm sure it's the only thing missing. It was the map I've used on most of our trips—just a standard road map, nothing special. I'd marked on it in a few places, nothing that could give anybody any usable information, but it struck me as funny that it was the single item stolen."

"Maybe it wasn't. Maybe you put it somewhere else. Did you check at home and in the other car?"

"Immediately. I remembered glancing at it just before we left. I know it was in the glove compartment."

Vernon pushed at the white stubble on his chin. "Yeah, it makes me uneasy too, but unless we get the police in on this, we're not likely to know. Oh, well, I guess we just wait and see what happens." He leaned over to the bedside table and poured the last of a can of Coke into a Styrofoam cup. "You know, I've had a lot of time while lying here to think about all we've been through chasing down this dream of mine. It hurts all the more now that we seem to be so close to an answer, but then I realize how far we have to go, and there's nothing to guarantee that any of this will pan out."

"No one offered us any guarantees."

"No, they didn't." Vernon took a noisy sip from the cup. Somewhere down the hall a patient cried out. Vernon continued, "At least I've still got my mind," he observed. He sat the cup down. "Clay, I had an idea the other night. I was just sitting here watching television when it popped into my head."

"I've had most of my good ideas while doing something mindless," Clay agreed.

Vernon lowered his voice. "Hand hid the money in a cave."

It was an idea they had discussed before. "A cave? How did you settle on that?"

"I understand we have no hard evidence to support that, but it's logical. I'm sure of it."

"Based on intuition alone? That doesn't sound like you."

"Maybe not, but it's time for a little radical thinking. Let's reexamine the facts. We found the site of Kingfisher's camp, we located the path Hand and Neptune took when they rode west, the same route as depicted in the waybill. From the stone doorway at Solomon's Temple, the waybill indicates that they continued to the southwest, passing a marker tree. They used its sign to direct them to the western margin of Lookout Mountain. From there Neptune caught sight of either Lookout Valley or Big Wills Valley and probably Sand Mountain beyond."

"That all sounds plausible." Clay had heard this analysis many times.

"Now, unless you return to Solomon's Temple and bushwhack across miles of woods looking for that marker tree, and that's assuming it's still standing after 150 years, then we are going to be hard pressed to find out exactly where they descended the western margin of the mountain."

"Agreed. You said that before and if we don't know where they left the mountain, then we have no final point of orientation. The balance of the waybill may or may not relate to the description in the journal."

"Exactly. If we assume that Neptune's description does not correlate with the latter part of the waybill, then we must either give up, or we will have to try another approach. Namely, we would have to work backwards, using the spirit of the description combined with the impression we can gain from the map. I know this is starting to sound a bit shaky, but stop and think about it. Hand, and perhaps his brother, visited the cache repeatedly. They wouldn't have simply buried the money because it would have been too much trouble to dig it up every time they wanted to make a deposit. From Neptune's description, the hiding place was not near any inhabited place, so a house or cabin is out of the question. Most people when they hide something of value want it sheltered, not out in the open. In those times there was no mining in this part of the country so any hole in the ground would have to be a naturally occurring one, in addition to the fact that caves around these parts are a dime a dozen."

Clay reached for a piece of hard candy, butterscotch, lying on the table and began to unwrap it. "It does make some sense as you say."

"And two other things. Neptune wrote that Hand had roamed the mountain as a boy, so he knew its secrets for a lifetime and . . . ," he said, now raising on a finger to emphasize the final point. "He needed a place where the other Cherokees wouldn't go even if they knew of its existence, a place to be avoided. It just so happens that caves in the Indian religion were viewed as entrances to the underworld, inhabited by monsters and evil spirits, places dangerous to mortal men. Medicine men were the only ones who went there, and they chanced it only by invoking their most powerful magic."

Clay sucked on the candy. The flavor spread out and coated his throat. "Men like Kingfisher."

"Exactly," Vernon answered with passion. "And remember

this." He took a small note pad and ballpoint pen and made two sketches. "Recognize these?"

"They're from the waybill."

Vernon circled the first symbol, the image of what appeared to be a winged snake. "This is a monster. An anomalous animal, part bird and part serpent. It's called an Uktena. Lanny Potts mentioned it when we first started this thing. And I believe this symbol . . . ," he continued, circling the second symbol, a sort of inverted chevron, "is the cave entrance itself."

Clay took the pen and drew a series of lines both straight and wavy, again representations of the lines on the map. "And this is the canyon Neptune talks about and the stream."

"Undoubtedly."

Clay sat back in his chair. "You make a strong case for it, but something worries me."

"What?"

"A cave in 1830 might be kept a secret, but I doubt that the secret would have lasted. Most of the caves around here are both known and explored. If Hand had just left his money lying around inside a cave, it is highly likely by this day and time that any treasure hidden there is long gone."

"That's true, but you make two big assumptions."

Clay smiled, "I know. Either the money was hidden inside the cave and/or the cave itself is undiscovered." He stood up and shook his head. "And we haven't discussed the issue of Hand's brother."

Vernon shook his head and smiled. "Yes, Jiya is a problem for us—a big unknown. From the looks of Dr. Weatherford's notes, he realized that also."

"You have to admit that Jiya may well have claimed his share too."

"That assumption is entirely possible, but we will never confirm it until we find the cave."

"Always the optimist."

"Somebody around here has to be. I can't help myself." As

Clay pushed his chair aside, Vernon said, "And son, . . ." This form of address was unusual. Clay stopped his preparations for leaving. Vernon pushed himself further up onto his pillows. "I just want to thank you for all of your help. I doubt that I would be alive today if it weren't for you."

"Well, Dad, it was something that had to be done." An uncomfortable silence followed. Finally Clay stepped toward the bed and embraced his father.

Vernon reached for a Kleenex to wipe his eyes. His voice broke with emotion. "I just don't know sometimes. Since your mom died it's like I've been on another wave length. Thank God you're crazy enough to listen to me."

"Come on, Dad, you're not out of this yet. And don't worry for a minute that we're not going to finish this waybill business. You'll be back on your feet in no time."

Vernon managed a half smile. "Yeah, sure." He looked down and tugged at the sheet. "You'll have to excuse me. I just got to feeling sorry for myself."

After Clay was gone, Vernon turned on the radio, a symphonic broadcast, and took one of the pieces of candy for himself. He put the pad and pen away and from the drawer at the bedside withdrew a letter from Sara Weatherford. He adjusted his glasses and began to read it once again.

— ·— ·— ·—

Clay did not return directly to the farm that night, for his father's impassioned confidence had deeply moved him and he felt restless and unsettled. A lifetime of memories cascaded through his mind's eye. He drove down the deserted streets of Mathis Ford, past the darkened shops and the lonely war memorial on Main Street, up the hill and past the padlocked Yard, past the silent schools and churches, and past the modest homes of boyhood friends and the empty sidewalks down which he had run a thousand times, until he found himself stopping before his father's empty home on Sevier Avenue. He turned off the headlights and the motor and sat in the car for a long while staring out through the windshield, watching a parade of images materialize on the glass in front of him. He pictured himself and his brother pitching ball on the front lawn and remembered his sister's laughter as they played tag with their favorite dog, old Buck, who lay buried in the long-neglected garden. As his perplexity deepened, he witnessed a vision of his mother's smiling face and vividly recalled the soft sound of her voice. He turned away from her ghostly image and wiped the moisture from his eyes with the soft flannel of his shirt sleeve. He thought of Lillian as he opened the door and then of Carolina as he stepped onto the walk.

The lamp in the entry was on as usual. It was controlled by a timer and came on automatically at sunset. He walked into the kitchen and checked the refrigerator since he had only snacked at the hospital. He poured a glass of orange juice and followed it with a container of blueberry yogurt and a banana. The grandfather clock in the hallway struck ten o'clock. He washed his hands at the sink and walked to Vernon's study.

The clutter in the study had increased during the course of their search. The central table was covered in books, papers, and pamphlets stacked upon layers of maps. Clay stood by the table and slowly pivoted on his heel, following the lines of the bookcases halfway around the room until he found what he wanted. It was a book his father had shown him once entitled *Native American Mythology*. He pulled the book from the shelf and flipped through the pages to the index. He scanned several pages before stopping on page 42 to read aloud,

The belief system of the Cherokees divided the universe into three basic divisions. The upper world was thought of as a series of arches or palisades which represented order and perfection and contained the perfect deities and their attendant spirits, the most powerful deity being that of the sun. The underworld stood for disorder and chaos, where all things were opposite to the upper world, and which was the home to monsters and ghosts. Lastly, the middle world, the home of man, which was a great rocky island surrounded by water, suspended from the vault of the sky by four great cords, inhabited by principles and beings which were a balance of, or compromise between, the upper and lower extremes. The upper world was unobtainable by mortal man or beast since it was the world of spirits, but communications, such as caves and the mouths of springs, did exist between the lower and middle worlds, and such entrances were to be challenged only by those possessing the most powerful magic.

He reread this last sentence and turned the page.

The inhabitants of the middle world were in turn divided into three categories: man, the animals, and the plants. Each creature or plant in this world was the imperfect reflection of a corresponding ideal to be found in the upper world. In general, man and animals were enemies, while man and plants were friends, the latter explaining the reasoning behind the Cherokee practice of medicine. Each living entity had a soul which upon death became a ghost which entered the spirit world above to join its progenitor. In the animals, this ascent was not accomplished until after a series of reincarnations, usually seven, the most magical numbers to the Cherokee coincidentally being four and seven. However, if the entity met death in an improper fashion, without the proper ceremony, the ghost might remain in this world to torment the killer. Because of this belief, the Cherokees developed elaborate prayers and magic to protect them from such ghosts.

Since all mythology is based on man's inherent, culturogenetic need to find order, to explain what he sees, the animals, as well as the plants and man himself, were classified and given attributes necessary to maintain the order of the animal society. For example, the rabbit was the trickster, the seducer, the deceiver, and is the most commonly mentioned animal in Cherokee myths. Since the American Indian was not literate, his systems of classification were limited to memory, so that exceptions to these rigid classifications became commonplace. In order to maintain a balance and to perpetuate order, special, or anomalous, animals and plants were recognized. They were exceptions to the aforementioned rules. Obvious examples were the bat, which possessed characteristics of both the birds and the mammals, and the turtle which had four legs, but spent its life in the water like a fish. Should these anomalies be taken to the extreme, a monster, an abomination, was the result.

The most horrific of all monsters was the Uktena, a giant spotted serpent, its body as thick as a tree trunk, possessing the wings of a bird and the antlers of a deer. It could be found lurking in high mountain passes or in the deep pools of rivers waiting in ambush for its hapless victims. Its blood was poisonous and only fire could contain it. Beneath the seventh spot behind its head was its heart, the only vulnerable part, and an arrow directed into this spot could inflict a mortal wound. In addition to its size and ferocity, its greatest defense was the Ulunsuti, a magical crystal growing from the crest of its head. The reflection from this crystal, which was completely clear, except for a bright red streak running through its center, was so bright that any hunter approaching the creature would be instantly blinded and left to wander into the monster's grasp. However, should a brave hunter be clever enough to kill the creature and avoid its poison, the Ulunsuti was the most powerful of all magic and could bestow powers to its owner above those of any other man.

Clay looked about on the table and found a piece of scrap paper and placed it in the book to save his place. Maybe it is a cave, he thought, meaning the final series of symbols. But where in the hell is it? I would need to know the location of all the caves in the area even to make a guess.

He stepped back to the closest bookcase, where he removed a copy of the Holy Bible and turned to the first page of the Book of Numbers. Concealed here was a folded copy of the waybill itself, which he carried to the desk. For the first time he attempted to put together all that he and Vernon had learned from the fateful expedition to Solomon's Temple. Once again he spoke his thoughts out loud, and as he did so he sketched them on a legal pad.

"From the rock portal, Hand and Neptune rode west and rode down off the mountain the same day." He copied the symbol of the tree and the eye onto the pad. "It's for certain I'll never find the tree, so, . . ." He tapped the pencil on the paper. "Either the eye is another symbol, or it's a lookout, a view from the brow of the mountain meant to give direction to the next part of the map." He pushed away from the desk and walked back to the table where he curled back several maps before pulling out one from underneath the stack. It was a detailed relief map of northwest Georgia and northeast Alabama done in several colors. As he spread the map, an unsteady pile of papers fell onto the floor at his feet and scattered in all directions. He ignored them for the moment, but before he returned to the desk, he stooped to gather them up. The majority were a hodgepodge of information, handouts, pamphlets, free mailings, and the like, picked up by Vernon during his travels. As Dovie said, he never threw anything out. As Clay placed a handful of material back on the table, something about the topmost piece caught his eye.

It was a pamphlet printed on poor-quality paper. On the front was written in bold print "Bill's Hang Glider Nirvana." Below the title was a black and white picture of a hang glider about to be launched from a high cliff. The picture's perspective was from the rear of the glider so that the prospective customer could have some idea of the chasm into which the pilot was about to launch himself. Something about this nondescript picture made a connection with the waybill. The series of lines following the eye symbol, if turned horizontal, closely resembled the indented silhouette of Fox Mountain shown in the picture. The circle could be the setting sun. Clay opened the pamphlet, but the only picture inside showed Nirvana Bill, a rough-looking character with a walrus mustache, strapped in his glider. The address at the end of the short text listed a post office box in Chattanooga and gave a phone number. Clay glanced at the shelf clock. He would have to try Wild Bill in the morning.

Shall we not yield him, in costly devotion,
Odors of Edom, and offerings divine,
Gems of the mountain and pearls of the ocean,
Myrrh from the forest, or gold from the mine?

—REGINALD HEBER, "BRIGHTEST AND BEST SONS OF THE MORNING"

January 1987

Clay finished adjusting his tie and walked back into the bedroom. Carolina was standing before the window, dressed only in her underwear, staring out at the array of lights that stretched away from them in all directions. Here and there, some at great distance, pillars of light, a few from among Atlanta's forest of skyscrapers, thrust themselves from the invisible black envelope of the trees that covered most of the city. There was no sound to accompany this expansive display; they were too high above street level, sealed into their room by double panes of glass and roll upon roll of thick carpeting. He walked up behind her and placed his hands gently at her waist.

"Don't you think you should get ready? We have reservations for nine," he said, putting his lips close by her ear.

She did not turn to the question, but answered as if day dreaming, "It won't take me but a minute—my hair and makeup are done." She wandered into the bath and returned as promised.

"You're beautiful," he called after her.

"I know it," she tossed over her shoulder.

They did not speak as they rode down in the elevator and walked through the lobby of the hotel. Standing at curbside, enduring the cold wind while waiting for the valet to bring the car around, he noted, "You seem thoughtful tonight."

She turned and looked at him. "I am. We need to have a talk."

"Okay," he answered.

They pulled onto Peachtree Street, headed south, and caught the first traffic light across from Lenox Square. "We need to talk about normalizing our relationship," she said.

"You make it sound as if we were involved in some sort of diplomatic intrigue."

"Diplomatic, maybe, intrigue, probably." He remained silent, waiting for her to continue. "Clay, I could write a book on unusual relationships, primarily from a negative point of view, but over the past few month ours has evolved into something entirely new to me. Outwardly, it is wonderful. Emotionally, I have never felt better. Physically, I am fulfilled . . ." She pulled down the visor and checked her face in the weak light of the makeup mirror. The faint odor of her perfume filled the car. She was gathering her thoughts. "It's what is not said that's the problem, and I'll take most of the blame for that. I made the mistake of handling this relationship as if it were meant to be permanently clandestine. I can understand why I did it, I mean, after all I went through in my divorce, my dependency problem, my screwed-up relationship with my brother, it all fits. But what I mean to say is, what I'm really searching for with you, what I really want more than anything in the world, is a normal, loving, caring, giving relationship. A fantasy perhaps. Just like in the movies. I realize such things seldom happen in the real world, especially in these days and times, but I cannot resist looking for the ideal." She turned in the seat to face him. "I have reached a point in my life where I'm ready to settle down."

"Go ahead. I'm listening," he said quietly.

Her voice hardened a touch. She meant for him to hear exactly what she was saying. "Please, don't jump to conclusions. This isn't some ploy of mine to bring up the subject of marriage. What I'm getting at is honesty. I can truly say that I have probably never had a completely honest relationship in my life. It was always a series of games, cat and mouse, man and woman, and the bond of matrimony provided me no excuse for restraint. I have made mistake after mistake. I have exhibited incredible stupidity at times, and God knows I've paid the price."

The traffic through Buckhead was heavy even for a Saturday night. Crowds of young people, partygoers, stood at the street corners. Clay cleared his throat, but still did not comment on what she had said.

"Clay, I'm still not sure how much we have in common, or exactly why we've stayed together, but I sense a chance for happiness with you, and I want you to feel it too. This is all so new to me that I am not sure how to go about it without scaring you off. I don't mean to sound the romantic, I am responsible for my own way in life, and I'm not asking for you to be my parachute, but I have to make some decisions."

"Yes."

"I want to bring everything out in the open. I'm willing to meet you halfway, even more than halfway on this. No more sneaking around. No more phone calls by the side of the road. No messages delivered via a third party."

"That's fine with me," Clay said amiably.

"Are you that sure of yourself?"

He was uncertain of how to respond. "I think so. I mean, I'm not sure exactly what you mean."

"What I *mean* is you and your father."

Uh, oh, he thought, before answering out loud. "Again, I'll need for you to explain yourself," he replied, stalling for time.

She turned again in the seat, directing her gaze once more to the passing street scene. "I don't know exactly what's going on with you two, but I have enough sense to know that this whole Indian thing is not on the level. I saw the look in your eyes that day in the field when you started to drag me up the mountain. It was like you were obsessed with it. Then at the hospital with your Dad, I overheard one of the nurses say he was injured in a hunting accident. Now that doesn't exactly jibe with what you told me.

You said you were coming down here to visit with your daughter that weekend. Now what the hell am I supposed to think? Here I am, sitting here talking about honesty, I've got the big problem and all, I want to open up, and I find myself calling your credibility increasingly into question."

"This is getting pretty heavy," he said, beginning to squirm under the heat of her inquiry.

"Well, perhaps that's because it *is* heavy," she said emphatically. "What else would you call it—a serious adult discussion?"

They reached the restaurant and turned into the drive that directed them to a covered parking deck at the rear of the building. She opened the door herself and walked ahead, her heels making sharp clicking sounds against the concrete. He checked their coats and spoke to the maitre d' while Carolina stepped into the powder room, probably to regain her composure. She smiled at him when she returned, and they were seated in a booth. "Would you like a cocktail?" their waiter asked.

"Scotch and water," Clay said. He always drank scotch when he was anxious.

"I'll have an old-fashioned," Carolina answered. "Tell him to make it sweet." Another man filled their water glasses. "Have you been here before?" she asked Clay.

"Once—years ago."

The lighting was low, but the room was not dark. The walls were covered with murals—hunting scenes. The conversation level was appropriate. The help came and went in a controlled, professional manner, always available but not overly solicitous. They looked over the menu in silence until the drinks arrived.

"Your turn," she finally said.

"Carolina, I have always been as honest as I am capable of being as far as my feelings for you are concerned. It frightens me to think of losing you. I'll be the first to admit that my past relationships with women, in particular my failed marriage, have also left something to be desired. I am perfectly willing to cooperate with you in any manner possible, and in no way do I want to jeopardize our intimacy, but," he punctuated his declaration with a swallow of his drink, "there are certain things between my father and me that I've had to keep a secret."

"Secret?" she said sarcastically.

"Yes, secret, and let me explain myself so that there is no misunderstanding." Clay was getting a bit hot himself. "Over the past two years or more—I really can't remember—I've helped my father with his research. He is pursuing a point of history of immense interest to him and will be to others once he follows it to its conclusion. I will have to admit it is an obsession with him and has become somewhat of the same with me. Other people may not share this interest, or may misinterpret it, and their misunderstanding could inadvertently destroy all that we have accomplished. We are close to the end of our search—at least I think we are. I only ask your patience. Any secrecy that you may have detected does not concern you or my feelings for you. Much of what my father and I have discovered no one else knows about, so believe me, you are not the only one excluded from our so-called secrets."

Carolina was thinking while he talked, he's not going to tell me about this. He has no intention of confiding in me.

Before she could formulate an answer, he reached out and touched her hand. "Carolina, I love you. Just don't push me too far on this point. We should *both* be allowed a few secrets." He saw tears welling in the corner of her eyes. I've got to give her more, he realized.

"Oh, Clay, I love you too," she said, but her voice broke. She put the menu aside and wiped her eyes with a crisp linen napkin.

Clay had come to a decision. I'm either in this, or I'm out of it, he thought. "There is no book," he said suddenly. "I lied to you. The truth of it is we're searching for a treasure," he said. "A buried treasure." He took a large swallow of scotch.

She stared at him in disbelief. "A treasure?"

He nodded in agreement as if reluctant to say the word again. "It may be a wild goose chase, but a lot of our evidence would indicate otherwise."

"You mean to tell me y'all have been sneaking around all over the countryside getting shot at because of a buried treasure?" Her tears turned to a sarcastic laugh.

"I know it sounds screwy, but that's because you haven't been involved in it."

She pulled her hand away and swirled the crushed fruit in her drink with the cocktail straw. "I don't know that I want to be involved in it. This is getting entirely too weird."

"Well, I've told you, and you're still not happy."

"Clay, I'm very happy, but I'm just a little mixed up right now. This is not the sort of revelation a girl can prepare herself for. Believe me, I hope you find this treasure or whatever, and I can assure you of my discretion."

He picked up the menu and opened it. "Why don't we change the subject. We're fast on the way to destroying the evening. So what have you selected?"

"I'm in the mood for seafood. Perhaps I'll order the snapper." Whatever he's looking for it must be pretty valuable, she mused. If he's telling the truth, and the story is too outlandish to be otherwise, then it's certainly not worth ending the relationship. Although it went against her grain, she quieted her anger and counseled for patience—slow down, see what happens. You'll learn everything in time.

■ ▪ ▬ ▪ ▬ ▪ ▬

May 1987

Vernon was sitting on the back screen porch reading the evening newspaper when Clay arrived. His son was carrying a large cardboard tube, the sort used for the transport of large posters or maps.

"I've got the material from Huntsville and Chattanooga," Clay announced as he sat down on the wicker couch covered in a faded canvas.

"Let's have a look at it."

Clay removed several maps and papers from the tube as Vernon scooted his rocker alongside. "I have marked here, with red crosses, the approximate locations of all known caves within the radius of our search. I superimposed a blow-up of the waybill on a topo of Lookout Mountain and came up with a couple of likely points of descent. Undoubtedly, Neptune and Hand camped along either Lookout Creek or, less likely, Big Wills Creek the second night. I also called the hang glider place and they told me that this picture is taken from this point right here. It's called Cloudland Point. The view is to the northwest. The cut between Fox and Sand Mountains is represented by this V."

"So, how many caves are there?"

"At least sixteen."

"Good grief. And how many of those even roughly fit the profile?"

"Maybe five, but even that is a big assumption since Neptune's descriptions of the later landmarks are vague at best. One that sounded good by its location alone begins with a deep pit—sixty feet, so that one's out."

"What's your second choice?"

"Several of the others appear to be heavily traveled." He then pulled a piece of paper from among a tight roll of others. "But take a look at this one. It's called Barley's Cave—evidently after the guy who discovered it. The entrance is not exactly in a canyon as described in the journal, but is more on the back side of Fox Mountain above a streambed. It is also at the western extremity of the search area."

Vernon studied the map of the cave's passages. The copy had come from the National Speleology Society in Huntsville and was dated 1971. "I'm interested. What's the scale here?"

"I think that one is one hundred feet to the inch." Clay watched his father carefully scan the map, then added, "I haven't told you the best part."

"Go ahead."

"Check out the notation I have underlined." In the last line of the description, written in bold type was the statement "Admission only by permission of owner."

"What does that mean? Is it a commercial cave?"

"No, thank God. I called this spelunker in Chattanooga who had actually been in the cave during its mapping. It is a newer cave, as they say. It was mapped in the late sixties—about three miles of known passages. Anyway, it was a real popular cave for a few years, but the owner of the land, a farmer by the name of Comer Woodall, took a disliking to all the traffic and closed the cave off. No one much has been in it since."

"What did he mean by 'closed it off'—dynamite?"

"No. He fitted a metal gate over the entrance. Has a padlock on it evidently."

"And Woodall has the only key?"

"Presumably."

"How far is the entrance off the pavement?"

"About two miles as the crow flies. Woodall's farm is here—up this dirt road. The path to the cave follows this streambed."

"Have you contacted him?"

"Why bother?"

Vernon raised his bushy eyebrows and pursed his lips. "What are you getting at?"

"Well, I could be nice and call him, and if he said no, go anyway. If he were to say yes, and I subsequently found anything of value, he would certainly want his share, wouldn't he? Neither way is the best way."

Vernon rested the map on his lap and started to laugh. "Ha! Good thinking. You may get the hang of this after all!"

— · — · — · —

Carolina was not sure why she even bothered to tutor Tommy Byers. He was not very bright, and he hated Spanish, but he needed the course for college, and his parents were friends of the family. The three-day-a-week schedule was becoming painful for both of them. She checked her watch before she left the house. She could still call Clay at work and make it to town by 4:30.

The operator knew her voice without the need of inquiry, "I'm putting you on hold, Miss Rose."

Clay was outside and took a full minute reaching the phone in the main warehouse. "What's up?"

"I just wanted to know if you had decided about next weekend?"

"Honey, I don't think I'm going to be able to make it."

"Remember—honesty."

"I know, but I have to do some fieldwork on the project." This was the code word now used for the waybill and all of its implications.

"And that doesn't include me?"

"Carolina, you're the one that told me you weren't that interested."

"I can't deny that," she agreed reluctantly. "Where will you be going?"

"Down into Alabama—west of you."

"Are you going to be camping out again?"

"Probably."

"Oh, Clay, please be careful."

"You know I will. I'll be back home on Sunday, and I'll call as soon as I walk through the door. If you get worried, call my dad—he knows the specifics. If you want, you could drive up here Sunday and stay the week."

"Maybe I will."

"I'll leave the key in the usual place. Bye, bye. I love you."

"Bye. Love you too." As Carolina held onto the receiver for a moment, dealing with her anger and disappointment, considering what was said, she heard a second click following Clay's hanging up, the sort of sound one hears when a second party is on the line. It's just the operator, she thought, dismissing it. As she drove out of the driveway, she considered the meager prospects for full employment. No need to worry about that today, she thought. Turning the car toward her appointment, she remembered her friend Janie's offer in Chattanooga. She said the man was a little old, early fifties, but a date's a date. Anyway, it was better than sitting at home with her brother.

— · — · — · —

After studying the maps for a while, Clay came upon an approach to the cave's entrance that would bypass the Woodall farm. Another secondary road came even closer to the cave, but a ridge rising several hundred feet above the proposed parking place intervened. There were few houses along the road according to the topographical map, but it was many years old, and its accuracy as far as dwellings were concerned was questionable. He would just have to appraise the situation on site. In addition to his usual camping equipment, he took along fifty feet of half-inch nylon rope, although the profile of the cave showed no elevation of more than twenty feet in its upper levels. He took along a battery-powered headlamp attached to a plastic hard hat, preferring it to the traditional carbide, as well as some basketball knee pads, and, of course, tools, bolt cutters, and a hacksaw for opening the padlock and gate. If this was the cave, Hand would not have ventured very far into its interior, and if it looked promising, Clay could always return to the truck for the metal detector. After conducting a running debate with his conscience for some days, he decided to take a pistol, a twenty-two-caliber automatic, and took the extra time to hide it inside the spring mechanism of the front seat. Just before he left he called Vernon to say, "I want to make sure you know where I'll be."

"Yes. You'll be checking out Barley's Cave first, and if you have time, Lightning Ridge Cave and then Pendigrass Cave, in that order."

"Right. And I told Carolina to call you if she gets uptight. She may drive up here on Sunday."

"Did you tell her where you're headed?"

"Only in general terms, and she still doesn't know exactly what we're up to."

"You're a braver man than I," Vernon said. "I don't see how you've kept the lid on it. She must be a damn patient woman. Your mother would have had it out of me the first unexcused weekend."

Clay drove south on Friday afternoon taking the interstate highway south toward Birmingham. The walls of Lookout Valley and then Big Wills Valley rose on both sides like ancient citadels and would continue to for the next fifty miles. Lookout Mountain lay to his left, the vast Sand Mountain plateau to his right. He passed through Trenton, the site of old Lookout Town, the Cherokee town that served as a sanctuary during William Hand's convalescence. Somewhere, tantalizingly close by, perhaps just a few miles from the interstate itself, was the site of the cache, be it a cave or a cairn or a hole in the ground. He looked up to the alabaster cliffs, the unbroken expanse of trees mounting the flanks of the mountains, and began to measure the number of possibilities, trying to calculate his chances of success. They seemed impossibly small. He grew impatient with the radio and turned it off.

He pulled off the four-lane a few miles past the Alabama line, filled up with gas, and bought an orange soda and a package of peanut butter crackers from a machine. He made small talk with the attendant, an acne-faced kid in his early twenties, and extracted from him the necessary directions. The turnoff was not five miles away. As he slowly pulled from the station eating his last cracker, a tan-on-tan police cruiser went by him going in the opposite direction, manned by a single officer. They exchanged steering wheel waves as they passed. The cruiser slowed as the patrolman watched Clay's truck recede in the rearview mirror. He had long ago learned to read license numbers in reverse order. The sequence matched that of a notation clipped on his dash. He did not tarry, and after briefly questioning the boy at the pumps, turned around to follow the red camper truck with the Tennessee plates.

Clay found the approach road without any trouble. It proceeded for about two miles, passing the same houses shown on the map, before reaching a dead end against the ridge separating him from Barley's Cave. The closest house was about a quarter mile away. A sign was staked in front of the house and advertised "Organic Vegetables," but Clay saw no evidence of its owners. After a quick examination of the turnabout and a short walk into the woods, he returned to the camper, for he had no intention of staying the night—it might provoke an excessive amount of attention. He had lived long enough in this part of the country to know how people take notice of strange vehicles and for that reason had planned to stay in a public campground about twenty miles further down the highway.

The policeman had not followed him onto the dirt road, knowing full well it was a dead end. To have followed would have meant detection and alarm, and like his quarry, he did not intend to be noticed. After backing across the grassy shoulder to aid his concealment, he called in and then sat quietly watching for Clay's return, patiently awaiting a move, and when it came, he headed south, making note of the time.

EL DORADO

*He that has never suffered extreme adversity,
knows not the full extent of his own depravation.*

—Charles Caleb Colton, *Lacon*

The naive green of spring was by now well established throughout the valley, and Carolina was glad for it. The invigoration of fall was fine, and winter was always a challenge, but along about March, she was ready to do away with the sweats and the gloves and go back to shorts. So taken was she by the warmth and renewal of this particular afternoon, and having no definite plans for the weekend, she added a couple of extra miles to her usual run, ending atypically by coming up behind the barn on the road leading to the lower pastures, the same road she and Clay had taken when searching for the blasted stones. As she approached the barn, she decelerated, planning to walk the rest of the way to the main house. Her mouth was dry, and spying a water faucet, she paused on impulse to drink. The tap was low to the ground, causing her to kneel to reach it, which made her invisible to anyone near the barn. As she swallowed, she caught the irritating sound of Bait's voice.

"Come on, Leon, get your ass in the truck! Ole Charlie's got work for us."

She did not care for Bait. He was polite enough, but she did not like the lascivious looks he gave her, especially when she was in her running gear. He was her brother's creature and was not to be trusted. She peeked through the stack of wood and watched Bait carry a shotgun to the white truck parked in front of the barn.

Leon started the engine, raced it a couple of times as was his habit, and then spun the tires in a cloud of flying gravel and dust. Strange, she thought, knowing full well it was past six o'clock. It's Friday—those two should be long gone by now. By the tone of Bait's voice, she knew he was up to something, and that something somehow included a gun and her brother. She began running toward the house.

Charlie usually held council in his study, but Doris was gone and had taken Carolina's nephew with her. He met Bait in the kitchen, Leon waited in the truck, and they began the discussion there. Carolina entered by way of the unlocked front door. She tiptoed across the slate entry in her running shoes and listened from the hallway. They were in the kitchen as she had anticipated, but she could not make out what they were saying. She slipped off her shoes and laid them aside on the rug. To gain a better ear for the conversation, she crept down the hall and slipped into the guest bathroom, closing the door to all but a crack.

Seconds after she had stepped from the hall, the two men entered it, turning the corner toward the study. She caught only part of what was said.

"What's he doin' way over there?"

"How the hell should I know? All he said was that he was camping out and working on a project."

"Well, do you want us to check it out or what?"

"Bait, I don't know whether this hard dick is somebody to worry about or not. I just want to know what he's up to and if it concerns me. I need to know if he's undercover."

"We can get it out of him," Bait said smugly.

"That's what I'm afraid of. Now listen real close to me, Bait—I don't give a damn about him and my sister, but I sure don't like him snooping around. He just might stumble onto something. All I want you to promise me is that you fellas will stay clear of the law. There'll be no gun play this time—understand?" The door to the study closed and the voices were muffled once again.

Bait would probably leave by the kitchen, the way he had

come in. Carolina slipped down the carpeted hall, past the study door and into her brother's suite of rooms, which spread across the rear of the new wing. She waited a moment to see if she had been heard and then returned to put her ear against the door.

"Here's where he's supposedly camped, and here's where the patrolman saw him first. He's in the same Dodge pickup with Tennessee plates."

"Howard told you that?"

"Let's just not say where I got the information."

"I suspect he's settled in for the night."

"That's probably a pretty good assumption," Charlie said. "But he could be away from there early, so you'd better get your shit together tonight."

"I'll call Horace."

"I thought you scared him off."

"Not when there's money involved."

"I'll be around all day tomorrow, or leave a message on the machine and I'll call in."

"Don't you worry about a thing, Mr. Rose."

No reassurances would remove the worry from Charlie's mind. He had heard them before. "Okay. Just keep your finger off the trigger this time. Now get to it."

Carolina heard footfalls and literally jumped around the corner into her brother's bedroom. She heard the back door slam and the sound of the truck engine and peeked around the corner. The hall was empty, but she heard the refrigerator door open. Anyone in the kitchen would have a clear view of her leaving the bedroom. She was thinking of going out a window, when she heard her brother's topsiders slap against the kitchen tiles. It was a characteristic sound, one that both identified the person walking and the direction of their travel. He was headed toward his bedroom! The door to his closet, a huge walk-in, stood open, and she quickly stepped inside it and slipped behind a line of plastic clothes bags. You fool, she thought. Hiding in your own house. He can see my legs plainly if he looks. She was perspiring heavily. The stagnant air smelled of wool and naphtha.

Afraid to move a muscle, she listened to her brother moving about in the next room. Several minutes passed. Carolina heard a faint tapping sound, metal on glass, a razor on glass. She could not hear him sniffing. Music came on, some light jazz, and with it further footfalls. At long last she heard, through the wall, the equally characteristic male sound of urine falling into the toilet, followed by the flush, and then the heavenly patter of the shower. She slipped from her hiding place without looking back and walked nonchalantly by the kitchen.

This was all very peculiar. Although his name was never mentioned, she had the overpowering suspicion that the two men were discussing Clay. This game, and she could no longer avoid calling it that, had taken on a surprising and disturbing turn. Why were they interested in him? Because of her? Because of her brother's baseline paranoia?

She continued on to her room and locked the door behind her. For all the good it would do, she thought. She sat on the bed and closed her eyes and tried to regain some semblance of control. Her inquisitive nature had gotten her into this, but it would certainly not get her out. Her thoughts raced ahead, unfocused, out of control; fear, the purest of the primal emotions, the one that cannot be denied or postponed, was now loose in her brain. The implications of what she overheard were clear, but what to do about it? She stood and walked to her vanity and began to shuffle things about, looking desperately for Vernon's number.

— · — · — · —

Bait and Leon and Horace had arrived outside the campground before dawn. Bait was driving and positioned the truck under a grove of pines to wait. As they sat quietly in the cab, Leon drank his first beer of the day, an act of intemperance which he defended by declaring it to be Saturday. Horace ate two honey buns and continued to complain of hunger, while Bait smoked cigarette after cigarette. About eight o'clock, just as Leon had stepped out of the truck to get another beer, Clay eased by the campground office and turned north onto the highway. "I'll bet-cha he's goin' back to where that cop spotted him last night."

"What cop?" Horace asked. "I don't want nuthin' to do with no cops."

"Cool it. The cops ain't goin' to bother us. Charlie'll see to that."

"And Charlie still don't know what this feller's looking for?"

"That's what we aim to find out," Bait said, turning the key in the ignition. He had changed trucks, using one without the farm's name on the door panel.

They did not see Clay turn into the dead end, but a thin haze of pale dust still hung in the air, marking the passage of his truck. Bait pulled over and waited about ten minutes before following. The unnamed ridge rose precipitously in front of them, marking the likely end of the road, but not knowing that for sure, Bait took his time. As they approached the last house, the one advertising the vegetables, a man walked out to the road. He was tall and lanky and wore overalls, and his hair was pulled back into a pony-tail. Bait slowed down and then stopped in front of the house. "Mornin'," he said.

"Mornin'," the man echoed.

"Does this road go through?"

"Naw. It runs out about just around the curve up there."

Bait smiled and explained, "We're just lookin' for some place to hunt this fall. Who owns the land up on the hill?"

"A bunch of different people, but Mr. Woodall, he lives over the hill, owns most of it."

"Thanks, friend. Take it easy."

The thin man watched them drive off and listened until their motor died. By the sound of it, they had stopped before they came to the end of the road. He checked the mailbox since he had for-gotten to do it the day before and walked back into the house to fix breakfast. Funny, this was more traffic than he usually saw in an entire week.

The rope was heavy, but by slinging it across his chest and shoulder, bandolero-style, it was manageable. The day had already grown hot. Clay wore his plastic hard hat and managed to stuff all of the tools, extra batteries, and such into a single pack. Lastly, he slid a roll of maps and notes into one of the side pockets and double-searched the truck to make sure he had left no clue as to why he was here or where he might be going. It was 8:30 in the morning when he set off into the woods.

Clay found a moderately used trail that began where the road ended. He decided to follow it, since it seemed headed in the direction in which he wanted to go. It led him to the top of the ridgeline after a short, steep climb, but from here it veered to the left, continuing uphill, away from his destination, which lay somewhere to the right, below him. He abandoned the path at that point and cut diagonally down the slope through heavy underbrush, brushing spider webs from his face at intervals, and soon found himself alongside the streambed shown on the topographical map. Like many of the streams in this limestone country, it was dry most of the time, its course filled with a jumble of rounded gray boulders. Clay sat down on one of these and pulled out the map, looking back over his shoulder in an attempt to estimate at what point he might have crossed the ridge. He made a comparison of this place with the one described by Neptune. Although it did not look exactly right, he had not located the cave either. It was all a matter of perspective.

He swatted at a swarm of gnats that buzzed about his ears, and soon surmised that he was upstream from the cave entrance, which was described on the map legend as lying somewhere on the far side of the ravine. He shouldered the rope once more and climbed the slope ahead of him for a short distance before turning downstream. The hillside, heavily wooded with oak and hickory and clumps of laurel, was studded with boulders and at irregular intervals, low limestone cliffs and outcrops, ideal cave country. Not long after he turned and walked parallel to the water course, he came upon a fissure at the base of one such cliff. It emitted a steady stream of cool air, the respiration characteristic of cave systems, but it was far too narrow to allow entry.

Perhaps two hundred yards past this fissure, he came upon a

faint path leading up from the creekbed. It led him around an outcrop of rocks, and there it stopped in a small clearing. At the center was barred gate, more like a trap door, fixed onto the rock. He saw now that the cave, by its position behind the rocks, would have been impossible to detect from below. The original entrance appeared oblong, but had been closed in by a barrier of melon-sized rocks fused in concrete. The rusted gate was about the size of a ship's hatch and was mounted roughly horizontal to the ground where it was secured by two padlocks, one on each side. Clay could see no hinges. He would have to use the hacksaw.

It took him most of an hour to get the twin locks off, but the gate itself pulled free easily. The expected column of cool air blew steadily in his face. Clay pulled a hand light from this pack and shined it into the hole, but could tell very little other than the tunnel appeared to go straight down. The cave map had indicated a nonvertical drop of about twelve to fifteen feet at the entrance. He tossed a pebble into the blackness, and it struck something almost instantaneously. After securing the rope to a tree and unloading most of what was in the pack, he turned on his headlight, slipped on a pair of leather work gloves, and started his descent.

Once through the hatchway and away from the glaring sunlight, his electric beam became much more effective. He was on the wall of a chamber, the limits of which he could not tell, whose floor was composed of mounds of loose, irregular rock. The footholds were not the best and would have been extremely difficult to manage without a rope, but the scope of his vision steadily increased as his eyes adjusted to the darkness. In spite of his poor technique, he reached the bottom without mishap and paused once again to consult the map showing the layout of the cave, noting that the only exit to this room was somewhere along the opposite wall. By working around the periphery, he estimated the shape of the room to be roughly circular, about twenty feet in diameter. The floor was covered entirely in breakdown, rocks fallen from the ceiling or walls over the passage of time, a regular haystack of stone, the sort of place that would defy a careful search. Several smears of white, discarded carbide marred the monotonous brown rock and were the only visible signs of previous visitations. He knew immediately that he would need the metal detector if he was serious about searching this room.

As Clay surveyed the beginnings of the cavern, he began to analyze what he saw from another point of view. William Hand could have descended on a rope as he had, but the ascent, especially if he carried any weight, would not have been easy. Clay mused on that point. Of course, he could have had a ladder for that purpose.

The chamber was wet, uniformly damp, and any organic or ferrous metal would have been reduced to dust long ago. There were several other points that did not add up—the canyon below the cave was not as formidable as that described by Neptune, but then such emotional descriptions are always highly subjective. In addition, the canyon shown on the waybill, if its description was consistent with the others, seemed to be of grander dimensions than what he found on his hike to this cave. All in all, he did not feel good about his chances, but since he was already here, he might as well have a look around.

The exit from the entry room was located exactly where described, and consisted of a narrow crawlway about fifty feet long. At this point Clay was able to stand, finding himself in a second, more narrow room, a huge crack really, perhaps four to five feet in width with a ceiling of indeterminate height. Several worn stalagmites and a small, muddy flowstone were the first formations that he had encountered. He walked for several hundred more feet, and the crack narrowed into another crawlway, which he followed for some ten minutes. When it ended, he found himself in a much smaller room where ahead of him, down the passage, the floor disappeared. To continue he would have to chimney, using his back and feet only, along the two walls. Hand could not possibly have come this far. His curiosity satisfied, he turned back toward the entrance.

As Clay had predicted, the hand-over-hand climb back to the

surface was not an easy one, especially since the soles of his boots were now slick with mud. Halfway up he came to the best of the footholds, where he rested in the shaft of sunlight falling from the hatchway overhead. The last few feet were the worst, but at last he was able to grab the metal frame of the gate and pull himself up.

Clay was so exhausted by the climb, so intent on getting up without falling, so blinded by the natural light beyond the entrance, that the image of a man, his face covered by a red bandana, did not register. Before he could react, someone grabbed him by the back of the shirt and jerked him free of the cave, sending his hard hat and light flying, propelling him upward and then forward before driving his forehead and face into the ground. Stunned, Clay offered no resistance as someone pulled his arms behind him and pressed his neck to the ground with his knee.

A voice said, "Don't move sucker, or we'll break 'em." Clay lay perfectly still, his face burning from the friction of his landing, as his wrists and feet were tied together. As the knots were tightened the pressure on his neck eased.

Another voice, a sharp, nasal voice said, "Well sir, why don't you tell us what the hell you think you're doing up here?" Clay could not formulate an answer. The same voice said, "Why don't one of you get this here trespasser to speak up?" Clay at that point was pulled free from the ground by his bound arms. Excruciating pain shot through both shoulder joints.

"Just cavin'," he hissed through clinched teeth.

"We know that, smart-ass." To make a further point of his answer, someone kicked him hard in the ribs. A burst of white light passed before Clay's closed eyes, and he awoke with his face pressed against the ground. Someone had poured beer over his head, perhaps in an attempt to rouse him.

The same irritating voice began again, "Now, lover boy, I want you to know, we didn't climb halfway up this goddamned mountain to get a breath of fresh air." Something, a foot maybe, gently touched his thigh to emphasize the point. "Are you beginnin' to get my drift?"

"Who are you?" Clay asked. He started to roll over, but someone prevented it by putting pressure between his shoulder blades. These men were not dealing with a simple trespasser. His mind raced over the possibilities—who are these fools—dope dealers, moonshiners, thieves?

"Just never you mind. You can just call us caretakers." Several people, maybe three, laughed.

"This is state land, ain't it?" Clay managed.

"Yeah, it's state land," a new voice said, "And I'm Mister Game Warden." There was more laughter.

The different voice came closer until it was right over him. The voice grabbed Clay by the hair and pulled his head backwards. He tried to catch a glimpse of the man, but could only see a pair of black army-issue boots and the cuffs of his jeans. Then, as a befitting climax to the abuse, he felt cold metal against his cheek. "Okay, Mr. Hardigrew, we've had just about enough out of you. Have you ever seen what a twelve-gauge can do to a man's head?"

How in the hell do they know my name? Maybe they rifled his truck. Clay was terrified. "Look fellows, I ain't tryin' to give you a hard time. Gimme a break! I swear I thought this was state land. I'm just an old pot hunter, out looking for Indian stuff. There's no need to be hard on me, why, I'm not greedy at all." He tried to laugh. "I'll be happy to share with you whatever I find."

"Since when does a person look for arrowheads with a metal detector?" said the man in the black boots. That confirmed it—they had been in his truck.

"That's not all I look for," said Clay. He tried to sound agreeable, compliant. "You name it, I'll put the detector on it. Why, I look for 'most anything old—you know coins, Civil War stuff, . . ." They released his head in midsentence.

"Yeah, yeah, sure. But I just don't believe you're tellin' us the whole truth. Do you boys?" The other two voices answered negatively. "What do y'all think we oughta to do to loosen this boy up?"

A deep voice, a slow voice answered, "Why don't we put the little shit-eatin' rat back down in his hole?" That brought the biggest laugh yet.

They blindfolded him and finally rolled him over. His ribs screamed in pain with each breath. "Come on, boys, I didn't mean no harm. Y'all don't want to do this."

"Aw, shut up, pussy," one of them said, as they cuffed him hard on the ear with the palm of a meaty hand.

They untied his hands to take off his pack and then retied them to his front and around his waist. Using a slip knot, they then fastened his own rope around his chest and under his arms. They untied his feet and two of them grabbed him by his shirt sleeves and pulled him erect, causing the blindfold to loosen.

The hard voice, the one in charge, now assumed a sissified, childlike quality, "All right, now, Miss Smartmouth, back down you go." Clay faced his tormentor and caught a glimpse of a face at the extreme periphery of his vision. He noted the angular scar above the mask and the unmatched eyes. Ugly bastard, he thought.

Clay tried to resist, but the pain in his side was so severe that he found it impossible to do much more than cooperate. They pushed him forward and someone said, "You want to go down easy or do you want to make it hard on yourself?" He let them guide his feet into the entrance, and they tightened the rope around his chest until he could hardly take a breath. "You sure you don't want to talk?" Clay wanted to say yes, but he still clung to the hope that he might somehow get out of this predicament. As they forced him over the edge, his feet came free and he rotated sideways, banging into the ungiving rock of the cave's wall. "I'm lookin' for gold," Clay shouted upwards. "Indian gold."

More laughter followed his admission. He hit bottom hard and lay still. He heard the gate being put back into place and then silence. He reached up and pulled off the blindfold to see the last of the light disappear from overhead. They had placed some sort of covering over the grate! He was now enveloped in total, absolute, and utter darkness. To his singular good fortune, they had given him enough slack such that, after groping and reaching about on the floor of the cave for a time, he was able to sit down and loosen the rope from around his chest. He leaned back with his eyes closed, since having them open made not the slightest difference, and began to work at untying the ropes that bound his wrists.

There is, indeed, no such thing in life as absolute darkness; one's eyes revolt and hasten to fill the vacuum by
floating in sparks, dream-patterns, figures whimsical and
figures grotesque, shifting, clad in complementary colors,
to appease the indignant cups and rods of the retina.

—GELETT BURGESS, "CONFESSIONS OF AN
IGNORAMUS," *THE ROMANCE OF THE COMMONPLACE*

Carolina was frantic by the time she located Vernon's number. She got no answer. Unknown to her, he had accepted a last-minute invitation from his older son, John, to spend the night with him and his family at their lake cabin. She redialed several times over the next hour with the same result and even went to the trouble of phoning Clay's office in hopes someone might answer. She then had information locate John Hardigrew's number, but once again she was stymied. Short of calling the police, Carolina had now exhausted all of the possibilities. She lay back on the bed and began to consider the extent of her plight.

Despite the reality that she remained ignorant of the circumstances leading to Vernon's injury, she now had reason to suspect Bait and Leon were somehow involved. She also knew that her communications with Clay had been monitored, and that her brother, most likely by way of one of his damned connections—probably Howard Suggs—had found some way to follow Clay's movements. But what was the purpose of all this? To what end? Charlie was undoubtedly up to something, and by now Carolina had developed her own suspicions. She put together his frequent trips to Florida and his time at the airstrip, his problems with money, his tolerance of Bait, his unreasonable paranoia and reclusiveness, and came to a conclusion she had hoped to avoid.

She stood up and walked to the window. She began to think

further about how much of this was conjecture and how much was fact. Rationally, she decided that no immediate answer would be forthcoming and that as she had originally thought, her primary concern right now must be Clay's welfare. Bait was capable of anything under the influence of anger. The rest of this story would come out in time.

Carolina went downstairs after she showered and changed clothes and began to prepare dinner. Be cool, she thought. She asked her brother beforehand if she could fix him anything, but he declined, saying that he was going to the country club with friends. As he left by the back door, she toyed with the idea of following him, but decided against it, figuring that whenever Bait called back, which would most likely be tomorrow, the message would come by way of one of the house lines. She tried phoning Mathis Ford several more times to no avail, but finally gave it up and settled down with a book to wait.

Charlie got back after midnight, and the phone did not ring until nine o'clock the following morning. The caller was her matchmaker friend in Chattanooga telling her that the blind date had fallen through. She lingered over breakfast, then shuffled into the den, and when asked, simply said that she did not feel well, using the sort of sullen feminine tone that stifles any further inquiry. Charlie left the house for a while, explaining that he was going over to a neighbor's to check some stock. She had no idea if this was true or not, but once again elected to wait it out rather than follow him.

About 10:30, long before he returned, the phone rang. This time it was Bait.

"Miz Rose, could I speak to your brother, please ma'am?"

"Why, he just stepped out, Bait. Could I give him any message?"

"When did he say he would be gettin' back?"

"Bait, I really can't say. He didn't tell me. He took the pickup so he could be going 'most anywhere. I'd be glad to give him a message."

For a moment only static coursed through the wires, then he continued, "Well, I'll just have to call him back later."

"Are you at home?" she inquired innocently. "I could have him call you."

"Naw, I ain't where I can be easily reached. I'll just have to try back in a few hours."

She came close, but that was not good enough. At least she knew when he might call back. She dialed Tennessee once more, but still got no answer. On impulse she punched in Clay's number, but only the machine was home. The recorded sound of his voice was unsettling. She left no message. On the chance that she might need it, she stepped outside and checked the amount of gas in the Jeep. The day slowed to a crawl.

Charlie returned around two and turned on a baseball game. She stayed in her room, not wanting to tell him of Bait's call. At 2:30, the phone rang again. Once more it was one of her friends, this time inquiring about one of the horses. Not sixty seconds after she put down the receiver, it rang again. She shouted down the stairs and around the corner, "Charlie, it's for you!"

She had every intention of listening in on the call, but Charlie outsmarted her.

"Yo, Mr. Rose, this is Bait."

Charlie did not give him a chance to say anything further.

"Bait, call me right back on the office line." She was had. Without access to the office line, the only one of which was in Charlie's study, she could hear nothing of what was said. She heard the telephone ringing—twice only and then it stopped. Barefoot as before, she slipped down the stairs and into the hall. The door to the study was closed. Should she try it again? She crept forward. Not a sound. Nothing. Abruptly the door opened. She and her brother stood face to face. He smelled of alcohol.

"Something I can do for you, sweet sister?"

"I just wanted to make sure you got the phone."

"Thanks. It was just Bait about a piece of machinery."

"Will you be here for supper?"

"Don't count on me. I've got a couple of things cookin', and chances are I won't be here. And by the way, Little Charlie will be staying with the Barnetts another night."

She turned and went through the kitchen and continued on to the pool. She considered taking a swim, but did not want to change. She walked around the periphery, silently cursing her brother and his cohorts.

■ ▪ ▬ ▪ ▬ ▪ ▬

Clay spent the first hours in the cave, or at least that is how long it seemed to be, trying to suppress the urge to panic. Once he worked his hands free, he had nothing to distract him from his predicament. His watch lacked a luminous dial so that in the absence of light it became useless. Equipped with a quartz movement, it did not even provide him with the reassurance of a mechanical tick. He had worn a sweatshirt and had been allowed to keep his gloves, but in time the subterranean cold began to gnaw at his skin. He stepped up and down for a time, but grew tired, and by feeling about in the dark was able to make a seat among the stones, where he huddled in silence.

The silence was particularly difficult to tolerate. He had tried to self-administer a pep talk, but the words carried no weight or resonance, the cave just swallowed them up, and they seemed only to magnify his loneliness and fear. After a few sentences he grew quiet again. He tucked his shirt into his trousers and cinched up his belt and drew his knees against his chest, which seemed to make a difference in his overall comfort. The pain in his side had subsided to a dull ache accentuated by deep breathing, and his various abrasions seemed to have gone numb. In this withdrawn, low-energy state he waited, fantasizing about a rescue, expecting either the return of his tormentors or, after twenty-four hours or so, the arrival of a rescue party led by his father. He kept his eyes closed much of the time, finding it preferable to the sensory deprivation that enveloped him. He watched the points of light that all human beings carry there and tried to follow and make some sense of them. Sometimes, by accident, they took on familiar shapes and somewhere during those dark hours, he slipped into what he would later recall as sleep.

The next light that Clay saw did not come from within him, but was external. It was a curious, cold, detached light, unto itself, providing no illumination beyond its own bright circle. He felt the rocks at his back well enough, and the cold continued pressing in around him, but this light was contrary to his usual senses. Over a time it moved, and he realized only then that it was very far away. He fixated upon it, watching the sphere of light draw ever closer. He found it amusing that he did not see the light as at all unusual, that he did not view it as completely absurd and dismiss it immediately, but instead welcomed its coming as a diversion from the monotony and loneliness of his confinement.

As its clarity grew, he could see something at the center, also moving, a living thing with a trunk and limbs. Growing ever larger, this organism within the light took form and became a man, a beautiful man, bronze-skinned and smoothly muscled, running toward him with reckless speed. The man's black hair grew long to his shoulders and was unbound and blew in response to some unfelt wind. He was clothed only in a loincloth and bore a flint knife and medicine bag at his hip. In his left hand he gripped a bow, a long powerful weapon, taller than a man, made of dark wood and strung tight with twisted buckskin. The halo of light slowed and then stopped altogether, suspended directly before Clay. He was filled with wonderment as the bronze man stepped forward, raising his right hand, the palm open and exposed. His dark eyes, and indeed much of his face, were cloaked in shadow, but Clay could see that his lips were moving in speech, silently, without a whisper of sound.

The stranger went through a series of curious mannerisms and gesticulations, primarily with his hands and arms, finally ending this ceremonial posturing by clutching a crystal talisman suspended from around his neck. Turning in profile, he began to speak again, this time with his arms extended as if in supplication, giving the impression that a third, as yet unseen, party was present. He then crouched onto one knee and drew a single arrow from the quiver on his back. The shaft was of the same black wood as the bow, and the feathers that would guide it glowed with an ominous light of their own, a deep red, the color of dying embers.

Patiently the man waited in this position, turned away from Clay, staring upward, and finally, his patience rewarded, a remote object appeared far above, moving in broad, unhurried circles, spiraling toward them, slowly descending until Clay could make out its wings, impossibly broad wings, and the unmistakable silhouette of a giant serpent. The hunter notched the arrow and drew the cord to his cheek and sighted on the monster. The arrow arched skyward, trailing behind it a shower of phosphorescence, converging on the serpentine form with unimagined speed and an uncanny accuracy. As the missile struck home, the creature disappeared in a burst of unnatural fire, all traces of its flight obliterated in a shower of giant emerald scales, each the span of a man's arms.

The bowman took the amulet from around his neck and held it aloft, turning slowly to each of the four points of the compass. As the crystal circled about his head, oscillations of light appeared from within its center. Having identified the axis of its greatest activity, the archer strode forward along this invisible line, pushing aside the wreckage of the beast, the litter of scales, the massive pieces of shattered bone, the strips of smoking flesh to that prime point where the talisman's strobe of light was transformed into a single, piercing beacon. Casting the crystal aside, he stooped before the severed head of the serpent and drew his knife from its sheath. From between the great horns that adorned the creature's skull, he extracted an object that flashed as brilliantly as any diamond, a colorless crystal veined with red, an enchanted stone stained by the blood of the dragon, infused with a magic more potent than any imaginable.

The champion grasped the prize in a closed fist and beckoned for Clay to follow him. He then rose from the ground as if levitated and without knowing how or why, Clay joined him, unfettered by the weight of humankind, all seeing, all knowing, embodied with the power of flight. They sailed over forests and rivers and expanses of sand, across oceans and endless rivers, and after a great distance came upon a monolith of black rock, a single, fractured spire, climbing in rough tiers until its summit disappeared among the clouds. Midway in this rock was a door, a mighty door of oak and iron, burnished by the eternal work of the elements, and secured with a thousand golden locks. The magician flew low by the door and brushed it with the monster's crystal, causing the locks to burst and fall away as the great door swung free to reveal a blackness as deep as any in Clay's prison, the coldness of a hidden place that had never known the sun, a place to be feared and shunned by man, and they flew into it, the two of them, and were lost.

— ∙ — ∙ — ∙ —

About two hours after Bait's second call, his truck turned down the road to the barn. Carolina was sitting in the den when she heard Charlie leave by the front door. She jumped to her feet and watched him from the entry as he opened the door to his car. Convinced that whatever they would be talking about would concern Clay, she then ran to her room and quickly slipped into jeans and a dark blue shirt. She grabbed her car keys and pocketknife from the bureau and exited the house by way of the back door.

She trotted down Ajax Road for a short distance and climbed the fence. By approaching from the rear she was less likely to be seen and made it to the wall of the barn without discovery. Most likely the meeting was being held in the barn office, and she crept to one corner and listened. Charlie's Ford sedan and two pickups were parked out front. Horace and his brother stood by one of the trucks. The only window to the office was on the front of the barn, and they would be able to see her plainly if she approached from that direction.

Retracing her steps, she quietly entered the barn by one of its rear doors, the one hidden behind stacks of feed. She looked along the row of stalls and saw no one. From this angle she could not see the door to the office, an advantage she utilized in creeping to an unoccupied stall not twenty feet from her goal. The door itself was partly closed so that she could not see inside, but the voices were plain. Charlie and Bait were talking, but she could make out nothing of what they were saying. Their dialogue went on for ten minutes. She thought about leaving the shelter of the stall, but once again there was no place of concealment should they exit the office.

Suddenly the door opened and Bait walked out. Charlie was right behind him. "You say he's been down there since ten o'clock this morning?"

"Yeah. About ten."

"Damn," Charlie said. They walked outside and stood beyond the double doors.

"It'll take us about an hour and a half to drive back over there," Bait said.

"I'll follow you in the white truck."

"It's got our name on the side," Bait observed.

"Well, if anyone's that interested, they'll be just as likely to look at our tags," Charlie retorted. "Do we need anything?"

"We ought to take more light and maybe some more rope."

Carolina ducked as they reentered the barn. She glanced around the empty stall, praying the equipment they needed was to be found elsewhere. She listened to them banging around outside and then heard the motor to one of the trucks start. They were leaving! She looked again as the white truck backed up. As soon as it cleared the door frame, she ran to the front of the barn.

It took her perhaps four panicked minutes to run to the house, start the Jeep, and follow them. Although she was hitting close to eighty miles per hour on the straightaways, she knew they were still several miles ahead. This meant nothing until they intersected Route 143, where they would be faced with two choices, right or left. Clay had told Carolina he would be in Alabama, which was to the west, allowing her to blow through the intersection without a second's hesitation. She recklessly passed several cars and at the twenty-minute mark, just before cresting the mountain, spied a white truck in the distance and slowed her speed. As they approached a curve, she caught sight of a second truck, a truck with only one functional brake light, and assumed that it was Bait's. This small mechanical dysfunction allowed her to follow at an even greater distance.

By shortly after seven o'clock, Bait pulled into the gas station where the policeman had first seen Clay. He bought gas, a pack of cigarettes, and some vending food, and Leon used the restroom. The station was close by the exit from the interstate, and Carolina rejoiced once more in her good fortune that they did not see her. She turned away from the station, crossed over the four-lane, and waited for the men to continue. Their stop prompted her to notice her own gauge—less than one-quarter of a tank. They had been on the road for just over one hour.

Charlie and Bait compared notes as Leon finished his business.

"How far is it?"

"About three or four miles to the turnoff."

They left once more, and the Jeep fell in behind them. Bait turned on his headlights, which made it even easier, but Carolina did not follow suit, figuring she would wait until it was absolutely necessary. Because of the position of the dirt road leading to Clay's truck, and the distance at which Carolina was following, she did not see them turn off. The trees along the road concealed their lights, and Carolina drove past and continued on for several miles before she realized she had lost them. Unfortunately, she had by now passed several more roads and was forced to investigate all of them. The first two dead-ended into farms, and the third degenerated into a rough logging road that began climbing the side of the mountain. She doggedly followed it for some distance before giving up. A full half hour passed before she found the correct turn. The sun was now below the mountain and the forest was in shadow.

Once again, Carolina was fortunate. Because of her detour and the delay it caused, her brother and his henchmen had had time to clear the trucks. The parking area did not allow for concealment, and realistically, she no longer saw it as necessary. She looked in the glove box and found a small flashlight, but when she switched it on nothing happened. Rather than search anymore, she used what light was left her and found the trailhead, walking as rapidly as possible uphill toward the crest. By the time she reached it, breathless with the effort, the sunlight was almost gone. She stopped to listen, but heard nothing—no footfalls, no men's voices. She was just turning to continue along the trail when she heard a single faint shout to her right, down the hill, somewhere among the trees. She listened again for a time, but again heard nothing. Should she follow it? The trail was plain. The voice was her solitary clue. She cautiously moved downhill, off the trail, making every effort to step silently among the dry leaves.

Her eyes soon became more accustomed to the growing darkness, and she made good progress, slipping only once or twice on concealed rocks. Halfway down, she heard another shout, closer this time, again off to the right and below her. She saw no sign of their lights. At last she reached the creek bed and began to move cautiously across the uneven rocks. The going was tougher here, the footing more unpredictable, and she stopped frequently to listen. After moving ahead several hundred yards, she saw a brief flash of light among the trees, and for the second time since beginning this mad chase, she felt afraid. She touched the knife in her pocket, but then chided herself for counting on such a pitiful weapon. Her options were few at this critical juncture, considering that she had no idea of what lay ahead, much less of how to deal with it. She was completely committed to helping Clay, no matter the consequence, and could not turn back. Clinching her teeth, she climbing toward the light.

Once again she saw a flash among the trees and for the first time detected bits and pieces of disconnected speech, men talking. She edged along the hillside on all fours, feeling her way toward the commotion, moving from rock to rock, tree to tree, staying as low to the ground as humanly possible. The light became steady now and the speech more consistent. She made out Bait's voice above the others.

Carolina reasoned that from her present position below them, there was little chance she would see or hear what was going on. She must either be lateral or above them, since there seemed to be a mass of rock interposed between her and the lights. She was now very close. Creeping over the moist leaves on her elbows and knees, she patiently moved higher until at last she crawled into a profusion of ferns and lay still. Just below her lay the trunk of a recently fallen tree that, rather than resting flat on the uneven ground, leaned steeply against its healthier neighbors. Between this conveniently hanging trunk and the mass of ground cover that grew under it, she caught her first glimpse of the horrific drama taking place in the clearing before the cave's entrance.

Had she not known in advance the identity of the characters on stage before her, they would have remained unrecognizable. The dark figures, the projections of exposed rock, the dense forest only partially revealed by the darting illumination of the electrically generated lights, gave the appearance of some misbegotten, neolithic encampment peopled by primal men.

Bait, his scarred face and beard once more hidden behind a bandana, stalked about the clearing, waving his hands in the air, his grotesque marionette's shadow rising and falling across the rocks, his voice now hoarse, his demeanor threatening, explosive.

"Okay, my friend, I'm only going to ask you one more time, what in the fuck were you doin' down in that hole?" Impatient for a reply, he walked over to a man sitting at the center of the group and slapped him on the side of the head. Carolina could not hear the blow, but, by the recoil of the man's head, she felt its effect. Despite the blindfold, she knew the bound man was Clay. Her fear dissipated in a surge of rage. The man did not speak, and Bait drew his hand back to strike again.

At the edge of the light, another figure, Charlie, his face also covered, stepped forward and grabbed his arm. "Go easy," he said. He then squatted by the seated figure and began speaking in a low tone. "Mr. Hardigrew, I think we could all agree that you are at our mercy. We are not anxious to hurt you, but we really need to know what you are doing here. Now you can tell us, even in the most general terms, and we will leave you be, or you can continue your resistance and experience considerably more pain than you already have. I don't know what it is that you are hiding from us, but I assure you that we will not give up until you share it with us. Now tell us about the maps."

Clay appeared defeated. He sat sprawled on the ground, his back against the stone, the glare of several lights in his face. Dried blood was caked across his forehead, and he inhaled in short gasps, splinting to save the pain in his chest. He knew he had to give them something, or they might kill him. It was not worth that particular sacrifice. "I'm looking for a particular cave," he croaked.

"Why?"

"It may be on an old map."

"Interesting, but you wouldn't have gone to such trouble for the map alone. What's the big deal about this cave?"

"I'm not entirely sure. It may contain treasure."

The word treasure brought a stir to the two men lounging about in the background. One of them was smoking a cigarette, the other held a shotgun. As they moved closer, showing renewed interest in what Clay had to say, she recognized the shapes of Horace and Leon. Their faces were covered also, and despite the brutality of the interrogation, Carolina could not believe how ridiculous, how surreal, they looked.

"What sort of treasure?"

"Cherokee treasure."

"Gold and silver?"

"Maybe. The map doesn't say."

"Is this the cave?"

"I don't think so. Too hard to get in and out of. Too wet, too."

"So that's what the metal detector is for?"

"Yeah. Can I stand up?"

"Sure." For the first time, Carolina could now see that his hands were now tied in front of him. He paced about, bent from the waist as if in pain. "I've looked through the maps in your pack and still don't see the one map you're referring to."

"That's because it's not there."

"And where is it?"

"At home. I don't need it. I have it memorized."

Charlie, who was also standing by now, turned away and whispered something to Bait. He began with Clay again. "Why were you up on Lookout Mountain?"

"Same reason. The map showed an old trail across the mountain, and I was trying to find it." Clay stopped his pacing. "I guess that means y'all are the fellows we bumped into up there?"

"Pretty good guess," said Leon, a comment that drew a nasty look from Bait.

Clay continued, "How did you know I was here?"

Bait chimed in, "I think you got it a little mixed up, old buddy. Just answer the damn questions. Don't go askin' any."

Charlie was uneasy. He whispered something to Bait and returned to the shadows. Bait grabbed Clay by the shoulders and forced him back to the ground. Carolina felt something crawling on her cheek and slapped it away.

A full minute of silence passed as Charlie considered the situation. The Cherokee gold business sounded like some crackpot scheme and was not worth his effort. He needed to make sure that Clay was telling the entire truth. He could understand why Clay and Vernon were sniffing around up on the cliffs—from there they could get a bird's-eye view of his whole operation, but that did nothing to explain why Hardigrew was now eighty miles away crawling around in some godforsaken cave. It simply did not make sense. He could certainly not count on his sister for any more information, and despite the fact that Clay had not acknowledged him, recognition could not be far away. In addition, they could now be blamed for Vernon's injury, whatever the circumstance. The most important consideration was to discourage Clay from making further unauthorized tours of White Rock Farm. He briefly whispered another instruction to Bait, and stepped back to observe its implementation.

Bait got right down in Clay's face. "Mister, we don't cotton to folks who snoop around. We just want you to know that you ain't welcome in these parts and to stay the hell out. Understand?"

"Whatever you say. I'm not about to disagree with you."

Bait, as quick as a snake, popped Clay on the forehead with the butt of his hand, almost knocking him over and dislodging the blindfold. "Are you real sure?"

"Yes," Clay groaned.

"And one more thing. Which one of these caves was you going to look at next?"

"There's a couple of them. . . ."

"That ain't good enough," hissed Bait, drawing back his foot to deliver another blow to Clay's ribs. Until now entirely passive and unable to see the impending blows, he caught sight of Bait's boots from under the blindfold. Hearing the swish of the blow, Clay lunged forward and blocked the kick with his arms. The move threw Bait off balance and in that instant Clay grabbed the offending leg with his tethered hands, lifting and twisting it further into the air and in doing so caused the attacker to fall onto his back. Before Bait could roll away, Clay was on top of him, somehow managing to pin the squirming man with his body. In an effort to free himself, Bait began to pummel Clay about the head and shoulders with his fists, but could not land a solid blow. Instinctively, his hands tied, seeking to return the pain being administered to him, Clay bit into Bait's stomach with all of his might, eliciting a prodigious scream from the deserving victim. "Ohhhh, shit—get this son of a bitch off me!"

Horace and Leon immediately reacted, but were at first unsuccessful in separating the two men. Clay hung on like a snapping turtle. They each struck him several times, once kicking him in the legs, all to no avail. Bait continue to yell mightily, until Horace bodily lifted Clay from the ground as his brother punched him hard in the neck. Clay, who was now temporarily insensitive to pain, was rendered breathless by this punch and was forced to release his hold. Bait jumped to his feet, pulling up his shirt in the process. "Look what that bastard did." A large lesion, a perfect impression of a human bite, appeared on the right side of his abdomen. Minute mounds of blood welled through the damaged skin. "Bit a goddamn plug out." He let the shirt drop and approached the motionless Clay.

Carolina had watched the elevating level of violence and, from the hatred in Bait's tone, realized that he was now capable of killing her lover. "Stop it!" she screamed, her throat so dry that her protest was painful. "Leave him alone!" At the sound of her voice, the four assailants froze. Two flashlight beams swung toward her hiding place. She stood up concealing the open knife behind her hip. Lowering her voice, she said, "Charlie, it's me, Carolina."

By the time she stepped to the edge of the circle, Leon and Horace had melted into the darkness and Bait had retreated to the perimeter of the clearing.

"What in the hell are you doing here?" Charlie said, lowering his mask.

"I might ask you the same question. What are you trying to do, commit a murder?"

"We aren't about to murder anybody."

"Is that so? Looks like things were pretty out of control to me."

She then knelt over Clay and helped him roll onto his side.

She pulled away the blindfold and brushed the matted hair from his eyes. A thin rivulet of blood issued from each nostril.

"Clay, can you hear me, it's Carolina."

He opened his swollen eyes. "I hear you."

She rose and brandished the knife in her brother's face. "Charles Rose, I don't know what in the world you're up to, and frankly I don't really care, but why don't you and your chickenshit friends just get out of here and leave him alone?"

"Now, listen to reason, Carolina, this guy isn't exactly what he seems to be."

"How would you know, you paranoid cokehead? Happens to be everybody here isn't what they seem to be. I know about those night flights. I've heard the planes. Do you think I'm that stupid? Now get out of here before I blow the whistle. I mean it—NOW!"

"Careful, Carolina. You may be getting in way over your head." The thought of killing the two of them right there flashed through his mind, but he quickly figured that he would never get away with it. Too many loose ends. Finally he turned and said, "Come on, Bait. We've got what we want."

"Well, maybe we have, and maybe we haven't," Bait added in mild protest, and from the sullen stare he aimed at Carolina, she was certain he would have killed them both without the restraint provided by her brother. As the four men retreated into the darkness, Carolina picked up a stone and hurled it at their backs, giving physical vent to all of her justified anger, honestly hoping it would somehow connect and knock Bait senseless. Fortunately, her puny effort was wide, and they ignored it, allowing her to return to Clay, who by now had managed to sit up. She had forgotten how dark it was without a light.

"I can't believe they're gone," he mumbled, hardly able to speak. "I think you saved my life."

"I know," she said, placing her arm around his shoulder.

"Oh, no, you don't," he said rubbing his head. "I just about went crazy down there. I started seeing all sorts of crazy stuff. The pain is only the half of it. God, am I thirsty. How about getting my hands free and checking my pack to see if that water bottle is still in there." It was nowhere to be found. "What time is it?"

"I can't see my watch," she answered apologetically. "I'd guess that it's about ten o'clock."

"We've got to get back to the truck."

Carolina saw no need to repeat the obvious. "Can you walk?"

"I'll just have to," he said, and with her help made it to his feet. The starlight was considerable by now, and they made their way across the streambed without any trouble. Carolina stepped into a pool of standing water that went over the top of her shoe, but otherwise their progress was steady, and within fifteen minutes they had crested the ridge and started on the path leading down to the parking lot.

"My damned side is killing me," Clay groaned.

"Do you think they might have broken something?"

"I wouldn't be surprised."

The keys to Clay's truck had been in his ransacked pack, but another search failed to find them. Fortunately he had an extra set hidden in a magnetic box attached inside the front bumper, but when he turned the ignition nothing happened. Even the alternator lights were dead. He checked under the hood.

"What a nice bunch of guys. They took my battery," he observed.

"Don't worry," she said. "At least we've got the Jeep. We can come back in the morning."

For some reason, Charlie had not tampered with her car, and before another hour passed they were checked into an inexpensive motel outside Fort Payne. Clay sat in the car while Carolina went into the office. He did not want to explain his appearance to anyone.

"Here, take my credit card," he told her. "One look at me and the police will be on their way over here."

Clay undressed as soon as they found their room. He stood before the mirror in his shorts, surveying the damage to his body.

His right eye took most of the damage. His wrists were deeply abraded and caked with dried blood as was his forehead and nose. His lower lip was swollen, but otherwise intact. Both knees were swollen, and bending them was fast becoming impossible. His chest and side, for all the pain, were only reddened. Over one of the lower right ribs, he located a spot that was exquisitely tender. "If I broke anything, it's right here," he indicated. After a shower and a change into a clean set of jeans and a T-shirt, he felt only marginally better. Carolina drove over to a fast-food restaurant and brought back cheeseburgers, fries, and three gigantic Cokes. Once finished, he lay back on the bed.

"Come here and kiss me," he said.

Carolina lay down next to him and kissed him on the forehead.

"Thank you. That may be the only place on my body that's not sore." He opened his bleary eyes and reached out and touched her cheek. "I really thought I was a goner. Those guys with your brother were animals."

"Take these aspirin and go to sleep," she whispered, stroking his wet hair.

Clay awoke the next morning in agony, stiff and unable to roll out of bed without her help. To watch him move was painful. Carolina ran a tub of hot water, he soaked, and took some additional aspirin.

"Don't you think you need some x-rays or something?"

"What if the rib is broken? They can't do anything about it, so why bother?"

They ate breakfast at a Waffle House. His appearance brought several long looks from the clientele. "I ran into a door," he told the waitress. She told him she was sorry.

"I never thought orange juice and coffee could taste so good," he observed.

"So are you going to tell me about what happened or not?"

He put down his juice and looked into her blue eyes. She wore no makeup.

"You're beautiful," he said.

"And you're a fool. Now tell me about it."

He realized that further deception was out of the question. He stirred some cream into his coffee and began. "Carolina, a couple of years ago, while in New Orleans, I ran into an old friend. With his help I purchased a gift for my father's seventieth birthday. This gift was a box of old things, a kind of time capsule I guess you would call it, just the sort of thing my crazy father would like."

"Like father, like son," she commented between sips of coffee.

"I guess so. Anyway, inside this box was a silver pocket watch engraved in Cherokee and among the papers was a map—a waybill, we call it. My dad became convinced that this presumed map—it was all in symbols so you couldn't read it—was a treasure map, a guide to a cache left by some rich Indian named William Hand before he shipped out to Oklahoma. In the beginning I couldn't take my dad's speculations seriously and for a long time I just humored him, thinking it was just a lot of interesting nonsense. Then some of the pieces came together—things that were more than coincidence, things we could document, and we could prove. The key piece of evidence fell into place when he obtained an old diary from a doctor who lived in Arkansas."

"What was it about?"

"Well, that's a story in itself, but in brief it was an account written by an escaped slave, that, you might say, collaborated everything that we had suspected. It actually described William Hand's cache of gold."

"And that's what brought you to the farm?"

"Yes, we were just driving around checking out leads."

"Pretty lucky, wouldn't you say?"

"That's an understatement. But you know what the luckiest thing of this whole affair was?"

"What?"

"That old photograph of your aunt's. That's what gave me the clue as to what the map was trying to say. It gave us a starting point."

"So you really believe that there is buried treasure somewhere around here?"

"There was at one time. Whether it still is, remains to be seen."

"You've been through a lot for this, haven't you?"

He looked out the window. A tractor trailer truck was moving away from the gas pumps across the street. "You know, it's funny. You're the first person other than my dad that I've spoken to honestly about this. When I actually sit down and analyze what has happened, all the people we have talked to, all the chances we have taken, all the hours we have spent on the road, I continue to find my own story hard to believe. I could say I was in it for the money, but then again I don't even know that there is any money. As you said before, I am obsessed with it. Totally obsessed. The very idea of it became far more real than any fantasy." He shook his head in disbelief. "And now, here I am, sitting in some greasy spoon, feeling like one of those trucks out there just backed over me, while my father, the man that started all of this, is sitting at home an invalid. After all of our searching, my dad's accident and my almost getting killed, I still don't know where the treasure might be, or whether it exists at all."

She smiled. "Your father wouldn't like being called an invalid."

"No, he wouldn't."

"Well, treasure or no treasure, at least you found me," she smiled.

"Carolina, I'm sorry for all of this," he replied earnestly. "I'll make it up to you somehow. I want to thank you again for saving me last night—those guys would have probably killed me."

"I think you said that before, but your gratitude is accepted."

"Who was the redneck with the funny eye that slapped me around?"

"They call him Bait. He works for my brother, and you aren't the only one who would like to get even with him. He's a tough customer—mean as a snake."

"I remember his voice. I am almost sure he's the same guy

who shot at us at Solomon's Temple." Clay broke his bacon into pieces and mixed them with his grits. He took a mouthful and then a swallow of coffee. "But what makes no sense to me is, why did your brother go to all that trouble to track me down? What's he so damned scared of? He's taken as many risks as I have."

Now it was Carolina's turn to come clean, to relate her version of the truth. She bit her lip, unsure of exactly how much she should say. It seemed to be a moment for frankness, but she held back, deciding to keep any suspicions to herself. "He's just a mean, spiteful person. I think he suspected you were looking for something, which in a perverse way was fairly astute, but why he came after you, I'm not sure. Maybe he got obsessed with it too."

Clay was not buying her explanation. He cradled his coffee in both hands and stared directly at her. "I don't believe you, Carolina. You know exactly why he did what he did. I may have been beaten half to death, but I wasn't that out of it. I distinctly heard you say something about airplanes. Now, why don't you quit bullshitting me and tell me what old Charlie's up to?"

Carolina was had. She lowered her eyes. "Drugs. At least I think it's drugs. I don't have any hard evidence, but I do know it's something illegal and somehow it involves the airstrip."

Clay sat down his empty cup. "That would certainly explain his paranoia." He picked up the check and examined it for a moment. "What do you think we ought to do about it?"

Carolina finally looked up. Her eyes were now red and her voice broke, "I don't know what to do. I feel trapped."

"Do you think I should turn him in, handcuffs and twenty years in the slammer, or should I just forget it? Let bygones be bygones?"

She could not answer him. A tear made its way slowly down her cheek. "Oh, Clay, I'm scared. I may not care for him, but he's still my brother. I don't want to see him in prison."

"I'm not sure he's worthy of such pity from so beautiful a woman," Clay said, offering her a fresh napkin. She accepted it and dried her eyes. "Are you going back to the farm?" he continued, once she had regained some semblance of composure.

"What else can I do? I have no money, no house, and a boyfriend who lives out of the back of a camper."

Clay left the question open. "We can talk about this later," he said, as he laid a couple of dollars on the table for a tip.

Carolina did not press the issue, but said instead, "Are you going to continue with this treasure thing?"

"I honestly don't know. I felt it was insane at the start and my experiences of the last twenty four hours have only reinforced my original impression. I ought to just give it up. It's worse than a needle in a haystack."

They bought a battery and a few more supplies and returned to Clay's truck. The installation was easy in spite of the pain in his chest. Carolina sat in the cab, awaiting the signal to turn the ignition. As he was finishing tightening the second cable, he was startled to find a man standing by the truck. Clay stopped his work and said, "Morning."

"Somebody take your battery?" It was the vegetable man from around the corner. He wore a broad-brimmed straw hat, the kind with a clear, green celluloid insert in the bill.

"Yes, they did."

"Too bad. I figured something was up. Why there's been more traffic down this road the past day and a half than we usually see in a month."

"Really."

"Yeah. There was one bunch—three guys in a blue Chevy truck—that looked pretty rough. I betcha they was the ones that took your battery."

"Probably."

"You a caver?"

"Yeah."

The man smiled. He had a broken front tooth. "Looks like you took a little fall."

"Goes with the territory," Clay said, resuming his work.

"Which cave was you lookin' for?"

Be careful, Clay thought. "I used to go in Barley's Cave over the ridge here, but the owner closed it off. I just was scoutin' around, thought I might find another entrance."

"Yeah, that's too bad. Old man Woodall just don't take to people bein' on his property." The man then stepped around the front of the truck and peered over Clay's shoulder. "Looks like you about got it."

"Yeah. Hope it works." He signaled Carolina, and the engine turned over and caught. Clay closed the hood and brushed off his hands.

Then, for no apparent reason, other than to make conversation, the man said, "I see you got one of them metal detectors." Clay nodded his head in agreement. This fellow was observant. "Ever find much?"

"Bullets mostly," Clay said, moving toward the driver's door. "An occasional old coin." Carolina exited the truck, making room for Clay.

As he was climbing in, the man said, "I had a friend that found an old coin around here once."

Clay closed the door and rolled down the window. Unable to resist the further inquiry, he replied. "Oh, really. Whereabouts?"

The curious man pointed north. "Up north of here, on Sand Mountain as I recall. Kind of weird too, it was one of them pieces of eight."

Clay stopped one line of thinking and began another. "You say, a piece of eight?"

"Yeah, you know, like in the pirate movies."

Clay was uncertain as to whether they were talking about the same thing. "Did you actually see this coin?"

The man smiled again, pleased that Clay was suddenly interested in what he had to say. "Oh, sure. It was the size of a silver dollar." He held his fingers, thumb and index, in a circle. "Silver with Spanish writin'."

Clay opened the door and climbed out again. He glanced at Carolina, who stood stoically on the passenger side with her arms folded. "Let me make sure I've got this right. You have a friend who found a silver coin on his place, and the coin was covered with Spanish writing?"

The man's mouth twitched at one corner as he talked. "That's right, except it wasn't on his place. As I was sayin', that was another strange thing, he found it up *on* the mountain, in the woods somewhere. Ya see, there was an airplane that crashed up there, and he was helpin' out in lookin' for it and somehow found this coin."

"And you can't remember exactly where that was."

The man seemed genuinely sorry when he said, "Naw, I wasn't with 'em that day."

Clay now became effusive with his friendliness. "That sounds mighty interesting. I wouldn't mind goin' up there and running my detector around a little bit. Where might I find your friend?"

"Why he don't live around here no more. He moved his family up to Manoa a couple of years ago."

"Where's that?"

"Up in Tennessee. It's a commune."

Carolina covered her mouth with one hand. Clay cleared his throat. "Would you happen to have his address?"

"Not exactly, but my wife will. She and his wife were real close and write from time to time. If you want to stop by the house, I'll have her look it up for you."

"That would be mighty nice of you. Climb in and I'll give you a ride."

El Dorado, a kingdom somewhere between the Amazon and Peru. The name derives from an ancient custom by which once a year the king is covered in oil and then powdered with gold dust, thus becoming El Dorado, the "Golden One." In spite of all their riches, the people of El Dorado are not at all greedy and consider their treasures to be superfluous. The only use they have for their gold is as a thing of beauty, to adorn their palaces and temples; otherwise, they regard it as something far inferior to food and drink.

—ALBERTO MANGUEL AND GIANNI GUADALUPI,
THE DICTIONARY OF IMAGINARY PLACES

Carolina left the Jeep by the fire station in Trenton, and during the time it took to drive to Chattanooga, Clay had a shaking chill, and the pain in his chest changed in character. Only in response to Carolina's pleading did he agree to stop at an emergency room, by coincidence the same one that had initiated treatment on his father. He told the emergency room physician that he had fallen while rock climbing.

"Better than hang gliding," the doctor observed, while looking at the x-ray. "None of those walk in here. It looks like you've busted the right eighth rib, and I think a spot of pneumonia is developing under it. That's the very reason we don't bind people's chests anymore. You allergic to penicillin?"

They gave him an injection, a prescription for further antibiotics, and told him he needed to check in with his family doctor the following day. "Why don't I drive you on home?" Carolina said as he shuffled through the automatic doors leading to the visitors' parking lot.

"No. We need to follow up on this Manoa thing while the trail's hot."

"Now Clay, you know that's not true. You've been through enough for one weekend. Do you really think this fellow with the coin is going to move away tonight, just because he heard you were coming to see him?"

"Probably not, but I can rest in a motel as well as I can at home. My brother will just want me to come in to work."

They stopped at the crest of Monteagle Mountain for the night, but saw little of the community beyond the interior of the motel. Carolina went out for two milkshakes and a sack of burgers. According to the scale in the emergency room, Clay had lost four pounds during his ordeal in the cave. He ate his fill, took the second of the antibiotic capsules along with a pain pill, and collapsed onto the bed. He was asleep before Carolina could wash her face.

Upon awakening, Carolina left the Fred Astaire movie she was watching to run Clay yet another tub of hot water. He tried once again to reach his father, but there was still no answer. It was by now six o'clock Sunday night, and for the first time in the past two days he felt concern beyond that of his own safety. He had no basis for such a feeling other than from habit he expected Vernon to be home by this hour. He then called his brother, but instead talked to his sister-in-law. "John drove your Dad up to the airport on some sort of business. They said they were meeting someone, but didn't say whom," she informed him. "Do you want me to have him call you?" she asked.

"No, just tell them I got tied up down here in Alabama and won't be into work tomorrow. I'll try to get him at home later."

As he hung up the phone, Carolina said, "You're lucky you work with family. Anyone else would have fired you long ago."

Clay winced as he repositioned the pillow. "How true, how true," he agreed. "I'm basically no good to anybody." He pulled her toward him and said pitifully, "I need your help."

"How is that?"

"I've just experienced a flash of insight," he announced. Carolina was anticipating the worst. "I've decided to write a travel guide called 'The Treasure Hunter's Guide to Cheap Motels and Restaurants of the American South,' and I'll need you to edit it."

She pushed him away. "Oh, you're full of it. Anyway the title's much too long."

"Seriously, I'm hungry again."

"Do you want me to bring you something, or does the poor pitiful patient feel up to going out for his dinner?"

"Let's go out."

Clay took another pain pill as they walked out the door, and chased it with a beer he discovered behind the seat of the truck.

"Do you think you ought to mix all that?" Carolina asked.

"One beer isn't going to hurt me," he said indignantly.

Carolina drove them to a place she had noted on the way into town, "Sturgent's Kountry Kitchen." The restaurant served buffet-style and Clay opted for the "All You Can Eat—$8.95" special, which included a dessert bar. He fell asleep in the car on the way back to the motel. She guided him back to bed, where he remained until nine o'clock the following morning. He made a declaration of improved health while standing over the toilet, but Carolina was suspect. She had purchased a thermometer while filling the prescriptions and took his temperature while he sat up in the bed.

"Ninety-nine eight," Carolina reported. As Clay stepped into the hot shower with her, she watched his pale skin flare in the hot water and noticed that ten hours of sleep had not erased the subtle lines of fatigue around his eyes.

She cupped his face in her hand and said, "You look terrible. Are you sure you don't want me to take you home and let you rest up? You can see a doctor and get some more sleep. We can find this commune place next weekend or next month for that matter. It's not going anywhere."

Clay would have none of it. In contrast to the night before, his voice flared in anger, "Dammit, Carolina, lay off!" He stepped backward, out of the stream of water. "You don't understand what I'm feeling. I've got that . . . that premonition again." He was recalling the vision he had experienced in the darkness of the cave. "It's the same weird sensation—no, it's more than that—there's no hocus pocus about this one. This is no dream. It's a solid lead. I just know it. If you can't stand to watch me follow this thing through, then I'll drive you back to your car." She left the bathroom rather than confront him.

Clay would not look at her as he toweled dry by the bed. He wrapped the towel around his waist and picked up the phone. She ignored him in turn by reading the paper. Vernon finally answered.

"Clay, where in the world are you?"

"In some motel in Monteagle, Tennessee."

"What are you doing there?"

"It's a long story, but . . . ," Clay then related his account of the night in the cave, the beating, his encounter with Charlie Rose, and the discovery of the Spanish dollar. "Carolina seems to think her brother is running drugs and he suspected me of being a federal agent."

"Drugs—my God. And they broke one of your ribs?"

"That's what the doctor said. But don't worry, I'm better already."

"Did you call the police?"

"Not yet. I can't decide if I want to or not."

There was a silence at the other end of the line. When Vernon answered, his voice was filled with remorse. "Clay, I'm terribly sorry. I feel responsible for this. Why don't you come on home? You can pursue this coin thing when you feel better. It's not worth it."

"Dad, you're starting to sound like Carolina. I'm not going to let y'all talk me out of this. I refuse to give it up. I think I'm getting close and I'm determined to finish this search once and for all. When I finally walk away from it, that's it, I'm not looking back."

Vernon spoke very softly, "Son, you do what you need to do, but please don't take any unnecessary chances. God knows it makes me feel even worse not being able to help you. I want you back in one piece. One cripple in the family is enough."

"Dad, I appreciate your concern, but I'm not about to change my mind. Just stop for a minute and consider all we've been through. I wish you were here, but let's face it, you're not. It's up to me now."

Vernon paused so long at the other end that Clay wondered for an instant if he were still on the line. "Okay, I concede. It's all yours. Just be careful is all I ask."

"Well, if it makes you feel any better, let me promise you I'm not about to do anything stupid. I just want to talk to the guy."

"That sounds reasonable enough. Now tell me again where you'll be going from there."

Clay repeated the directions to Manoa. Carolina was peeking at the conversation from over the paper.

"And this is the fellow that found the coin on Sand Mountain?"

"That's what I was told."

"Damn. It sounds like more than a coincidence, doesn't it?"

"That's what I said."

"Okay. Please keep in touch."

"We will. Carolina's got your number."

"And Clay . . . "

"What?"

"I've got some other news."

"What's that?"

"Sara Weatherford is here. That's why John and I were in Knoxville."

"Well, Dad, that's great. I didn't realize you'd kept in touch."

There was a pause at the end of the line before Vernon continued. "Clay, we're going to be married."

Clay was dumbstruck. "Why, I had no idea. Well, Dad, that's wonderful. When?"

"We don't know yet. I proposed by phone last week. We might drive down to her place in Florida."

There was a second faint hitch in the conversation. Clay asked, "Does she, uh, know about the diary?"

"Yes and no," Vernon chuckled. "Yes, she knows about the diary. No, she doesn't know exactly how I found it. I simply told her that I chanced upon it while searching about Eldon's office."

"Good thinking."

"A husband has to have some secrets. Anyway, she's very enthusiastic about it. Wants to introduce me to some of Neptune's descendants and all."

"Well, I'm relieved. You never cease to surprise me. Carolina and I send you both our best."

"Thank you, son, and good luck. If anybody can see this thing through, you can. I'm counting on you."

"Don't worry. We can't miss."

Carolina tried to be cheerful during breakfast, but Clay remained morose and uncommunicative.

"So this is the doctor's widow from Arkansas that Vernon is going to marry."

"Yes. This whole situation gets more complicated with each passing day," he said with a frown.

"Are you in pain?" she asked.

"No," he said tersely. "No more than last night. Look, I'm sorry I blew up at you in the shower. This whole situation is about to drive me crazy, but I just can't give it up now."

It was a morning of threatening clouds and unexpected gusts of wind. A thunderstorm struck as they descended the mountain. After the rain passed, layers of ground fog filled the many hollows, and Carolina felt as if the dark clouds would soon recondense inside the cab of the truck itself. They drove toward Manoa in silence.

After two hours of secondary roads and lonely intersections, they entered the nondescript hamlet of Deaconville. Situated in the midst of the rolling farmlands and woods characteristic of middle Tennessee, its central attraction appeared to be the Big Dipper Drive-In. They stopped for a Coke and a Dipper Burger, and Carolina sought additional directions from the freckle-faced girl manning the window.

The woman pointed down the highway and said, "About ten miles, you can't miss it."

Twelve miles past the town limits, they came upon a simple wooden sign routed with the single word, Manoa, and above it, a well-rendered horn of plenty. Below was an addendum, a smaller sign added to the first, announcing "Visitors Welcome."

As Carolina turned into the drive, Clay said, "Truce."

"Okay," was her only reply.

The passage of the rain had cleansed and brightened the vegetation, and to the right side of the entrance was a broad, well-tended pasture, containing a herd of dairy cattle. Once beyond the field and inside the trees, they passed what appeared to be a house, a ramshackle frame structure with a geodesic dome incorporated into the roof line. Three small boys, eight to ten years of age, were tossing pebbles into a puddle at the roadside. One wore a tie-dyed T-shirt. Several additional signs led them onto a poorly drained gravel parking lot before a larger building that superficially resembled a dormitory. It was identified by a brightly labeled proclamation reading "The House of World Friendship." Numerous other buildings were to be seen scattered among the trees; some appeared to be dwellings, the others utility buildings of various sizes.

A half-dozen other vehicles were parked in the lot, and a woman descended from the covered porch as they stopped. In stature she was extraordinarily thin, and her long brown hair was pulled tightly to the back of her head. She wore a denim work shirt and a pair of wide-cut jeans bearing heavy embroidery around the cuffs.

"Welcome to Manoa. My name is Deborah," she said, raising her hand in greeting.

Clay reciprocated introductions and said, "We're looking for Winslow Mims. We called yesterday and talked to a lady here who gave us directions. What was her name, Carolina?" He remembered her name perfectly, but chose to be indirect.

"Lucy, I believe."

"I'll have to check and see where Winslow is today," the hostess said. By the inflection of her voice, they could expect a wait. "Why don't you come inside and have a look around?" She escorted them into an informal reception room and offered them a seat in one of several worn, overstuffed chairs. As she was leaving she said, "And help yourself to the cookies."

Clay walked along her line of sight to a large plate of cookies, each the size of a saucer. He picked the smallest one to sample.

"What kind is it?" Carolina asked.

"I can't say for sure. Cashew-oatmeal maybe? Whatever, it's really good." He picked up a second one and handed it to her, while keeping a third one for himself.

The rough-paneled walls were covered in pictures and framed newspaper clippings, along with slogans and articles of one kind or another espousing various causes or explaining the philosophy of Manoa and its inhabitants. Carolina walked over to a prominent display standing on a nearby table, parallel columns of cubbyholes holding a multiplicity of pamphlets. She picked up one dealing with passive solar technology. Clay walked to the rear of the room and looked beyond the wide doorway into another larger room filled with long lines of tables—a dining hall. The faint smell of the kitchen hung in the air.

"I've read about this place before," said Carolina. "I just couldn't remember the name. A girl I knew at school visited here once."

A bearded man entered the room and introduced himself simply as Albert. "I understand you are looking for Winslow."

"Yes, we are. We were given his name by Quentin Walker, an old friend of his."

"Winslow is working in the dairy today. Why don't you follow me?"

They left by the front entrance and followed a path through the trees. They passed a playground for children and a whimsical house adorned with several dozen whirligigs. Clay asked about an unadorned rectangular building marked as "Soy Dairy."

"One of our communal industries. We manufacture tofu." Albert pointed out another unnamed building beside the one in question. "And that's where we grow our bean sprouts."

"You don't say. Very interesting." Clay glanced at Carolina and raised his eyebrows. "I know everyone asks this question, but how did Manoa come to be?"

Albert, who had cultivated a soft, mesmerizing voice, smiled a quiet smile and began his canned reply, "In 1969, a busload of individuals left Oregon seeking an alternative lifestyle, a way of living at peace with the natural order. Their leader was a psychologist and teacher, Harold Lysom, who, more than anyone else, was the one that decided to end their odyssey here."

"How did he happen to choose this spot?"

"He felt a special energy emanating here."

"I see." Clay glanced to Carolina a second time. "How long have you been here?"

"I came here in 1975. I'm originally from Canton, Ohio."

"Home of the Football Hall of Fame."

"Yes, I believe it is," the guide answered without any further elaboration.

"Is Mr. Lysom still living here?" Clay continued.

"Oh, yes."

Albert led them past an extensive vegetable garden, three plastic-sheathed greenhouses, and the first of two large barns. They walked inside the second of these where two men and a single woman were working. Albert asked one of the men where he might find Winslow, and the man pointed to the rear of the building. There, in a brightly lit workroom, with a milking machine partially disassembled in front of him, was yet another man, dressed in a khaki work shirt and sporting a magnificently bushy mustache. Albert once more asked where they might find Winslow.

"He was helping me earlier, but we weren't doing much good, so he said he was going down to the pond for a few minutes."

"Find out what the trouble is?"

"It's the main pump. We'll have to order another one."

Albert led them from the confines of the barn and into the open woods. "Winslow is our best mechanic and . . . ," he gave dramatic pause, "one of our freer spirits."

"Are you telling us he can be hard to find?"

Their guide turned slightly and smiled his enigmatic smile but declined for the moment to say anything further. The path descended slightly, crossed by a small, untended field with a margin of beehives, and then, through the trees, Clay caught a glimpse of green water. The pond appeared to cover several acres. Tied to a rickety dock in front of them was a small rowboat partially filled with rainwater. Beyond it duckweed grew in the shallows and a wood duck box leaned into a mature clump of cattails. The banks of the pond were entirely grown up with alder and willow, but on the far side, roughly opposite the dock, this dense undergrowth was broken by a grassy clearing. Albert indicated that they should follow him in circling the edge of the pond.

To one side of the clearing and unappreciated due to the angle of their arrival, stood a tepee, life-sized from what Clay could see of it.

"What's this?" Carolina asked.

"Oh, it's from our early days. We keep it here as a private place, a memorial of sorts."

Standing before the tent, staring out at the silver surface of the water with hands clasped behind his back, was a man with flaming red hair.

"Yo, Winslow." The man turned. His beard was the same color as his hair.

"Howdy, Albert."

Winslow was a very big man, big arms, big hands, big face. He appeared to be in his early forties and smiled broadly at their approach, a big unrestrained smile, of the sort usually confined to children. The sleeves of his faded flannel shirt were cut off just above the elbow, and in his left hand he held a small bouquet of wildflowers.

"Sorry to disturb your meditation, but these folks here are looking for you."

"No problem. Just pickin' some flowers for the table."

Clay made introductions once again, and Albert excused himself and disappeared back the way they had come.

"Lucy said that you were a coin collector?" Winslow began.

"Not exactly," Clay replied. "I am a spelunker, a caver, but I am also interested in Indian and early American artifacts. I happened to run into your friend Quentin, and he told me the story of your finding a Spanish coin."

"Yessir, a real Spanish dollar, eight reales, minted in Mexico City in 1795," Winslow said with some authority.

"You seem to remember it well."

Winslow's smile faded and he said, "It ain't the sort of thing a person would soon forget."

"Do you still have the coin?"

"No, 'fraid not. It's long gone. Sold it to a dealer. Didn't get much for it. Turned out they aren't all that rare."

"Do you remember where you found it?"

"Yes, but it's been a long time gone."

"Tell us about it."

"It was back 'bout eight or nine years ago. I was living up on Sand Mountain then, and a light plane went down in a storm. Well, they couldn't spot it from the air, but a deer hunter claimed he heard the plane having trouble, and a bunch of us volunteered to help look for it. It was in the winter, cold as a witch's tit as I recall, and me and another guy were walkin' up on Savage Creek when it started to rain. We continued on up the hill and picked up another creek, when all of a sudden the wind started blowing down this canyon like four hundred hells, and we got up under this big rock to get out of the weather. Anyway, we was just sittin' there feelin' sorry for ourselves, and I happened to look down and there it was."

"The coin?"

"Yeah. It was just laying there in the rocks waitin' to be picked up. It was so tarnished that it looked almost like a rock itself, but the shape of it caught my eye. I took it as a sign."

"And you only found the one?"

"We looked all over for some more, but that's all we came up with."

A fish struck near the center of the pond and concentric waves circled toward the banks. "Do you think you could find that place again—the place where you found the coin?"

"I probably could, although all those rocks start lookin' the same once you're up in 'em."

"I could make it worth your while."

Winslow began to swing the flowers back and forth at his side as if the offer made him nervous. "You know, I'm pretty busy around here. I got a family and all."

Clay did not let up. "How much?"

"And I'll have to check with my wife and some of the others."

"We'll only be gone for the day." Winslow's resolve wavered. "Would one hundred dollars do it?"

The big man smiled. "Sure. When do you want to get started?"

"How about first thing in the morning?"

"No problem." He offered his free hand and said, "Deal?" They shook hands. "Y'all got a place to stay?"

Carolina stepped up for the first time, "Why, no, we don't."

"Well, then, why don't you stay with us? We got some guest quarters, really more like a bunkhouse, and the food is real reasonable if you're keen on vegetables."

"You don't look like you suffer for it," Clay observed with a grin.

Winslow patted his ample midriff and replied, "No, can't say that I do." He walked over and closed the flap on the tepee.

"What did you mean, when you were speaking of the coin, that you took it as a sign?" Carolina asked.

Winslow smiled again and pointed toward the water, "Like that fish." Clay and Carolina looked out over the pond, but there was no fish to be seen. He continued, "The fish that jumped. He was probably telling me to be careful. Nature is all around us, and it talks to us all the time, but few of us want to listen."

"If the fish told you to be careful, why did you agree to come with us?"

"Sign or no sign, I need the money. I can still be careful, can't I?"

Carolina continued with her original question, "What sort of sign was the coin? It certainly wasn't a sign from nature."

Winslow laughed this time, "That's right, pretty lady. It sure wasn't, and it brought me nothin' but a whole lot of bad luck."

"How so?" Clay asked.

"I can't be too specific other than to say I didn't feel the same as long as I had it."

"And your luck changed when you sold it?"

"After a while it did. I was glad to get rid of the thing." From his tone, Winslow let it be known that he preferred not to discuss any further mystical implications of his find and began walking back toward the barns.

Not to be deterred, Carolina fell in immediately behind him, and persisted with her gentle interrogation, "Winslow, would you mind if I asked you one more little question?"

"Not as long as it ain't got nothin' to do with that damn coin."

"I simply wanted to ask you, what does Manoa mean?"

He kept on walking, talking over his shoulder, "It was the capital of El Dorado, the lost kingdom of gold."

All the wealth he had gathered in the days gone by
They placed in the cavern then left him to die.
Many years have gone by, and the legend's still told,
And the white man's still searching for Chief Sawnee's gold.

—FOREST C. WADE,
"CHIEF SAWNEE," CRY OF THE EAGLE

A feeling of apprehension churned in Clay's gut the entire night. As he lay there in the dark, staring at the ceiling, his mind was tantalized by the remote chance of success, while at the same time the voice of reason dictated otherwise. When combined with his pain, this conflict proved a potent stimulant, and even pharmacological aid produced only a fitful sleep. He awoke to find himself an energized sleepwalker, physically exhausted while his mind raced on, refusing to show any sign of fatigue.

Their accommodations, a barren pine-paneled room in one of the outbuildings, were more than adequate, although he and Carolina had been forced to occupy separate beds. He awoke with the sunrise and lay awake for a full hour before finding enough energy to rise. They did have access to a shower down the hall, a no-nonsense fiberglass stall with an attendant notice reading, "Conserve energy and water—please limit to five minutes." His body temperature remained normal, and Carolina, acting as nurse, dutifully dosed him with antibiotics according to schedule. They ate breakfast in the dining hall—stone-ground cream of wheat and honey, homebaked bread, and a variety of fruits. Clay left a donation of thirty dollars in lieu of actual payment, a custom which was frowned upon, and they walked to the truck carrying their single grip.

Carolina was wearing Clay's last clean T-shirt. Winslow, sporting a blue ball cap with a gold *M* above the bill, was waiting for them as planned. His hair stuck out from under the hat like a flaming doughnut, appearing somewhat like a blue-collar Bozo the Clown. He wore spotlessly clean overalls, and seemed slightly embarrassed when Carolina complimented him on his appearance. "My wife always wants me to look smart around strangers. I guess women are supposed to have all the manners."

Clay let Carolina drive while he lay down in the back of the camper. When reviewing the maps with Winslow, he found that the locale where the doubloon was found was at least ten miles outside the search radius he and Vernon had established. The location spoke once again of the varying scale of the waybill and the inexact nature of Neptune's description. The canyon in question was somewhere along the western edge of Sand Mountain where it abutted the Tennessee River. "I'll know it when I see it," was about as specific as Winslow offered to be.

Towers of cumulus clouds rose ahead of them, the forerunners of afternoon thunderheads. The spring had been unusually dry and warm, and Clay wondered if the weather had chosen this very day to change. He pulled the metal detector free and checked the earphones and leads. Satisfied with its operation, he fell asleep. Several minutes later, after crossing the Tennessee River, Carolina pulled onto the shoulder, and the change in road sound roused Clay from his sleep. With the river at their backs and Sand Mountain looming over them, the three adventurers studied a well-marked road map spread across the tailgate of the pickup. Winslow dragged his finger along one line and then another before saying, "We go on like we're going until we turn here on State Road 161. It's no more than five miles to the turnoff after that."

Carolina pulled back onto the highway at Winslow's direction. Clay continued to study the map. "Remember all that talk about luck?" he said. He was also looking at a much-folded copy of the waybill.

"Yes," she answered.

"Well, if we ever find that pot of gold, luck will have led us to it. I would have never found this place in a million years without bumping into Winslow's buddy. Dad and I weren't even in the ballpark. The distance between the eastern edge of Sand Mountain and the canyon we're looking for is almost twice the distance we had figured."

"No need to feel ashamed about it," she said. "Luck, be it good or bad, is a part of most equations."

The road eased away from the river, and they drove past scattered small farms and scores of ubiquitous house trailers. Just after passing a two-pump country store, they left the pavement and drove down a dirt road for several more miles. They passed into a hollow, a broad, level erosion cutting deeply into the flank of the mountain. The valley narrowed rapidly, and the road ended abruptly before yet another trailer. The screen door hung open and there were no cars to be seen other than a derelict Pontiac, stripped of its wheels and left stranded upon short stacks of concrete blocks.

"I used to know the boy that lives here," Winslow said.

"Let's hope he still does," commented Carolina, sounding none too confident.

As Clay and Winslow prepared to unload the camper, a brisk wind swept up the valley, and the sky suddenly darkened. The low rumble of thunder followed the wind, and a huge mass of black cloud filled the western horizon.

"Why don't we sit here for a few minutes and see what it's going to do?" Clay suggested, choosing to temper his impatience in the face of the approaching storm. He and Carolina remained in the cab while Winslow stretched out in the truck's bed.

"You still got that premonition?" she asked.

"I really feel more uneasy than anything. I just want to keep moving."

"How's the rib?"

"The same, although I'm feeling better in general. Winslow can carry the heavy stuff."

The wind picked up, pushing the tops of the trees in all directions. Clay glanced through the rear window. Winslow had his hands behind his head and appeared to be dozing. A few oversized raindrops smacked into the windshield and then, without the least warning, a wave of pea-sized hail fell upon the metal hull of the camper body. The clatter of its impact caused Winslow to sit bolt upright.

"Great, just great," Clay winced. "I guess this is the bad luck."

The falling ice continued for another three or four minutes, and then the rain picked up, a solid sheet of rain, obliterating the landscape around them, the only illumination coming from bursts of light somewhere overhead. Winslow tapped on the glass and Clay turned to face him. His eyes seemed to protrude from his face, and he mouthed some words that could not be heard above the din of the storm.

"What's he trying to say?" asked Clay.

"I think he's saying this is a bad sign," Carolina replied. "Or maybe it's some sort of prayer."

The rain persisted another ten minutes and then stopped as abruptly as it had begun. The sky lightened to an uneven gray. A litter of torn leaves and twigs covered the road and the patches of bare earth before the trailer.

"Storm make you nervous, Winslow?"

"Maybe. I'm just glad it's past. Reminds me too much of the last time I was up here—only a lot warmer."

"Don't worry. Look over there, blue sky's a-coming," Clay said, pointing to the west while trying to sound optimistic.

"Yeah. I see it."

They unloaded the rope, the filthy day pack, a camp shovel, and the metal detector. Winslow took a special interest in the detector. "I always wanted to operate one of these gizmos."

"How far is it, would you say?" Clay asked.

"Two, three miles, I reckon. There used to be a path started behind this trailer. It leads up this draw, along the dry creek."

Clay shouldered the pack with a grunt and said, "Y'all get started. I want to lock the truck."

This small lie was necessary to cover his reaching under the front seat to find the hidden pistol, the same one he had fired at Bait. He quickly cinched up the pack, locked the doors as promised, and ran after the other two.

They first encountered a heap of trash festooned with a discarded washing machine, but once past this mess they walked in a mature forest, largely undisturbed by human activities. The trail soon left the rocky streambed and cut sharply to the right to begin a steep climb. The sun broke through at their backs, and their shadows came and went with the passage of clouds. The temperature, which had dropped with the storm, began to rise again, and the air slowed and thickened with humidity.

Winslow talked steadily as they walked. "I'm originally from Muscle Shoals, but my first wife was from Bridgeport, and we moved back over here after I got out of the navy."

"How long were you married?"

"About three years."

"Any kids?"

"No. She wouldn't have any, which, looking back on it, was good for the both of us. I wouldn't have been much of a daddy in those days."

"How'd you end up in Manoa?"

"Another woman. I'm afraid I'm stuck with this one," he chuckled.

They passed by a large white oak tree that gave the illusion of having split a large boulder. "I remember that tree," Winslow remarked.

The heat was beginning to make Clay light-headed, and his legs felt wobbly. "You've got a good memory. How much further?"

"Hmmm, seems like about a mile, but it could be two. I ain't never been much good on distances in the woods. This trail starts to peter out soon, and anyways we didn't stick to it toward the end."

Clay stumbled once and almost fell. "You gonna make it?" Carolina said, slowing to take his arm.

"It entirely depends on how much further we have to go," he answered weakly. "I can't handle much more of this climbing without some rest."

As Winslow has predicted, the trail for one reason or another became less distinct and was overgrown at intervals by masses of chest-high blackberry bushes. Winslow plowed ahead, seemingly impervious to the brambles. Clay and Carolina doggedly followed him, heads down, trying to ignore their growing discomfort until they entered a clearing of sorts; a large tree had been uprooted, tearing a hole in the canopy, giving access to a partial view of the valley below. Rather than enjoy the scenery, Winslow stared intently into the undergrowth. "Wait here," he grunted. He put down the metal detector and stomped off into the woods, disappearing almost as soon as he stepped from the trail, seemingly intent on bushwhacking straight across the steep incline.

"Come over here and sit down," Carolina said. "You need to rest when you can or you'll never make it." She pulled a can of Coke from the day pack before he could stop her, but said nothing of the gun. "Let's split it." The drink was warm, and the carbonation burned at his mouth and throat.

"I hope to God he knows what he's doing."

"Whether he does or not, I have the feeling that old hippie will come through for us," she said.

A full twenty minutes later, Winslow was back, sweating like a steer, having soaked through the sweat band of his cap. "Come on, I'm pretty sure I found it."

Clay struggled to his feet and pulled the pack after him as Carolina shouldered the heavy coil of nylon climbing rope. After an indeterminate and painful distance, they encountered a cascade filled with a turbulent stream of water, runoff from the thunderstorm.

"We need to go down this cut and then across," Winslow indicated, nodding below to where the stream's descent became more reasonable. They crossed without major difficulty. Clay slipped once again, but was able to catch himself with his hands. Winslow took no notice of this mishap and continued on, straight up the slope without even so much as a glance to his rear. The ascent became so steep for a time that they were reduced to using saplings and rocky outcrops as handholds. After a climb of two hundred feet, they entered the mouth of a narrow, hanging canyon, where the stream to their left disappeared under a boulder field and man-sized rocks sprouted among the trees like giant mushrooms.

Winslow finally halted his reckless charge, stopping to remove his hat and wipe his florid face on his sleeve. Clay bent from the waist, resting his hands upon his knees, while trying to catch his breath. The pain in his chest was excruciating. Carolina stood next to him, slumped under the weight of the rope. "I'm sure this is it," Winslow said. "Seems like it was up to the right, but with all the leaves out, it's hard to say."

He moved forward into the rocks by himself and was soon calling to them. His shout encouraged Clay, who felt the surge of a second wind as if for the first time since leaving Manoa, he was certain of where he was. He reached out and gripped Carolina's wrist and said, "Come on, we can't wimp out now, this could be it."

Winslow was waiting for them under a deeply eroded rock overhang. The lip of this natural shelter was framed in wild grapevines, several of which looped down to curtain the broad opening. The floor was dry and covered in a veneer of rock flakes exfoliated from the roof overhead. The tubular egg cases of countless dirt daubers clung to the ceiling, and clusters of spent hickory shells were scattered along the back wall.

Clay squatted down in the cool shadow. He said nothing for a moment, no thank you, no superlatives, no exclamations, until, reaching overhead to touch the rock, he began to recall once more Neptune's experience, attempting to conjure up the images formed around the words, casting aside his assumptions in favor of the reality of this place, trying to fuse the present with the obscure and distant past.

"This is where I found it, all right." The spell was broken. In lieu of an immediate response, Winslow repeated the declaration, "I said, this is where I found it. Right here. Ain't no doubt about it."

"Does this fit?" asked Carolina.

"It fits very well," answered Clay. "The canyon, the ledge, the coin, it all fits." He looked to Carolina and blinked. "It just doesn't seem possible, after all this time."

Winslow took the harness of the metal detector from around his shoulder and pushed it toward Clay. "Why don't you fire this thing up? That's what we busted butt to come up here and do, ain't it?"

"You do know how to work it, don't you?" Carolina asked.

"We're about to find out. It worked well enough in my back yard." Clay duckwalked from beneath the overhang and fastened the harness of the detector across his shoulder. After attaching the earphones, he swung the searchcoil to and fro and dialed the adjustments. When satisfied, he moved the phones to around his neck and said to Winslow, "Now show me again where you found the coin."

Winslow crawled the length of the shelter before answering, "I was hunkered down just about right here and looked down and there it was."

"Move over and let me run the detector through there." Carolina and Winslow stood back as Clay swept the coil over the layers of splintered rock and dust. Immediately the headphones began to whine. "This is too easy. I've got something." He localized the signal, and Carolina began to dig at that point using the folding shovel. She worked slowly and after about six inches hit solid rock. "I don't see anything," she said.

Clay unhooked the detector and began to sift the dirt she had excavated. "Look," he said, displaying a cylindrical brassy object in the palm of his hand. He rubbed the adhering dirt away on the pocket of his shorts.

"Looks like a bullet," Winslow observed.

"A thirty-thirty shell casing," Clay said. "At least we know the machine works." Continued searching beneath the overhang produced no further signals.

"Now what?" Carolina asked.

Clay studied the site and thought for a moment, recalling Neptune's account from memory, ". . . *and we climbed for such a distance that I thought the fall must have rendered him mad. When almost all breath had left me we passed between several large boulders and came to a high cliff face where scattered among the rocks were a vast number of coins.*" He looked up the canyon and said, "It's up there somewhere, probably against this side of the cliff."

"What are you talking about?" Winslow asked, realizing that there might be more to this than meets the eye.

Clay knew that at some point he would have to share more information with his guide. Until now, Winslow had displayed good faith, and the same intuition that had led them this far told Clay that the man could be trusted. However, his need for candor was balanced by the reassurance of the pistol buried at the bottom of the pack. "Winslow, it would take too much time for me to tell you the whole story, but just suffice it to say that I have good reason to believe that there may be other coins besides the one that you found here." He zipped the pack as Winslow collected the heavy nylon rope. They resumed climbing.

There was no level ground in the canyon; the floor rose steeply on both sides of the watercourse, irregularly palisaded by outcrops of limestone and rubble fallen from the cliffs above. Just how far Neptune ventured from the shelter was uncertain, but Clay was confident from the symbols on the waybill that the cave, if it existed, lay close at hand. He reasoned that by climbing away from the water course and skirting the foundation of the cliff, the description in the diary and the symbols on the waybill would somehow coalesce. The one definitive point of reference was that as depicted in the map, this canyon bifurcated as it narrowed. The cave symbol was centered midway along the southern wall.

"I hate to be contrary, but do you have any idea where you're going?" Carolina asked.

"Trust me."

They came to a small rockslide, and Clay raised an open hand. His head swam from hyperventilating. "Let's rest for a minute and let me think about this," he gasped, as he sat down on a convenient rock.

"Do you mind at least telling us what we're supposed to be looking for?" Carolina asked. Her T-shirt was soaked through and smeared with streaks of grime.

Winslow's face had grown explosively red. A stream of perspiration dripped from tip of his nose. "Oh, man," he wheezed. "You're sure gettin' your money's worth out of this old boy."

Clay was unmoved. He tried to ignore the boring ache in his chest. Blood pounded in his ears. "This canyon is supposed to fork up ahead. At that point the main cliff should veer further to the right. We should find large boulders, larger than we've seen until now and probably a pile of broken rock much like this one." He wiped his eyes on his sleeve. "Let's go."

Not fifty yards beyond their resting place, the cliff did turn slightly, and Clay spotted a prominent point of rock jutting above the trees like the prow of a ship. "Look close now. This could be it." They paused at the foot of another slide, this one older, faded, starting to disappear under pockets of shrub and ground cover. Its bulk was piled against and around a series of automobile-sized rocks. Clay dropped the pack, and stood gazing across the slope before turning to trace the eighty feet of rock rising vertically above the slide. "This looks right." He shook his head in agreement with his own conclusion. "Yeah, this could be it. Y'all just have a seat and have that shovel ready."

Clay readjusted the detector and began to work his way across the jumble of broken limestone, overlapping each pass of the coil, trying to make sure that he left no area of ground uncovered. The tough shrubbery made his efforts more difficult, but he did not hurry. It took him a half hour to cover the near side of the slide and during that period of time, he was isolated from all other stimuli—the headphones assured that—causing him to focus only on the signal, the monotonous baseline whine that reflected the state of the electromagnetic field generated by the coil. Finally, as he neared the top, near the cliff base, he shouted, "I've got something here!"

The maximal amplitude of the signal lay to one side of an oblong patch of grass-covered soil. The soil proved to be only eight inches deep overlying a layer of compacted shards. Winslow attacked this debris with the shovel, and the clanging of steel against stone echoed down the narrow ravine. Carolina sifted each spadeful of dirt by hand as Clay stood by.

"Look," was all that she said when she encountered the first coin. Clay thrust both fists into the air and began to hop up and down, at least as far as his broken rib would allow. He poured water from a plastic bottle over the coin. After the dirt was carefully brushed away, Winslow declared it to be a Spanish dollar. "Looks to be Mexican silver. 1797. Yessirree. Seein's believin'," he declared.

Carolina could only shake her head and repeat, "I can't believe it, Clay. It's just like you said it would be."

Clay redonned the phones and continued the search. Over a period of forty-five minutes, they located five more coins, all Spanish dollars, buried from six to ten inches below the ground. The coins were scattered at irregular distances across the top of the slide, all within thirty feet of the canyon wall, consistent with Clay's assumption that they had come to rest as the result of a fall. He persisted down the far side of the slide, but found no more coins. Once he was confident that the area of William Hand's fall had been covered, he removed the harness and called up to the others, "I'm gonna have a look up ahead."

Staying as close to the cliff as possible, he walked to the end of the side canyon, a distance of about a quarter mile. Other than a few minor fissures, he saw no evidence of a cave or other obvious hiding place. As he started to return, pondering the mystery of Hand and Neptune, a great weariness swept over him. The sum of the years followed in its wake, all the clues, all the false leads, all the assumptions, and then in quick succession, a series of images raced through his mind, each more vivid than the last, leading him toward a conclusion: *"He said he had gathered eagle feathers here as a boy. . . . scattered among the rocks were a vast number of coins. At his instruction, I retrieved these coins and placed them in the box broken by his fall."* He found Carolina and Winslow lounging in the bright sun with the equipment piled between them.

"Well, you did it," she said, smiling broadly.

"Better, *we* did it," he replied.

"Anyplace else you want to look?" Winslow asked.

Dreamily, as if talking to himself, Clay walked to the mass of the mountain rising above them and looked up, "There's a cave here somewhere. There has to be."

"I doubt you'll find it up there," Carolina commented wearily.

The surface of the limestone was worn by water and spotted with lichen. Smooth as concrete, it was broken at twelve feet by a narrow ledge. There, the climbable rock veered left, bending upward at an angle approaching sixty degrees, interrupted by handy ledges and cracks, some wide enough to support vegetation, air gardens of shrub and stunted pine. At thirty-five feet a spartan colony of trees mixed with laurel sprouted from the cliff face, indicating a wider ledge perhaps, and above it the rock turned and vaulted skyward at ninety degrees. "We need to get up there," Clay said.

"And how in the Sam Hill are you supposing to do that?" asked Winslow before taking a swallow from the water bottle.

"You need to boost me up to that near ledge, or vice versa. Whoever climbs up first will need enough muscle to pull themselves up. Once secure to that point, the rest looks like an easy scramble."

"So you think the cave's up there?" Carolina said.

Clay turned to the two of them. "William Hand, the one-time owner of these coins, hid a cache of money somewhere in this canyon. My information says that he fell at a spot like this, something we confirmed by finding these coins. In addition, the map shows two symbols, a darkened circle drawn next to a Cherokee monster, called an Uktena, a symbol of the underworld. I believe these tell us that a cave is located somewhere in this cliff and that Hand fell during a rainstorm while climbing down with his money. The strongbox he was carrying broke open with the fall, which explains the coins we found."

Winslow, seemingly ready for most anything, replied, "Well, you've sure been right on until now, and I'm ready to help you out, but it ain't gonna be as easy as you say gettin' up there."

After some discussion concerning Clay's ability to pull himself up to the ledge, he elected to squat and let Winslow stand on his shoulders. Only with great effort and Carolina's help was he able to rise to his feet under Winslow's considerable weight. Steadying himself against the rock, Winslow grabbed the ledge, swinging one leg up until his heel caught. He hung in this awkward position for a moment, then let his leg fall free. "This ain't gonna work. I'm afraid I wasn't built to be no acrobat," he said.

"Is there anything you can get a rope around?" Clay grunted through clinched teeth, shuddering with the effort.

"Maybe. Let me down."

"My pleasure."

Winslow removed his shirt and tied it around a spherical stone the size of a baseball. He then secured the rope to this weight and, by swinging it around his head like a lariat, managed, after several mighty attempts, to loop the rock and the trailing rope around a small tree. Whether it would support his weight remained to be seen. He mounted Clay's shoulders with the help of the rope and within a few seconds was standing on the ledge. He hauled Clay up with ease, followed by the pack and the coil of rope. Taking advantage of every available foothold, the two men worked their way along the steep incline until confronted by a thicket of tangled undergrowth clinging to the mountainside. Using the contorted trunk of a scrub oak for support, Clay managed to gain a precarious seat on the uppermost ledge. He secured the end of the rope to the same tree with a bowline.

"I've got to rest for a minute. My damn side's killing me again." he told Winslow. The ledge was several feet wide and more or less horizontal. Clay pushed aside a low shrub and, by leaning backward, touched his shoulder to the rock. As he reclined in this awkward position, something incongruous caught his eye. A few yards to his right, the homogeneous texture of the cliff's substance was broken by a fissure. The air flowing from this opening in the rock bore an unmistakable coolness.

"Do you see anything?" Carolina called up from below.

"Yes," he replied as he rolled to his hands and knees and began worming between the cliff and the wiry mass of vegetation that filled the ledge. "Stay put for a minute," he called back to Winslow. Upon reaching the fissure, he broke off the last few resisting branches with his gloved hands and at long last confronted his private demon. There it was. Within arm's length after all this time. A narrow opening emitting a powerful stream of subterranean air.

He tried to swallow, but could not. "The cave—it's here. I found it," he croaked.

"He found it!" Winslow echoed. "You want me to pull up the rest of the stuff?"

"How about handing me the pack, then go back down and help Carolina with the detector?"

While waiting for his companions to return, Clay switched on the headlamp and peered into the blackness of the cave's entrance. He savored the rush of cold, sterile air. Strangely enough, he did not relish the moment for its promise of imagined treasure, nor did he recount his many ordeals in reaching this hidden place, but instead regressed to a memory from his childhood, of a book telling of an ancient tomb, of a catacomb overlooked by eons of grave robbers, his standing by the broken seal, pausing to regale in that shortest of moments which flashes brilliant just before the final victory, the exhilaration felt at the instant of life's foremost checkmate.

He then thought of his father and their last conversation and was saddened that he could not share this remarkable achievement with the man most responsible for its undertaking.

Clay removed his spectacles and carefully wiped away the dirt and condensation. He felt unusually calm and focused. A small mound of rocks was piled across the cave's entrance, and he went to work to remove what little obstruction remained. Whether the rocks were placed there to close or conceal the entrance, he could not say.

Winslow and Carolina soon reached the ledge in tandem; Carolina with her hair secured in a blue bandanna, Winslow with the detector draped across his back. Clay pulled two hand lights from the pack and distributed them. He felt as if he should say something momentous, but the words were not there. Finally, taking a deep breath, he said simply, "Stay close."

The initial passageway gently descended, curved faintly right, and then leveled out. Clay examined the ceiling, dragging his finger across the thin layer of carbon coating the rock. The carbon residue implied an open flame, a torch or tallow candle. "Watch your heads!" he called behind, remembering that neither of the others wore hard hats. He pushed the pack ahead of him.

After crawling sixty feet, the tunnel abruptly opened into the wall of a chamber, the dimensions of which were at first indefinite. Clay could clearly see the floor below, a drop he estimated at six to eight feet. He descended feet first, sliding down the face of an inactive flow stone to reach the bottom, where he turned to assist the others.

From this vantage the room was roughly circular, at least forty feet in diameter, with a ragged dome of a ceiling. In contrast to most caves in the area, perhaps owing to its position so far above the water table, the interior was unusually dry. At an angle of sixty degrees from their point of entry was the only apparent exit from the chamber, a narrow horizontal crevice along the base of the wall. The walls were otherwise featureless. The level floor was likewise, other than a uniform layer of beige dust. The same arid climate of the cave that allowed the accumulation of the dust imparted to it a most fortuitous quality; it recorded any disturbance to its surface in a most exacting manner. Recorded before them, fanning out from the base of the flowstone, was an unmistakable array of human footprints.

The majority of the prints led diagonally across the room to a broad shelf of rock that hugged the opposite wall. The symmetry of this feature made it appear manmade.

Winslow muttered in wonderment, "Shit fire, would you look at that?"

"What is it?" Carolina whispered.

"Pots," Clay said softly. "And some sort of statue." He slipped the pack from his back. "Don't anybody move. We want to do this right."

The welcome coolness of the cave's entrance was now a chill. Backlit by Carolina's beam, Winslow's head and beard were shrouded in columns of steam. Clay extended his arm and said, "Winslow, hand me the metal detector. We'll have to cover the whole room. Here, Carolina, hold my helmet and give me light."

Clay adjusted the earphones and then stepped forward, sweeping the coil before him. "Y'all stay right behind me. We don't want to disturb anything until we cover it with the detector."

The tracks forming the ill-defined path appeared to be of several vintages, many indistinct, merely depressions in the dust, while others appeared as if formed not an hour before. The apparent age of any given track did not necessarily conform with its contour, since many of the sharper, and presumably more recent impressions, were curiously indistinct, without a definitive heel. By contrast, several of the least distinct tracks bore a deep heel, as one might see on a boot.

"What do you make of these?" Clay asked, pausing in his search.

"Some of them look so fresh and rounded—like moccasin tracks," Carolina said in wonderment.

Clay glanced toward the shaded outline of her face, "Easy now."

"Well, they do."

"This damn place gives me the creeps," Winslow said. "This ole freak has always been partial to sunshine."

Clay twice adjusted the detector before continuing his slow advance across the room, following the faint indentations in the dust. The silence was so complete that Carolina was aware of the sound of her own breathing. Clay shuffled forward until he drew near the stone platform.

"Bring the lights," he said in a strange voice. "Walk where I walked."

Carolina and Winslow crowded at his back. The statuary had assumed the form of a bird, an unearthly creature carved from dark stone, perhaps eighteen inches in height. Flanking it were a number of earthen vessels, the largest shaped into the image of a man—or was it an animal—the likeness of some living thing possessing large eyes, a beaklike nose, and a grotesque expression. Lying before this effigy was a disc crafted from flint as well as a long bone, a femur, large enough to be a man's.

"Holy Jesus," Winslow mumbled.

"It looks like an altar," Carolina said. "What do you think it means?"

"I have no earthly idea," Clay answered, "But these objects are not here by accident. I have a feeling this room was used by someone long before the appearance of William Hand."

"The Indian?" Winslow asked.

"Yes. The man I've been following," Clay answered. "He cached some money in this cave one hundred and fifty years ago."

"What's that along the back?" Carolina said, directing her light to the rear of the platform. "It looks woven."

Clay stepped forward and went to one knee. "As best I can tell, it appears to be what's left of a wicker basket."

"What would that have to do with Mr. Hand?"

"Again, I can only speculate. But from what I know of Chero-kee myth, it would take a very brave man to venture into this place. They believed that caves were entrances to the underworld, places inhabited by evil spirits and all sorts of monsters. Only a medicine man with the most powerful magic would ever think of coming here."

Clay then swung the electric coil across the array of artifacts. "I'm getting a strong signal."

Carolina followed the muffled whine of the detector and pointed, "You're over the big pot in the center. Something must be inside!" She handed Winslow her flashlight and slipped around Clay. It took both hands for her to lift the effigy jar from its pedestal. Winslow projected the beam from both lamps into the interior. Something reflective caught the light.

"Would you look at that," Carolina murmured in amazement.

"I don't know that I'm ready for this," Clay said, hesitating to take what was offered him.

"Go ahead," she whispered.

He reached into the narrow opening at the top of the vessel and a tingle of energy coursed through his hand as he touched something ice cold. He grasped the heavy disc gently and lifted it for all to see. It was a coin, a golden coin, as bright and lustrous as the day it was struck. He centered it in his trembling hand.

"Well, I'll be damned," Winslow said, stupefied by what he had just witnessed.

"Is it the coin you wanted?" Carolina asked.

Clay brought the treasure toward his face. He blew across its surface and held it closer to the light. Reading aloud, he said, "Georgia Gold, 1830." He then turned the coin over, "Templeton Reid Assayer, Ten Dollars."

Carolina looked inside the vessel once again and said, "There's something else here."

Clay reached inside once more and withdrew a glassy object that was transformed into a transparent crystal by the artificial lights. A faint vein of red curled through its center.

"It's a crystal," Winslow mumbled.

"A divining crystal."

"Oh, man, old pots, bones, and now a magic crystal." Winslow said. He swayed back and forth as if suddenly uneasy. "Let me tell you, I know something about crystals and that one is real special—some sort of powerful magic. We ain't got no business foolin' with it. We need to show respect and leave it be."

"Your instincts are correct, Winslow. I plan to leave it. It was not meant for us," Clay said, returning the crystal to the vessel.

"I hate to keep repeating myself, but what is the significance of all this? Why was only the one coin left? And what's with these pots? Was it meant to be some sort of offering?" Carolina said, flashing her single conical beam across the rough hewn altar.

Clay shrugged and continued, "Who's to say? This is not at all what I expected. Maybe we missed something. Let's have another look around."

He retraced their steps using the detector, while Carolina and Winslow covered the walls and ceiling with their lights. At one point close by the entry, Clay suddenly crouched and began digging at the floor.

"Did you find something?"

"No. I didn't find a damn thing. This dust is not more than a few inches deep. Let's have a look at the other passage."

The fissure leading from the treasure room was barely eighteen inches high. Clay pushed his way several yards into it before it narrowed even further. He could see no sign of anyone's having preceded him.

"It would take a rat to crawl through here!" he shouted.

He backed his way out and pushed himself into a sitting position, slumping against the cold stone. He rubbed at his aching rib and allowed a groan. The circle of his headlamp fixed itself to the floor and did not move.

Carolina knelt beside him and placed her arm around his shoulder. "Clay, are you okay?"

"Somebody beat us to it."

"What?"

"You're right about those footprints. Somebody's been here since Hand."

"Who?"

"Hell if I know. Hand took his share. Maybe his brother came for his. Could be there's other people involved in this we don't even know about."

"You have to admit any of that is possible."

He continued as if he did not hear her. His chin remained on his chest. "I somehow thought it would be different. I had it all laid out in my mind—a chest of gold coins, a king's ransom, fame and fortune." He exhaled a great sigh and looked up, his light dancing across the rocky dome. He then laughed, "I feel like God's own fool! Is it possible to be elated and disappointed at the same time?"

"Sure," she said, "Every high has its low."

Clay rose to his feet. "There's a lesson here that I need to learn. But what is it?" He wiped at a moist eye hidden in darkness. "Like you say, 'What does it all mean?'"

He switched off the humming detector. "I think whoever placed these pots here was a believer. They had faith in the crystal and the mythology that provided its power. I don't think William Hand gave a damn. He was pragmatic to a fault. He simply needed a secure hiding place and, buddy, this is it. How he found out about this world-class hole in the wall will probably remain a mystery to all of us. Perhaps he chanced upon it—Neptune mentioned that he hunted here as a young man. Maybe the old shaman told him about it, who knows? But, why he left this gold piece, or if he left it at all, is the final irony in this story. Could be it was an offering as you said—a token meant to honor the spirit of his ancestors and assure his own good fortune," Clay mused. "We are fortunate to be standing here at all. I guess it's only fair that we not know all the answers."

Carolina carefully returned the effigy to its original position. She turned to Clay and hugged him in spite of the bulky detector slung over his shoulder. "Oh, Clay, don't worry about all the answers. Just be happy with what you've accomplished here! That's all you need to care about."

Winslow pulled at his beard. "Man, I thought I'd seen it all, but if this ain't about the weirdest thing I've ever been in on. . . . It's just like somebody left all this here for us to find."

Clay closed his fist on the golden coin and said, his determined voice tempered with finality, "Perhaps he did."

— · — · — · —

Mathis Ford
One Week Later

Clay was dreaming again, a pleasant, meaningless fantasy that would never reach the threshold of a memory. The bedroom was much too warm and he pushed back the sheet and rolled onto his right side. The still air smelled of old quilts and seasoned furniture and he found the silence comforting. He lay still for a time in that neutral position and listened for the pad of the cat, but was unrewarded by her approach. Beyond the single dusty window, the gray of dawn gave way to polychromatic sunlight and the promise of a new day. Soundlessly he sat up and studied the attitude of his sleeping lover, before circling the rumpled bed to kneel beside her. He caught her particular scent and gently kissed her upon her closed eye and drew back and whispered, "Carolina."

She did not change her expression or open her eyes, but inhaled deeply and exhaled, "Good morning."

He stroked her black hair and pulled some of it against his cheek. "Did you know that I love you?"

She reached out blindly and touched his forearm. "Yes."

"And I want you to stay here with me."

She opened her sleepy eyes, then raised the coverlet and drew him into the warmth and said, "If you want me to." She then kissed him in return and put her mouth close by his ear, "Is that a proposal?"

"Yes, it is a proposal."

She stiffened in his embrace and pushed away, throwing back her head to clear the hair from her face, a profoundly provocative move under any other circumstances, "That's not funny. It's much too early for that kind of talk."

"It's not meant to be. Somehow it wouldn't seem appropriate over lunch."

Carolina was now wide awake. "Clay, are you serious or what? Do you really want me to live with you?"

"Yes, that's what I want. I want you to move in with me and marry me and stay with me forever."

She flopped down on the pillow and stared at the ceiling. "I wasn't prepared for this. This is getting too serious."

He raised himself onto one elbow. "Very serious."

"Why the sudden change of heart?"

"I don't know. I just woke up this morning and realized how important you are to me. Call me impulsive."

"Why are you so sure? I'm pretty unstable, you know, and my history is ghastly."

Clay sat up again. "That doesn't matter. People matter. You matter to me. My family matters to me. Today matters to me."

"Was it finding that coin?"

"Perhaps, or at least in part." He repositioned his pillow. "But that's behind me."

"You said it's worth a lot of money."

He shrugged his bare shoulders and said, "I was told it is, but that's not what we're talking about."

"Money always matters."

Clay set his jaw and began speaking to the room, "Not right now, it doesn't. It doesn't matter worth a damn when it counts. Is money really going to make you love me any more than you already do? Let me tell you something. For a long time, I haven't known who I was, or where I was coming from, or where I was going. I haven't stood for anything. I haven't wanted to stand for anything. I was selfish. I abdicated my responsibility for living."

"Slow down. Aren't you being a bit hard on yourself?"

"I don't think so. This waybill thing has been more than a treasure hunt. It provoked me to do things I would have never done before. It caused me to lie, to cheat, and even to steal. It made me look within myself and far beyond myself. It has worked a deep change on me, Carolina—I've walked with ghosts and they've touched me. They've touched my heart and my mind. Why not ask the dead what they think of Mister Reid's coin, or for that matter, all the earth's treasures and our dreams of it? They would laugh in our faces. This experience has made me see the flimsy nature of our being here at all."

"You're getting pretty wound up."

He clutched at the sheet and said, "Maybe I am. Maybe I need to be, but I plan a change and I want you to be part of it."

She pulled him back to the pillow and laid her arm across his chest. "Oh, Clay, don't ever forget that I'm on your side. This ordeal has changed both of us."

"Yes, it has." They were now face to face. He watched her pupils focus his image. "Well, what's your decision?"

She smiled. "You know I'll stay with you."

"I thought you would." He pushed his finger across her soft lips. "This may not be the best time for this, but have you thought anymore of what we should do about your brother?"

"Yes, I've thought about it. No, I haven't made any decisions."

"May I make a suggestion? Tomorrow I'm going to see my lawyer. I will give him a draft of a letter I will also be sending your brother by registered mail. Other copies will be deposited at my bank and with my brother. The letter will inform him that we will be getting married in the near future. It will dictate to him that you would like to negotiate a reasonable cash settlement for your share of the farm as soon as possible. Lastly, it will imply in the vaguest of terms that we are both aware of his illegal activities and are prepared to act on our suspicions should he ever again bother either of us. Of course, I will let him know of the disposition of the copies so that he will not be tempted to act against us to prevent their exposure. If I do not receive a response within one week, I will contact the authorities."

"You've already written the letter, haven't you?"

He lay back down on the pillow. "Yes, I have. Does that change your mind about me?"

"No, not about you." she said. "A letter may even be too forgiving. I just don't know if he'll be reasonable."

"The way I see it, he doesn't have an option."

"You're assuming he's a rational person."

"That is the assumption. Whatever his response, it's something we'll have to live with for a long time."

She moved closer to him. "Yes, we will."

The land shall not be sold in perpetuity, for the land is mine; for you are strangers and sojourners with Me.

—LEVITICUS 25:23

EPILOGUE

The Snowbird Mountains, North Carolina
August 1987

The hawk left a summer thermal and was slowly spiraling downstream along Santeetlah Creek when it saw the rabbit cross the rectangle of grass and enter the garden. Whatever deficiencies the creator may have designed into this single-minded creature, its eyesight was not one of them, and it locked onto the unsuspecting animal from a thousand feet above, collapsing its wings toward the end of the dive, increasing its speed severalfold, striking with such force that the rabbit's spine was broken on impact. With talons firmly implanted in the now flaccid prey, the bird, its wings flapping mightily, struggled to ascend from among the tangle of bean vines, when from around the corner came a bright green lawn tractor driven by Ike Corn. To the red-tail's credit, the unexpected appearance of the man did not weaken its grip, and in a matter of seconds, it was under the cover of the hemlock trees across the creek and then gone.

Ike stopped the machine and dismounted, and for a time watched the spot where the bird had disappeared into the foliage. The distraction past, he unloaded two rolls of chicken wire from the trailer behind the tractor as well as an armful of wooden stakes and two sacks of fertilizer. He cut open one of the sacks with his knife and began to walk up and down the rows of his garden spreading the fertilizer by hand. When satisfied with its distribution, he stepped over to a small pump house and threw the switch that pulled water from the creek and distributed it to the drip irrigation system. He was driving the first stake to a new fence when his wife called to him from the back door.

"Thomas's here," she said in Cherokee. A telephone was ringing in the background.

He dropped his tools and walked to the front of the house to meet his brother, who was standing alone in the driveway, next to a new pickup truck.

"When'd it come in?" he said, referring to the truck.

"Yesterday."

Ike walked around to the driver's side door and peered into the cab. He made a low whistle, a sign of approval. "Automatic?"

"And air conditioning."

"How you gonna keep your boy away from it?"

Thomas laughed and raised his fist and said, "He knows better."

"Did you get a hitch put on?" Ike asked, walking to the rear of the truck to check for himself. Answering his own question, he continued, "What in the world you plannin' on haulin' with that thing? You're gonna have to take me fishin' now."

"What are you talkin' about? You're the fellow with the boat."

"Well, it's a mighty nice truck is all I can say."

"Thanks." Thomas reached through the driver's side window and removed a manila envelope. "I got something for you."

Ike accepted the envelope and opened the clasp. "What's this?"

"Another installment from the coin dealer in Philadelphia."

Ike looked at the check and smiled. "This is a lot of money."

John just laughed. "And that's not the last of it."

"What'd he suggest we do with the rest of them?"

"The lawyer says we ought to just sit on most of them. Keep it quiet as long as we can. It'll keep the prices up."

Ike reclosed the clasp and said, "I figure he knows best."

"I guess." Thomas then cast his brother a sidelong glance. "Anyway, we've always got that little insurance 'policy' you left behind."

Ike looked down and kicked at a rear tire, "Don't give me no trouble now. You know damn well I had my reasons."

"Sure, sure. I can go along with that."

A pause followed. Ike turned toward the house. "You wanna come in and sit down for a while?"

"No, I can't this afternoon. I've got to get over to my sister-in-law's for supper."

Ike raised his eyebrows in mock sympathy. "Y'all goin' to church in the morning?"

"Probably."

"Maybe we'll see you there."

Ike watched the dust dissipate along the road and walked back to his garden. His wife was by now sitting in the shade at the edge of the grass, sewing on one of his shirts.

"I saw a hawk take a rabbit in the garden just before Thomas drove up," he said.

"Really," she answered, without looking up or missing a stitch.

"Yessir, it about got hung up in the bean plants."

"Just think, if you could make a deal with that old hawk, you wouldn't have to mess with puttin' up a fence."

Ike smiled and began banging on the stake once more.

Neptune's Account

The text of this book is set in Waverly, with part titles in Bernhard Modern; and was composed by Graphic Composition of Athens, Georgia. The printing was done by Thomson-Shore of Dexter, Michigan, on Glatfalter Supple Opaque. The endpapers are Equinox by Simpson Papers. The spine of the book is bound in Record Buckram, the boards in Natural Sailcloth, both by Holliston Mills. The book was designed by Atlanta graphic artist David Laufer.

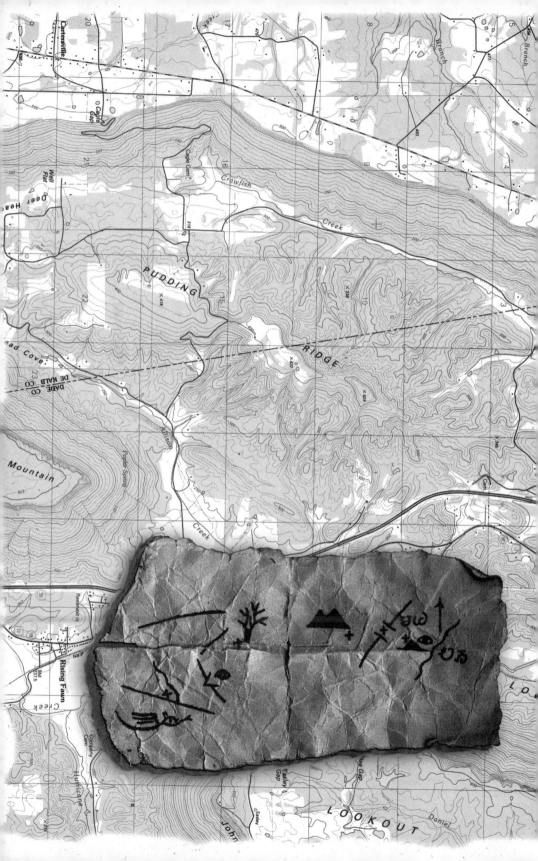